SOLOMON'S AGATE

DAVID LIVINGSTON

To Sally Caroline and Rip
My Winning Trifecta

PROLOGUE

How can a person not believe in Karma?

For many thousands of years, people have searched for answers to questions that are unanswerable, at least in this world. Is there a God? What is the meaning of life? What happens when you die?

All the cultural refinements and scientific achievements to this point in the known world have brought us no closer to the answers. Ancient civilizations are just like us. We are just like them. Just the way it is.

Legend has it that somewhere in Sub-Saharan Africa a few thousand years ago, there was a treasure trove of precious stones and jewels buried deep in the "Lost Mines" of King Solomon. The mines may or may not be real, but the ancient stones and prayer beads that we can wear and hold in our hands today, some of which are said to be from those lost mines, are not only real, but are full of the mystery and karma of many generations of our ancestors, who made them, wore them, and held them in their hands, many, many years ago.

PART 1

Gib

CHAPTER 1

The 7th at Aqueduct was a Maiden Special Weight for 3 year old fillies going 6 furlongs. They were alive to 2 of the fillies in the last leg of the Pick 3. The fillies were "Tiara" and "Awesome Sis". Awesome Sis was by "Awesome Again", out of the obscure mare "Sister Act", and was a first time starter.

After a quarter, Awesome Sis was relaxed on the rail in fifth. She maintained her position until the top of the stretch, then swung out three wide and easily cruised past the 3rd and 4th place fillies, who were both tiring badly. She then found another gear and accelerated through the stretch to win by a length and a half. The Pick 3 paid a handsome $819, thanks to a 19 to 1 shot who got loose on the lead and wired the field in the first leg. Especially impressive was the fact that they had singled the first leg, had 3 runners in the second and 2 in the third, for a cost of $12 per ticket. They had it ten times. So, for the only bet of the day, they had invested $120 and collected $8,190. Not bad. Not bad at all.

Gib Carter breathed out, relaxed and had another beer. He would be drinking something different later, probably an Alsation white wine, maybe even Champagne. He was getting quite comfortable as a successful American businessman with a beautiful European girlfriend, quite comfortable indeed. Another beer, a fresh shirt, a quick call for messages, and then at 7:00 sharp they would meet in the lobby. The dinner alone would undoubtedly be exquisite, but something even more enticing awaited afterward, Natalya Petrova.

Natalya Petrova was the 31 year old daughter of a wealthy Eastern European banker, at least that was her story. In fact, she was a 35 year old Russian high school dropout who had learned at an early age that there were advantages to being a beautiful woman, and it was obvious to anyone and everyone that crossed her path that Natalya Petrova was indeed a beautiful woman. Gib had met her two days earlier in the posh bar at the Four Seasons Hotel. He was in New York as a last minute replacement for Roger Boardman, the Chairman and CEO of his firm, Boardman & Company. Boardman & Company was an investment banking and wealth management firm headquartered in New Orleans, with regional offices in Little Rock, Memphis, Mobile, Birmingham and Atlanta. The firm was started in 1952 and had grown slowly but steadily, and now was a very respected advisor to wealthy families, private companies and small corporations, primarily in the Southeast, but also with a small but growing presence in New York City. The New York City trip was not really one that required the head man to be there, so Roger Boardman had asked Gib to go in his place. Gibson Carter was Chief Investment Officer for Boardman & Company. He had known Roger Boardman when they were both fledgling stock brokers at Merrill Lynch in Little Rock in the mid 80's. Boardman had always respected Gib, and they remained good friends and business confidants through the years, although their career paths had led them to different firms. When Boardman took over as CEO of the firm his father founded, one of his first calls was to his friend Gib Carter. He asked Gib to come to New Orleans to discuss the possibility of joining Boardman & Company as Chief Investment Officer. Roger Boardman knew Gib Carter was a decent, honest man, and truth be told, he had always known that Carter was not cut out to be a stockbroker, at least not the kind of stockbroker that the big firms were looking for. They wanted an aggressive, self assured sort of guy, one who looked and acted like a financial advisor to wealthy clients. What they wanted even more was for that guy to be able to leverage his relationships with those wealthy clients, their families and friends. Gib was smart, likable and level headed, but aggressive he was not. Gib was not a salesman, but he was just the kind of guy Roger Boardman wanted as a business partner. After a series of meetings and a long weekend in New Orleans, Gib Carter became the new CIO of Boardman & Co. The timing was good for Gib. Fourteen months earlier he had lost his wife to breast cancer. His daughter and only child Nikki, was a law student at Tulane, another reason that Roger Boardman had figured Gib might be ready to make the move to New Orleans. He had lived his whole life in Mobile, and it was time for a change. It had been a tough couple of years. At 52, he was ready to begin the next chapter of his life. He had a good day at the track and he was having dinner with Natalya. Gib Carter suddenly had a little swagger, and it felt good.

The evening could not have been better. Gib and his new friends toasted their success at the track, swapped war stories and had an all around big time. Gib couldn't remember when he had had so much fun. When the check came, he signaled to the waiter that dinner was on him. If he had stopped to think about it, he almost certainly would not have done so. Roger Boardman was not one to entertain in this fashion and he would probably not be happy that Gib was doing so. Before the waiter could hand the check to Gib, however, the gentleman to his left intercepted it. He was the quietest one in the group, but he had a pleasant demeanor and seemed to enjoy Gib's company. Gib thought that the gentleman was with one of the large European banks, but he wasn't sure and he didn't want to ask at this point. He had spent the day with these people and had just finished dinner with them. It would not be a good idea, he reasoned, to bring attention to the fact that he did not remember the gentleman's name, so he just said thank you and gave a sincere nod of gratitude.

As good as dinner was, the after dinner activity was better. Gib and Natalya made love in every position he had ever tried, which didn't take long, and then proceeded to go through her repertoire, which lasted for hours. The next morning Gib was up early, as usual, and strolled out to the lobby to enjoy his normal routine of coffee and the morning paper. When he returned to the room Natalya was still in bed, waiting for him. She reached up, pulled him toward her and proceeded to make Gib forget every word he had ever read in the Mobile Press Register, Times Picayune and Wall Street Journal.

Gib had two more nights in New York, and he wanted nothing more than to spend them the same way he had spent the last two, in bed with Natalya Petrova. He had only known her for three days, and he was quite sure there was some sort of back story that went along with the curves and the smile, there always was. Gib was from Alabama, but he was no fool. He knew there could be trouble ahead if he expected more out of Natalya than just a good time. He knew that the chance of his having any kind of relationship with her after this week was slim. He knew these things, but he also knew there were really no guarantees in life, and he was stone cold certain that there was a chemistry between them that was real, and special. Of course.

At lunch the next day, Gib was joined by one of the bankers from dinner the previous evening. His name was Pietro Ferretti and he was from Sardinia. Gib knew little else about him, but he liked him. Pietro was relaxed and friendly, and had been in the group at the races at Aqueduct the day before.

"I had a great time yesterday", said Gib. " I believe I need to come to New York more often".

"I can't argue with that", replied Pietro, in his Italian accented English. "This is quite a city. I like it for business, but also for pleasure. Speaking of pleasure, you have spent some time with Natalya, I think she really likes you".

"Not sure about that", replied Gib, somewhat modestly, "How do you know her"?

"I don't really, she's very nice, but I don't know much about her. Apparently her family is in the banking business. I met her here for the first time. She was with the Russian guys when we met. They were all laughing and having a good time. I just assume she's friends with them through business, but I don't really know".

It was obvious that Pietro wasn't aware that he had spent the last few evenings with Natalya. so Gib changed the subject.

"A few of the guys are going back to Aqueduct today, are you going also"?

"Not today". replied Pietro, "I have a conference call this afternoon. How about you"?

"Definitely, I love it there. Plus, I've listened to enough opinions about the financial markets for one trip, so I'm headed out there right after lunch".

"Good luck" said Pietro. "Maybe I'll see you this evening".

Gib, true to his word, took a cab to Aqueduct right after lunch. The other guys planned to get there in time for the last three races, so he had plenty of time to relax and enjoy the races before then. He bought a racing form and settled in. He wasn't much of a gambler, but handicapping the races and betting a few bucks almost didn't seem like gambling. In fact, he had often thought that the horse track and the stock market were really the same thing. It was all about picking winners, and it really didn't matter how you did it. Both required discipline. Both required research. Both required work. But most of all, they represented the same risk versus reward decision making process. You evaluate your choices, you pays your money and you takes your chances.

The first two races were losers for Gib, but he managed to pick the winner of the third race, a 4 to 1 shot that paid him $50.00 for his $10.00 win ticket. He bet a long shot on the next race, skipped the 5th race, then lost the 6th in a photo finish. His buddies from the conference showed up before the 7th race. They all got a beer and then walked to the paddock to check out the horses.

As Gib watched the horses being saddled in the paddock for the next race, his mind drifted and he found himself thinking of Natalya. She was so beautiful. Her fair complexion and silky dirty blonde hair were matched by a lithe body that was as close to heaven as anything Gib could imagine. She was spending the afternoon at the spa with some of the other girls. She had told him earlier, with a sly smile, that she would have a drink waiting for him when he returned from the track. The bugle sounded, bringing Gib back to the present, as the horses and riders were called to the track for the post parade.

"Who ya like Gib"? one of the guys asked him, as if Gib had been studying the racing form all afternoon and had some insight into the race.

"That gray sure is pretty", Gib replied, an observation that any third grader on a field trip could have made. Then he added, "but the eight horse looks good in the hind quarters and is bred for the distance, so I'll probably put him on top of the two favorites in the exacta".

Gib wasn't as sure of his opinion as he acted, but he really had noticed the eight horse in the racing form. The part about the hind quarters was borderline bogus. He had a horseplayer friend at home who sometimes made that comment and it sounded good, so he went with it. When the eight horse came home first by three lengths, followed by the favorite, Gib, along with his buddies, had nailed the exacta. Sometimes it works out.

The last two races were both losers for the guys, but because of the exacta in the seventh they were going home with a few extra bucks in their pockets. Instead of heading straight back, they decided to stop off at a local watering hole down the street from the hotel. After ordering a round of drinks and making a toast to each other, they settled in and talked of money and politics, gambling, women etc. Guy talk. These were rich men. They managed money, a lot of money. They took Gib in, and Gib appreciated that. He was a smart, successful money man himself. He was the Chief Investment Officer of Boardman and Company. He belonged. They drank and talked and laughed, then drank some more. Gib had arrived. As he got up to visit the men's room, he realized that an hour and a half had passed, and it had seemed like ten minutes. He looked at his phone and saw that he had missed a call from Natalya. On the way back to the table, he stepped outside and called her.

"Well, are we having fun yet"? Natalya asked, before Gib said a word.

Gib paused, he wasn't sure how to respond. He had known her less than a week. Surely she wasn't chastising him for having a few drinks with the guys.

"Yes we are, as a matter of fact", Gib said, with a tone that just very slightly hinted at irritation.

"Okay then", Natalya replied, then laughed. "Want some company"?

This threw Gib off a bit. Natalya wasn't mad, she seemed genuinely happy that he was having fun with the guys. He definitely wanted company, but later, not now. He was boozing it up with some of the investment world's elite. Roger Boardman would be proud. After all, he figured, this is exactly why Roger suggested that Gib go to New York in the first place, to meet people. And these weren't just people, these were the big boys. They controlled, among them, tens of billions of dollars. They were the portals through which firms like Boardman and Company accessed the big money. The pension funds, the huge institutional accounts, the private accounts of the super rich, and who knows what else.

Before Gib could respond, Natalya continued, "I'm with three of the other girls, and we're crashing the party, we can't let you guys have all the fun".

Again Gib paused, but just slightly, "bring it on" he said.

When Natalya and the other three lovelies hit the local watering hole, the whole place took notice. Gib stood and started to make an attempt at introductions, but Natalya bailed him out by simply saying, "you boys know where a girl can get a drink around here"?

Half the guys in the place raised their hands immediately and started a chorus of hell yeah and other affirmative responses. They all laughed, then the girls had a seat and ordered a drink. The party had begun.

The next morning was tough for Gib. His head was pounding and his memory was fuzzy. He had had a three beer head start on the other guys yesterday, and about an eight beer head start on the girls. He knew they had visited a nightclub and there was dancing involved, but that was about it. He was lying in bed next to Natalya, so he knew he must have done something right. Today was the last day of the conference. He was scheduled to participate in a panel discussion on alternative investments right after breakfast, so he forced himself out of bed and got ready.

Lunch was buffet style, in a room adjoining the main conference room. Gib sat with a mixed group of people, most from Chicago. The panel discussion had gone well, in spite of the hangover. It had not gone unnoticed during the week that Gib had buddied up with the power brokers from Europe and Asia. Gib could feel his lunch companions hanging on his words, so he obliged them with a casual discourse on alternative investments, expanding on the topic of the morning session.

A younger lady from Chicago asked Gib:"Do you and your firm see opportunity in Eastern Europe"?

"Absolutely", he responded. "There is a growing, educated middle class there, and they all want the latest technology, so we have taken equity positions in some of the newer, more innovative tech companies in the region. In addition to tech, we're big on Natural Resources. We just made a large investment in the Timber Industry in China. Large American pensions and endowments are actively looking for ways to get growth outside of the U.S. stock markets, as we discussed this morning. Eastern Europe, as well as South Africa I might add, are good markets for us".

"How do you manage currency risk"?

"We are not hedged. We believe that the increasingly global nature of the markets, and resulting liquidity and transparency, have facilitated trading for us and other firms, without the need to add the cost of hedging for currency risk, at least in the short term. We certainly respect the currency risk, however, and have no problem with hedging if and when it is in our opinion it is smart to do so".

Gib realized that he could have answered the question in a much more concise manner, but what the hell, he was now the expert in global alternative investing, his opinion counted, he was a player.

The last night of his New York trip didn't go the way he would have liked. He and Natalya had cocktails in the bar at the hotel. She had one glass of wine and switched to sparkling water. She was having a business dinner with the group from her bank and it required her complete attention. Gib wanted to ask about her after dinner plans, but decided against it. She seemed to be distracted by work, and besides, he had to be ready for an early flight the next morning himself. He knew Roger Boardman would want a full report soon after he returned. He walked her through the lobby to the elevators. They were alone, so Gib kissed her, and she buried her head in his chest.

"This week has been wonderful" she said. "Will we get a chance to do it again"?

" I hope so", replied Gib, "how about next weekend in Paris"? They both laughed softly.

The elevator door opened. As several people walked past, she squeezed his hand, smiled, whispered goodbye, and turned to get on the elevator.

Gib was busy the next couple of weeks, meetings, phone calls, all the usual stuff. At the monthly firm officers' meeting, he gave a full recap of the New York trip, along with comments about the people he had met and spent time with, which included some of the big hitters from Europe and Asia, but did not include Natalya Petrova.

Three weeks after he left New York, on a drizzly Tuesday afternoon, the phone rang on Gib's desk. It was the Boardman & Company receptionist, "call for you Gib, someone named Natalya from some bank".

Gib's heart skipped a beat. "Thank you I'll take it", he said. He had not exchanged contact information with Natalya in New York. She had said that she wanted to, but that her bank was very strict about personal calls and emails, and that her cell phone couldn't take calls from a foreign country. Gib wasn't so sure about that, but he didn't press her on the issue. He paused for a moment, then picked up the phone. "Hello".

"Gib, it's me, Natalya. I hope it's okay that I called".

Gib's face broke into a wide grin. "Of course, I'm glad you did. How are you"?

"Good. Pretty busy lately, I think I need a break, which is sort of why I called".

"Sounds good so far", Gib said, trying to sound calm. "Tell me more".

"You may think this is crazy, but I want you to come to a special party, in Greece. It's an engagement party. You may remember one of the guys from New York named Konstantin. He's marrying a girl from Greece. Her name is Resa Athanasuleas. Her family is very wealthy. They're having a party for Resa and Konstantin at a fabulous beach resort called Sani Resort. They suggested that I bring a date, so I'm inviting you. If you can't come I understand, but I hope you will".

Gib's mind was racing. He hadn't talked to Natalya since he left New York. He wasn't sure if he would ever talk to her again, and now she's on the phone inviting him to a luxury beach resort in Greece.

"Wow", he said, unsure exactly what to say next. He wanted to say yes, yes, yes, but it would be crazy to accept such an invitation without knowing more details. "When"?

"In two weeks", replied Natalya, in her seductive, accented English that made Gib want to head to the airport immediately. "All of the arrangements are handled, you just have to say yes. There is a private jet in Chicago that belongs to Pietro Ferretti, I think you met him in New York. He's there overseeing a project for the next two months. If you agree, he can come to New Orleans and pick you up. He'll bring you here and take you back. The resort is incredible Gib, and we'll have the weekend together".

Two weeks later Gib was on board a sleek Gulfstream G150, headed to Greece. Pietro Ferretti was accommodating in every way. He told Gib that he had some work to finish up during the first part of the trip, so Gib settled in with the Wall Street Journal, a couple of magazines and the more than occasional thought of what was in store for him at Sani Resort, where the coast of Greece meets the sparkling azure waters of the Aegean Sea. A couple of hours later, they were enjoying a glass of Argiolas Costamolino Vermentino, a refreshing, crisp white wine from Pietro's homeland of Sardinia. It almost didn't seem real. Sipping wine high above the Atlantic, casually chatting with a rich Sardinian, en route to a beautiful seaside resort and an even more beautiful European goddess named Natalya. This was a world he didn't know, or at least, a world he had never known before. He was happy, he was comfortable with himself. He really didn't need, and didn't think he would ever want, all of the high priced luxuries that he was enjoying with his new European friends. But it was fun, no doubt. Actually, it was more than fun, it was seductive. He had been reminding himself that this couldn't last, that at some point things would return to their normal state, and instead of jetsetting across the Atlantic, he would be back in New Orleans, enjoying a PoBoy and looking forward to tailgaiting at the next Saints game. That was his life. He knew that and he liked that. He reassured himself that what he was doing now was what any of his buddies would do if they had the opportunity. He worked hard. He had been through a lot with the death of his wife two years ago. He was having fun. No need to question it. He reminded himself of the conversations he had had with Nikki during the weeks and months after her mother died. "Don't be so hard on yourself", she had said. "It's not your fault she got sick. Give yourself a break and enjoy your life. Before long you might meet somebody new, and if you do it's okay, you deserve it". He knew she was right, but this seemed a little over the top. But then again, maybe he was just feeling guilty for being happy. Maybe he just needed to relax and enjoy it, the good life.

The Sani Resort was spectacular. A refuge from the real world. A playground for those who prefer elegance and style over glitz and glamour. A thousand acres of pine forest, beaches, olive groves and citrus orchards, along with four luxury hotels and world class amenities. Gib's room was more of the same. Simple, understated elegance. But there was a problem. No Natalya. He had come to this place, half way across the globe, at her invitation. Where was she? He didn't expect her to meet him as he stepped off the plane, but he also didn't expect to be staying in a room by himself. As he started to hang up his clothes, he heard a faint knock on the door. He hesitated, thinking that it was probably someone with the hotel staff, and then he went to the door and opened it. She was as beautiful as the first time they met, maybe more so. Her pure creamy skin had taken on the warm bronze glow of the sun. Her eyes were dazzling. She giggled. He took her in his arms, a honey bee returning to the hive. She kissed him and pressed her body to his. Making the soothing sounds of lust and love, they shared the next hour as though the world had stopped turning, and they alone were cradled in the serene, soft folds of a cashmere dream.

The next day was a blur. Breakfast, followed by a bike ride along one of the nature trails, a quick lunch, a fishing excursion and then dinner and dancing under the stars on a spectacular cliffside patio. Afterword, Gib and Natalya collapsed together on the bed in Gib's room, and slept to the sound of the waves rolling in on the beach.

The following day was the big event of the weekend. The veranda and the adjoining lawn and garden were transformed into a magnificent party venue. There was a covered bandstand, a large dance floor and lots of beautifully decorated tables. Greenery and beautiful flowers of every description were everywhere. It was a scene that reminded Gib of Don Vito's daughter's wedding reception in the opening scene of his favorite movie ever, The Godfather. A fact that only added to the surreal nature of the weekend.

A group of the guys headed out mid morning to the shooting range to shoot sporting clays. They invited Gib, but he declined, deciding instead to hang out by the pool and do some reading and relaxing. He was an avid reader, for both business and pleasure, and it felt good to slow down a little and get involved with a book. It also gave him the opportunity to do some thinking. Gib was a thinker, and lately things had moved a little too fast for him. He was in transition. That was a good thing, but he wanted to make sure he was headed in the right direction. New job, new home, new friends, and here he was sitting poolside at a world class resort on the coast of Greece. Hard to find a lot wrong with that. Maybe that was the problem. Maybe it was too perfect. Maybe he should take a step back and make sure it was all real. There were a few things, actually there were more than a few, that had crossed his mind during the time since his trip to New York. Gib was a level headed guy, no doubt about it. He was the type that listened. He was a little on the sensitive side. He was slow to trust. He was really good at seeing through the stuff that doesn't matter, and uncompromising about the stuff that does. He peeled back the veneer on a person as well as anybody. Problem was, it can be pretty tough to peel back the veneer on yourself, and Gib knew that he needed to do just that. The things that had crossed his mind needed to be identified and dealt with. Gib knew that. He was pretty clear on that. The bigger problem was one which he was not so clear on, partly because he didn't want to be clear on it, couldn't be clear on it, nothing clear about it, too powerful to be clear, too strong. Natalya.

After lunch, some of the guys got together to talk business, and Gib was included. It was a small group, only five men. Two from Russia, including Viktor, the older gentleman who had paid for dinner in New York, one of the Athanasuleas brothers from Greece, Pietro Ferretti from Sardinia and Gib. Viktor did most of the talking. Gib had been wondering how these people were connected. He first met them in New York at the investment conference, so he knew they had those ties, but there was never any discussion about the investment markets that he had heard. In fact, there was never serious discussion about anything. There was plenty of banter, especially while drinking, but no business talk. They were smart, they were rich, they liked to have fun. Maybe that was it, all there was to it, just buddies having fun. But Gib knew better. In his gut he knew there was more, and he was pretty sure he was about to start finding out about the rest.

Gib, calm easygoing Gib, was nervous. He wasn't quite sure if it was the good kind of nervous, like a 15 year old Gib trying to summon the courage to call Melanie Pennington and ask her to the prom, or the other kind, the kind that warns of danger ahead.

In the investment world, size matters. Brilliant minds, trained by other brilliant minds, spend many hours using those talented brain cells trying to accomplish one thing: to make rich men richer. The guy with a few hundred dollars to invest is on his own, or maybe gets advice from a friend, or someone far away on a telephone, or a hungry salesperson. The guy with a few million dollars to invest gets the royal treatment. The deep pockets make the rules. The deep pockets play by their own rules, and the deep pockets get deeper, just the way it is.

Sovereign Wealth Funds have deep pockets, really deep. A Sovereign Wealth Fund is a state owned investment fund. The money in the fund can come from many different sources, but whatever the source, the money belongs to a specific country, and is controlled by the people who control that country. There are rules and regulations, such as those set up by the International Monetary Fund when it published The Santiago Principals, which address the need for transparency and prudent governance. However well intended, the rules matter very little. Sovereign Wealth Funds do pretty much whatever they want to do.

Boardman and Company, on Canal Street in New Orleans, LA, USA, invested money for plenty of rich people, pensions and endowments, but not for Sovereign Wealth Funds. Boardman and Company managed a total of 2.7 Billion dollars. The largest single account was an oil company pension plan worth 48 million. That was about to change.

At the Sani Resort, on the Greek coast, the conversation began. Viktor spoke first. "Gib, we have a proposition for you. I'm going to tell you about our group and what we have in mind for you and your company. First, I want to give you some back ground. You are welcome to ask questions at any time, but I think that as I continue some of the questions you probably have will be answered, so I'll give you the complete story and then we can discuss whatever is unclear".

Viktor paused, Gib said "Okay, sure".

Gib relaxed a little. Viktor was speaking to him with respect, and although his tone was serious, it was not the least bit threatening. It seemed obvious to him that whatever this was about, he was not in any kind of danger.

"We work for Stezlaus Bank in Moscow. It is a private bank with impeccable credentials. It does not have a presence on the International banking scene, because it's not a commercial bank. It's owned by the Russian government, and it's sole purpose is to facilitate the management of Russia's Sovereign Wealth Fund, along with the task of executing trades and providing trade settlement services to all of the many entities with which the fund does business. As you might expect, it's quite a complicated operation. The fund itself is about 200

Billion Dollars. It's hard to put an exact number on it because it changes every day. The fund generates over 30 million dollars a day in new money that needs to be invested. The money comes from interest payments, dividends, maturing debt, stock sales, private equity deals, you get the picture. We're always looking for ways to invest the new money, and that's where you come in. We'd like to invite you and your company to be one of our investment partners. We propose that we start by giving you 200 million dollars to invest. It's not necessary for you to agree right now. We understand that you'll want to do your due diligence, and we're happy to help in that regard in any way we can. We've done our homework Gib. Boardman and Company is well respected, has never had any regulatory issues and keeps a low profile. Of course, you already know all of that. What you might not know, is that the world of Sovereign Wealth Funds needs firms like yours. Diversification is very important to us. The large global firms are capable, of course, and they have a good portion of our assets, but they are very large and very political. They don't listen. They always have some exotic new product for us to try. We don't like that. We like to keep it simple. We like to deal with people we can trust. Anyway, I've talked too much. It's your turn".

Gib didn't respond right away. Then he slowly cocked his head and said "run that by me one more time".

Viktor gave him a puzzled look. Pietro laughed, easing the tension, and said "it's an American saying, it means to repeat what you just said".

Viktor grimaced slightly. "The whole thing"?

Pietro then laughed harder, "no Viktor, I think just the part about the 200 million dollars".

Viktor relaxed and smiled, indicating that now he understood.

They spent the next hour discussing the details of their proposed new partnership, then Gib found a private office and called Roger Boardman. It was late morning in New Orleans, and Roger was in his office, about to leave for lunch. Five minutes later he asked his secretary to cancel his lunch plans. By two o'clock that afternoon Roger Boardman gave the okay to Gib to accept the investment account from the Sovereign Wealth Fund of Russia. Before the end of the work day in New Orleans, Boardman and Company received a wire transfer from the Stezlaus Bank in Moscow, for 200 million dollars.

Chapter 2

Natalya looked stunning, as usual. She was sitting at a table with a lovely Greek girl, her date and another couple Gib didn't recognize. Natalya smiled broadly when she saw Gib. He leaned over and kissed her, lingering just a bit. Natalya made the introductions. The Greek girl was Resa's cousin, the young man was her fiance. The other couple were friends of the family from Istanbul. All appeared to be having a good time. Dancing, singing and merrymaking were the order of the evening. Natalya pulled Gib onto the dance floor, pausing only briefly to allow him to take a gulp of Champagne. The night was alive.

Around midnight, fully engaged in the spirit of the occasion, Gib whispered something in Natalya's ear, then grabbed her hand and led her to a tucked away spot on the closely mown lawn area past the bandstand. The moon was bright. He pulled her close and they kissed with the passion of two teenage lovers in the summer moonlight of the Mediterranean. They dropped to the soft turf, removing clothes as they went. Their bodies glistened, their hearts pounded. As Gib looked into her eyes, Natalya reached down, guided him into her and made a low, contented sound that makes life itself worth living.

Breakfast came early, but Gib was okay with it. He wanted to spend some time with Viktor. After coffee and toasted Alevropita, a rustic Greek feta tart, they sat together in a corner of the hotel lobby. This time it was Gib who started the conversation.

"I got an email confirmation from Roger that the wire transfer came in late yesterday, that was quick".

Viktor shrugged slightly, "we don't like to waste time, time is money. As I mentioned yesterday, today there will be another thirty million to invest, it can be a challenge".

Gib didn't respond, he was still having a little trouble getting his head wrapped around the big numbers, and the casual manner in which Viktor discussed them. Viktor, ever aware, sensed this.

"Gib, we are not trying to...hit a homerun...with this money".

He paused and looked expectantly at Gib. Gib realized that Viktor was not waiting for a response, but was almost sheepishly looking for acknowledgement from him that he had used the American expression correctly. Gib just smiled and nodded.

Viktor continued, "the most important thing to us is that the money is secure. We want it to grow, of course, but we prefer steady, predictable growth, rather than taking chances. We like Boardman and Company, and we like you, just as you are. Don't think that you have to prove something to us, you've already done that. All of the documents have been signed and are in good order. This investment is only one tenth of one percent of the total value of the fund. Just do what you do. Don't worry".

"We do appreciate the trust and confidence Viktor. The next time you are in the States, I hope you will visit us in New Orleans and allow us to properly show our appreciation. In the meantime, will you be my main contact at the bank"?

"I'm rarely actually at the bank. I will have someone contact you so that you will have an inside person there. They will help you with pretty much everything you might need. I will talk with you as we go along, and officially at least twice a year, when we have our account reviews. Outside of that, our relationship will be casual, and hopefully we'll see each other from time to time. I suspect that we might, given your relationship with Natalya, but what do I know?, I'm just an old man. But, I will admit, it wasn't always that way". Viktor had a gleam in his eye and a knowing smile. Gib felt good.

Lunch was not what Gib expected. The weekend had been sensational, especially with Natalya. Everyone was preparing to leave Greece, and he assumed that lunch would be something quick and easy. He was wrong. At twelve noon, everyone was ushered into a large ballroom. There was a spread that was worthy of the royal family. The best of everything. Gib wanted to have a quiet lunch with Natalya, but that wasn't happening. As he walked into the room, he noticed that the tables had name places. He walked nonchalantly among the tables, checking it out. On a table on the far side of the room, there was a place for Gib Carter, right next to Natalya Petrova. Each table had platters of fresh seafood salad, wonderful fresh bread made that morning, soups, fresh fruit, cheeses and more.

As they were seated, Gib felt a tinge of melancholy. It was similar to his last day in New York. He would be leaving in a few hours, and he wasn't sure when he would see Natalya again, if at all. This time was different though. He felt closer to her, more connected, and he was sure she felt the same way. The weekend had been almost perfect, but it was about to be over. They would soon be thousands of miles from each other. Being with Natalya made him happy, made him smile. He didn't want it to end.

She felt the same way. Her feelings for Gib were very strong. He made her happy, made her smile. But there was a difference. Natalya could see the big picture. She knew things he didn't know. He had entered her world. She wanted him in her world, but she knew there were problems with it. She had considered that maybe, just maybe, she could become a part of his world. He wasn't married, he had money and he had a real life in a place she hadn't been, but knew she would like. But that was not reality. Reality was that he was leaving and she was staying. Reality was that they did live in different worlds, and it was going to stay that way, at least for now, and probably forever. Reality also was that she had a nagging thought. She knew things he didn't know, things that could be bad for him, and she knew, deep within her she knew, that she should tell him.

Gib didn't know exactly how to say goodbye to her, so he made it short and sweet. As he turned to walk away, she said his name. He turned to her. She took his hand in hers, slowly brought it to her lips and kissed it. As she did, she looked into his eyes. "I can't wait to see you again my darling", she said softly. Gib held her gaze, not wanting to leave.

The ride to the airport was mostly in silence. Pietro knew that Gib probably needed some time to re enter the world of the here and now. He was happy for Gib, but also a little concerned. Pietro liked Gib. Everybody liked Gib, especially Natalya. He could see that, and what's not to like about Natalya. Beautiful, charming, seductive, she was the total package. Pietro knew a little bit about women, having a history of his own. That history perhaps is what gave him pause. Two people having a good time is one thing. Two people in love is something different. Love makes fools of us all.

At the hangar, there was a delay. The jet had to be refueled. Gib wondered why that hadn't been done before now. They'd been in Greece three days. He was irritated. That wasn't like him. He didn't say anything about it, he just felt it. Pietro realized that the trip home would be a lot better if Gib would maybe say a word or two, so he facilitated.

"Let's have a drink Gib, it's got to be five o'clock somewhere".

Gib just looked at him, then said "better make mine a double".

An hour, and two double scotches each later, they were in the air. What started out as a long ride home had quickly turned into two buddies on a road trip at 25,000 feet.

"How bout some horse racing"? said Pietro. "We can bet the European tracks right now".

He booted up his laptop, connected to the internet, and a few keystrokes later he was looking at the field for the first race from Goodwood in England. Goodwood, a beautiful, bucolic like countryside race track with an air of British sophistication, did indeed look inviting. A few more keystrokes and the wireless printer on the plane began spitting out pages of the Daily Racing Form. Twenty minutes later they made their first bet of the day, a straight win ticket on a two year old colt with a good pedigree making his first start. He ran well but couldn't catch the leader in the stretch. As they looked at the second race entries, Gib decided he needed his own online wagering account. He fired up his laptop, opened an account with TurfSports, an American online horse race wagering platform, and put $500 in his account with his credit card. Just like that, he was in business.

After two more scotches each, Gib and Pietro found their groove. The fourth from Goodwood was an allowance race for fillies and mares, age 4 and up. Gib and Pietro couldn't agree, so they made separate bets, which both lost. Not wanting to wait thirty minutes for the next race from Goodwood, they bet the next race from Kempton Park. Gib picked his first winner of the day, an eight to one shot that won in a photo. Pietro cashed his first ticket in the next race from Goodwood. And so it went, two guys having a big time drinking and gambling.

It was about that time that Pietro Ferretti had an idea, a burst of inspiration. Pietro Ferretti, flying high, living large, loving life, maybe a wee bit in the grasp of a not small quantity of single malt scotch, thought about Shanghai.

Charlie "Shanghai" Morris didn't have any of Gib's newfound swagger. He didn't want any swagger, not his style. Shanghai was a weird dude, but a brilliant weird dude. He grew up in a housing project in Boston. His mother was a smart, pretty young woman with a history of making bad decisions. She liked to party. She liked to drink and do drugs. She liked men. She didn't know who Charlie's father was. When she was 29 years old she ran out of options, and she and Charlie moved into the housing project. She tried to straighten up and make a life for herself and Charlie, but it never really worked out. At the age of 10, Charlie started hanging out with a group of Chinese/American kids in the project. By age 12 he was part of their gang. He managed to graduate from High School, but the odds were stacked against him. He had multiple run ins with the authorities, skipping school, drinking, etc. He was arrested, along with three other guys, in a drug bust at a friend's house. He gave the cops a fake name, and when they asked where he lived he said "Shanghai", and laughed. He landed in jail for 18 months. When he got out he returned to the only life he knew, in the projects. But now Charlie had street cred, and he was the smartest guy around. He read voraciously, often spending hours at the public library, and he was a genius with numbers. He needed money, but didn't have a job. He sold some weed to make a few bucks, but he knew that was dangerous and he had no intention of going back to jail, which if happened again would probably mean he'd go to the big house. The big house was bad. It was not an option.

One of his buddies worked parking cars at Burnham Glen Casino, and he told Shanghai he could probably get him on there too, at least part time on the weekends. It was an hour and a half by train from the projects, but it was a job. Foxwoods had a very strict drug-free policy, no second chances. Shanghai waited a few weeks, passed the drug test and started parking cars at Burnham Glen Resort and Casino two nights a week. The guys at Burnham Glen liked Shanghai, and Shanghai liked them. A month into his new gig he was parking cars at Burnham Glen five nights a week. One busy Saturday night, a pit boss at the casino came out to the valet station and asked for a volunteer to be a "runner" inside in the sports book. Saturday was the biggest night for the valet guys, and nobody spoke up. Except Shanghai. He was curious about the action in the Sports Book and wanted to check it out, so he volunteered. He never returned to the valet station. The Sports Book absolutely fascinated Shanghai. He worked every chance he got and when he wasn't working he was hanging out. It amazed him that so many wealthy guys bet so much money on so many different things. He knew a little about football, basketball and baseball, but not much. Sports didn't get discussed a whole lot in the projects. What he did know was numbers. And probabilities. And the way people think and act when they get drunk. He knew Burnham Glen was making a helluva lot of money off of these drunk rich guys, and they showed up every weekend, like clock-work. Shanghai wanted in on the action. What he didn't know, at least not yet, was that there were a lot of guys much higher on the food chain already in on the action. And some of them were bad people. Very bad people.

He started as a number cruncher. Every Sunday night during the NFL season he would compile statistics from that day's games, double check them, then condense them and put them into the format that the Foxwoods guys wanted them. By Monday morning the guys at Burnham Glen had posted the odds for every NFL game that week, and had started taking action. Shanghai didn't mind the work at first, he liked numbers and he was just glad to be a part of it. What he didn't care for though, was the fact that he would do all the work, give them what they wanted, and they would just talk to each other, set the odds and the cash rolled in. They didn't always win, of course, but they were on the right side more often than not. That fact, plus the "vig", the props, teasers and parlays all added up to a handsome profit during the busy NFL season. At least for those guys. Shanghai was doing okay, had steady work and a good reputation, but he was only making an hourly wage, plus an occasional bonus after a really good week. He knew he was as smart or smarter than those guys, but he didn't know football very well, and he was pretty much lost when it came to interpreting the data and making an odds line. That all changed for Shanghai on a Saturday afternoon in February, right after the Super Bowl. Some of the guys were planning a trip to Vegas for some R&R and invited him to join them. Vegas was awesome and he loved it. Saturday morning the group took a one day side trip to Santa Anita Park in Southern California, for a day of horse racing. He had watched some of the horseplayers at Burnham Glen and it intrigued him, but then again, everything at Burnham Glen intrigued him. He had been so busy compiling statistics from NFL games that he hadn't paid much attention to the other stuff. During the short flight from Vegas to LA, he opened a "Daily Racing Form" for the first time. He was immediately hooked.

He didn't understand what he was looking at, but by the end of the day he had figured out a few things: 1. Thoroughbred handicapping involved a lot of numbers, was very difficult and required hours of intense study. 2. He hadn't seen a single person at the track that day, including the "professional" gamblers in his group, that seemed to be a true expert. 3. Horse race betting was a pari-mutuel wagering game. He didn't have to play against the "House", like football. Instead, he was playing against the other horseplayers, and they weren't very good. Charlie "Shanghai" Morris had found his game.

For the next six months, Shanghai was a machine. He read books on thoroughbred handicapping, watched every race from Aqueduct, Santa Anita and Gulfstream Park every day. He watched race replays on his computer every night and studied the charts. He handicapped races, thought about races, read about races, listened to the experts' opinions on races, but he didn't bet on races. Shanghai was disciplined. He knew that a very small percentage of horseplayers, he heard the number was 2%, were long term winners. He watched the guys in the Racebook at Burnham Glen. He listened to their opinions and bad beat stories. He paid attention to everything, but he didn't bet. He continued crunching numbers for the guys in the Sportsbook, managed to get a raise and moved into a small apartment close to the casino. In due time, Shanghai began to

reap the rewards of his hard work. After spending hours studying the racing form, he would make one or two bets. Some
days he would bet more, but not often. There were days when
he studied for hours and didn't make a single bet. What he did
do was win. Not always, but enough to show a solid profit. The
guys in the Sports Book took notice. He was tight lipped, but
they knew he was putting in action on the ponies and cashing
tickets. In October of that year, a couple of weeks before the
Breeders' Cup, the Super Bowl of horse racing, the manager of
the Sports Book made him a proposition. The big money boys
at Burnham Glen would bankroll Shanghai. He would handicap the races and make all of the bets using their money. He
would get 10% of the profit, if there was one. If they lost, he
got nothing but lost nothing. It was a no brainer. Shanghai got
to work. The first day of the Breeders' Cup was pretty much a
disaster. They didn't cash a ticket. The second day, the bigger
day of the two for gamblers, started out the same. Shanghai
was pressing. Going into the fourth race of the day, he started
questioning himself. He wasn't used to this, gambling for other
people, and in such large amounts. He was out of his comfort zone. The fourth race was a turf race with a million dollar
purse. All the best turf horses were entered, thirteen of them.
Shanghai liked turf racing, even though there wasn't a lot of
it in America, and had had success with it. Twenty minutes
to post, Shanghai was scared. He loved the race, had a strong
opinion on one of the European horses, listed at 26 to 1 on
the tote board, and had planned to key that horse on a trifecta
ticket with several others. Problem was, almost nobody else

liked him. He wasn't even mentioned by the experts in the pre race analysis. He opened at 12 to 1 and had slowly drifted up to 26 to 1, not a good sign. Everything pointed to another losing race for Shanghai and his investors. Everything, that is, except his gut feeling. So, Charlie "Shanghai" Morris faced the decision that every horseplayer faces at some point, trust your initial opinion and listen to your gut, or do the "safe" thing and follow the logic of others. He walked in a circle, looked at the board, closed his eyes and tried to think clearly. It was no use. Time to fish or cut bait. He stepped to the window and bought a trifecta ticket on the fourth race using the European longshot, with two minutes to post. The first half of the race went as expected, the horses spread out along the rail. In turf racing, the horses seem to glide around the track until they enter the top of the stretch, then the fun begins. As they passed the quarter pole, there were five horses within a few lengths of the lead, then a break of five lengths, then the rest. One of the trailers started moving up on the outside. At the eighth pole he looked to have the leaders measured, and was closing rapidly. Even more rapidly, on the inside along the rail, came another closer, wearing the black and red silks of a European import. The finish was very close, but the inside horse prevailed. Shanghai's heart was pounding. He had nailed it. A 26 to 1 shot, on top of a 15 to 1 shot, on top of an 8 to 1 shot in the trifecta. The trifecta paid $19,709 for a $2 ticket. He had a $30 ticket, which payed him $295,635. His hands were shaking. He got a beer. And another. He walked outside, back inside and back outside. Finally, he sat down and looked at the ticket. His heart slowed down. As he walked to the window to cash the ticket, he thought about how crazy it was that he had a ticket in his pocket worth almost three hundred grand.

Half way across the Atlantic, Pietro Ferretti said "let's have some fun Gib".

"I thought we were already having fun", Gib replied, taking another slug of scotch.

Pietro chuckled, "yes we are my friend, but I'm in the mood for action. Are you familiar with Burnham Glen Casino in Connecticut, a short drive from New York City"?

"I've heard of it" said Gib.

"Well, our guys, Viktor and the boys, have friends there. There is an eccentric fellow named Shanghai that they know. He's a horse race handicapper and he's very good. He's the one that gave us the Pick 3 bet at Aqueduct the first day we met. They say all he does is handicap thoroughbreds. The guys at Foxwoods have some sort of deal with him. When they bring in the high rollers they give his picks to them so the big boys can cash some tickets on the ponies. This makes them happy, and when the high rollers are happy the money flows. When the money really flows, it flows to the table games, which makes the Foxwoods boys happy. It's brilliant".

Gib gave Pietro a cockeyed, almost full drunk look, "what happens when his picks don't win"?

Pietro sat there, stone faced, as if he'd never considered that possibility. Then he leaned in toward Gib, his head slightly askew, and with a straight face and thick tongue said, "how the fuck do I know"? and then leaned back and laughed the kind of laugh that easily comes with a gut full of good scotch whiskey.

Gib, of course, started laughing also, which only made the Sardinian laugh harder. For a good two or three minutes, there was nothing else, only laughter. Chest heaving, uncontrollable laughter. They both managed to slow down and take a few deep breaths. Then the conversation continued.

"As I was saying Gib, this guy is good. Let's find out if he has any picks today we can use. With that, Pietro called someone at Burnham Glen. He didn't say a name, he just said "hey, this is Pietro, does our friend have any picks today? I'm travelling and want to make a bet or two". He listened for a minute, then said "okay, just thought I'd check, thanks anyway". He was about to end the call, but hesitated, as if listening to something the other person was saying at the end of the call. He then said "okay, tell me about it". Another few minutes, and Pietro was off the phone. "No luck", said Pietro, "Shanghai doesn't have picks every day, and today is Monday, so a lot of the tracks are closed anyway".

Gib wasn't fazed. "Not all of them. It's five minutes to post at Delaware Park, second race. I kinda like the five, Lady Bandini, a longshot at twenty one to one". Lady Bandini never threatened and finished next to last, twelve lengths behind the winner. It was a similar story at Suffolk Downs and Finger Lakes. Then, back at Delaware Park, Gib cashed on a five to one shot, collecting $120 for his $20 win ticket.

"Why don't you bet some real money"?, chided Pietro, who had just dropped $200 on the same race at Delaware Park. "If you're gonna run with the big dogs, you gotta step it up my friend. Twenty dollar bets are for wimps. I believe I'll have another drink".

Gib joined him, taking a break from his computer screen. As they sat and sipped their scotches, Gib said "tell me a little more about this Shanghai fellow, sounds like an interesting character".

"He is," replied Pietro, "but there's not much more to tell, at least that I know. I've never met him, apparently he keeps a real low profile. I have heard stories though. Some of Viktor's buddies are real gamblers. I'm talking big time". Pietro paused, "this is just between us girls", and looked at Gib for acknowledgement.

"Of course" replied Gib, "no problem there".

Pietro continued. "These guys have so much money they can hardly count it. They have been known to win or lose multiple millions at a time. They spend a weekend at Burnham Glen and never leave the casino, barely leave the tables. They play craps and blackjack, and I'm sure other stuff that I don't know about. They have a private room, private dealer, cocktail waitress, everything and anything they want. They bet on soccer, baseball, football, basketball, whatever is on television, they bet on it. The biggest bets they make though, at least that I know about, are on Shanghai's horse racing picks. They don't make those bets with the casino. They have an arrangement with an offshore group that takes their horse racing bets".

"Wow, how does that work"? asked Gib.

"Well, once again, it's simple but brilliant", said Pietro. "The offshore shop is very private and selective. The only bets they take are really big ones. I'm not sure, but I think Foxwoods even uses them to lay off some of their sportsbook action when it gets out of balance and they want to lighten their exposure. These guys are big time. Anyway, their policy on horse racing is that they pay track odds, so whatever the prices are at the track, that's what they pay. For example, if a 3 to 1 shot wins and pays $8.20, they pay $8.20. Nice and simple. Plus, since the bets are not actually made through the parimutuel system, like they are at the track or on line, the offshore shop doesn't pay taxes or fees of any kind. It's totally private. With me so far"?

"I think so", said Gib.

Pietro continued. "Since they don't pay taxes or fees, they make more on the losing bets than the tracks do, and they pay out the same as the tracks on winning bets. That means they have an advantage. In the long run, that advantage is worth a lot of money. Now, Shanghai is a smart guy, really smart. One of the things he brought to the attention of Viktor and his buddies, is that the fact that the offshore shop pays track prices is also a disadvantage to the offshore shop in some cases, as I'll explain. In parimutuel wagering, the track is required to pay a minimum return of $2.10 on a winning $2.00 bet. Now, there are times, as you know, when a heavily favored horse is bet down to really low odds, at times to the point that it seems ridiculous to even consider betting on the favorite, because even if he wins he's only going to pay $2.10. Still with me"?

Gib nodded and said, "yeah, and I think I might see where you're going with this".

"Good", said Pietro. "Now, when this happens, and a heavily favored horse's true odds would result in a winning price of less than $2.10, it creates what is know in the business as a "minus pool". Also, in horse racing, each type of bet has it's own, segregated parimutuel pool. In other words, a bet placed to win goes into the pool with all other win bets, and the same with place, show, exacta, trifecta and all other types of bets. They all have their separate parimutuel pool. The result of all this, is that there can be situations in which the bettor has an advantage over the house, so to speak, in these separate pools, if they are able to recognize these situations and take advantage of them. That's where Shanghai comes in. He watches for opportunities like these and when he spots one, passes along the information to the guys at Foxwoods, who then pass it along to their best customers. In fact, when I called Foxwoods earlier today, they told me about just such an opportunity this Thursday at Gulfstream Park. I didn't get the details, because these guys are out of my league. What I do know is that there is a race at Gulfstream Thursday in which there is a really short priced favorite, probably one to five or something close to that. This horse figures to get extremely overbet in the show pool, creating a minus pool. Therefore, because the track is required to pay a minimum of $2.10 for each winning bet, you can bet the favorite to show, and if he hits the board you collect the same amount, $2.10, that you would have made by betting to win. So, when you boil it all down you get this: A large bettor can make a 5% return on his investment in the time it takes to run a horse race, as long as his horse finishes at least third in the race. Keep in mind, these guys are making huge bets, and they look at it as an investment that will return 5% to them in less than two minutes".

"Damn", said Gib. "But doesn't the offshore shop understand the concept of minus pools and that they're at a disadvantage when they occur"?

"Of course", said Pietro, "but they don't occur often, and most of their clients aren't aware of them anyway. Of course, they also don't know about Shanghai, and they make plenty of cash on the rest of the bets put in by the high rollers, so it works out".

Gib was quiet for a minute. He was rolling the concept around in his head. It made sense, seemed logical. Gib's strength as an investment professional was his keen sense of risk adjusted value. He was never willing to take on risk without the expected return to justify it. Finally he said, "these guys must be making some pretty good money doing this. Come to think of it, it's a lot like the bond market. There are always inefficiencies that can be exploited, but it takes someone with the required experience and investment acumen to make it work. There is an edge there for the person able to see it and act on it, but it's a small edge, and it's really only meaningful when there are large sums of money involved. However, when big money is involved, a small incremental advantage can be worth a lot, a whole lot".

Pietro just looked at Gib and grinned. "Exactly".

CHAPTER 3

The next day was tough for Gib. The scotch, the jet lag and the busy long weekend were taking a toll on his energy level and attention span. He had almost made it through the day, when he got an unexpected call from Chicago. It was Pietro.

"Gib, my man, you sound a little tired. You should go home and get some rest".

"I'm headed that way", said Gib. "What's up"?

"Well, I wasn't sure I should call you today, but I have something to run by you and wanted to give you time to think about it if you're interested".

"Okay", said Gib.

Pietro continued. "There is a Villa in Tuscany that is owned by a group of people, some of whom you know, including me, that is available to members of the group, by reservation, throughout the year. The membership group is really nothing more than a bunch of guys that like to hang out and have fun together, as well as get away for a quiet week or weekend a few times a year by themselves, or with a friend or two. The group is loosely organized. We have a party for the whole group twice a year, Spring and Fall. The other weeks are available to be reserved by members. The members with the most seniority get the first picks. There are fifteen members. Each one of us gets three weeks a year, that's forty five weeks. Then we have the two parties, so that leaves five other weeks that are available. Those five weeks go to the highest bidder. It's not a perfect system, but it works pretty well. The group has been together for a long time, over fifty years, There has been turnover in the membership, but not much. Anyway, a gentleman from Switzerland, who you don't know, has just announced that he is leaving at the end of this year. His wife has health issues. His children are grown and have no interest in being a part of the group. You don't have to tell me right now, but I'm calling to see if you are interested in buying his membership share. The cost is $415,000. I don't know what he paid for his membership share years ago, but it was a lot less than that. Look, Gib, I'm not trying to get into your business. You're a good guy, and I just thought it would be fun to have you as part of the group. Also, I know that you and Natalya have gotten really close, and I have a feeling that she would be pretty thrilled to have the chance to share the Villa with you. Of course that's none of my business, I'm just giving you a little added incentive. This is not an official invitation, that has to come from the group, but everybody likes you, and I think they would be happy to have you. Let me know what you think. If you're interested I'll tell you more of the details, but that's basically it".

Gib sat there. He was too tired to think about such a proposition at that moment. "Okay Pietro, I'm glad you called. Sounds really good, let me sleep on it and then we can talk again".

"Okay", said Pietro. "I only called today because I wanted you to know right away. Just call me back when you feel like talking more about it".

"Alright, great, thanks".

Less than two hours later, without changing clothes or eating a bite of dinner, Gib was sound asleep. The next morning Gib felt like a new man. He had slept hard. He was starving. Breakfast wasn't part of his routine, but you would never know by the way he attacked the first meal of this day. Bacon, three eggs over easy, grits, biscuits and gravy, orange juice and coffee, all disappeared in the span of about ten minutes, including the time it took to locate the hot sauce two tables over. When the carnage was over he returned to normal, and started thinking. The conversation from yesterday with Pietro was in his mind, but on the periphery. The first order of business was to get back in the groove at the office. The investment markets wait for no man. Early morning in New Orleans is the middle of the trading day in Europe, and the end in Japan. A trade not made could be an opportunity lost, just the way it is. It was a constant challenge. Gib loved it.

Like it or not, good or bad, for better or worse, Gib also loved Natalya. He hadn't fully acknowledged it to himself, not officially, but that didn't matter. He was a goner. He arrived at the office early, did his reading and fired up his computer.

There it was, it made his heart flutter, an email from Natalya Petrova. "Hi there. I miss you already. Please tell me that you miss me too". He immediately replied, "I miss you too".

He met with his traders at 7:30, as always. They reviewed their open positions and their cash, and made a plan for the day. Total cash was over three hundred million, way more than normal, largely because of the two hundred million in new cash that had come from the Stezlaus Bank in Moscow. It had been the topic of conversation all day Monday. Everyone was proud of Gib for bringing in such a large account, and from the Sovereign Wealth Fund of Russia, of all places. Gib downplayed the significance of it, but it didn't go unnoticed that he did have a little extra spring in his step. After the meeting, Gib returned to his office and began catching up on phone calls. He ate lunch at his desk. Before he knew it, it was after five o'clock and the office was almost empty. He stopped on the way home and bought beer and a deli sandwich.

As he unwound from the business of the day, his thoughts inevitably turned to Natalya. Then, as if on cue, the conversation with Pietro left the periphery and took center stage. He had a thought. At first it was a fleeting thought, then something a little more. He pushed it aside. It came back. He dismissed it as crazy. It danced around a little and lacked true cohesion, but it didn't go away. It lingered.

Sleep didn't come easily this night. Gib's mind wouldn't allow it. The lingering thought had to be addressed. At five AM on Thursday, after only a few hours of fitful sleep, he sat on his back porch with a cup of coffee and began the inevitable debate with himself. His practical side said that he should ignore the stuff about the Tuscan Villa, concentrate on his work at Boardman and Company and let his relationship with Natalya develop as it may. Things were going well in New Orleans, very well, no reason to put himself in a possible financial bind by investing over $400,000 in a piece of real estate half away across the globe that he had never laid eyes on, much less stepped foot in. The lingering thought wasn't as much a thought as an idea. A crazy idea that made no sense. In fact, it was indefensible, totally lacking credibility in any sense of the word. And it was risky. There was a tug of war going on inside him. The practical versus the risky. The practical side had all of the facts and logic. The risky side had Natalya. Case closed.

At 8:30 Thursday morning, Gib called Pietro in Chicago.

"Good morning Pietro, you got a few minutes to talk"?

"Of course, I hope it's about Tuscany".

"Well, no. I like that idea, I'm very interested, but I have something else to ask you right now".

"Okay", said Pietro, his curiosity piqued.

Gib continued. "You mentioned the other day on the way home that this fellow Shanghai had a race picked out today that he thought would present one of the minus pool situations that we discussed".

"Yes", replied Pietro, "I remember, in spite of the scotch".

"I think it was at Gulfstream", Gib continued, "If it's not too much trouble, could you check and get the details for me? I love the concept, and I might want to invest a few dollars in it, providing of course that your guy Shanghai still recommends it".

"Sure, I'll check it out and send you a text, is that okay"?

"Perfect", replied Gib.

Within the hour, Gib received the text from Pietro. Gulfstream Park, 9th race, the four horse, Helsinki, to show. Gib went to the Daily Racing Form website and looked at the race. Six horses were entered, Helsinki was the two to five morning line favorite. It was the feature race of the day, a $50,000 Overnight Stakes that was added to the card to accommodate Helsinki's connections. They wanted a tune up race before they shipped him to Churchill for the Stephen Foster Handicap, a Grade One stakes race in mid June. Two of the six horses were big longshots entering the race off of layoffs. Two more were respectable allowance runners who were trying to pick up a piece of the purse in a short field. Only one other horse presented a legitimate challenge to Helsinki, and he would have to run a big race to even come close. It looked like a no brainer that Helsinki would at least hit the board.

The lingering thought had become a crazy idea, then it was more than that. Gib Carter, who always did the right thing, had developed a plan, a workable plan, that normally would never even cross his mind, because it was not the right thing. It was a wrong thing, but Gib managed to convince himself to do it anyway, and oh, what a tangled web he would weave.

Gib took an early lunch and walked to the riverfront. There he sat on a bench and reviewed the plan. He made a mental checklist. Number One: He wanted Natalya in his life.

She was far away, both in distance and circumstances. They could have a long distance relationship, but he wanted more, and he knew she did too. He was willing to take a risk to be with her. Number Two: He needed $415,000. That would get him in the club, and three weeks a year or more with Natalya at a Tuscan Villa. Number Three: This is where the plan crossed into dangerous territory. Gib was Chief Investment Officer of a firm with over two billion dollars in assets. He was sitting on three hundred million in cash, which needed to be invested now. His job was to use that money to make smart investments, ones with a favorable risk versus reward proposition. He had convinced himself, however skewed the logic, that race number nine that afternoon at Gulfstream Park presented just such an opportunity.

Gib knew that Pietro's buddies made large horse racing bets directly with an offshore shop of some kind. He didn't know much more than that, and he really didn't want to know much more. What he did want to know, without a doubt, was that the offshore guys could be trusted. He grabbed his phone, called Pietro again and got voice mail. He asked Pietro to call him. Gib skipped lunch, he had no appetite. At about 1:30 Pietro called. Gib wasted no time.

"I want to make a bet on the Gulfstream race, can you arrange it"?

"I'll try", replied Pietro, "shouldn't be a problem".

"Alright", said Gib, "tell me again exactly how it works, betting with the offshore group".

"Okay, well, as I said before, the bets are made through Burnham Glen, they are the ones that have the connection. The money doesn't go into the mutuel pools, it goes directly offshore, by wire. Winning bets are returned the same way, by wire, directly to the place of origin, quick and clean".

"Can you trust these guys, both the offshore guys and Burnham Glen"?, asked Gib.

"Of course", said Pietro, "this is serious business, this is not a fly by night operation. What's up with all the questions? you seem to be a little uptight about it".

"Just making sure about the offshore part. If it's an offshore operation, how can I know, without any doubt, that my money is safe"?

"Well, you're doing business with them already, in a way".

"What do you mean by that"?

"Look Gib, I'm not trying to convince you of anything. You can make the bet or not, your choice. Viktor and the boys like to gamble, so they set up a way to do it. They do it for Burnham Glen, and they do it for high rollers that are friends".

"So Viktor bets his own money"?

"Yes, so do I. No big deal".

Gib paused, "I want to bet ten million".

Pietro paused, "ten million, you gotta be kidding me, nobody bets ten million on a fucking horse race. Are you kidding me or are you fucking crazy"?

"Neither", answered Gib. "I'm an investor and this is a good investment. Can you arrange it"?

"I don't know man. I don't know". Pause. "I'll call you back".

It took a lot of discussion and a lot of cajoling, but at around 3:00 Central Time, 4:00 at Gulfstream Park, a ten million dollar bet was made on the four horse to show, in the 9th race at Gulfstream. It would have raised some eyebrows with the offshore guys, it was a large bet, even for them. But it didn't, because they didn't know about it.

Gib didn't have long to wait before finding out how his most recent investment had performed. It was forty five minutes to post. Gib left the office, went home, opened a beer and had a seat on the sofa, with his laptop connected to TurfSports. com. The four horse was one to five on the tote board, so far so good.

As post time neared, Gib had a hard time sitting still. Finally, the gates opened and they were off and running in the 9th race at Gulfstream. The race was a mile and a sixteenth. The first quarter was uneventful, the pace was even, the four horse appeared relaxed, in third, just two lengths off the lead. The half went in forty eight and change. As they approached the quarter pole, Helsinki moved up on the outside of the leader. As they hit the top of the stretch, the two of them were neck and neck, with four lengths between the two leaders and the horse in third. In mid stretch they were still battling, still two ahead of the rest. At the sixteenth pole, just over 100 yards from the finish line, it was clear that it was going to be very close. The four horse was weakening. Now in second, he just had to hang on to the wire. Gib's heart was pounding, and for the first time, he started to panic. He yelled at the computer screen, telling the four to hurry. He was now in third. As they hit the wire, Gib could hardly breath, he couldn't tell, it was a photo finish. The photo was for third, between a longshot who had gotten through on the rail, and Helsinki, the one to five favorite. After what seemed like forever, the result was posted. Helsinki finished fourth, beaten by a nose.

Gib sat, stunned. He buried his head in his hands. It wasn't possible. Couldn't be real. But it was real. He had just lost ten million dollars of somebody else's money. His hands were shaking, he felt sick, the world was crashing in on him. He went to the liquor cabinet, poured a brandy, knocked it back, then had another. He splashed water on his face. He paced. He had a big problem.

He didn't leave the room for almost three solid hours, except for one trip to the bathroom. He just sat there, and stood there and walked in circles. He kept shaking his head in disbelief, wishing it wasn't real. He couldn't think straight. He was paralyzed with fear. At some point, he wasn't sure of the time, he made a decision. He had to get a grip. He drank several glasses of water and took two sleeping pills. Somehow he managed to crawl in bed and, thankfully, got a few hours sleep. By dawn the next morning, he was showered and dressed and trying to calm down and think straight, but it wasn't easy. He had to do something, and fast, but right now he needed to slow down enough to begin to think through his predicament. First of all, he knew he had some time before anyone at Boardman and Company would notice anything was wrong.

He had wired the money to a numbered account somewhere offshore. Exactly where, he didn't know, but if anybody asked, he could come up with a reasonable sounding name. The ten million dollars itself would not raise any red flags, after all, he had over three hundred million that needed to be invested. The ten million would be on the balance sheet as an alternative investment. It would stay that way for another couple of weeks at least. Once a month, every alternative investment had to be marked to market, that's when it would get hairy. So, at least he had a little time to try to figure something out. Secondly, Pietro, Viktor and the boys would surely be sympathetic to his plight. They were gunslinger types themselves, after all. Maybe they would help him out by making him a short term loan, or even covering the ten million themselves until he could work out a way to pay them back. Not a great option, but at least something. He was in a helluva bad spot, no doubt about it, but now he was starting to think through his options, slim as they were, with a clear head.

At 7:30, Gib called Pietro. He dreaded it, but he knew he had to start somewhere. He got voicemail, so he hung up and sent a text, asking Pietro to call him. He called the office and told them he was going to be out most of the day, and to call him if anything came up that needed his attention. Nobody asked any questions, Gib was the golden boy. He got a text from Pietro saying he was in a meeting and would call in about an hour. It was a long hour. Gib knew he needed to stay busy, so he got a legal pad and started making notes and writing down questions he had for Pietro. Finally, he got the call.

"Thanks for calling Pietro, I fucked up big time. You got time to talk about it"?

"Of course", replied Pietro.

"Well", said Gib, "what the hell am I going to do"?

Nothing. Not a word from Pietro for over five seconds, way too long for a normal pause. Not good.

"I wish I had a good answer for you Gib, but I don't, the money's gone".

"I know the money is gone Pietro", Gib practically shouted, then a long pause, "what about this Shanghai fucker?, is that real, or is all of that just some made up shit Pietro"?

"He's real, everything I said is real. I know it doesn't matter right now to you Gib, but you weren't the only one that lost big on that race. I'm sorry brother, I really am, but it happens that way sometimes".

Gib knew Pietro was right, but he didn't like the way it sounded. He was all set to talk to Pietro about it, now it seemed pointless. Gib said nothing for what seemed like an eternity, then he said "let me ask you a question Pietro, and I want a straight answer".

"Okay", replied Pietro.

"Is there any chance the race was fixed"?

"No", said Pietro, without hesitation.

Gib said nothing for a long time, then hung up the phone. Pietro Ferretti now had a problem of his own. A big problem. He should have known better. There was no offshore bookmaking operation, not in the traditional sense. There was indeed an offshore account, a numbered account, but there were no bookmakers there. It was just one of the many ways in which Stezlaus bank and the boys from Russia laundered money. When someone made a wager, they simply paid off if it was a winner, and kept the money if it was a loser. Just like any other sportsbook. The difference was that they didn't try to make a profit, although they certainly did. They were in business to take in clean money and pay out dirty money, simple as that. They didn't care if they were on the wrong side of a bet, as long as there was action, and plenty of it. They even preferred to take small losses instead of winning big. They wanted happy clients. They wanted cash flow. They didn't want any problems with pissed off gamblers.

When Gib insisted on making a ten million dollar bet, Pietro saw an opportunity. His own cash flow was not great. Ten million would help. After thinking about it for all of about fifteen minutes, he hatched a plan. He gave Gib an offshore account number that he controlled and only he knew about. He had Gib wire the cash to that account. If the horse racing bet was a winner, he, Pietro, would simply forward the cash to the bogus bookmaking operation, they would simply pay the winning bet back to his secret numbered account, and he would send it to Gib. If it were a loser, Bingo. Pietro suddenly had an extra ten million bucks to do with as he pleased. No risk, and a possible huge reward. When Helsinki finished fourth in the race, the unlikely scenario worked out, and suddenly he was ten million bucks richer. He immediately transferred the money out of the phantom account into another numbered account in another bank in another offshore banking haven, somewhere in the Caribbean. About as untraceable as it gets. His good fortune soon turned against him, however, in a big way. Funny how that works. In his haste to set up his get rich quick scheme, he failed to consider the fallout from Gib being snagged for ten mil. Bad mistake. There aren't a whole lot of people who can lose ten million dollars and go on about their business as if nothing happened. There are some of those, but it's a small club, and Gib Carter wasn't in it.

Suddenly, Pietro began to worry. Within the hour, he made a call of his own, that he also dreaded, but knew he had to make. To Viktor. He told him the story. It was a short conversation. The part about Gib losing ten million was bad enough. When Pietro told Viktor that Gib was asking about Shanghai, it got worse. The call ended, as usual, on Viktor's terms.

"Lay low, keep the fuck quiet and hope that's the end of it. You dumb fuck".

That wasn't the end of it. No way. Gib had questions. Gib wanted answers. He started thinking through everything he knew about these people, his new friends. He called the Stezlaus Bank in Moscow and got a recording, closed for the weekend. He went to the website, impressive building, lots of important sounding language. There was a listing of officers and managers. No Viktor. No anybody that he had ever heard of. No Natalya. He thought. He called Pietro again, no answer. He didn't bother leaving a message. He went for a walk, trying to calm down and think. His phone buzzed. It was Nikki, his daughter. He remembered they were supposed to have lunch today. He sent her a text, apologized, told her they would have to do it next week. As he thought, he knew what he had to do. He called Burnham Glen and booked a room for two nights. It crossed his mind that he shouldn't bring attention to himself, maybe book a room somewhere nearby instead of at Burnham Glen, but dismissed it as being paranoid. No reason they should know who he was, he hadn't had any contact with them. The money was wired directly from Boardman and Company to the offshore shop. He wanted to pay a visit to Burnham Glen, and that's where he was headed.

He was wrong. They knew who he was. Viktor called them. He alerted them to the fact that there were some people not happy with Shanghai, especially Gib Carter. By the time Gib's flight left New Orleans, a plan was in place. The drive from JFK to Burnham Glen was a little over an hour. The casino had a fleet of passenger vans that shuttled people to and from the airports in the area. Gib didn't have any checked baggage, just a carry on. He had decided on the flight that he should take public transportation to the casino, wanting to be as inconspicuous as possible. As he walked through the baggage claim area at JFK, he noticed a man standing near the exit, wearing a uniform with a Burnham Glen name tag. He was an older black gentleman with a pleasant looking face. There were several people standing with him, apparently casino guests, talking and laughing. Gib relaxed a little and walked toward them.

"Are you headed to the casino"?, he asked.

The driver smiled and said "yes, and you are welcome to join us, we have two more coming, then we're on our way".

A moment later, a couple walked up and joined them, looking to Gib like Burnham Glen regulars. Gib, being the only person by himself, sat in the front with the driver. The van was equipped with a full bar, and the group wasted no time getting started on their weekend. Gib declined a beer or cocktail, but did accept the offer of bottled water. Less than ninety seconds after taking the first sip, he was out. The van never left the airport. They took an access road to the entrance that read International Freight Shipments. The driver removed the Burnham Glen name tag from the front of his shirt and slid it in his pocket. At the security gate, the attendant checked the number of passengers against his list, and waved them through. Next stop was a huge hangar along the periphery of the second group of buildings. A small sign near the entrance read Moscow Industrial Transport. The van pulled alongside the hangar and waited, within minutes they were directed to drive to the rear of a large transport plane at the head of one of the runways. As they approached, the back of the plane opened and a hydraulic lift platform was lowered to the ground. The van pulled onto it, was lifted, and, after a double check by the crew, drove into the back of the transport plane. Less than 25 minutes after leaving the baggage claim area, the van and all of it's occupants, all but one of whom were Russian nationals, were in the air, headed to Moscow.

When they reached altitude, those occupants left the van and took their seats for the long trip home. An hour later, at the intended spot, the plane reduced speed and dropped altitude. A small cargo door opened. Quickly, unceremoniously, a wire mesh bag wrapped in steel cable was dropped into the deep, dark water of the North Atlantic. Inside was Gibson Carter, sound asleep.

Gib's apartment was a detached garage that had been converted to an apartment after Katrina. It had been rented for three years to one of the oil services companies, as a temporary home for executives and other key personnel during their work assignments in New Orleans. It was owned by a vice president at Boardman & Company. Gib moved in and signed a one year lease his first week in New Orleans. It was tasteful, modern, and unsecured. The two man team entered with no problem at 2:00 AM. They systematically examined every square foot. When they were satisfied with everything else, they focused in on the laptop. Why Gib had not taken it, they didn't know and didn't care. Very carefully, they copied the hard drive, then scanned and recorded every internet search and web site visit ever made.

They left quickly and silently. Gib's smart phone, wallet and carry on bag were carefully searched and incinerated, within half a mile of the baggage claim area of JFK, where he was last seen.

CHAPTER 4

Nikki Carter was disappointed. She enjoyed spending time with her father. They tried to get together every week. They would email each other back and forth, usually trying to agree on a restaurant to visit. New Orleans was such a great food town that it wasn't always easy. It often took several days of emails to come to an agreement. She loved the new, cutting edge places. He liked the hole in the wall joints. There were plenty of both to last a while. She was proud of him. It took some time after her mother died, but he gradually regained his quirky sense of humor and pleasant, easy going manner. Her friends loved Gib. They would hang out and tailgate at Saints games, before and after the game. He would occasionally meet them for happy hour on Friday afternoons. The last few weeks had been different, though. He was always busy with work. He had been to New York and Greece, and now he was in New York again. She knew that his job required him to travel some, and she could tell he enjoyed it, but she wanted him to slow down a little. It also had crossed her mind that he might have a new girlfriend. If so, she was glad. He deserved it. She had to admit to herself, though, that it would almost certainly be different between them if he did start dating somebody. She was an only child, Gib was her rock. It would be really weird sharing him with another woman. As she got off the street car, she told herself to chill out, her father's last minute trip to New York meant that she had to change her plans, big deal, be happy for him, don't be selfish.

Nikki was 25, in her last year of law school. No steady boyfriend, but she had no trouble getting a date. She was slim, with straight dark hair and brown eyes. Breasts were on the small side, but that was just fine with her. She was brilliant, in the top five percent of her class. She had the kind of self assured manner that made her easy to like, kinda like Gib. She had a small circle of close friends, male and female. Her best friend was from Honduras. Her name was Gabriela. Nikki met her in the library at Tulane. Gabriela was born in Honduras but grew up in New Orleans. She had twin brothers, four years younger, who were in school at Loyola in New Orleans. She lived with her family in a wonderful old house on the fringe of the Uptown area. Her aunt and her grandmother lived there also, along with her mother and brothers. Her father lived and worked in Honduras with his brother, running the family seafood business. Gabriela was a year older than Nikki, and was in her last year of Medical School. She worked part time in the library, and had helped Nikki with a research project in her freshman year. Nikki appreciated Gabriela's intelligence and work ethic. They became friends very easily. Gabriela invited Nikki to dinner at her home. Nikki sat at a table with everyone in the family, seven people in all. They were all talking at once. Nikki became part of the family. She would eat dinner with them, hang out with them, spend weekends with them. They adored her.

Gib missed the meeting with his traders Monday morning. Not like him. By lunch time Roger Boardman was concerned that nobody had heard from him. At 3:00 he left a message on Nikki's phone, asking her to call him. She returned the call after class at 4:30, sounding concerned.

"Roger, this is Nikki, is everything okay"?

"I'm sure it is, I don't want to worry you, but Gib wasn't in the office today, and we haven't heard from him. Do you know where he is"?

Nikki looked puzzled. This wasn't one of his poker buddies asking, this was Roger. "I thought he was in New York". It wasn't a statement as much as a question. She was at a loss. He went to New York on business. Why didn't Roger know that?

"Did he say he was going to New York"? Roger asked.

Now Nikki was concerned. She told herself to relax, not to jump to conclusions, not to automatically think something was wrong. "Yes, we were supposed to have lunch Friday, he cancelled because he had to go to New York on business. Is that not right"?

"I don't know. He didn't say anything about it to me", said Roger. "And nobody at the office seems to know anything about it. Are you sure it was a business trip"?

"Well, he said it was", she replied.

Both Roger and Nikki knew this was a problem. Neither had ever known Gib to tell a lie. Neither could even imagine it. He said it was a business trip, but there was no business trip. How could that be? "I'm going to go by his apartment", said Nikki.

"Okay", said Roger, "call me as soon as you can".

Gib didn't answer her knock on the door, so she used her key and went inside. The apartment looked normal. Nothing out of place. No indication that there could be something wrong. His car wasn't there, but that would be expected if he had left on a business trip. She wanted to check his computer, but didn't know his password. It just didn't make sense. She had left messages on his phone, no way he would ignore her. She sat on his sofa and tried, unsuccessfully, to reassure herself that everything was okay.

Nikki felt the first wave of real worry. Her mind started going to unpleasant places. Her mother was gone, taken by the monster called cancer. Now her father seemed to have disappeared into thin air. She had to get a grip, but it was hard. It was unfair. Her father, Gib Carter, was the most decent man she knew. No way he would just leave. No way. She had to do something. Had to figure out why. She slowly walked through his apartment, trying to think. She went in his bedroom, everything was okay. She was trying to keep it together. As she opened the door of his bedroom to leave, she looked at his closet door. She had already looked there. She knew it was a waste of time, but she opened it. Everything in place, neat and orderly. The door to the closet was almost closed when she had a thought. Gib's dirty clothes hamper. She went through his dirty clothes. She picked up a cotton shirt. In the shirt pocket there was a folded piece of paper. She opened it. There were three words. Burnham Glen, Viktor and Shanghai. She didn't have a clue what they meant, if anything.

Nikki suddenly was full of dread. This was something that happens on a made for television movie, not in real life. And certainly not in her life. Or her father's life. They were regular people. No drugs, no nasty divorces, custody battles, lying, cheating, backstabbing. None of that stuff. Her father was a hard working, kind, stand up guy. To her knowledge he had no enemies. Maybe she was overreacting. Maybe he was on a crazy weekend trip and was having so much fun he stayed an extra day. Maybe he did have a girlfriend. It was only Monday afternoon, why was she getting so worked up? She was thinking these things, trying to keep a cool head. All the while, her gut was telling her something different. In no uncertain terms. And was not to be denied. Better to put her big girl pants on and deal with it. She had always heard that the first twenty four hours after someone goes missing are critical. She couldn't just wait and make sure there was a reason to be concerned. By that time it could be too late, and she would never forgive herself.

Her Google search of Burnham Glen immediately produced the homepage of Burnham Glen Resort and Casino, a huge hotel and casino complex in Connecticut, two and a half hours from New York City. Nothing about it was familiar to her, and not a likely destination of Gib Carter's. She called Roger. He answered immediately.

"Any news"?, he asked without hesitation.

"Not much. The apartment looks normal. I did find a piece of paper in a shirt pocket with the word Burnham Glen written on it. Does that mean anything to you"?

"Not really. I've heard of it, that's about all."

"Same here", said Nikki, "also on the piece of paper were two other words, Viktor and Shanghai. Either of those mean anything"?

"No" he replied in a soft voice, with just a bit of an unintended air of foreboding. Then he said in a stronger voice. "Actually, the name Victor could possibly mean something".

"It's Viktor, with a k", said Nikki.

"Hold on a minute, let me check something", said Roger. He pulled up scanned copies of the documents they had just executed involving the Russian Sovereign Wealth Fund. On the last page were the signatures, Roger Boardman, Gibson Carter, Yuri Vladiskos and Viktor Gromyko.

A week before, the name Viktor Gromyko meant absolutely nothing to Nikki. Now it could mean everything. Roger immediately thought he would call Stezlaus Bank in Moscow, but it was about 2:30 in the morning there. He would call as soon as the bank opened. Instead he called Burnham Glen Resort & Casino, where happy hour was in full swing.

"Good afternoon, this is Roger Boardman calling from New Orleans. I'm trying to locate one of my business partners, Gib Carter. It's urgent that I talk to him, he has a family emergency. He doesn't answer his cell phone. I'm thinking he could be somewhere in the casino. Could you get someone to check for me. We're quite anxious to talk to him".

"Hold please Mr. Boardman, I'll try to get someone to help".

A couple of minutes later a gentleman at the concierge desk was on the phone. "This is Carlos, how can I help you Mr. Boardman"?

"I'm trying to get in touch with Gib Carter, he should be either in the hotel or casino, it's very important that I talk to him".

"One moment". Then a pause of a couple of minutes. "I don't see that we have a Gib Carter registered with us. Is it possible that he's registered under a different name, or maybe even at another casino in the area"?

"No, it's Burnham Glen, please check again, it's Gibson Carter, from New Orleans".

"Certainly sir". Another, longer pause. "I'm sorry, but we don't have anyone by that name registered with us. It doesn't appear that he has ever been a guest here. Perhaps for some reason he's at another hotel, I can check if you like. I can inquire by email to all of the other properties in the area, if that would help".

Roger sighed. "No, that's okay, thanks for trying".

He hated telling Nikki that he had struck out at Burnham Glen, but he did. She kept her focus. He told her to try and get some sleep, and to meet him at his office at 1:00 AM, for the call to Moscow. Sleep was not an option for Nikki. She called

Gabriela. When she answered, Nikki lost it. She tried to talk, but the words wouldn't come. Gabriela waited, and tried her best to stay calm herself. Something was wrong, really wrong. Nikki was not the type to lose control. She reacted instinctively.

"Take your time Nikki, I'm not going anywhere, okay"?

"Okay", replied Nikki, barely able to get it out.

"Nikki, where are you?, I'll come get you".

"At my father's apartment".

"Is he there"?

Nikki tried to respond, but it was useless. She was crying in a way that no one should ever have to cry. Gabriela was beside herself with fear and concern for Nikki.

"Stay put Nikki, I'll be there in a minute".

Gabriela didn't bother to knock, the door wasn't locked. Nikki was sitting on the sofa. She looked at Gabriela. Gabriela hugged her, tears flowing, without a word. She thought she could feel Nikki relax a little, which was a good thing. After a few minutes, Gabriela asked, "what's wrong Nikki?, what has happened"? Nikki took a deep breath, and told her everything.

At 1:15 AM, Roger Boardman made the call. It went straight to voicemail. Same thing at 1:25 and 1:35. The 1:45 call was answered, in Russian. He was a little taken aback, but only for a moment. He proceeded in English. "Good morning, this is Roger Boardman with Boardman & Company. Is Viktor Gromyko available"? There was no immediate response. He wasn't sure if it was because of the question or the language.

"I'm sorry sir, who did you say was calling"? The language was no problem.

"Roger Boardman, Boardman & Company, from the U.S., New Orleans".

The reply was not immediate, which was painfully obvious. It was as if the receptionist was trying to decide how to respond. "One moment sir".

The next voice was that of an older male, heavily accented. "Mr. Boardman, I'm Nickolai, please excuse us, we are training a new receptionist. Who is it that you're looking for"?

"Viktor Gromyko", said Roger, growing impatient.

"We don't have a Viktor Gromyko at the bank, sir, is there something I can help you with"?

And so it went, no Gib, no Viktor, no nothing. Roger hung up. Didn't say goodbye. Didn't care. He turned to Nikki and Gabriela. The look on Nikki's face made him want to curse himself, curse the world, curse God. Roger didn't know what to do, so he just hugged her.

Gabriela insisted that Nikki come with her to her house and try to get some sleep, or at least eat breakfast. Nikki wasn't interested in either. She said she was going to her apartment, alone. Gabriela knew it was pointless to argue. She reached in her purse, took something out and gave it to Nikki. Nikki needed sleep. It was a sleeping pill. She made her promise to take it when she got home.

Tuesday afternoon at 4:30, Nikki woke up, in Layton, Connecticut, just down the road from Burnham Glen. She had left Roger's office and driven straight to the airport, bought a one way ticket to Boston, then taken the train to Burnham Glen. She walked around, the place was massive. She decided not to stay there, but instead paid cash for a room at a cheap hotel nearby, using a made up name. She had no luggage. She lay on the bed to rest for a minute, and slept for three hours. Gabriela answered on the first ring. She was both furious and relieved. The furious part would melt away, but it would take a few minutes. The relieved part was much stronger.

"Thank God, where are you?, we've been worried sick".

"I'm in Connecticut".

A pause, a sigh, then in a softer, lower voice. "What are you doing in Connecticut? are you okay"?

Then a deep sigh from Nikki. "Yes, I'm okay. I'm sorry Gabriela. I couldn't just stay and do nothing, and I knew you would try to stop me, so I just left".

Gabriela wasn't sure what to say next. "Nikki, are you sure you know what you're doing? I mean, I know you're upset. I'm upset. If it were my father I don't know what I would be doing. I'm just worried for you, and I'm worried that you're alone. Look, Nikki, if something has happened to your father, if he's in some sort of trouble, maybe you should talk to the police. I'll go with you. I'll come to Connecticut. Please, just think through it".

Nikki was silent. She was thinking. Then she spoke, calmly. "There's something wrong. It doesn't make sense. He's a good man. He's not confrontational. He's happy in New Orleans. Something had to happen. He wouldn't just leave and not tell me anything, and he wouldn't just ignore my calls and texts. If I talk to the police, they'll have to start from the beginning and ask all the questions I've already asked. They don't know him.

They'll start to investigate, but that takes time. I'm here, now. I'm going to Burnham Glen. I have to Gabriela".

"Promise me this", Gabriela replied, "if you don't find out any more than you know now, by tomorrow, you'll talk to the police".

"Okay", said Nikki.

She tried to freshen up, then took the shuttle to Burnham Glen Resort & Casino. She had no idea where to start, so she walked in, looked around and headed to the large bar at the rear of the main casino floor. She sat at the bar, asked for a bottled water, then ordered a glass of white wine. She was anxious, but not scared. She realized that she was sitting in the wrong spot, facing the bar, her back to the casino floor. She casually moved around to the end of the bar, and sat with her back to the wall. Another glass of wine. She was looking, and thinking. She caught the bartender's eye and he walked over to her. "I'm looking for someone", she said with an almost sheepish half grin. "I know it's crazy, but I only have one more day here, and anyway, I sort of don't know his name".

The bartender looked amused. "Might be kinda tough without a name".

Nikki pressed on. "I somehow ended up with his shirt, and this piece of paper was in the pocket". She showed it to him. The words Burnham Glen, Victor, and Shanghai.

He shook his head. "I have no idea, but he must be quite a guy". He clearly found it all a bit humorous.

Nikki decided on a different approach. The bartender was losing interest, and had drinks to serve. As he turned to walk to the other end of the bar, she said, "Who has been here a long time? Like, an employee who knows everybody".

He kept walking, not acknowledging the question at first. Then he stopped and turned to her. "Clarence, the valet manager, he knows everybody". She smiled. He smiled, and shook his head.

Clarence was easy enough to find. Partly because he was an older black gentleman at the valet stand who was obviously in charge, and partly because he had a name tag that read Clarence Young. He was the kind of person every hotel or nightclub or casino should have at the front door. He was a natural. He was happy. He had a big smile. It seemed like he did indeed know everybody. Nikki sipped her wine and watched him from just inside the large main entrance to the casino. He directed the traffic in front of the main entrance. Those using the valet service got the red carpet treatment. Those picking up or dropping off someone were relegated to the far outside lanes, and they had to keep moving. Limos were wild cards, some were big time, some just took up space, and so it went. Nikki had a good feeling about Clarence, so she decided to wait until things slowed down, and then try to talk to him. That took a while. If it had been a weekend night it would have been later. As it was, just before 11:00PM, Nikki walked over to Clarence.

"Mr. Young, my name is Nikki Carter. Could I take just a minute of your time? I'm looking for someone and I'm hoping you might be able to help".

Clarence, the master of smooze, replied with a devilish smile and his signature quick wit. "What in the hell kinda man wouldn't want to help out a pretty girl like you? Call me Clarence sweetheart".

"Okay, Clarence, thank you. I'm looking for my father. I think he was here a few days ago, but I'm not sure, nobody seems to have seen him. I found this piece of paper in his shirt pocket". She handed it to him. "Any chance you might know one of those names, or have any idea what those three words could possibly mean"?

Clarence studied the folded piece of paper. His grin replaced by a more serious expression. He had been around the block, more than once. He sensed a quiet desperation in Nikki's voice and saw worry in her eyes. He wanted to give her good news, but he just shook his head slowly. They were standing in front of the valet stand. The valet guys were having to walk around them. Clarence motioned with his head and stepped to the side and behind the busy area.

"Tell me about your father. Why are you looking for him"? It was the kind of question Nikki should have expected, but it took her off guard.

"I'm worried about him. I don't know where he is". She paused, but he said nothing. "He's missing".

She said it as if she were saying something out loud that she hadn't been willing to admit before. Her eyes began to fill with tears. She bit her lip. Clarence put his arm around her and together they walked into the hotel, and took a seat in the corner of the lobby, as far away from the casino entrance as possible.

"Can I get you something, a bottled water maybe"? Nikki looked at him and breathed out.

"I think I need a drink".

Clarence Young was 61 years old. He had felt his share of heartache. He never knew his father. His mother left him with her parents while she took off headed who knew where to do who knew what. He adored his grandmother. She died when he was fifteen. His grandfather was a good man, but he was old and tired. Clarence managed to graduate from High School, but then the trouble started. He was involved in a bar fight that ended badly. A nineteen year old boy was stabbed to death. He wouldn't talk. He served five years, even though he didn't do it. After prison he joined the military, put in twenty years and retired. He started to work at Burnham Glen when he was forty eight. He had married and divorced while in the military. He had a daughter, 29, who was somewhere in California. She called him once a month or so, promising to come visit soon. He was still waiting.

Nikki told Clarence what she knew. He listened. He was torn. This young lady needed help, but he had no idea how to help her, and he didn't want to get involved. He looked at her. He thought of his daughter, and knew he could not just send her on her way. Then he had a thought. He was still holding the piece of paper. He looked at it, then he spoke to her, almost in a whisper, without looking directly at her.

"There's a bar called Neeley's, it's about a mile from here, on Farley Ave., take a cab. Be there at 12:30. Don't know if I can help, but I'll buy you a drink". He stood, still without looking at her, and walked back outside.

Clarence was sitting in a room in the back of the bar. It was a private room where some of the guys got together once a week and played cards. They also watched ball games there, got together for special occasions there, and so forth. The room, the bar and the apartment above the bar were owned by Rufus Neeley, Clarence's best friend and confidant. Clarence was uncharacteristically uptight. He knew he was entering dangerous territory. The boys at the casino had been good to him, but he knew the score. He minded his own business, showed up for work on time and hustled to take care of the people. He had paid his dues. The gig was good. He made a little money and had lots of friends. He was willing to overlook some things. Life is tough when you buck the system. Ben there, done that. Better to take care of yourself and your people, and let other folks do the same. He didn't dwell on it, but he knew there was some heavy duty shit going on behind the scenes at Burnham Glen. Big money don't play. These boys were big money. These boys don't play.

So why was he sitting here in the back room of a bar, about to share some information with a young lady he had never met until two hours ago? A white girl. Pretty sure not one of his people. The answer lay somewhere inside the man. The memory of feeling alone, wondering why his parents didn't want him. Of knowing what it's like to be the underdog, to be just another poor black kid with nobody and no prospects. Of feeling cheated and not worth much. Of being born unlucky, of wanting to be understood, and loved. Somewhere, among all that.

She walked in the bar precisely on time. She hadn't taken more than a few steps, when a pleasant looking gentleman approached her. "You looking for Clarence"?

She nodded. She followed him to the back room. Clarence stood, and smiled warmly. "This is Rufus, he owns the joint".

"Nice to meet you", said Nikki.

Rufus nodded and asked "what would you like to drink"?

They spent about five minutes chit chatting, then Clarence began. "Like I told you, I don't know if I can help you. But I'll listen. Tell me about it".

So she did. He didn't interrupt once. Clarence had a bad feeling. He wished like hell he didn't, but he did. He wasn't sure what to say, so he did what he knew was best. He laid it out there.

"Nikki", his voice was a little shaky, he wasn't used to that. He cleared his throat. "What I'm going to tell you is not what you want to hear, but it's not going to do you any good for me to beat around the bush". Nikki's facial muscles tightened. "There are some bad people at Burnham Glen. I don't know what happened to your father, but it doesn't sound good. That doesn't mean something bad has happened, but it does mean that you are dealing with some really dangerous people. That's why we're talking here instead of there. I don't have any idea who Viktor is, but I have an idea about Shanghai. There is a guy who used to work at Burnham Glen, they call him Shanghai, not sure what his real name is. He worked as a valet for a while, then he moved inside to the Sports Book. He was kinda different, but he was a hard worker. Never got into trouble that I know of. Anyway, he's a really smart guy, and from what I hear, he's an excellent horse race handicapper. They say that the big money boys at the casino pay him to handicap horse races for them. How it works I'm not sure, but I hear that he's doing well at it".

Several seconds passed as Clarence gave Nikki the opportunity to say something, but she didn't. He continued. "Shanghai is not the type to cause trouble. Just the opposite really, he keeps a low profile. He comes around every now and then to say hello and have a couple of drinks. The guys like him. It doesn't make sense that he would be involved with anything related to your father, unless somehow it was connected to horse racing".

A long pause, Nikki's mind was in high gear, thinking. She spoke. "I gotta talk to Shanghai".

Clarence knew this was coming. He had thought through it himself. This was a tough spot. He had already decided how to handle it.

"Okay, Nikki, listen to me. These are some bad damn people. They don't care about you. They don't care about me. All they care about is themselves and their money. If you want to go talk to Shanghai, I'm not going to stop you, but I don't think it's a good idea and I'm not going with you. Once they know I've helped you, it's over for me". He told her the address, she wrote it on a pamphlet she had picked up at the casino. "What you should do is call the police and ask for their help. It's not a good idea to go by yourself Nikki. Let them go and talk to Shanghai".

Nikki looked at him. "Will you call me a cab"? is all she said.

When the cab arrived, Clarence went to Nikki and wrapped his arms around her. She was trying her best not to cry.

Nikki walked into her room just before 2:00 AM and collapsed on the bed. She didn't look at her phone. She was sure Gabriela had tried to reach her. She appreciated her. She knew Gabriela was worried, but she had to do this. She slept til daybreak, got up, showered and put her clothes back on, the only ones she had. The shower helped. She looked online and got directions to the address Clarence had given her. It was only five blocks away. She would walk. She was starving. The hotel had a free Continental Breakfast. Not the best but good enough. After coffee, breakfast and a scan of USA Today, she was back in her room. Still only 8:15 AM, too early to pay a surprise visit to Shanghai. She sat and thought. Doubts started to creep in. Clarence was scared of the Burnham Glen people. That stayed in her mind. If he was scared of them, she should be too, she knew that. But it was her father, and no way was she backing out now. Still, she needed to be careful, to be smart. She had to trust her instincts. After her talk with Clarence, she didn't think Shanghai himself was a threat to harm her. In fact, it's possible that Shanghai didn't know who Gib Carter was. She would knock on his door, and hope he was home, alone. If he wasn't home, she would give it a couple of hours and try again. If she didn't find him and talk to him by lunch time, she would come back here. She would try again after work hours, if she still had no luck, she would call the police. She wanted to call Gabriela now, but she knew she couldn't tell her what she was doing. She would wait.

As she walked up to the door, her pulse quickened. She told herself to slow down. She took a deep breath. She knocked. No response. She looked around. Knocked again. Nothing. She was trying to decide what to do, when she heard something, not much, but something. The door opened partially, and she was face to face with Charlie "Shanghai" Morris. She froze. Her mind went completely blank. She had spent so much time worrying about what could go wrong, she never thought about what she would say if he opened the door. Several awkward seconds passed.

"Can I help you"? he asked.

"Ugh, I ugh, I'm sorry, are you Shanghai"? She wanted to stop right there and do a retake, like they do on a movie set. She felt like a bumbling idiot.

He gave a slight shrug. "Yep".

She thought her awkward stammering would make him wary, but it actually did the opposite. She was totally non threatening. She seemed shy, unsure what to say. She was very pretty. He couldn't care less why she was there. He knew a good thing when he saw it, and she was a good thing. "I'm Nikki Carter, would you mind if I ask you a couple of questions"?

"Go ahead", he replied, then, "would you like to come inside first"?

Again Nikki was a little caught off guard, but this time she didn't hesitate. "Okay, thank you". She took a seat on the end of the sofa. He sat in a chair opposite her. "I'm sorry to intrude.

I'm looking for my father, Gib Carter. Nobody has seen him for a few days. It's not like him to be out of touch, and I'm very worried. He was supposed to be on a business trip to New York, he flew there last Friday, and he just sort of disappeared". She took a deep breath, and showed him the piece of paper. "I found this in the pocket of a shirt he left at home".

Shanghai took it and looked at it. His stomach tightened. He didn't know Gib Carter. He didn't know Viktor. He did know something was wrong. He looked up at Nikki. Gone was the good thing.

She spent an hour and a half with Shanghai. It was no fun for either of them. He felt bad for Nikki. She was searching for her father, and he felt pretty sure it was not going to turn out well. He wanted to help. He also wanted to live. He told her the truth. He didn't know Gib, never heard of him. He had never heard of Viktor, and he knew that if his instincts were correct, he was glad he hadn't. This is just the kind of stuff he was trying to avoid. He had gotten a look at what goes on behind the scenes at Burnham Glen. That was all he needed. Let them have their money and big egos, their fast paced lives, their lies. But maybe he was no better than them. They were paying him. He was helping them. Did he really think they used his horse racing picks just to make a few bucks for themselves? Did it matter? Were they doing anything illegal? He didn't have all the answers, but one thing was clear. Something had gone wrong. This beautiful girl was hurting, and there was nothing he could do to help her.

Nikki walked back to the hotel, dejected. It was time to call the police. She had promised Gabriela. She didn't bother to check messages, she just made the call. Gabriela answered in a sad voice. She was relieved and very glad to hear from Nikki, but she had to give her some bad news, and it broke her heart.

"Nikki, are you okay"? She said yes, but didn't sound convincing. "Have you talked to anybody here"?

"No", answered Nikki. Not knowing why Gabriela was asking the question, and not caring. "I guess we should call the police", said Nikki, with total resignation.

The sound of Nikki's voice made Gabriela dread even more the conversation she had to have with her.

"Nikki, the police are already involved. I have some bad news, and I'm sorry I have to tell you, especially on the telephone". Nikki now was fully alert, and braced herself for what she thought she knew was coming. What she heard next was not what she expected. In many ways it was worse.

"There is ten million dollars missing from Boardman and Company's Investment Portfolio. They're saying that your father wired ten million dollars to an untraceable offshore account the day before he disappeared. They've issued an international warrant for his arrest".

Nikki sat, dumbfounded, and as low as a person can be. She wanted to lay down and never wake up. She had no desire, none, to spend another day in this cruel world.

PART 2

Ernie

CHAPTER 5

Ernie Cole was 68 years old and looked every day of it. He had been a successful young bond trader on Wall Street, but that was many moons ago, and it didn't end well. It appeared to most people to be a typical case of "too much too soon". Ernie apprenticed as a teenager at the Wall Street firm where his father was a senior partner. He finished college in three years and then graduated with an MBA with honors from Tuck School of Business at Dartmouth. He immediately joined an investment banking firm as a junior analyst, and quickly established himself as one of Wall Street's young, bright minds. The trouble started, as it so often does, with a very pretty young lady. Her name was Catherine Lanahan. She was blonde. She had long slender legs. She had porcelain skin, high cheekbones, hypnotic eyes and an overall air of supreme confidence. He met her in the lobby waiting for the elevator. She smiled at him. He never stood a chance.

He slept with her on the third date, if you can call it that. A date that is. He had mustered the courage to ask her for a drink after work one Friday. She suggested they go downstairs to the bar in the first floor of the building. A group of young people met there on Friday's after work. They were a mixture of people from different firms in the building, but they all had one thing in common: They were the new breed. Ernie was born into it. His father was a Wall Streeter. His father made more money in a single day than most men made in a month. He had a driver. He had a "Place" in Tuscany, where his wine cellar was full of old Brunello. He was on the boards of three different Fortune 500 companies. His father was a Wall Streeter. Ernie was part of the new breed on Wall Street, but he wasn't a Wall Streeter. Ernie had another side. He loved the challenge and complexity of the financial markets. He liked being the smart guy. He liked having money, but Ernie had another side. He kinda wanted to live in the city and take the subway. He thought it might be cool to hang out more and listen to live music. He liked the vibe of the street. He didn't care a whole lot for suits. He didn't want to have to keep his shoes shined. He liked the money, money was freedom. Ernie's father was a Wall Streeter, Ernie was not.

They sat at a table in the back, on the left side, where the young people gathered. She knew most of the others and introduced them to Ernie. He was immediately accepted. He was young, good looking, confident and hanging out with Catherine Lanahan. After five beers and an obligatory shot of Patron, he was in the groove. The guys loved Ernie, the girls did too. They all laughed and drank and had a big time, these young titans of Wall Street. At around 8:30, the party started to break up. He and Catherine moved next door to the restaurant, were seated, and promptly ordered a nice bottle of Italian white from the Piedmont region. The conversation flowed effortlessly. Two hours and a second bottle later, they left the restaurant. Each took a cab, Catherine to the apartment she shared with three other girls, and Ernie to his father's Brownstone overlooking Central Park. Before they parted company Catherine kissed Ernie on the lips, just once, before she got in the cab. She didn't say a word, but as the cab pulled away from the curb, she was looking at Ernie, and smiling.

The second date was a bit more formal. Ernie invited Catherine to a reception and dinner honoring the head of the New York Federal Reserve Bank, who was retiring after 22 years in that position. He was going in place of his father, who was out of the country. Catherine looked stunning in a black dress and diamond necklace. Ernie and Catherine looked like they belonged together, each of them poised and confident. Ernie couldn't help but notice the looks that Catherine got. Hell, he was looking at her too. As they walked onto the dance floor after dinner, hand in hand, he felt like a kid in junior high school. As they faced each other, the band started playing a slow number, he put his arms around her and she melted into him. She laid her head on his shoulder and closed her eyes. He caressed the back of her neck. When the song was over she looked at him. They kissed. He could feel the electricity from head to toe. As the next song started they didn't move. They just stood there gazing at each other and whispering softly. The world around them ceased to exist. The band took a break and everyone cleared the dance floor. They walked outside, got a fresh glass of champagne, and mingled with the other guests. At the end of the night, limos were waiting outside to return the guests to their homes safely. Ernie escorted Catherine to her door. They kissed good night, both breathing deeply.

As they say: The third time's the charm. The following Friday, Ernie and Catherine once again joined the group down-stairs for drinks after work. Once again they drank too much, but instead of having dinner in the restaurant, they took a cab to Ernie's father's place. He put on some music, opened a bottle of wine and started to fill a large pot with water to start cook-ing one of his favorite pasta dishes. When he turned to look at her, she had kicked off her shoes and unbuttoned two buttons on her blouse. As he poured them a glass of wine and looked up again, she had unbuttoned number three. He slowly moved to her, and finished the last few buttons for her. He parted her blouse, reached back, managed to unhook her bra, and began kissing her breasts. He then, slowly, pushed his hand past her stomach, and down further until he felt the heat and wetness between her legs. She trembled. He felt like Superman.

The next couple of months were more of the same. Ernie and Catherine hanging out, going out and making love. Lots of making love. And why not? They were single adults with careers, but other than that neither had responsibilities to slow them down. Weekends were usually free, they had money, they had time, life was wonderful. Ernie began to let his thoughts wander off to a place they had never been, to the idea of marriage, and a family. He was fully in love with Catherine, and he couldn't imagine his life without her. Six months into their relationship, Ernie's firm sent him to Zurich, Switzerland for ten days. The firm had a small office inside of one of the large Swiss banks. It was there to serve the firm's European clients. There was one full time Swiss Investment Advisor there, and two assistants. Twice a year, someone from the New York office would travel to Zurich and spend time learning the nuances of doing business there. It was valuable experience and often led to other opportunities in Europe. Ernie knew it was a pretty big deal that he was asked to go, especially at his age. There was never any question that he would go, but he was not happy about being away from Catherine for that long, especially so far away.

Zurich was fabulous. He stayed at the Baur au Lac, a luxury hotel in the heart of the city. Everything about it validated his status as an up and coming player in the game of high finance. The office was equally impressive, old wood and leather, expensive rugs, artwork. Ernie enjoyed all of it, but by the fourth day he was ready to get back to The Big Apple, to Wall Street, to Catherine. He called her every night, but because of the time difference it was afternoon in New York and it was hit or miss when she had the chance to talk. The fifth day in Zurich, he woke up early so that he could call her during the evening hours in New York. She didn't answer, it went to voicemail, he left a sweet message. Three hours later he checked his phone, nothing. He skipped the scheduled lunch, grabbed a sandwich and walked to a nearby park adjacent to the Bahnhofstrasse, the famous pedestrian street that is home to world class shopping and some of Europe's most important banks. He called again, voice mail. This time, instead of leaving a voice message, he texted her. The text message was again sweet, but not as sweet, and it was short. Ernie wanted her to call, text, something. That evening Catherine called, it was just after lunch in New York. As soon as he heard her voice, Ernie thought something was different. Not something overly obvious, hardly noticeable really, but something. They chatted for about ten minutes, then she had to go. Ernie paused to allow her to say something else before she said goodbye. He wanted to hear her say "I love you", "I miss you", "I wish you were here right now so I could hold you and kiss you and make love to you for hours non stop", but she didn't. She just said good night.

The rest of the trip was no fun. He did fun things, ate fabulous meals, met with rich people, saw a bunch of old buildings, took a day trip to the Alps. None of it mattered. Nothing mattered, except getting back home to Catherine. If indeed that were possible. He had a sickening feeling that the Catherine he left in New York was gone. Not literally, but gone just the same. Actually not the same at all. If she were gone, literally, gone to another place, he could go to that place. The sickening feeling was that she had gone to a place that was out of reach by any means of transportation. A place that existed, but not for him. He tried to think of other things, but it was no use. He scolded himself. He asked himself, "why did you fall in love with her? how could you possibly allow another person to have your heart and do with it what she might"?

He awoke on his last day in Zurich with a fresh attitude. He was heading home. The people in Zurich liked Ernie and were impressed with him. He had no doubt there would be opportunities later, in Zurich or elsewhere. But now he was going back to New York, and he had a beautiful girlfriend there waiting for him. Ernie had a positive outlook on life. Always had. No reason not to. Who knows if he was born that way, or his environment made him that way. Probably both, but no matter how the self confidence got there, it was there. He was smart, but had never been the smartest guy in the class. He was athletic, but others were more so. He was handsome, but didn't have movie star looks. What he had was an iron will, and that iron will trumped all of the other attributes a man could have. But it didn't trump Catherine Lanahan.

Ernie had never known heartbreak. In fact, he had never really known pain or suffering of any kind. He had been born lucky, as they say. He had no siblings. The Cole family was wealthy. His father was something of a rarity, a rich man with a kind heart. His mother was crazy as a loon. She drank too much. She was rich, but she didn't act like it. She had a small antique and book shop in the village, but she didn't keep regular hours. She loved old books. She would buy what she loved, regardless of the price, and she was reluctant to sell any of her favorites. Writers and artists of all types would stop by her shop just to chat, or maybe take a nip of something. Ernie's full name was Ernest Hemingway Cole. It was between that and F. Scott Cole. Ernie's father was okay with either. His mother was torn, but as she held her baby boy the first time after going home, she glanced across the room and her gaze fell upon a first edition of Death in the Afternoon. Ernie it was. His parents divorced when he went away to college. He loved them both and he always knew they loved him, so the divorce didn't change their lives a whole lot. His father worked all the time. His mother hung out and drank, same as always, only now they lived apart.

His first few days back at the firm in New York were hectic. It was as if they were letting him know that, although he had spent the last ten days working in Europe, he was still a junior analyst. Ernie felt much better about Catherine and his relationship with her now that he was back. She had met him at the airport when he got home. They went to his father's place, had a quick drink, made passionate love and spent the night together. When the weekend rolled around they hung out with friends, went to a movie, the regular stuff. He intended to bring up the uneasiness he had felt in Switzerland, but now it seemed unnecessary. Things between them were just fine, so he let it go. Catherine Lanahan was a smart girl. In addition to being smart, she was beautiful. She was also a bit cunning. Ernie was her man. She loved Ernie, but not just for being Ernie. She loved the whole deal, including Ernie. If you took Ernie away from the deal, she would still love the deal. If you took the deal away from Ernie, well, the world would keep turning, but no way would Ernie and Catherine be breathing the same air.

The next few months flew by. They spent Christmas and New Years apart. She went skiing with some girls from college.

He went to Connecticut to be with his father and grandmother. His father had just finished cowriting a book on charitable giving, and needed some down time. That was just fine with Ernie, he needed a breather himself. After a week though, he was more than ready to get back to the city, to his routine, to Catherine.

In late February, Catherine invited Ernie to go with her to visit her mother and her new husband in Little Rock, Arkansas. Ernie wasn't thrilled with the prospect of spending a weekend in Arkansas, but he was glad that Catherine wanted him to go, so he did. Frances Lanahan hadn't spent much time in Arkansas herself. In fact, she had never been to the state until she met Jake Delaney. He was semi retired from the family timber business. He had been divorced for almost two years but hadn't dated much. He met Catherine's mother Fran while visiting the California wine country during a business trip to San Francisco. They drank wine, had dinner two nights in a row, and by the third day had begun a romance that was still going strong two years later. When they started talking marriage, he was surprised that she was okay with moving to Little Rock, but she was. She kept her apartment in Boston. He was fine with that. They traveled a lot. She fit in well with his friends, and she kept her closest friends in Boston. Catherine was thrilled to see her happy with their life in Little Rock, and was looking forward to the visit.

They arrived on Friday afternoon. It was chilly, but not as cold as New York. Ernie liked Jake right off the bat. He had the self assured manner of a man who had known success and was comfortable in his own skin. He was happy to let the girls carry on as they do, and seemed to genuinely enjoy being the host. He fixed drinks, showed Ernie around the house and eventually made his way to the back patio to prepare to grill steaks for dinner. He invited Ernie to join him, and soon they were swapping stories and laughing like old friends.

Jake's youngest son Richard, who lived in a condo near the university, joined them for dinner. Richard was a first year medical student, and had the same pleasant personality as his father. Ernie had met Frances a couple of times before in New York. He liked her, but had not gotten beyond simply being Catherine's boyfriend. He was okay with that, figuring that eventually, as they spent time together, they would be closer.

Jake not only grilled the steaks, but prepared the entire meal. He made risotto with wild mushrooms, a fabulous spinach and radicchio salad with grilled bread and goat cheese, and had even made a Madeira reduction for the steaks. Everything was delicious. For dessert they sipped a late harvest riesling that he had gotten in Napa, along with a pistachio and dark chocolate terrine. It was a meal that was every bit as good as any Ernie had in Europe or New York. The conversation during dinner was lively. They all had opinions and didn't mind expressing them. Ernie wasn't used to being at the family dinner table, much less one as enjoyable as this. As the evening progressed, talk turned to plans for the next day. Catherine and her mother made it known that they had already planned a long overdue shopping trip together. That surprised nobody.

Jake wondered why they even bothered to announce it. Richard looked at Ernie.

"What you gonna do while they shop"? Ernie just shrugged and made an exaggerated fake frown. "Why don't you go to the track with us"? Richard said.

"What track"? Ernie asked.

"Oaklawn Park, in Hot Springs. It's been there over a hundred years. It's great. You'll love it. It's a thirty minute drive from here".

"Better tell him Lobo's going", said Jake, "and probably Big Tony".

"He'll love em", said Richard, "they can be a pain in the ass, but they're fun. He'll love em".

"I'm liking this idea" said Ernie. "Let's do it".

Ernie was up early the next morning, as usual. As he walked into the kitchen to fix a cup of coffee, he noticed a newspaper on the counter. As he looked at it he saw it was the Daily Racing Form. There was a note on it. "First post is 1:00, we'll leave at 11:30". Ernie opened the Racing Form, and entered the world of thoroughbred horse racing.

Hot Springs, Arkansas is a town with a past. A colorful past. Gangsters, gambling houses, booze, fast women, and horse racing. Oaklawn Park opened in 1905. The Mayor declared an official half day holiday so people could go to the track. The gangsters and gambling houses are long gone now, but the love affair with horse racing, over a hundred years later, is still going strong. Hot Springs is not just a town with horse racing, it's a horse racing town. You can buy a Daily Racing

Form at the gas station. Restaurants have pictures on the walls of horses and horse people. Going to the track in Hot Springs is not just accepted, it's embraced. The population of Hot Springs is about 35,000. A typical Saturday crowd at Oaklawn is over 20,000. On some big days it has been over 50,000. More than a love affair, it's a serious relationship.

Lobo, as usual, spent time Saturday morning making his picks for the day using the newspaper. No Daily Racing Form, no tip sheet, no program, no nothing. He made his picks based on jockeys. He was sitting at the kitchen table with the newspaper in front of him when Richard and Ernie walked in.

"Good morning", said Richard, with a little more enthusiasm than normal.

"Mornin", replied Lobo, barely looking up from the paper.

Richard said,"this is Ernie, Catherine's boyfriend from New York. Ernie, this is the one and only Lobo, my favorite uncle".

"Your only fuckin uncle", replied Lobo, still not looking up. "Good to meet you Ernie".

Ernie chuckled, "good to meet you too".

Ten minutes later, after picking up Big Tony down the street, they were on their way to the track. Tony looked just like Ernie had imagined he would. He was built like a lumberjack with a beer gut. Richard drove, Ernie sat in front. Lobo and Big Tony were in the back.

"Ever been to Oaklawn Ernie"?, Big Tony asked, in his usual straightforward manner.

"First time", replied Ernie. "Looking forward to it. I'm gonna stick close to Lobo and see if I can learn a few things".

Lobo smiled. Big Tony laughed. "Shit, good luck with that".

As soon as they stepped foot inside the track, Ernie was hooked. They didn't bother buying reserved seats. The only ones left weren't any good, and they didn't want them anyway, especially Big Tony. The reserved seats at Oaklawn are on the small side, and Big Tony was big. Big Tony also liked to talk. The reserved section was okay for talking to those people within about a five or six foot radius. Big Tony's radius was several times that.

Barely through the gate, as if on cue, Big Tony stopped and turned to the others, arms outstretched, "this is my house" he said, emphatically and with just enough bluster to get the desired effect.

Lobo shook his head slowly and walked off, muttering, "fuckin redneck".

Ernie had been at the track less than five minutes, and he was laughing harder than he had in the past year on Wall Street. Big Tony, with Richard along for the ride, gave Ernie a tour of the Track Level section of Oaklawn Park, with a final stop, of course, at the corned beef counter. Corned beef sandwiches are one of the most popular traditions at Oaklawn Park. Thinly sliced, piled high on rye bread, slathered with horseradish and mustard, they sell them by the thousands. You don't eat lunch before you go to Oaklawn, you wait til you get there and eat a corned beef sandwich. Part of the deal. Lobo walked up, having secured his mutuel ticket for the early Daily Double. He looked at Ernie.

"I see Tony didn't waste any time finding his favorite lunch counter. Let's go to the paddock and have a look at these Nags".

The lady behind the counter, a feisty looking redhead with a glint in her eye, said "you got some winners picked out Lobo"?

Lobo, master of glib, with no facial expression answered, "does a fat baby fart"?

She chuckled, Ernie laughed and they all headed to the paddock, Big Tony already thinking about the next corned beef sandwich.

The track level at Oaklawn Park is a microcosm of society. Each strata of racetrack hierarchy is represented. At the top are the horse owners and their friends. They only enter when they have a horse running in the next race. They walk to the paddock, meet with the trainer and admire the horses, especially their own. They dress and act like rich people, because they are. Below them are the beautiful people. The ones that dress and act like rich people, but they aren't quite there yet. Next is the upper middle strata. There are lots of these at Oaklawn, dressed as if they're attending a college football game. Next is the lower middle, which are regular people enjoying a day at the track. Then you get to the great unwashed, the characters, the young, the old and everything in between. The ones that smoke cigarettes, have tattoos, wear any old thing, laugh and argue and cuss and scream for the number four horse to please please please hurry up and get to the wire. This strata is the heart and soul of the track. For every stone faced horse owner that bets $100 to win on his horse, there are fifty of these characters betting $2 each to do the same thing, and they do it with their own unique style. And passion.

The magic of the track is that when the horses leave the gate, all the class distinctions melt away. Everyone is in the same boat. Everyone is the same. Please please please, run you sombitch run. From a distance, an onlooker would peg Ernie Cole as a part of the upper strata, which, technically, he was. The soul of Ernie Cole, however, was, and forever would be, firmly in the camp of the great unwashed.

Lobo barely missed the Daily Double when his horse in the second race got stuck on the rail and didn't get through until it was too late. Ernie cashed his first ticket in the fourth. A five dollar straight up win bet on the second choice. He collected twenty five bucks and immediately announced "beers are on me".

"Fuckin A" said Big Tony and immediately put his arm around Ernie and half dragged him to the nearest beer stand. He got two beers and stepped to the side. Ernie looked around to make sure the other guys wanted one too. When he turned back around Big Tony had one beer left, and it had a very short life expectancy. Ernie laughed once again and shook his head.

"Give me four beers please" he said. He handed one to each of the others and lifted his for a toast. "To my first winning horse race bet, most of the profit from which is now residing in Big Tony's stomach". Lobo nodded and drank up.

Richard said, "I sure hope you cash a few more tickets", and drained his share of the proceeds.

"Let's go to my spot" said Lobo.

Big Tony made an exaggerated eye roll. "Nobody wants to go to that bullshit spot. The reason it's your spot is because none of these other twenty thousand fuckin people want that spot, including me".

"That's exactly why I like it numbnuts", Lobo retorted, "It's the only place I can get away from your bogus ass".

With that, Lobo led the way to his spot, followed by Richard and Ernie. Big Tony took a seat on the steps outside and turned to the next race in the program. Lobo's spot was on the rail, as far down toward the first turn as you could get. There was no entrance or exit gate nearby, so there was no traffic and rarely any people at all, which was the whole point. It was quiet. You could see the horses leave the gate and start running straight at you. As they got closer, you could hear the sound of hooves hitting the ground. When they got right in front of you and started into the first turn, the sound was powerful. The hooves hitting the track surface had a percussion like sound, deep and rhythmic. You can hear the horses breathing heavily, and sometimes you can also hear the jockeys shouting and sweet talking and whatever they do to get their horses to run like the wind. As the horses roared by and the sound started to die away, Ernie said, "Lobo, that was cool. I felt like I was in the Civil War, facing a cavalry charge".

"I know what you mean", said Lobo, "it really makes you appreciate the size and strength of the horses, and the courage it takes for those little fuckers to ride em. I'm thirsty, let's grab a beer".

As is usually the case when guys are drinking and having fun, time got away from them, and the four of them decided to go in together and try to nail the trifecta in the last race. After much deliberation and even more than the usual back and forth, they sent Richard, the least drunk of the guys, to buy the ticket. It was dusk and the crowd had thinned. As the horses hit the top of the stretch, there were four horses within a half length of the lead. Three of the four were on their trifecta ticket. The other horse was a nine year old gelding named Super Nova who looked on paper to be one step away from the glue factory. As they neared the wire it was obvious that Super Nova was going to finish in the top three, killing their trifecta. Richard was screaming and hitting his leg with his rolled up track program, as if he were a jockey trying to get to the wire first. Lobo and Big Tony were watching him as if, instead of being a jockey, he was trying his absolute best to win the world's biggest dumbass competition. Super Nova finished third, at forty to one. Richard was dancing around and whooping it up.

Big Tony couldn't take it. He screamed. "Richard, you dumb fuck, we didn't win the race. Shut the fuck up".

Richard leaned his head back and shook it from side to side, like a man possessed. Lobo and Big Tony looked at each other. Big Tony said "Richard we're leaving, you dumb drunk fuck".

Richard, now with his head back, his eyes closed, and a shit eatin grin on his face, calmly reached in his shirt pocket and held out the ticket. Big Tony grabbed it, looked at it, then looked up at the tote board. The trifecta paid $2,842, and they had it. Big Tony grabbed Richard in a bear hug and they danced around in a circle. Ernie started whooping and hollering. Lobo looked on with a drunk smile as big as Alaska.

The Longshot Saloon is a pitching wedge shot from the entrance to Oaklawn Park. After cashing the ticket, which included having to sign a form that allowed the track to withhold income taxes, the last thing the boys wanted to do was get in the car and drive home, so they didn't. They walked across the street. A celebration was in order. Big Tony went to the bar and brought back four beers and four shots of tequila.

"Here's to my buddy Richard" he said, as he knocked back the tequila. Never mind that thirty minutes earlier he had called Richard a dumb drunk fuck. "That was unbelievable. How did you do it? We never even mentioned that old broken down bag of bones. You're the best fuckin handicapper in the world".

Lobo looked at Big Tony. "Damn right he is", and knocked back his shot of Tequila.

The cab ride back to Little Rock wasn't cheap, but it was necessary. They rolled in at 3:00 AM. The women were not there to greet them. Ernie and Catherine had a 1:05 PM flight to New York. Catherine woke Ernie up at 7:00. Jake and Fran were taking them to breakfast at Capital Hotel in downtown Little Rock and Catherine wanted to make sure Ernie could answer the bell. He could, but barely. He almost fell out of the shower twice, each time just managing to steady himself before he hit the deck. Catherine didn't have a whole lot to say while they were getting ready. Ernie and Catherine had never had a fight, hadn't even come close. Ernie was pretty sure that streak was about to end. For now, though, he was still smiling to himself at the thought of all the fun he had the day before. When he walked into the den of the Delaney home that morning, he felt about the same as he looked, haggard. He was functioning, barely, and nowhere near peak efficiency, but he was a trooper, and issued no complaints.

"I warned you about Lobo and Big Tony", Jake said, with a grin.

Ernie found himself a little relieved at that, the grin. "Shoulda listened", said Ernie.

Jake continued, "You want coffee?, we're going downtown to breakfast, but we have plenty of time".

"That would be great", answered Ernie.

Coffee in hand, they walked out to the screened porch, where Fran was reading the Sunday paper, all dressed and ready to go. "Good morning Fran", Ernie said in a normal tone of neither deference nor apology.

"Well, good morning to you Ernie", in a tone that clearly indicated that either or both would be at least appreciated, if not expected. There was a moment of palpable silence that was broken by Jake, who, with laser like insight, sensed that Fran thought Ernie, as Ricky Ricardo would have said, "had some splainin to do".

"So Ernie, tell me about the last race yesterday, sounds like you guys cashed a pretty nice ticket".

"Sure did", said Ernie, "you would have been proud of Richard, he added a longshot to the ticket at the last minute, and that's what won the cash. Big Tony was pretty happy about it".

Fran was not a fan of Big Tony, to say the least, so Ernie had unwittingly added another check mark on the negative side of the scorecard. Catherine joined them on the porch, just in time.

Jake's attention turned to her. "There she is", he said, "good morning pretty girl".

"Good morning" replied Catherine.

She was indeed pretty, if not beautiful, and that fact was certainly not lost on Jake, or Fran or Ernie for that matter.

The breakfast was over the top delicious. Ernie actually began to feel almost normal. The flight home was uneventful, Ernie even managed to sleep. By Wednesday, out of necessity, Hot Springs Arkansas was relegated to somewhere near the back part of the memory bank. Wall Street has a way of doing that.

She gave him the news on a Wednesday evening. They were having dinner alone at his place, which was a little unusual but she had suggested it and he went along willingly. She looked at him and said "Ernie, I have some news".

Ernie looked at her and after a few seconds said "okay".

"I'm pregnant", said Catherine, with a hint of a smile.

Ernie had no reaction at first. He was processing the information. They hadn't talked about getting married, much less starting a family. "Are you sure"? he asked.

"Yes, I'm sure", she replied. "I went to the doctor this morning".

"Holy shit", said Ernie. " Damn, what are we gonna do"?
Catherine looked at him. "Let's talk about it".

Talking about it was just a formality. Catherine had already thought it through, and decided. She wanted the baby. She wasn't sure at first, it would change her life forever, and she was so young. Terminating the pregnancy would be the easy choice, and it was tempting, but every time she thought about it she got a sick feeling in the pit of her stomach, and she knew there was no way she could go through with it. Of course she knew Ernie would be a good father. And, of course, his family was rich. There was that. She wanted the baby.

Ernie sat on the sofa, elbows on knees, chin in hands. There's often a very fine line between good and bad, love and hate, courage and cowardice. Life is like that. Try as we might, we don't totally control our destiny. We can shape it, influence it, wish for it, beg for it, work for it. We can't control it. Just the way it is. If all the people in all the world stood in a line, beginning at the South Pole and ending at the North Pole, with the most cynical and cunning at the beginning, and the most hopeful and idealistic at the end, Ernie would be somewhere in the Northern Hemisphere, maybe Guatemala, maybe further north. His father was kind, but pragmatic. His mother was brilliant, creative and a shade off kilter. In his mind he was a tougher version of his father. In reality, he was a kinder version of his mother. His mind was at work, he was thinking it through. It mattered not.

CHAPTER 6

Hayden Cole was born a week before Christmas. His mother and father had married the first weekend in May, on Kentucky Derby Day. For a wedding gift, Ernie's father gave them the luxury apartment overlooking Central Park. They were already living there, now they owned it. They were very happy for the first couple of years. Ernie working on Wall Street, Catherine working part time at the law firm and caring for Hayden. He was a beautiful child. His face was Ernie, but his cobalt blue eyes were Catherine Lanahan. Ernie was crazy about Hayden. He talked to him as if he were an adult. He took him to the park, played with him, read to him, held and kissed him and marveled at the way he soaked up the world around him.

The trouble started when Hayden was two. Ernie naturally thought they should have another child. Catherine had always skirted the issue. She didn't make it clear that she did or did not want another baby. That in itself should have told him what he needed to know, but Ernie, being a male, didn't get it. He brought it up one weekend as if it were a new, happy topic. No more skirting. She shot the idea down as quickly as Annie Oakley drawing down on a dinner plate from thirty feet. Discussion over. Catherine was strong willed. Ernie knew that and liked that, but this shouldn't be a battle of wills. He respected her wishes, but he didn't always understand the underlying reasons for them. He told himself it didn't really matter.

Ernie had been playing golf some on the weekends. It was fun and got him away from work. He was a decent player, having learned as a kid from the golf pro at Westchester Country Club. Spring was starting to show, and the guys planned a weekend getaway. They left early enough Friday to get in eighteen holes. Then they grilled steaks, drank, smoked cigars and played poker. Guy stuff. They had planned to play thirty six Saturday, but they missed their early tee time, so they played twenty seven. Saturday night was more laid back. They had pizza delivered, talked and drank beer. There were eight guys, two foursomes. One of the guys was Ernie's best friend, Finn "Crackhead" Peterson. He got the nickname at a poker table somewhere, never fully explained. Finn Peterson's father was not rich. Just the opposite. Finn and his two sisters grew up in New Jersey. His father was a butcher. He made his way to Wall Street on guts and determination. He met Ernie in a bar at Dartmouth. Ernie had a date, Finn had the night shift.

Finn was the smartest guy Ernie new. They were very much alike. They argued vehemently, each conceding nothing. They competed in almost everything. They were also different, each having qualities that the other admired without overt acknowledgement. Mostly, though, they were true friends. They trusted each other, and it was understood that when they talked as friends, just the two of them, about something that meant something, they spoke from the heart, the unvarnished truth. Sunday morning early, before anyone else was up, Ernie and Finn had just that sort of conversation.

"Why you so disappointed she doesn't want another child right now? You got plenty of time. She'll probably come around. If not, it's not so bad only having one is it"?

"Well, I couldn't be happier with Hayden. He's a blessing. I'm very grateful. It just seems so natural to have another child. I would like for Hayden to have a little brother or sister. It would be great. I know it's not me that would have to carry the baby for nine months, go through labor and all that, but it would be such a joy. I guess I'm just a little disappointed that she doesn't feel the same way as I do about it".

"I understand Bro. Just be glad for what you got. As I say, you got a pretty good gig".

"Yeah, I know".

Silence.

"What the fuck is buggin you then? You're acting like you have the weight of the fucking world on your shoulders. For no good reason that I can see. What's wrong? Tell me".

Ernie was shaking his head, slowly. "I don't know. Nothing really".

"Fuck that. Something is bugging you and you need to tell me what it is. Why are you acting all morose and shit? I hate to tell you, but you're not the first one to have have stuff go wrong in his life. Quit acting like a fuckin martyr and tell me what the hell is goin on".

Again, Ernie slowly shook his head and sighed, followed by a short muted chuckle, not the happy kind, but the sarcastic kind that signals something not pleasant, something not what it should be, something wrong that needs to be confronted and dealt with. The ironic chuckle. The one that says ha ha isn't this a funny little thing, but really means fuck, fuck, fuck this is not the way I want it to be, why can't it just be the way it should be, I'm gonna have to get out of my comfort zone, isn't it silly, me having to do that, ha ha ha.

"Alright, let me get another cup of coffee". Ernie refilled his coffee cup and sat down as if he were about to address the Geneva Convention.

"This is just between us".

Finn gave the equivalent of an eye roll, and with upturned palms and a nod said. "Of course".

"This may sound crazy to you, but I have this feeling. Maybe intuition, maybe something subconscious that's just barely tickling my brain, I don't know. But it's starting to be more than that, and every time I dismiss it from the front of my mind, it circles back around and reenters from the back, quietly, but it's there".

Finn, shaking his head yet again. "Okay, okay, it's not necessary to go all Sigmund Freud on my ass. Something's bugging you, we've already established that. What the fuck is it"?

Another one of those chuckles. Pause.

"I'm questioning my relationship with Catherine. I can't get this thought out of my mind that maybe she's manipulating me and I don't even know it".

"Okay, keep going".

"When I brought up the idea of having another child, it was weird. It was almost like I was asking the wife of a friend or a neighbor if there were plans for another baby. Just a natural question during the course of a conversation. But this wasn't that, this was my wife. I'm asking a serious question about a deeply personal and important decision having to do with the rest of our lives together, and I get a response that makes me wonder why I even bothered. It's like she's already decided and just hasn't clued me in yet. Maybe I'm just disappointed, but it doesn't feel good".

"That's understandable. I would feel the same way I'm sure. Maybe you should just drop it for now and bring it up again later. You know how women are. The next time it may be totally different".

"Maybe, but I'm just not getting a good feeling about it. You know, if she doesn't want another child, I'm okay with that. I would be disappointed, but it would be okay. Hayden is wonderful. I'd get over it. But that's not the way it is. I don't think she really cares what I want. I hate to say it, but that's the way I feel".

Finn just listened. He figured there was more. After a few moments, Ernie continued.

"Maybe it doesn't sound like much, but things are different than they used to be".

"Like what? What do you mean? Give me an example".

"We used to have so much fun, just hanging out and doing stuff. Going to cool bars and restaurants, seeing shows, riding bikes, whatever we felt like doing. There was no plan, it was just life and it was fun. Now, I realize that having a child changes all that, and it should. That's not the problem. There's just this feeling I have that all of the fun stuff might not have been as free spirited as I thought. Maybe there was an agenda. I was living life day to day, having fun and falling in love. Catherine was doing those things too, but along with it she was looking ahead, sizing up what might be in it for her down the road".

Finn looked at Ernie. "What the fuck are you talking about? They all do that. I would be questioning her more if she didn't do that. Sure, she wants the good life. What's wrong with that? So does every girl I ever dated, or tried to date. That doesn't make her a bad person, or a bad wife or mother".

"I know. But there have been things that make me wonder. I can't help it".

"Like what"? Tell me one thing".

The next thing out of the mouth of Ernie Cole would start a chain of events that would change his life forever. They say ignorance is bliss. Maybe so, but the truth has a way of always being there. The truth belongs to no one, no beginning, no end, while the provenance of blissful ignorance is a bad seed, buried, but still there, lurking.

"You remember when Catherine and I were dating and I went to Zurich for a week".

Immediately, Finn knew there was trouble ahead. He hadn't seen it coming, but now it was staring him in the face.

His mind was racing. He tried not to show it. He flashed back. A mutual friend was in the bar in the lobby on a Friday afternoon when Ernie was in Zurich, Catherine seemed a little too flirty with some guy he recognized, but didn't know. He mentioned it to one of Ernie's coworkers, who told him, with a look of disgust, that it was Catherine's old boyfriend, who also worked in the building. Within an hour they left together. The friend told Finn, but it was a brief mention. We all have secrets. Finn had a few of his own. Ernie was happy. Catherine was good to him. It was second hand information. Finn had kept it to himself. He knew that no longer was an option.

"Yes".

"A couple of times when I called or texted her, she didn't reply until hours later. Obviously there's a time difference, so I thought it was just the wrong time when I tried to call or text. One morning I got up really early and called her during the evening New York time. She didn't answer. I texted her the next morning New York time. She finally called me that night in Zurich, after lunch in New York. She sounded rushed and apologized for not calling back earlier. She said work had been very busy. There was something about that conversation that bothered me. Nothing in particular that she said, just her voice. It was different. I could hardly sleep that night. I kept thinking about how I had fallen so hard for her, about how I had allowed myself to be crazy in love and all of the sudden how bad I felt. At the same time, I knew it didn't make sense for me to be so sensitive, and that there was no reason to be acting like she had broken up with me or something. When I got back, things were great. We picked up right where we left off. I intended to talk to her about it, but then it just didn't seem to matter, so I didn't".

Finn looked at Ernie. He wished he was anywhere but right here, right now. No time to think it through. He did what he had to do.

"Okay, I'm going to tell you something. I didn't tell you earlier because I thought it was best not to. Maybe that was a mistake, but I thought it was the right thing at the time. A guy I work with told me he was in the lobby bar on a Friday when you were in Zurich. Catherine was sitting next to some other guy he didn't know. They were talking and laughing, and after a couple of drinks they left together. He asked who the guy was. He was told it was Catherine's old boyfriend. That's it. That's all I know. It doesn't necessarily mean anything, but I think now I should have told you. I'm sorry I didn't".

Ernie didn't flinch. He was thinking. He had flinched once already, in Zurich.

"That's okay. I'm glad you're telling me now. I should have trusted my instincts".

The divorce took two years. It wasn't pleasant. Ernie tried to talk to her at first, get the story. Catherine technically wasn't unfaithful. She wasn't married to Ernie at the time, not even engaged. They were dating. He was out of the country, she had a few drinks, things happen. In the legal world there is something called "the spirit of the law", a rather ironic acknowledgement that sometimes we must look past the written word to get to the reason for the written word. In a relationship, the rules are even less clear. Sometimes there is no law to follow, other than "the law of the heart". Catherine had not planned it, but it happened. She was a good wife and mother, but she broke the law of the heart. When that happens, some guys can talk about it, deal with it and get through it. Ernie wasn't one of those.

Catherine moved to Boston to live with her mother and take care of Hayden. Fran and Jake had had their own issues, and had agreed on a much cleaner divorce almost a year earlier. Hayden was four when they moved.

It broke Ernie's heart to have to live apart from Hayden, but he made the best of it. He was allowed to have him every other weekend, but there were restrictions, and Catherine made sure they were followed. She put Hayden in a private school. He made friends and got involved with school activities. He began to have occasional conflicts on Ernie's weekends. Gradually the weekends became less frequent.

In what seemed like nothing more than the blink of an eye, Ernie was a thirty two year old divorced man with an eight year old son. Another blink, and he was pushing forty. His Wall Street gig, to an outsider, was almost perfect. He wasn't a suit. He was a trader. Trading complex derivative products was his game. Success on Wall Street comes in many ways. Most people follow, or at least attempt to follow, the logical path. Graduate with honors, get a foot in the door, survive at first, pay your dues, advance to the upper echelon, reap the rewards. Of course, Ernie wasn't most people. He was Ernie. Right off the bat he wanted to be a trader, and a trader he became. The investment world is obsessed with information. Legions of bright, young people go to the best schools, go to Wall Street, make a lot of money, have status, live the good life, all without doing anything more than providing information to the risk takers. It's a good gig, if you're that type, one of those. Ernie wasn't. He was a trader. His father was a smart man, very successful, achieved a lot, got rich, had a great reputation, all without any major problems or setbacks. All without taking any risk other than what was required to be a success and live the life of one who had made it. His father was one of the elite. His mother was married to one of the elite, which entitled her to live that life, and she did, for a while. It was boring. It was empty. She eventually went in another direction. She decided to follow the less traveled path of those who, like her, are destined to be different. Who take a step into the unknown for the simple reason that they want to know what's there. They need to know what's there. It may be good, it may be bad, but it's not boring and it's not empty. One of the beauties of having children is the magical way in which we bring a brand new, unique person into the world. Try as we may, we can't change them. We can teach them, guide them and love them. We can't change them. They are who they are. It's a beautiful thing, but it can be tough on those who are different. Society is not kind to the outliers. Just the way it is.

Ernie had his father's penchant for achievement and making money. That was learned. But he was born with the soul of his mother, and that made all the difference, just as sure as the river runs to the sea.

CHAPTER 7

"**D**ouble espresso and a blueberry scone, please".

It was Saturday morning, she had just finished a three mile run through Audubon Park, Nikki was treating herself. It had been a tough week, the kind that almost made her second guess her decision to enter law school. All of the outside tables were taken, so she walked back across St. Charles Avenue and found an empty park bench. She felt better after running. It was almost always that way. It was not only good for the body, it cleared her head and had an overall calming effect on her. That was a good thing. Not just because of the stress of Law School, but also because of the emotional pain caused by the disappearance of her father almost two years before. She thought of Gib every day. A lot of days it was every hour of the day. There were fewer of those now. She was grateful for that.

The sun was starting to warm the morning air. It was the first Saturday after New Years. The weather can be iffy in January in New Orleans, but today was perfect. Nikki almost felt a little sliver of happiness working it's way into the picture. That would be welcome. The time since Gib's disappearance had been tough. The toughest thing was that she still didn't know. Didn't know how it happened, why it happened. Didn't know if he was alive. It had been big news, international news. She had worked tirelessly trying to get answers. She took a semester off from law school and did nothing but search for the truth. She came up empty. It took it's toll. Reggie helped.

Reggie Hodges was in Medical School at Tulane. Three days a week he worked in the campus counseling center. One afternoon he looked up to see a beautiful girl walk through the door with tears rolling down her cheeks. She looked vaguely familiar. When she calmed down and started to tell her story, he realized it was Nikki Carter, the Tulane Law student whose father had disappeared with ten million dollars. For the next year Reggie talked with Nikki almost every day. Some days he helped her work through the pain. Other days they just talked. Reggie was kind, and that's what she needed. He was also smart, level headed and funny. At first he had a girlfriend. That was good. Kept things straight. But his girlfriend began to resent the time Reggie spent with Nikki. Things got complicated. She left. Nikki knew that Reggie wanted to sleep with her. A woman knows these things. She was okay with it, was even excited by the possibility, but she also knew it would never be the same afterwards. Never is. Never can be. Just the way it is. For whatever reason, or none, she did it anyway.

They say that men have a hard time distinguishing between lust and love. It's true, but they don't have the market cornered on that trait. Nikki was eventually going to have to make a decision. She knew that. She just didn't know what it would be. Reggie forced the issue during Thanksgiving break. They were at his parents cabin in North Georgia, a beautiful spot on the Tallulah River. The fall colors were still hanging around. The family setting was comfortable and reassuring. He asked the question laying flat on his back on a giant river rock. She was sitting beside him looking at him. She said yes. They decided on a June wedding. Everyone was thrilled.

As she walked back to her apartment, Nikki was thinking about all the things she needed to do. The wedding was six months away and she had done nothing except set the date. But it was such a beautiful day. She wanted to be outside, maybe ride bikes in the park or invite Gabriela to play tennis. She was glad it was Saturday. No drama, no stress. That was about to change.

As she neared her apartment, half a block from the intersection of Prytania and Lowerline, she passed a woman on the sidewalk. It wasn't unusual to see an unfamiliar face strolling through Uptown, especially on the weekend, but this woman was by herself, appeared to be in her late thirties and was strikingly beautiful. Once home, Nikki grabbed a bottled water from the fridge and walked out onto the front porch with the Times Picayune to relax for a bit and enjoy the great weather before she showered and decided what to do with the rest of the day. As she opened the door, she was startled to see the same woman she had passed on the sidewalk, walking tentatively toward her front porch. Their eyes met. Neither spoke right away. The woman had kind, but sad eyes. Nikki looked puzzled but didn't feel threatened. The woman stood perfectly still, looking at Nikki. Then, in a soft but not weak voice, she spoke.

"Are you Nikki Carter?"

Nikki paused, then slowly nodded. "Yes".

The woman, totally calm and deliberate, spoke the words she had traveled several thousand miles to say. "I want to talk about your father".

Nikki's face turned pale. "Who are you"?

"My name is Anna Lishin, but your father knew me as Natalya Petrova".

After a long pause, which was inconsequential because in an instant her whole world had not just paused, but stopped and was about to be reconfigured, Nikki managed to speak. "Please come sit down".

Anna slowly, cautiously stepped onto the porch. They were eye to eye, less than two feet apart. The Russian's eyes filled with tears.

Nikki spoke softly. "Let's go inside".

Nikki was a sophisticated young woman. Well read. Intuitive. Self assured. In this moment none of that mattered. Nothing mattered. This moment transcended all of the normal course of things. It had been almost two years. Somehow she had survived. Now, here she was. A strange woman was on her doorstep, and had some things to say.

"Can I get you something, maybe a bottled water"?

"Yes, thank you".

It was obvious to Nikki that this woman, Anna, was in pain. There was emotion practically oozing from her every pore. She sensed the story wasn't going to be a happy one, but it was going to be real.

"Tell me more Anna".

Anna took two deep breaths. Nikki stayed calm and waited.

"I met your father in New York. We were both there on business, at an investment management conference. There was a group of about ten of us who had dinner together the first night. I sat across from Gib. We talked. After dinner we had drinks in the hotel bar. He was different than most of the other guys. We didn't talk business, we talked about movies and music. We spent the rest of the weekend together. It was wonderful".

Anna took a sip of water and another deep breath. Nikki was calm. Anna spoke English very well, but with an accent that Nikki thought could be Eastern European.

"I grew up in Russia. My family was poor. My parents sent me to live with my aunt and uncle in Moscow so I could get a good education and a job. It was a good plan, but I was young and foolish. I made mistakes. I left them when I was sixteen and went to live with my boyfriend. He was twenty two. He had money. It was fun for a while, but he was not a good person. I got pregnant. He was mad, said he didn't want children. I tried to leave but he wouldn't let me. We had a bad fight, it got physical, I lost the baby. After things settled down, I waited til one night when he was passed out drunk, and I left for good. I went to the only place I thought I could go, to the home of a friend my age. Her father didn't like it, but he took me in. He had two rules. One was that I could never date anyone in his family or business. The other was that I had to get a job. I lived in their house for almost four years. I worked in a coffee shop and gradually started keeping the books for the owner. I learned about business. After a couple of years, the man who had taken me in, who I now thought of as my adopted father, offered me a job as a bookkeeper in his business. It was a challenge, but I liked it and he payed me well. Eventually I moved into my own apartment in the city. After another year or so, I got the opportunity to fill a position at a bank, the Stezlaus Bank. It was difficult for me at first, but I managed to survive and learn the banking business, at least what I thought was the banking business". Anna paused, took another deep breath and a sip of water.

"Let's have a glass of wine", said Nikki in a flat, matter of fact voice. She was anxious to move the story along, but she was scared also. She thought a glass of wine would be good for both of them. She was correct. Anna continued.

"The first trip I made with the guys at the bank was a weekend in Hong Kong. They basically just took me along. I went to the dinners and a couple of informal cocktail parties, but for the most part I just stayed to myself. Nikki, I want to tell you something, and I want you to believe me". Anna's eyes filled with tears again, and this time they overflowed down her face. "I loved Gib. I loved your father".

The tears turned into a torrent, from both Anna and Nikki. Anna had used the past tense, Nikki was pretty sure sure she knew what that meant. She had to ask.

"Is he alive"?

Anna, with the weight of the world on her shoulders, simply shook her head. Nikki closed her eyes. At once she was both relieved and devastated. She had wanted answers. She got her answer. She held her face in her hands, then she leaned over and buried her face in a pillow. Now came the pain.

Anna, of course, had her own pain. The pain of regret. And guilt. Nikki's pain, in time, would go away. Anna hoped that hers would lessen, and it would, especially after travelling across the world to tell Nikki the truth. That mattered. That mattered a lot. But she couldn't tell Gib the truth, not in this world. She had had her chance. She hoped and prayed that maybe, maybe, Gib and Nikki would forgive her if she did what she knew she had to do. Tell Nikki the truth now. Tell it all.

Nikki raised her head and stared across the room at nothing. "Why did you wait until now to tell me"?

Anna tried to compose herself enough to answer. The tears kept coming. "I didn't know what happened until a week ago. I had an idea, but I didn't know. I was scared, and I'm still scared". The tears were dropping in her lap. "I'm so sorry".

Nikki turned to Anna, and without thinking, acting on gut instinct, reached to Anna and held her trembling hand. "I'm going to walk down the street and get some more wine. I want you to tell me everything". Anna slowly nodded.

Nikki returned with the wine, along with a container of homemade pimento cheese and a fresh baguette. The mood in the small apartment was improved, with both ladies feeling that the hardest part of the conversation was behind them. That would be the case, barely.

Nikki began as they resumed the conversation. "Do you know what happened to the ten million dollars"?

Anna took a deep breath but didn't blink. "Yes. It's kind of complicated, and I may not have all of the details correct, but I'm sure about the important stuff. First of all, this sounds crazy, and I'll explain, but Gib bet the ten million dollars on a horse race and lost".

Nikki, once again, was stunned, and couldn't help wondering if the nightmare would ever end. No way in hell this could be true. Anna continued. "I think it will help if I go back and tell you more about my job and the people I work with. I have thought a lot about this. It's not a good story, and I'm not proud of it, but I'm going to tell you the way it is. I owe you that". The mood once again was tense. "The bank I work for, Stezlaus Bank, is not just a bank. It is a bank, technically, but it's owned by the government and controlled by the Russian Mafia. The bank does all sorts of stuff, a lot of it legitimate, but it also handles huge cash flow transactions for both the government and the mafia. The bank uses outside investment management firms to manage the Russian Sovereign Wealth Fund, which is legitimate. That's how Boardman and Company got involved. The bad guys use the bank to handle money from gambling, drugs, prostitution and a lot of other things, including making under the table cash payments to government officials, which allow the whole thing to keep going. As I say, it's complicated".

Anna drank some wine and continued, worried about what Nikki must be thinking. "Nikki, you have to believe this. Gib knew nothing about the true nature of Stezlaus Bank. The guys from the bank that Gib dealt with liked Gib a lot. Their business with Gib and Boardman and Company was real and was not related to any mafia activity. Gib had integrity. We all knew that. It wasn't supposed to happen the way it did. I'm so sorry". The tears came again, in a torrent, just as before. Anna's whole body was shaking. "It was my fault Nikki. It was my fault, and I'm so, so sorry".

Nikki knew it was real. This was a broken woman. She looked at Anna, not knowing what to think, much less to say. It made no sense. Love her, pity her, hate her. All hung in the balance. She said nothing.

"I'm getting to the horse racing part". Anna said it as if she could read Nikki's mind. "I invited Gib to come to Greece for a wedding. He flew to Greece with Pietro Ferretti, a business associate of the bank. They flew together on Pietro's private jet. We had a wonderful weekend together. It was as perfect as it could be. At some point that weekend, one of the head guys at Stezlaus Bank, Viktor, talked to Gib and asked him if Boardman and Company wanted to manage a small piece of the bank's portfolio. After talking it through, they agreed on the business arrangement and the bank wired two hundred million dollars to Boardman and Company, with the understanding that Gib would oversee the investment process. It was a big vote of confidence in Gib". Anna paused. Nikki almost spoke, but didn't. "The trouble started on the flight home with

Pietro. The boys started drinking and talking. At some point, Pietro told Gib about the bank's connection with Burnham Glen Casino and about all of the big horse racing bets some of the guys make through the casino. I'm not clear on how it all works, I just know they talked about it. The day after they got home, Pietro called Gib in New Orleans to tell him about a real estate investment opportunity in Italy. I'm sketchy on the details about this too, but this is the way I understand it. A group of guys, including Pietro, Viktor and others, have a partnership group that owns a Villa in Tuscany. They take turns spending time there and they also hang out there together several times a year. It's kinda like a social club. I've never been, but I hear it's rustic and beautiful. Pietro asked Gib if he was interested in buying an ownership share and joining the group". Anna paused. This time Nikki spoke.

"How do you know all of this"?

Anna responded without looking at Nikki. "Pietro told me what I'm telling you. I went to Sardinia to talk to him, then I came here". Her eyes began to fill with tears again.

"Take your time. Keep going". Said Nikki.

Anna took a deep breath and exhaled slowly. "The part about the bet on the horse race is confusing. It doesn't sound real, but it is". Another pause. "This is the hard part Nikki. This is why I'm here". She looked at Nikki, "he did it for me".

Nikki could see the pain, the guilt. She could also feel the love, and she was beginning to understand what could have caused her father to make the decision that cost him his life.

Anna continued. "The way I understand it is this. Gib wanted to buy a partnership interest in the villa. The main reason was so that he and I could have a place to be together a couple of times a year. We could have figured out ways to spend time together, but this was just a few days after our weekend in Greece, and passion was high. We had no definite plans. The villa would change that. It was more than a couple of fun weekends. It was a commitment. Maybe with a different set of circumstances, less emotion and more time to think about it, he would have made a different decision. I have thought about that many times. He did something that made no sense, taking that kind of risk, bending the rules. Some people live their entire lives cutting corners and taking advantage of others. I know about this. I lived and worked with them. Not your father, not Gib. He was a man of deep character. He was a man of integrity. He deserved better. It breaks my heart".

Nikki was looking at Anna. This time it was Nikki who had tears running down her face. Anna managed to keep going. "The partnership interest cost about $450,000 U.S. dollars. The horse racing bet, which was supposed to be a sure thing, would have returned a five percent profit to the bettors. Gib needed $450,000. He bet ten million. The winning bet would have paid him $500,000, enough for the partnership and a little more for expenses and associated costs. The bank had just wired two hundred million dollars to Boardman and Company. Gib was the Chief Investment Officer of the firm. He and Roger Boardman were the only two people at the firm who had the authority to approve large trades. The general rule was that one of them had to approve anything over five million, although in practice approval was only requested when someone on the trading desk had a question about a trade. Most of it was routine. Gib had just landed the two hundred million dollar account from Stezlaus Bank. The trading desk was expecting to be busy investing that money, so when Gib approved a ten million dollar trade and gave the desk wiring instructions, nobody questioned it. Now, here's where it gets sticky. Gib had planned for the proceeds of the horse race bet to be split into two pieces. The original ten million would be returned to Boardman and Company. The five hundred thousand profit would be held in the offshore account awaiting instructions from Gib. When the deal on the villa was ready to close, he would wire the $450,000 to the seller and the other $50,000 would just stay in the offshore account, awaiting his instructions. Gib has the partnership interest in the villa and some extra cash for expenses. The two hundred million is intact. Nobody gets hurt".

Nikki stared straight ahead. They were thinking the same thing, these two women. Gib Carter had crossed the line and done something unethical, regardless of the reason. No way around it.

Two hours later the mood had lightened a bit. The pimento cheese and french bread were gone, and the second bottle of wine was destined for the same fate. The girls were talking about less serious things. Nikki had called Reggie and told him she didn't feel like going out and was going to just hang around her apartment. He wasn't really okay with the fact that she didn't at least suggest that he could come over, but he reasoned that she probably just needed some down time after a tough week. After their conversation, Nikki turned off her phone. Natalya Petrova was there. There was more to talk about.

"What was it like growing up with Gib as your father"?, asked Anna. "Tell me some stories". And so she did. Lots of stories and sweet and funny remembrances. Nikki did most of the talking. They both started to smile and laugh. It was nice. They both knew there was serious stuff still to come, and this was a welcomed respite.

After a while Nikki said, "I'm hungry, let's walk down to the Taj. It's the neighborhood bar. They have really good Pizza".

Anna looked at her and hesitated a bit. "Is it close"? she asked.

Nikki gave her a quizzical look. "Yes, just a few blocks. Would you rather not go"? Nikki couldn't help a tinge of disappointment in her voice.

"I would love to go", said Anna, "it's not that. She paused. "I just want to be careful and I don't want to put you in any danger".

At that moment Nikki realized she wasn't just looking at Anna, but also Natalya Petrova. She was warm, she had a pleasing Russian accent, she was smart and beautiful. She had traveled halfway around the world not just out of guilt, but because she wanted Nikki to know the truth about her father. She had done it for Gib. She had done it for Nikki.

The Taj Mahal was a vintage New Orleans neighborhood bar. Nikki had no idea who decided on the name, but it seemed

to fit. Everything about the place was unique. It had an ir-
reverent, sophisticated charm without trying to be anything
special. It was just the Taj. The only food served was pizza,
calzone and a house salad. The pizza dough and sauce were
made in the small kitchen, and they used only the best cheeses
and toppings. The house salad was simple chopped romaine
topped with chunks of feta, olives and cucumber, with house
dressing, no exceptions. There were no menus, other than an
oversized board that hung from the ceiling with a list of pizza
toppings. The house pizza was pancetta, green olives, mushrooms, caramelized onions and garlic, gruyere and parmesan,
with no sauce. The beer was draft, served in a frosted mug or
pitcher. If you wanted a bottled beer you got Dixie, super cold.
There was a full bar, but the wine choice was white or red, glass
or carafe. That's it. They tried once to expand the menu and
upgrade the table settings and decor. It lasted less than two
weeks, then they wisely went back to just being the Taj. That
was over twenty years ago.

They had to wait thirty minutes for the table, but that
was okay. Nikki ordered two salads and one house pizza, with
a pitcher of draft. Anna loved the place. She thought that it
would have been nice to experience the college life in a place
like this. She had always heard of New Orleans, but had never
had the opportunity to visit the city until now. The irony of
the situation didn't escape her. She had come to this place
with nothing in mind except having a very serious conversation with Nikki about one of the most difficult and unpleasant topics imaginable, the murder of her father. Yet, here they

were, sharing a pizza and a pitcher of beer in a funky New Orleans bar, thoroughly enjoying themselves and the carefree attitude of the place and the people around them. It also was a clear illustration to her that the human spirit is amazingly resilient and that Nikki Carter was solid and true to the core, just like Gib, and that made her smile.

After walking back to Nikki's apartment, the wine and pizza and beer took their toll, and both women fell asleep. Nikki awoke first. She showered and changed into jeans and tee shirt. It was still only four o'clock in the afternoon. Against her good judgement, or because of it, she walked back to the market for more wine. There was a lot left to talk about.

An hour later the girls once again settled in to their conversation. The carefree mood was gone, but that was okay. Nikki, although she understood where Gib crossed the line, and why, still didn't know what happened to him. Didn't know how he died. Didn't know how he was murdered. Was scared to know, but had to know. And it was time.

"Anna", said Nikki in a tone of voice that left no doubt about the seriousness of the question that followed, "how did he die"?

Anna, for some reason, was not surprised by the question and didn't hesitate with her reply. She looked at Nikki. "They drugged him and dropped him out of an airplane into the Atlantic Ocean. He was not conscious. He didn't suffer. If I could trade places with him right now I would".

Nikki closed her eyes and buried her face in her hands. She didn't cry. She said a silent prayer for her father, then opened her eyes. It was so horrible to imagine. She hoped and prayed that the vision she had in her head would not stay, would not haunt her. She knew that the best way to make that happen was to keep talking about other things and not dwell on how he died. She knew that, but she didn't know if it was possible. But she had no choice. She knew enough. Her father was gone. God rest his soul. Anna was quiet. She had been and still was trying to deal with her own grief and guilt. She said a silent prayer for Nikki, then reached over and gently held her hand.

Anna knew she needed to take the discussion in a new direction. "Nikki, nothing I can ever say or do will change what has happened, but I'm going to try to do the right thing now. Or at least I'm going to do what I think is the right thing. I'm not going back to the bank. I'm going to live with my father. He still lives in the small town where I was born. He's doing okay, but he's lived a hard life and physically he's not able to do what he once did. My mother died about five years ago. He's living now with one of my sisters and her family. They have struggles of their own and it's a strain for all of them. I have some money saved. I can buy a small house and he can live with me. I'll find a job. He can plant a garden and cook the meals. He has friends. We can live the simple life".

Nikki gave her a faint smile, and her countenance was one of approval. Once again the irony wasn't lost on either of them. Anna was going to live with her father, Nikki couldn't do that. But Nikki was a woman of character. She knew Anna was hurting, she felt Anna's sorrow and guilt, and that was no small thing.

Nikki poured them both a glass of wine. Anna continued. "I want to tell you more about Stezlaus Bank and who's behind it. I want you to know as much as you want to know about the people Gib got involved with. She paused. I want to tell you what I should have told him". Her voice began to crack and a tear once again rolled down her cheek. She took a deep breath. "As I said before, Stezlaus Bank is owned by the Russian Government. It has a legitimate function, which is to manage the assets of the Russian Sovereign Wealth Fund, and to perform all of the financial transactions of the fund. This is quite a large task and by necessity involves a lot of interaction with other banks, investment firms and businesses of all kinds, so there ends up being a huge volume of cash that flows in and out of the bank every day. Because it's not a commercial bank, it's not accountable to anyone outside of the Russian Government, which, as you might expect, has resulted in a lot of corruption and questionable dealings. Now, to further complicate matters, the Russian mafia and the government power structure are intertwined to the point that it's hard to separate the two. So, although Stezlaus Bank is owned by the government, it's controlled by the mafia. As crazy as it seems, there is legitimate business being done, such as with Boardman and Company, by the same people who are also laundering money and facilitating bogus financial transactions for the mafia. It's complicated, but it's the way it's been done for years, and it works for everybody involved. However, as with any business, things don't always go as planned. When Pietro Ferretti told Gib about the offshore gambling accounts and the connection to Burnham Glen, he crossed the line. He mixed the legitimate with the corrupt. Maybe it wouldn't have mattered if the horse racing bet had been a winner, but it wasn't, and so it did matter, a lot. Gib made a bad decision, a terrible decision. It was wrong and it cost him his life. But Gib was not a bad person. The people he got involved with are bad people, very bad and very dangerous. They don't just make a bad decision on occasion, they live bad lives". A very long pause. "They deserve to rot in hell". Anna made the last statement with the conviction of cold steel, with a stone face, looking straight ahead, not blinking, lips barely moving. The words hung in the air, unaltered and unchallenged. Then, in a much softer voice, with a tear rolling down her cheek, "and maybe I deserve to rot in hell with them".

CHAPTER 8

A nna sat motionless, as if the final curtain had dropped, and all that was left was regret and despair. Nikki moved to her and sat on the sofa facing her, Anna still looking down. Nikki reached, pulled her close and hugged her. She wrapped her arms around Anna and after a moment Anna did the same. They said nothing, continuing in a warm embrace that was comforting for both of them. Nikki lightly stroked Anna's hair and gently wiped the remains of a tear from her cheek. However unlikely, Anna and her father had shared something special, and now, in this moment, Nikki understood her father's longing for a life with this woman. Anna laid her head on Nikki's shoulder, sobbing, eyes closed. Nikki's soothing touch calmed her. They stayed that way for several minutes, Nikki continuing to very lightly and gently stroke Anna's shoulder. Nikki laid her head back and Anna nestled in, close to her body. Both women gradually drifted into a peaceful slumber.

Nikki awoke an hour later. She carefully stood, grabbed a blanket from a closet, put it over a still sleeping Anna and went back to sleep in her bed. Another hour, and Nikki awoke to a quiet apartment. The sofa where Anna had slept was empty, except for the neatly folded blanket. She looked around. No sign of Anna. No note. No nothing. Just empty space. Then the door opened. Anna had been sitting on the front porch, quietly soaking in the Saturday evening New Orleans vibe.

"I walked to the corner market for a cup of coffee. I didn't want to wake you".

Nikki was immensely relieved. She smiled. "I was worried that you were gone. I'm glad you're not". Pause. "You can stay here tonight, if you want to".

Anna was torn. She would absolutely love to stay. Have a relaxing Sunday breakfast with Nikki in New Orleans, maybe spend several days here. Exploring the city. Talking. Listening. But these weren't normal circumstances. There was danger. At least she thought there could be. No, she knew there could be. This day had turned out as good or better than she could have possibly hoped. Nikki was unbelievable, just like Gib. Their conversation had been both difficult and wonderful. There was more to say. There would always be more to say. But the most important things, thank God, had been said. It was time to go.

"Nikki, it's best that I leave now". She felt the emotion, the tears, trying to resurface. It didn't seem fair, it wasn't fair, to have to say goodbye so quickly. She moved to Nikki. Stood close. Handed her a folded piece of paper. "Take this. It's the name of a very bad man, the man at the top. I've never seen him, I've only heard the name, and that's only because I've listened carefully when the guys were drunk and talking among themselves without knowing I was near. He's not just the boss of Stezlaus Bank, he's the boss of everything".

"He's the Godfather", Nikki said. It was both a statement and a question.

Anna nodded. "He's the Godfather".

She knew that Nikki was going to need time to herself to sort through the stuff about her father. But now it was time to go. Anna reached over and held Nikki in her arms, feeling the warmth, feeling the love. Anna continued, "I've thought and prayed a lot about this. You have to be very careful. If they had any idea I'm here now it would be very bad news for both of us.

They have no reason to think you're a threat to them as it is, and I want it to stay that way. There will always be unanswered questions Nikki. I'm giving you this name because I want to have closure, but even more I want you to have closure. I can't decide what closure is for you, but I know that if you don't have it after today, there is a chance that at some time later you will look for more answers, and I won't be here. If I don't give this to you now, I won't have closure, because I will always think there is more I could have told you. I wish I could do better, but this is all I have".

Nikki took the piece of paper and slid it into her jeans pocket. Her eyes filled with tears as she looked at Anna but said nothing. Anna pulled Nikki to her and wrapped her arms around her, holding her tight, not wanting to let go. They stayed that way for a long time, then Anna pulled her head back and looked at Nikki. "You are wonderful. I will never forget you".

Nikki bit her trembling upper lip, fighting back the tears. "I'll never forget you either", she said softly. Then Nikki pulled away, and without looking at Anna, said "hold on a second", and left the room. She came back holding something in her hand and gave it to Anna. It was a leather bookmark with "Daddy" imprinted on it in less than straight letters. "I made this for him at summer camp when I was about ten years old. He never quit using it". Nikki smiled through her tears. "I was so proud of it".

Anna had managed to stay composed through the good bye, but no more. Tears streamed down her face as she wrapped her fingers around the bookmark. "I'll never quit using it either".

Both women walked to the door. They looked at each other, hugged tightly, and said goodbye. Nikki opened the door and Anna walked out, into the night.

Anna walked quickly to St. Charles Avenue. Within minutes she was on a streetcar headed toward Canal Street. The streetcar was almost full with people of all descriptions headed somewhere on a Saturday night in New Orleans. The mood was decidedly upbeat and festive, with lots of talking and laughing. This was good, it made it easy for Anna to settle in without being noticed. At Canal she left the streetcar, stopped briefly at a small grocery store where she bought a sandwich from the deli case. Then she walked to her room on the seventh floor of the Marriott. She had paid cash in advance for the room, and used a fake name and credit card to guarantee any room charges. She wouldn't leave the room until early the next morning. Then she would get a bite of breakfast, take a cab to the train station and board the 7:00 AM Amtrak departure to points north, using a ticket that also had been been purchased with cash in advance. In Birmingham she would leave the train, take a cab to the airport, catch her 4:30 PM flight to Atlanta, and then her direct flight to Moscow. She was travelling with a fake ID and passport. The flights had been paid in advance. She made it through customs two days before with no problem, although it had made her nervous. This time she knew she was good until she was back in Russia. She was more comfortable going through customs there, but she wouldn't relax until she was home where she was supposed to be.

The conversation with Nikki had been a huge relief. She had taken a chance by showing up unannounced, but it worked out. She hoped Nikki would have peace of mind and not be burdened too much by what happened to Gib. She already felt that her own burden had been lifted, or at least lightened to the point that she could live her life without the daily pangs of regret that had been with her the last two years. After a while she felt sleepy. She thought about Gib. They were happy thoughts. She had done what she had promised him in her prayers that she would do. Now she was going home.

Nikki locked the door and sat down. She laid her head back and closed her eyes. She took a deep breath and slowly exhaled. There was a lot to think about, but there was no way in hell she could figure it all out right now. It would take a while. Right now she just needed to rest and recharge. She didn't bother to get ready for bed, she just grabbed a pillow and curled up right where she was. Sleep came easily.

The next morning Nikki awoke in a new world, a better world. Gone were the questions about what happened to Gib, and why. Gone was the possibility, however remote, that he was alive and hadn't contacted her. Most important, she was sure now that her father was who she thought he was. He made a terrible mistake, he made a very bad decision that could not be excused. He did something that was wrong. But he had no malice in his heart, and his humble, kind spirit, the one that brought smiles of joy to her and many others, that part of Gib, her father, was still intact and always would be.

As she stepped into her small kitchen to make coffee, she stopped and reached into the pocket of her jeans. Written on the piece of paper was one name. A name totally unfamiliar to her. It meant nothing. It meant everything. Silas Greer.

CHAPTER 9

There aren't a whole lot of murders in Hot Springs, Arkansas. Maybe four or five a year. The air was crisp and cold the first weekend in February. The police chief wasn't happy to get the call.

"Chief, we have an apparent homicide. Kennesaw Manor Apartments, 420 Central Avenue. Gunshot to the chest. Sixty eight year old white male".

"So you've ID'ed him"?

"Yep. Kinda strange. Ernest Hemingway Cole".

PART 3

Ramos

CHAPTER 10

Fifty Years Earlier

Silvana Mantilla was a gentle, beautiful woman. She wanted nothing more than to be a good mother to her children and to help bring honor to her family. She was born and raised in a small town near Trujillo, Peru. She married young. Her husband was her childhood sweetheart, and for the first few years of marriage things were almost perfect. Their first child was a boy. They named him Ramos, a name that had been in her husband's family for many years. A few years after Ramos came two more children. At the age of 29 Silvana Mantilla had the life she always wanted, then it all fell apart. Her husband was very seriously injured when he fell from a faulty piece of scaffolding at the construction site where he worked. He survived the fall, but was permanently disabled physically and mentally. He suffered severe head trauma in addition to breaking his back. After a year he was able to walk with a cane, but it was difficult and painful. He had severe headaches and poor vision.

After two years he had surgery to try to relieve some of the pain, but it helped very little. He died less than a year later.

Silvana Mantilla was young and smart, but she had three children to take care of, no job and only a high school education. She managed to get hired as a housekeeper at Villa Pizarro, the sprawling home of Senor Juan Cortez Villegas, who owned a seafood export company and was the wealthiest man in Trujillo.

Juan Cortez Villegas was the sort of man you stayed away from, unless you were either rich and powerful, or female and beautiful. He did all the right things, said all the right things, knew all the right people, belonged to all the right clubs, gave money to all the right charities, and always smiled. Except when he didn't. When he didn't smile, he was to be feared. There were stories in Trujillo of lavish late night parties, fancy yachts, fast cars and women. There were also rumors, or maybe they weren't rumors at all, that Juan Cortez Villegas was head of a powerful drug cartel. Nobody seemed to know for sure. What was known for sure was that he was a charming rich man who always seemed to get his way.

Silvana knew all of the rumors about Senor Villegas, but she needed a job. As a housekeeper she would have very little contact with him, if any at all. She worked in the guest house, which was a cottage behind the main house. It had 8 rooms, a pool and a spa. It also had a full kitchen, laundry and all of the amenities of any world class hotel, which it basically was. In the mornings she would see to it that all of the rooms were cleaned and in order, then she would help in the kitchen or laundry if needed. On days when there were no guests she would help with projects. It was a good job and she was glad to have it. In late afternoon she would return home, fix dinner for the children and get ready for another day. She had Sundays off and usually would spend time with her extended family and let the children hang out with their cousins and friends. It was not an easy life, but it was a lot better than it could have been as a single mother of three children. After a year at Villa Pizarro, her friends encouraged her to start dating. Silvana was beautiful, and there were plenty of local men who would be more than happy to take her to dinner or to the movies, or to one of the local clubs. She knew they were right, but she was still a little reluctant. The world seemed hard, and she wanted her kids to be ready to face it. She had needs, she admitted that to herself, but the kids came first. There was, however, a small part of her that was excited by the prospect of meeting new people, new men. That small part of her, that little speck of a piece of her that hovered somewhere between the conscious and the subconscious. The little flicker of a fantasy of what could be, of what might be, that is essential to life itself, that involuntary yearning to be human, to feel alive, the feeling that defies logic, is not of the mind, but of the soul, that part of her, that small little sliver of yearning and desire, that is the one that proved to be the demise of Senor Juan Cortez Villegas.

The Villa Pizarro had two entrances, Silvana used the one for employees, service people, deliveries and such. It was monitored 24 hours a day by two armed security men, who verified all incoming traffic. The main gate/guest entrance was also manned 24 hours a day by two security men. Whenever occupied, the guest house was staffed by both a doorman and a concierge.

One morning, as she made her way from the employee entrance to the Guest House, Silvana noticed a lone male figure jogging along the crushed stone path that meandered through the manicured grounds. She knew it was Juan Villegas, out for his morning exercise. As he came closer, her first thought was to ignore him. After all, she had never even met the man. But as he approached, she realized that would not be possible, nor advisable. They were the only two people on the grounds at that moment. It would be awkward, maybe even rude, not to at least offer a greeting to her employer. It would be simple enough to make eye contact, say good morning, and continue on her way. He was jogging, so it wouldn't be necessary to make any attempt at conversation. She was glad of this. However, as if on cue, he slowed his pace as he approached, and started walking along the path, approaching the point where the path intersected the walkway, just ahead of her.

"Good morning" he said, short of breath from his jog.

"Good morning" replied Silvana.

There was an awkward pause. She wanted to be respectful, and wished that he would simply wish her a good day and continue walking. But he didn't.

"I don't think we've officially met, I'm Juan Villegas, and you must be Silvana. I appreciate your help with the Guest House, I've heard good things about you".

"Thank you", she said.

"Are you in a hurry"? he asked. Then, "I'm sorry, that sounded rude. What I mean is, if you're not in too much of a hurry, maybe you can join me for a short chat. You've been here almost a year and we've never had a conversation. Would that be okay"?

"Of course" replied Silvana, unsure what to say or how to proceed.

"Great", he said. "Give me a minute to towel off and grab a bottle of water. I'll meet you by the fountain in the courtyard. It's quite pleasant there in the early morning."

They sat at a table in wrought iron chairs beneath a canopy of trees. The courtyard was indeed peaceful and lovely, with the sound of the fountain and the chirping birds. Silvana thought that the setting was more conducive to meditating than talking, but in either case, it was certainly relaxing. He seemed to sense what she was thinking.

"My mother loved this spot", he said. " She would often sit out here at the end of the day with a glass of wine. Sometimes by herself, sometimes with friends. Most of the employees knew her and they made sure her wine glass never stayed empty for long. Inevitably she would offer them a glass and more than a few times it turned into a real party. It used to really aggravate me when that happened. I would scold her for drinking with the staff. She would just laugh and tell me to lighten up. She passed away last year. I sure do miss her. So, Silvana, are you happy at Villa Pizarro"?

She paused, then said "yes, very happy, everyone is really nice".

He then paused for a moment, and looked at her. She noticed his eyes, deep set and dark. He had a handsome face and an easy smile. He seemed nothing at all like the dangerous man that she had heard about. In fact, he seemed almost shy. He opened his mouth to say something, but before he made a sound there was a startling noise that made them both jump. It was a chainsaw roaring to life, soon followed by the unmistakable sound of a saw cutting through wood, and then a loud crash as the top of a tall tree fell to the ground. Then it was quiet again.

"I love the trees, especially the old ones", he said, "but we've had to remove a few this year because of disease. I hate to cut down a tree, but I guess it's necessary".

Once again the chainsaw began and once again the noise was deafening. As it paused the second time, he leaned in to her and once again started to speak. Only once again the chainsaw cut him short. He paused, a look of exasperation on his face, and they both laughed. He motioned for her to follow him and they walked toward the main house and stopped just off of the path near the gated entrance to the driveway.

"I probably should go. I have a meeting in an hour. It was a most pleasant visit, short as it was".

"Thank you Senor Villegas, have a good day", she replied.

He turned to walk away, then stopped. "Silvana".

"Yes"

"I have some guests coming next week. Mostly business men, but one is a young lady, much like yourself. She's the daughter of an old friend. She has a 14 year old son who is a very talented musician, he's coming with her to Trujillo to interview with the Music Academy here. Don't you have a son about the same age"?

"Yes, Ramos, he's 14 also".

"I would like to make them feel at home here. Maybe one evening next week you can bring Ramos and we'll have a casual dinner in the courtyard. The boys can hang out, go swimming or whatever else, there's a lot to do here".

Silvana wasn't prepared for this, and he sensed her uncertainty.

"Her name is Monica", he said. "She's a wonderful mother, as I'm sure you are. You can meet her when she arrives. Dinner is just an idea, but it would be fun and might help her relax. I think she's pretty anxious about the interview at the Academy. Any way, think about it".

"Thank you, I will", Silvana said, relieved that she didn't have to respond further.

The next Thursday evening, Silvana, Monica, Juan Villegas and the two boys sat at a round table in the courtyard. Silvana had wanted to decline the invitation, but Ramos liked the idea, and she thought that meeting Monica might be fun, so she had accepted.

Dinner was delicious, fresh scallops and shrimp, lightly sauteed and served with a fresh corn souffle and roasted toma-toes stuffed with buttery spinach and bread crumbs. Dessert was fresh fruit and an assortment of wonderful cheeses, along with a Tacama Semi Seco, a soft and sweet sparkling wine from the oldest vines in South America. Juan Villegas was a perfect host, he asked questions and listened attentively, his manner was akin to that of a proud big brother or maybe an uncle. Only, he wasn't related to either one of them. Sylvana had been discreetly watching Senor Juan Cortez Villegas. She was wary. She knew his reputation. When Monica was talking, Silvana looked at her, but at the same time she was looking at him, the way a woman does, out of the very corner of her eye. Never once had his gaze been on Silvana when it should have been on Monica. Never once had he given any indication that his intention was anything other than enjoying the company of two friends.

The boys had long since left the table and were hanging out in the guest house, watching television and talking. Young Ramos was impressed with the Villa de Pizarro, but he wasn't intimidated by it. It was obvious that Juan Villegas was a rich man, but what Ramos seemed to know, almost intuitively, was that he was more than that. That he had power, that behind the gracious manner and warm smile was a man that was used to getting his way. As they walked back to the courtyard, Ramos was thinking. He was a quiet young man, at least when he first met someone. He took his time with new friends, feeling his way along. His father died when Ramos was 10 years old, and he was the oldest child, so he was " the man of the house" as his mother would sometimes say. He loved and admired his mother. They gave each other strength. And great joy. He was proud to be the man of the house.

When the boys returned, Monica stood and extended both hands toward Silvana, who clasped them with hers and smiled warmly. "It's been a wonderful evening", said Monica, "thank you so much".

"We enjoyed it also", replied Silvana, "maybe we can do it again some time".

"There will be more opportunities", said Juan Villegas, "and I'm pleased that we had this time together. I'm a lucky man to have the chance to enjoy the company of two such lovely ladies".

The next opportunity took only two weeks. Monica once again visited Villa Pizarro, this time with both her son and husband. Their son had been accepted to the music academy, and the mood was festive. Sylvana was there again, along with Juan Villegas. Monica had suggested to Sylvana that she might want to bring a dinner companion, not knowing if there was a man in her life, but letting her know that if so he would be welcome and they would like to meet him. Of course there was no man, but the invitation again tweaked that little part of her that wanted there to be.

Juan Villegas needed no tweaking to remind him of his desire for Sylvana Mantilla. It was something that hadn't been far from his mind since the first day he met her. He thought he had seen a spark of interest the last time they had dinner with Monica, but Sylvana was careful to be discreet with her likes and dislikes, and she wasn't easy to read. That intrigued him even more. After dinner, the four of them moved to the patio area where they sipped after dinner drinks and listened to soft music. Sylvana wasn't used to drinking wine, She wasn't used to any of this. It was nice. She looked gorgeous and radiant without trying to be either. They talked of trivial things, simply enjoying the moment. They toasted to new friends and touched glasses. Sylvana's eyes went to those of Juan Villegas. His was a look of pure enchantment. As she lowered her glass she tilted her head slightly and smiled. Unwittingly or not, she could have tried for a hundred years and not given him a look that would make him want her more.

He invited her the next weekend to a small dinner party at the home of his closest friend, who lived in a fabulous old stone house in the hills overlooking the city. She knew this was the point of no return. She had not sought the attention from him, but she also had not discouraged it. He was charming, and treated her like a princess. He was interesting and fun. He was rich and handsome. She was beguiling. Maybe she should have known better. She did know better. She did it anyway.

The house was old and beautiful. They had dinner outside on the terrace overlooking the lights of the city. Adjacent to the terrace was a pool and stone cabana that included an outdoor kitchen and bar. The entire estate was surrounded by an old stone fence that blended perfectly with the house and grounds. The whole place looked like it belonged in a magazine of the most beautiful homes in Peru, which it was. After dinner, their hosts, with great fanfare, asked to be excused for an hour or so while they went to a neighbor's home for a short visit. The neighbor's elderly mother had passed away the day before, and they wanted to pay their respects. At least that was their story. After they left, it was just Sylvana and Juan Villegas, sipping expensive wine under the stars.

He looked at her with his sparkling dark eyes and said softly, "you are wonderful".

She felt her face flush, and the last bit of resistance melt into the night. He stood and held his hand out for hers. He led her through the back entrance of the house, and into a bedroom just off a small, cozy living area. She lost herself in the touch of a man who knew how it was done. The love making was passionate. She knew it would not be the last time.

The next day she felt good. There was no guilt, no second guessing the decision, no silly puppy love, she just felt good. There was also no plan, just the mutual consent of a man and a woman.

CHAPTER 11

Juan Villegas was not a complicated man. He grew up in a tough neighborhood. He had to learn at an early age to take care of himself. He and his family had no social standing. They worked and took care of each other, just like every other family he knew. As a young boy, all he knew was that the tougher you were, the better you had it. He was tough. He was not mean, but he showed no sympathy for those who were not willing to fight, to be a man. School was not hard for him, but like most of his friends, it didn't interest him. He managed to get by and finish high school, but that's as far as it went. At eighteen he went to work for a small local seafood company. He unloaded boats, cleaned boats, cleaned fish, helped make repairs, and whatever else needed to be done. Gradually he learned the seafood business. When he was twenty one he started driving a truck and making deliveries to the local markets and restaurants. Then he began to have management responsibilities. By age twenty five he was practically running the company. When the owner decided he was ready to sell the business and retire, Juan talked to some of his customers and within two weeks had put together a small group of investors who bought the business and hired him to run it. By age thirty he was twenty percent owner. At age thirty three he bought out his partners and became the sole owner. He expanded his markets, and soon was one of the largest seafood exporters in Peru. By age forty he was a rich and powerful man. He was politically well connected, and there began to be rumors that he used his seafood export business to do more than just export seafood. He was savvy, but not arrogant. He wasn't married, but he liked women and women liked him. He treated them well, until they got in the way, then he moved on. In his world, a woman was something to be admired and enjoyed, beyond that they had no place.

Sylvana was different. He had never had a relationship with a woman that worked for him. It wasn't worth the risk, especially since there were so many beautiful women elsewhere who sought his attention. That was what made Sylvana irresistible. She didn't seek his attention, he sought hers. His latest business trip was to Brazil. He stayed a week, and on five of the seven evenings he had the same companion, a stunningly beautiful young lady with a perfect body. She was ready and willing to please him in any way he wished. He made love to her, but there was no burning desire. He lusted for her body, but only in the primitive way that a stallion doesn't hesitate to mount a mare. Beyond that she meant nothing to him. She was just entertainment. She was too predictable, willing to do whatever she needed to do to gain the favor of a powerful and rich man. She wasn't Sylvana.

The next time they were together Sylvana noticed something a little different about Juan. After their lovemaking, which was as passionate as ever, he seemed to want to spend some time just being close to her, and not talking. She wondered if maybe he had something on his mind regarding business. That certainly wouldn't be anything unusual, his mind was always working, but it was unusual for it to intrude, even in a small way, upon their bedroom activities. One of the things that made their relationship work was that they both were able to detach themselves from the rest of the world while they were together. Today was slightly different. It was the first warning sign.

It wasn't Sylvana's fault, or it was. Depends on who's deciding. Her affair with Juan Villegas was not calculated, wasn't planned, but she entered into it willingly. Several weeks passed. They continued the usual pattern. They managed to find the time to be together a couple of times a week. There was almost never a time when she wasn't occupied either by work or caring for her three children, so it was a challenge. He began to suggest that maybe she could take short breaks at work and they could have time together at the Villa, there were plenty of places that were hidden away enough to allow it. She didn't really like the idea and resisted at first, but he persisted. She gave in, and they started making love in the Villa Pizarro.

Ramos suspected something was going on between his mother and Senor Villegas. He didn't know details, didn't want to know details, but he was pretty sure he was right. He understood, even at his young age, that Sylvana had needs, just like everybody else. He was okay with her dating someone, in fact, he wanted that for her. That was no problem. The problem was that she was involved with Juan Villegas. She never told him, and he never saw them together, but he knew. It wasn't something that he could talk to her about, which made it worse. Ramos hoped that it wouldn't last. He worried about it every day. Juan Villegas was a bad man. Juan Villegas was his mother's lover. Not good. Ramos would make excuses and cleverly find ways to spend time at the Villa, usually either walking his mother to or from work. The security people at the Villa knew him well, and admired his devotion to his mother. During busy times he even had small jobs at the Villa himself, usually working on the grounds helping to get ready for an important visitor. He kept to himself on those occasions, did his work and smiled graciously when he encountered someone. He made sure to stay clear of Juan Villegas, the lord of the manor, but he watched him, closely. Juan, like most people, was a creature of habit, especially inside his own compound. On days when his schedule allowed it, he exercised in the early morning, jogging along the path through the manicured grounds, alone. But not unseen.

The lovemaking lost a little of it's magic, which is, of course, usually the case. There were times when Juan tried to arrange a quick rendezvous but was unsuccessful for one reason or another, usually having to do with Sylvana's fear of discovery, or at least that's what she said. He started to be less understanding on those occasions. At times he would simply walk to the guest house and have a conversation with her, seemingly about work, while actually telling her when and where to meet him. He would often have papers in his hand which he would point to or he would make hand gestures that looked as if he were giving her instructions of some sort. It was a ruse. It made her uncomfortable. It began to be a problem.

Ramos had just turned fifteen and was playing soccer for the school team. His coach was a former member of the Peru National Team. The kids loved him. The first time Sylvana came to a practice, the coach couldn't keep his eyes off of her. They talked briefly after practice, and that weekend he called and invited her to dinner. They went to a small family restaurant that was popular among the locals. She loved every minute. He was charming and real. The next weekend the team had a game and Sylvana made sure they were there early. She had a brief chat with the coach, and after the game she stayed longer than necessary. Ramos, without hesitation, asked him to join them for dinner.

"I would love to", he looked at Sylvana, "but maybe you should ask your mother first".

They all looked at Sylvana, and in unison said "please Mother please".

Her smile was a million miles wide. "Okay", was all she said.

The evening was wonderful for everybody. The kids loved him and he loved them back. When it was time to go she followed him out and they talked for a long time under the stars.

The kisses they shared were better than anything she could imagine.

The next week Sylvana was alone in the courtyard and looked up to see Juan walking toward her. She had been dreading this moment.

"Good morning my dear" he said.

"Good morning", she replied.

"I have missed you", he said, "won't you join in my office for a chat when you finish what you're doing"?

They had been using code words in the Villa, and his office meant one of the small, out of the way bedrooms he liked to use.

"Okay", she said, "but I won't have long".

On the way there she tried to think of a way to tell him what she knew she had to, that the affair was over. She knew it was not going to be pleasant. It wasn't. The instant she told him, or more accurately, suggested to him that they shouldn't continue the arrangement, he became a different person. The smile was no longer a smile. She couldn't say she hadn't been warned.

That evening, Sylvana cooked dinner for the children and went to her bedroom early, telling them she was tired and wanted to rest. She took a bath and soaked for a long time, trying to relax, and trying to remove the filth of Juan Villegas. Her wrists were sore from his grip, the inside of her lip had a small cut, her whole body was sore and aching. Worst of all, she hurt between her legs, from his repeated angry thrusts. She told no one. The next morning she went to work at Villa Pizarro as usual. She kept to herself and went about her usual routine. At lunch time, she sat with the other employees at their usual spot at an outdoor table behind the guest house. She made sure not to do anything or say anything that would possibly betray her secret. The job at the Villa was very important to her and her family, so she acted as if nothing had happened, and silently prayed that it wouldn't happen again. It was with great relief that she learned that Juan Villegas was away on one of his business trips, and would be gone for a week. She needed the time to recover, to think.

Ramos knew something was wrong. He was close to his mother and attuned to her moods. Her pleasant, loving manner was there, but behind it was worry. He could tell. It was simply not possible for a fifteen year old boy to try to have a conversation with his mother about her love life, and he made no attempt, but he took extra care to reassure her, with his usual hugs and confident manner, that she could depend on him, always, no matter what.

The next time was different, no force, no anger. They made love, he apologized for before, she cried and said she was scared. He was sweet and kind and promised her there was no need to worry. She acted relieved and grateful, while indeed worrying about what would come next. She had to figure out a way to separate herself from Juan Villegas. There was no easy way. She told the coach she couldn't see him for a while. He couldn't understand. There was so much there between them, absolutely no doubt. Now he could hardly get her attention. She felt it too. It was right. But it was the wrong time. She hoped there would be a right time. There wouldn't be, and he would never understand.

Ramos would ask Sylvana how it was going at the Villa, but he never got straight answers. As the weeks and months passed, he became increasingly worried that his mother was trapped in a relationship with the most powerful man in Trujillo, and there was nothing he, Ramos, could do about it. Things were almost normal for a while, but it couldn't last. Juan asked Sylvana to meet him at his friends' home for a dinner party, similar to before except with a few more people. She didn't want to go, but she was scared not to. She told him she would go, but to please understand that she couldn't stay too late. She had to be home to put her children to bed. He was okay with that. He liked it that she asked him please. It disgusted her, but it got the job done. Surprisingly, the dinner was enjoyable. The people were very nice. It all changed when the other guests left and it was just the two of them. Juan was drunk, and he had no intention of saying goodnight to Sylvana just yet. She started to say goodnight, and he tried to take her in his arms and kiss her. She resisted. His drunk breath was hot on her face. She immediately became terrified. What happened after that was a blur. When it was over, he passed out on the bed.

She managed to pull herself together enough to make it home and crawl in bed. The next morning she stayed in bed. Ramos, fearing trouble, went into her room to check on her. She told him to go away and come back later. He insisted on talking to her. He pulled back the covers, looked at her bruised and battered face and began to cry. He held her and kissed her, then he turned and left. She would not see her oldest son again for seven long years.

Ramos had prepared for this day. He had talked to his uncle. It had taken a lot of convincing and all of the money he had saved working at the Villa, but his uncle agreed to help. Now it was time. He entered the Villa grounds early, by himself. It was unusual for him not to be with his mother, but he told the security guys she was not well and had to stay home. They let him in without a question. He began his usual work routine of tidying the grounds. He was anxious but not overly nervous. He took deep, slow breaths and relaxed his body. He was ready.

Juan Villegas was hung over, his head was fuzzy. He knew the morning exercise would help. He began to jog down the path at close to the usual time. He was not moving fast, and he slowed to a walk less than half way through his usual route. This was good. It would make it easier. Just past the guest house the path turned right and entered a garden area surrounded by beautifully kept hedges and covered by the sweeping canopy of trees. As he turned and walked through the entrance to the garden, Senor Juan Cortes Villegas was thinking of his plans for lunch. On these mornings, the ones shortened by the need to deal with the payback from the reckless behaviour of the night before, he could always find a measure of solace in a plate of the comfort food of his youth. He found it at El Coche Comedor, an old train car that had been turned into a restaurant and bar by his old friend Ricardo. The original was just the old car, cozy and quaint. Over the years Ricardo added a patio and a covered outside area that included a dance floor. It was decorated with all sorts of whimsical local art and strings of colored lights. On summer evenings local bands played long into the night. From late morning until late afternoon, the locals gathered for some of the best simple, traditional food served anywhere in Peru. Juan's favorite dish was Chupe de Camerones, a rich spicy broth with shrimp and corn. It's part seafood and part soup, very rich and delicious, and very messy. Juan would saddle up to a table and eat a large bowl full, along with plenty of crusty bread to soak up the broth, and a pile of napkins to take care of the collateral damage. It made his mouth water just thinking about it. The morning exercise helped his appetite, and the time that it took allowed him to anticipate a long lunch with his friend Ricardo at El Coche Comedor. It was a long lunch that, anticipated or not, would not happen. Not this day. Not ever.

Ramos waited until Juan was totally inside the garden area, and out of direct line of sight of the security building. He approached Juan Villegas from behind and quickly, quietly reached and hooked his left arm under Juan's chin and immediately pulled his head back in one violent motion. He made sure to apply intense pressure so Juan Villegas couldn't scream loud enough for anyone to hear. At the same time he quickly dragged him several feet away from the path. With his right hand, he reached around, and with his folding knife, which he kept very sharp, Ramos Mantilla slit the throat of the lord of the manor, forcefully. One motion was all it took. Blood spurted like a fountain. Ramos dragged the body further away from the path, and partially underneath the hedgerow. It would be easily found, but no time soon. The blood was a problem. Ramos used the outside faucet to wash his hands and arms. He rubbed leaves and dirt on his clothes to try to hide the bloody evidence. He hoped it would be enough. Casually, his heart pounding, he walked toward the front gate. The security guys were talking and hardly noticed. He made sure to give them a wave, but didn't look directly at them. He made his way through the gate and left the Villa Pizarro.

Thirty minutes later he walked into the police precinct nearest his home. A couple of the officers there had children in his school, and he judged both of them to be fair and decent men. He walked to the front desk and asked if either was there. Neither was, but the one he knew best was expected very soon. He waited. When the officer entered the precinct, Ramos stood. He politely addressed the officer. He was calm, steadfast and strong. "Senor Juan Villegas is dead, I killed him".

There was no trial, no suspense, just a fifteen year old boy who killed a man for abusing his mother and apologized to nobody for it.

His first day in prison was the scariest day of his young life. There were many people who didn't shed a tear for Juan Villegas. More than a few were happy about it, and admired Ramos for ending the life of a man who took and never gave. Problem was, the man was very powerful, and he had powerful friends. Not friends in the purest sense, for they were not the friends who share your life and pick you up at the train station when you return from a trip, even though it's late and raining. Not that type. These were the ones who like you, not because of who you are, but what you have, and what you can do for them, period. That type.

They put Ramos in a cell by himself and kept him away from the general prison population. His only goal was to make it to the next day. He thought if he could do that, he might be able later to think about life after prison, but not now, he had to focus on one thing, survival. He made it through the first day, the first week and the first month. The food was terrible, the bed was nothing more than a thin mat on a concrete slab, but the worst part was the loneliness. He taught himself a mental routine in which he remembered past events in his life, especially things that were funny and pleasant. He tried to recall conversations, focusing on each word and facial expression that he could remember from his family and friends. He thought about school lessons, soccer games, anything that would occupy his mind and keep him focused on life and not on his horrid prison cell. He was super aware and observant, constantly looking and listening and trying to learn everything he possibly could about life inside. He had little contact with anybody, even the guards. He was especially careful to watch the guards. They were the ones that had access to him. He knew there could be bad apples in the group, and if so, they could be a problem.

They allowed him one hour of exercise a day. He was taken to the prison yard, usually around mid afternoon, and there he could jog or exercise any way he wanted, alone. He craved that hour every day. It was the one and only thing he had to look forward to. The routine never changed. Two guards would come to his cell and take him to the yard. They stayed there, watching him, for the entire hour, at which point they returned him to his cell. He was allowed to stop on the way back to his cell for water at the water fountain, which he always did.

The trouble he always feared appeared there. He needed water. He was bent over drinking. Out of the corner of his eye he saw movement, then came a crushing blow to the back of his head. His face hit the water fountain with enough force to break several teeth and crush his cheekbone, almost before he hit the floor he was grabbed by the feet and dragged into an empty cell. Both guards watched anxiously, but did nothing. The attacker was big and strong. Ramos had no chance. But he wasn't unconscious. He kept his eyes closed and didn't move. There was blood everywhere. He relaxed his body as much as he possibly could and said a silent prayer.

The big man rolled him over and ripped open his prison clothes. Ramos knew that it took a knife blade to do that, and he had no doubt that he would not live to see another day. There was a pause, and he felt the big man's hands on his bare buttocks. As terrifying as it was to face the prospect of being violently raped, he had the courage to risk it over certain death. His eyes remained closed, his body limp. The first thrust of the big man was awkward, and did nothing. The monster started to thrust again, it was now or never. Ramos raised up and turned so quickly that the big man had zero chance to react in time. He used his right elbow and slammed it into the man's rib cage so hard that he heard the rib's crack. At the same time he yelled as loud as he possibly could, and kept yelling. He tried to stand but the man grabbed his arm and pulled him down, and at almost the same time he took the knife and made a wild, desperate stabbing motion which caught Ramos in the back and tore deep into flesh, bone and cartilage. The area around the cell was in chaos, prisoners were shouting, the guards began to panic. They grabbed the big man and half dragged, half carried him away. Other guards descended on the scene. They took Ramos, bleeding profusely, and quickly rolled him away on a stretcher. An ambulance rushed him to the ER, it was touch and go because of the loss of blood, but somehow he stayed alive.

It took him over a year to recover. He didn't remember the first few weeks. After that he progressed slowly, but steadily. He had multiple surgeries on his face. He was partially paralyzed from the back injury, but he gradually began to regain motion in both arms and legs. He was in bad shape, but was getting better, and every morning he thanked God for the gift of another day.

The warden vowed to identify the attacker and bring him to justice, but nothing came of it. The two guards were admonished and transferred out. The powerful friends of Juan Villegas were not pleased. Their plan had failed. There was, however, general agreement among them that Ramos Mantilla, lucky as he was, had been dealt with in a manner that would leave no doubt that it never pays to go against their kind.

When he had recovered sufficiently to return to prison, Ramos met with the warden and requested that he be allowed to enter the general prison population and not stay separated as he had been before. The warden was a tough but fair man. He respected Ramos for this, but he was apprehensive. He was not beholden to the underworld power structure of the cronies of the late Juan Villegas, but he fully understood their power. After thinking it through, he made it known to those that mattered that Ramos Mantilla had suffered enough. The young man had not uttered a word concerning his attackers during the entire ordeal. On top of that, it was hard for anyone to deny he had good reason to do what he did to Juan Villegas. The man had severely abused his mother. The investigation into the prison incident had gone nowhere partly because he wouldn't talk. Somehow young Ramos understood that the rules of the underworld were different than those of society, and that like it or not, those were the rules that he must follow.

He returned to prison as a seventeen year old young man, wise beyond his years. He still stayed to himself. He was rail thin, it had been tough to eat with broken teeth and a busted face. He had a scar that ran almost the length of the left side of his face, from above his cheek to his lower jaw. His left eyelid drooped slightly, giving him the unintended look of one who might be a little off kilter, even more reason for others to be wary. It was easy to pity the young man, but there is no pity inside the walls of prison. He wanted none. He got none. He was back where he started, trying to survive, one day at a time. His sentence was ten years. He had eight left. Plenty of time to think, and plan. Prison can break a man, can suck the very soul from wherever it resides. Can leave a man with no hope and no reason to care. It takes a strong will and the heart of a lion to fight off the demons. Ramos Mantilla's will was a block of granite, and inside him beat a heart that could stare down a pack of the fiercest warriors in the African wild and make cowards of them all.

Chapter 12

Nothing about life in the U.S. was easy for Silvana at first. She barely spoke English. She didn't drive. Almost everything was unfamiliar, but she adapted. Her two youngest children did amazingly well and that made her happy. But happy is relative, and she would never be truly happy, all the way happy, until she could wrap her arms around her precious Ramos and tell him how much she loved him and how so, so sorry she was. She didn't know if that day would ever come, and that was tough. Her brother had talked her into leaving Peru after the death of Juan Villegas. She was reluctant, but after what had happened she knew she would never feel safe there, more important, she could never be sure her children were safe, so she agreed to go. They left the same day Juan Villegas was killed. A man helped her. She didn't know him. Her brother told her she could trust the man, so she did. They went north to Ecuador and stayed there a week, then managed to pass through Colombia to Venezuela. When they reached Caracas, they were met by another man who Sylvana vaguely remembered from her childhood. The first man left them, telling Sylvana he was returning to Peru. She never even knew his name. The second man was a distant cousin who had grown up near her in Trujillo. His name was Luis. He looked after them for several days in Caracas, then boarded a large commercial fishing boat with them, headed for the port of New Orleans, in the United States. It was not an easy trip, but they made it without incident. Luis had provided them with passports and a work visa for her.

They spent one night in New Orleans before heading north. Luis took the opportunity to show them a little of the city. It was like nothing they had seen before. All the crazy characters, the old European architecture, the carnival like atmosphere. The children were fascinated and loved everything about it. Sylvana was too preoccupied with the sudden upheaval in their lives to even try to take it all in. She just wanted to get where they were going. Where they were going was Ferriday, Louisiana. A small town just across the river from Natchez Mississippi, in the low lying Mississippi River delta. They settled in quickly. It was a relief to Sylvana that there were familiar things there, especially other people from Peru. It allowed them to have a certain comfort that they otherwise wouldn't have had. It was still a new place and strange land, but part of the past was there too, and that was something to build on. Within a week she had a job as a housekeeper at a hotel in Natchez. She was able to ride back and forth to work with two other women who lived near her in Ferriday. They were both from Peru, and they became her best friends. They helped her learn English, although it was slow going at first. The kids started to school and picked up on the new language much faster than their mother. They also had several classmates from Peru, and that helped a lot. They managed to make it through the first year, and life in Ferriday began to be not just tolerable, but better than that. Their friends were as good as it gets. They had a place to call home and it began to feel like home.

The Peruvian community in and around where they lived was very close. They took care of one another. Often a group of them would work at the same place. It was good for the employer, because they were loyal, hard working employees, and whenever he needed to hire another worker, they usually had a friend who was ready to step in and work. They were also at a disadvantage, however, because many of them were undocumented and had very limited options for employment. Most were not well educated and had less than adequate English language skills. The result was that they took what they could get, and it was almost always at or near the bottom of the pay scale. At the core, though, they had a strong work ethic and an equally strong commitment to each other and their families. These traits served them well.

Ramos got stronger. He was still thin, and still had a noticeable limp from the nerve damage in his back, but he moved around better. His speech, which was affected by the face and mouth injuries, was returning to normal. The biggest change was that he was now living among the other prisoners, and he began to see a light at the end of the tunnel. He still mostly kept to himself, but now it was by choice. The other prisoners allowed him his space. He had earned the respect of even the biggest and the baddest, and everybody knew it. Nobody bothered him. He started working in the prison kitchen. There, as in all of prison life, there was a power structure. He willingly started at the bottom. That was one of the things about Ramos that the other inmates and guards alike noticed. He never sought to gain favor based on his place in the hierarchy. He just did his job. He was calm. Like everyone else, he was counting the days. His best friend inside the walls was a young man named Hector, who also worked in the kitchen. Hector was a year younger than Ramos. Like almost all young men who find themselves in prison, he had made some very bad choices. He was in a street gang. They hijacked a drug shipment and got caught. He was lucky. He only got five years. He had no clue about prison life. He was scared, but he was smart. He never said a word during the investigation, and had said very few since. Ramos liked that. He gave Hector advice, a little at a time. They earned each other's trust, and that would mean a lot in the days and years to come.

A week before her birthday, Sylvana got the best birthday present she had ever gotten or ever would get, a letter from Ramos. She read it, reread it and read it again. She ran around waving it in the air and shouting that her precious son was alive and well. It made everybody happy. She had no idea how he knew where she was, but it didn't matter, she got the letter and the world was a better place because of it. When she calmed down enough, she wrote him back and included pictures of all of the family. The next morning she mailed her letter and immediately began longing for another from him.

Ramos and Hector, although they both worked in the kitchen, didn't always have the opportunity to talk without being overheard. Today was a day they did. The two of them were unloading supplies from a truck at the back loading dock of the kitchen. They took a break and each sat on a wooden crate.

"Why'd you do it"? asked Ramos.

"Do what"? Hector replied.

"Try to rip off the drugs. Seems kinda crazy to me. Surely it wasn't your idea".

Hector slowly shook his head and frowned. "I don't know man, just stupid I guess".

"No, you're not stupid", said Ramos. "You made a pretty fuckin stupid mistake, but you're not stupid, so forget that answer. Why'd you do it"?

Hector looked at Ramos, paused, and again said softly "I don't know".

Ramos knew there was no need to go further with the question. He studied Hector. "Stick by me, you're going to be okay".

Hector believed him, and the moment would never be forgotten. He had been locked up for three years, but Ramos was just now finding his own place and figuring out the way things work among the inmates. He was careful not to let anyone other than Hector know what he was thinking. He gradually learned the system. Everybody wanted something. Most often it was drugs or sex. He stayed clear of those things. What he wanted was less tangible. He wanted information. It was surprisingly easy to get. All he had to do was listen. Just as in other parts of society, prisoners like to talk, and talk they did. It took a while, but Ramos learned everything about his attacker that he needed to know.

The light at the end of the tunnel began to shine brighter one morning when Ramos got the first letter from Sylvana. It was all he could do to make sure none of the other guys saw him crying. The love his mother had for him was the foundation upon which he would build the rest of his life. He told Hector about the letter. He showed him the pictures. Ramos was so proud that he actually walked around smiling for a couple of days, even though he tried not to. It was comforting to know that when it was time, he had a place to go. The letters didn't come directly from Sylvana, that would be too risky, no reason for her address to be on anything that could be seen. They first went to her brother, Ramos' uncle, and he sent them to Ramos with his return address. Same thing when Ramos wrote to his mother, the letter went through his uncle. He didn't like it that his uncle had to be involved. There was always the risk that there may be someone who still wanted revenge for the murder of Juan Villegas. He made it through two more years without any incidents. Hector only had a year to go. They didn't have the opportunity to talk as much as before, but they had already decided on the basics of a plan.

The closer Hector's release date got, the more important it was for them to agree on some things, and to make sure there was total commitment to the plan, to each other, to the future. Neither had a doubt.

"When you're out of this place, things are gonna change", said Ramos. " You and I both know that. If you change your mind about things it's okay, you gotta do what's right for you and your family. The only thing I ask is that you don't fuck around with that decision, you decide and that's the way it will be, no going back and no second guessing".

Hector looked at Ramos. His gratitude and admiration for him were never stronger. It was an honor for him to be his closest friend. His commitment was unwavering. It bothered him a little that Ramos felt the need to clarify it, but he understood. There was a lot at stake.

"I'll be there", said Hector. "On that day and all the days after. When I leave this place, a lot will change. That won't".

He held his hand out to Ramos. Ramos took it, clasped it and held it to his chest. "It's my honor my brother, I will never betray you".

After Hector left, the reality set in for Ramos. He had three more years. A lot of days to count. He kept mostly to himself, tried to keep busy and occupy his mind. One morning the unexpected happened. He was summoned to the warden's office.

"I have a deal to offer you Ramos. Apparently there is some concern among some powerful people that you may feel that you have unfinished business to tend to when your time is up. Whether you do or not is not my concern. What is my concern is that I've been told to offer you a deal. I don't like deals, and I damn sure don't like being told what to do, so I'm not happy about it, but I'm doing it. You've been a good prisoner. As far as I'm concerned you didn't need to be here at all, but that's beside the point. Here's the deal. You walk. You leave the country and don't come back. You'll be given money. No one will harm you. You leave in three days".

Ramos looked at the warden. Said Nothing. The warden broke eye contact, appeared anxious, looked again at Ramos.

"What are you thinking about? You walk in three days, you gonna say no to that"?

Ramos ignored the question and slowly looked away. His face was passive and he stared downward. He was in no hurry. After a long pause he spoke, lips barely moving.

"I walk in three days. Whether I leave the country or not is my business. I will harm none of these powerful people or their immediate families. If any harm comes to me, my family or friends, all bets are off". Another pause, then he turned and looked at the warden. "They can take their money and stick it up their ass".

The warden waited for more. That was it. He laughed a short, nervous laugh, then slowly nodded.

There was no more discussion. The three days passed quickly. There was no need to prepare, other than to get word to Hector, which he did. He had worked hard to strengthen himself, doing push ups, lifting weights and running when he could. There was no need for reflection or quiet contemplation. He was ready to go.

His first step as a free man felt good. He shook Hector's hand, then gave him a bear hug. They were both smiling. As he was getting in Hector's car, his eyes went to a gravel parking area adjacent to the paved lot. He walked over and stepped onto the gravel. The rocks crackling beneath his feet and the uneven texture of the surface were simple, beautiful reminders of the sound and feel of freedom. Hector drove away, Ramos never looked back. It was weird being able to talk freely, another small reminder of being out of the hole.

"I got all your stuff", Hector said, "you still good to go"?

"Yeah, still good", replied Ramos, without hesitation.

They drove as close as they could get to the spot Hector had scouted, then Ramos was off to set up camp. Simple as that.

"I can't wait to get the hell outa here. You keep me updated. I'll get the beer iced down". He paused as Ramos kept walking. "You okay"?

Ramos stopped, turned around and smiled. "I'm okay brother, just make sure you ice down plenty of that beer".

It took less than twenty minutes for Ramos to locate the spot and set up what little gear he had. It was next to an old barn or shed of some type that had been abandoned years ago. The roof was caved in and vines covered almost all of three sides. The other side is where he camped. The structure wouldn't be much protection from rain, but it gave him cover from wandering eyes, not that he expected any. He walked about two hundred yards from his camp site to a spot on the edge of the trees and looked across a large open pasture to a small farm house on the other side. He could see activity in the back yard, but he was too far away to make much of it. He held the binoculars to his eyes and looked again. There was a

dog and a man. He watched for a long time, lowered the binoculars and returned to camp. He wanted to hike and explore,
but he thought better of it and just settled in until dark. Just
after sunset he eased toward the edge of the pasture, hopped
the old fence and sat in the grass until darkness came. Then he
walked slowly across toward the house until he was almost to
the fence on the other side. He was very careful to be quiet and
unnoticed. He stopped and watched. The man was inside and
appeared to be cooking dinner. He didn't see the woman. He
hoped that she was away, that would help. Satisfied for now, he
walked back and laid down under the stars for the first time
in seven years. He awoke just before daylight. The morning
sounds were music to his ears, you don't hear a lot of birds
chirping in the big house. He watched. The man fed the dog
and went back inside. Mid morning the mail would come, and
that would be the time.

Jorge Veres was not born evil, he became that way by
choice. He had it tough as a child. Not fair, but not unusual.
There were many others in situations as bad or worse. Most
choose differently. He was big, he was strong. Those were his
ticket. He didn't beat up people for no reason, he did it for
money and status, although the status was dubious at best, and
the money was no king's ransom. But it had afforded him a
simple life on a small plot of land away from the city. His last
job was almost seven years ago and hadn't gone well. The boy
barely survived, but survive he did. That was a disappointment
to the people who paid him. Jorge was glad they simply allowed
him to retire and move on.

Jorge walked to the mailbox. There was a sales brochure from a travel company. As he turned and walked back toward the house, he opened it and admired the lovely beaches and palm trees. After a few steps he looked up and saw the boy, now a man, with an ugly scar and a crooked eye. Ramos didn't say a word, didn't move an inch, didn't blink. His look was pure and unflinching, his face relaxed, with no expression. He didn't want to do this, but he had to do this. Terror filled the big man. The evil had come home to roost.

They found him the next day. He was sitting on the gravel driveway, his back against the old truck parked there. His throat was slit. Protruding from his mouth was his severed penis, and his gonads lay in his lap. Ramos Mantilla was several hundred miles North, headed to Louisiana with his friend, Hector. There was an investigation, but it didn't last long. The powerful men kept quiet, and hoped that was the last of it.

The reunion was as sweet as both had imagined. Silvana cried tears of immense joy and gratitude. Ramos' tears were those of love and relief. The smiles and laughter lasted long into the Louisiana night. Among the biggest smiles were those of Hector Salinas, whose heart seemed to know that he also had come home. These were his people, his new life, his family. The younger ones were beside themselves with happiness that their big brother was home. The feeling in the close knit community of expat Peruvians was that something special was happening and that good things would follow the arrival of Ramos Mantilla.

Within a week Hector had a job, but it required him to live in New Orleans, at the Fairgrounds racetrack. He was hired by a thoroughbred racing stable as a groom. He had never been around horses, but he was quick to learn. He wasn't happy to be separated from Ramos, nor was he looking forward to living on the backside of a racetrack, but in time he adjusted to both. Whenever he had more than a day or two of free time, he went and stayed with Ramos and his family. They loved Hector and enjoyed his visits, Silvana and the kids would help Ramos and Hector learn English. It was slow going, but they both persisted until they were able to at least communicate on a basic level.

Along with learning a new language, Ramos had the added challenge of adjusting to life outside of prison. He entered prison as an almost sixteen year old boy, and left as a twenty three year old man. He had a lot to learn about a lot of things, and in time he would, but he had also already learned some things. Things that are timeless, and out of the reach of all but a few, and these were the things that enabled him to be the man he would become.

Chapter 13

Ramos took a job in the kitchen of a place called Mona's. It was a one stop grocery store and gas station that also served breakfast and lunch and was the gathering place for many of the people who lived in the area. There were hunting and fishing gear and supplies, hardware items and such. Mona was a larger than life character born and raised in Ferriday. She and her husband Bud ran the store until he took off ten years ago with the Mayor's wife, looking for greener pastures. The sign in front used to say Bud and Mona's, now it just said Mona's. If Bud ever considered coming back around, he would best think again. Ramos helped in the kitchen, chopping lots of onions and vegetables and prepping for lunch. After a while he started cooking at breakfast, then lunch. The ladies in the kitchen loved him. He was a quick learner and a tireless worker. The men weren't as quick to accept him, although they respected his work ethic. This didn't concern Ramos too much, but he noticed it, he noticed everything. Prison had taught Ramos not to be too quick to trust anybody, and to always be aware. He knew that his scarred face and droopy eye hinted at a back story that many men didn't want to hear, and that suited him just fine, he had no problem not telling it.

Delivery of produce and all perishable items happened early each day at Mona's, as in most restaurants. Ramos worked the early shift, so he often helped carry stuff from the truck to the work area in the back of the kitchen. Over time he got to know the delivery guys, and all about their job. The seafood was delivered by a company from Baton Rouge. Shrimp was by far the biggest seller of the seafood items on the menu. The shrimp Po Boy being the most popular. There was fresh fish on the menu some of the time, depending on what was in season and available. Ferriday was far enough North from the Gulf of Mexico that seafood wasn't as popular as it was closer to the Gulf. Locals were more likely to order fried catfish than fish from the Gulf. Mona had tried over the years to offer fresh Gulf fish more often, but most of the time they would end up with unsold fish at the end of the week, and it just wasn't worth it.

Peruvians love seafood of all types, and Ramos was sure that the ones who lived near Mona's would buy it if it was on the menu and prepared to their liking. He asked Mona if he could give it a try and she said okay, but only on a limited basis. The next morning he started asking the seafood delivery driver what different types of fish were available and at what price. Ramos' English was improving, but it was still choppy, and the young man was getting impatient with Ramos because he was asking so many questions. But he liked Ramos and appreciated his curiosity. He had an idea, and stopped Ramos in mid sentence.

"Why don't you come see for yourself? I'm driving to Morgan City the day after tomorrow, I'll get there early and drive back to Baton Rouge with a truck load of fresh seafood. You can ride with me and see what is coming off the boats, just like we do. If there is something you want you can buy it there and we'll bring it back, as long as it's a small quantity".

Ramos' eyes lit up with excitement. "Damn right I will. Just let me clear it with Mona".

Just South of Morgan City is Atchafalaya Bay, where the Atchafalaya River meets the Gulf of Mexico. Ramos was like a kid in a candy store. These were people he could relate to. People who lived near the sea. For two hours he did nothing but walk along the dock and see what kinds of fish were coming off the boats. Fresh fish, fish from the sea. He had one thing on his mind. Ceviche. Peruvians love Ceviche. It is prepared only with the freshest fish, which is cut up and marinated in citrus juice. It usually also is tossed with peppers and onions, and may also include any of a wide variety of spices. The citric acid in the juice "cooks" the fish pieces, turning them opaque to white in color and giving them a firmer texture. Ramos had no doubt that his Peruvian friends would order Ceviche at Mona's if it were available. Near the end of one of the docks were two boats with Spanish names, and he could hear the lively chatter of the men who worked them. He spoke Spanish to them and asked them about their catch. An hour later he was loading his fish onto his friend's truck, and they made their way back to Mona's, where he cleaned and iced the fish. He could hardly wait until the next morning, when he would prepare the newest menu item at Mona's, Ceviche.

Ramos was a little embarrassed that, although he had eaten Ceviche many times, he had never prepared it. He asked his mother for help, and she gladly gave it. The next morning she went with him, before sunrise, to Mona's. He had bought two types of fish. Spanish Mackerel and Amberjack. The Spanish Mackerel was the cheapest of the fish he saw, and the Amberjack was just something he decided to try. Sylvana showed Ramos how to filet the fish so that there was as little waste as possible, then she cut the fillets into bite size pieces and tossed them with fresh squeezed lemon and lime juice.

There were no orders for Ceviche that day. The locals weren't interested and the Peruvians were other places, working and living their lives. The next day was the same, until late in the afternoon. An older Peruvian man who lived near Ramos walked in with his daughter, a friend of Sylvana. They ordered Ceviche and Ramos was so happy he gave them each a double serving. They took the extras home and gave them to their friends. The next week Ramos made the same trip and bought fish from the same people. As he was leaving they stopped him and gave him a small container of freshly picked lump crab meat. They called it Lagniappe. Ramos knew Lagniappe was a term the people of Louisiana used and it meant " a little something extra", at least that's what he thought it meant. He was glad that his new fishermen friends appreciated his business.

The next day at Mona's, the Ceviche had a little something extra, fresh crabmeat. Louisiana people love their crab. All along the coastal areas of the state, people get together and throw a bunch of live crabs in boiling water. When they're ready they dump the crabs out on a table covered with newspaper and start cracking the shells and skillfully removing the tasty fresh crab meat. That afternoon Mona's served the first order of Ceviche to a non Peruvian. By the end of the week the Ceviche was gone. The following week the process was repeated, a larger quantity was made and the dish had a new name, Louisiana Ceviche. One afternoon, Mona told Ramos she wanted to talk to him. They sat in her small office with the door closed.

"Ramos, I have a proposal for you. Please hear me out, then we'll talk about it if you want to. I'm tired and I'm not getting any younger. This place is my life and I want it to continue. My son lives in Baton Rouge and is not interested. My daughter is interested but her husband is not, and they're too busy making babies anyway, God help um. You've been a blessing to me, and I admire you very much. I want you to take over Mona's. I want you to be the boss. I want you to be the owner. I'll stick around for a while, if you want me to. I'm not worried about the money right now, we'll work out the details. I've made a good living here. I'm proud of this place and want it to be here for a long time. I trust you. I hope you'll consider taking it over".

Ramos looked at her, a great feeling of relief washed over him. He knew the day would come when he would have a talk with Mona, he just didn't know what type of talk it would be, good or bad. Now he knew. He had no doubt that Mona liked him, but it takes more than that, and the rest he had been less sure about. He looked at her. A smile gradually made it's way across his face. The deal was done. He knew it. She knew it. The smile didn't leave. He kept looking at her and gave his response.

"The name stays the same".

Now her smile broadened. She reached out and embraced him for the first time ever. The next trip to Morgan City resulted in another added menu item at Mona's, but not a seafood dish. Ramos had lunch with his Spanish speaking fishermen before returning to Mona's. They sat a table under some trees near the parking area. Ramos noticed a basket of produce on the tailgate of a truck, and in it were red peppers shaped liked bell peppers. He walked over to take a look.

"You have Rocoto"? he asked, with a hint of excitement in his voice.

"Yes, I grow them", said one of the Central Americans, "you want some"?

Once again, Ramos called on Sylvana for her expertise in the kitchen, This time it was to show him how she made Rocotos Rellenos, another of the favorite dishes from his youth in Trujillo, Peru. The very thought of it made him want to tap dance across the floor. She started by cutting the top off of the Rocotos and cleaning out the insides. She then boiled them in salted water until soft and bright red in color. She sauted onions and garlic, added cumin and a few other spices. She cooked some ground beef, then added the onions and garlic, then added some beef broth and plumped raisins and let it all simmer. After most of the liquid was gone, she let it cool and added chopped boiled egg and black olives, then some crumbled cheese. She stuffed the peppers, topped them with more cheese, and cooked them in the oven until they were brown and bubbly on top. They were an immediate hit at Mona's. Louisianans love spicy food with a little bite. A Rocoto Relleno has more than a little bite. The Rocoto looks like a red bell pepper, but looks can be deceiving. They are very hot. Ramos served them with potatoes. The name on the menu was Rocoto Relleno with Scalloped Potatoes, a combination of Spanish and English, and everybody loved it. A week later there was something else new at Mona's, a garden, a garden full of small Rocoto plants.

As Ramos began to take over the decision making at Mona's, he had a situation he knew he had to deal with. He was the outsider. Things had been done the same way for a long time. Not everybody was going to be happy with the new way. He did what he knew was the smartest thing, but it was also the toughest and most risky thing. He went straight to the top. He went to the Cowboy.

Ronald Meeks was born and raised in Louisiana. He was shy and unassuming as a boy. He was smart, and after high school accepted an academic scholarship to Stephen F Austin State University in Nacogdoches, Texas, in Southeastern Texas, not far from his Louisiana roots. He hardly had a date in high school, and college started out the same way. Then he met Carla "Bug" Fuentes. Bug was beautiful. Her father was a

Mexican diplomat and her mother was the daughter of a Texas oil man. They tried to steer her toward the privileged life, but that wasn't Bug. She hung out with the fun crowd. They met in a Business Statistics class, both were smart. They worked together on a research paper. Ronald Meeks was bitten by the Bug. They started dating and his life changed. He began to learn Spanish. He hung out with an eclectic mix of Texas and South American students. He partied. He smoked weed. He spent time listening to music and making love to Bug. His grades suffered at first, but he managed to squeak by. During the summer after his freshman year, Bug helped him get a job working for her grandfather in the Texas oil fields. He started wearing a hat and boots. When he returned to school in the fall, the South American guys called him Vaquero, "Cowboy". The next summer Bug's grandfather began asking him to help him with some of his financial reports. Cowboy was very good with numbers, and had a savvy business mind. At the end of the summer, Bug's grandfather offered him a full time job.

Cowboy never returned to Stephen F Austin University, but he didn't quit learning. He studied law, accounting and international business through an online program offered by the University of Texas. He wasn't concerned about getting a degree, he just wanted the knowledge. Bug met someone else at school. It was okay, he figured it would happen. The years went by. Cowboy did well. He married a Texas girl and raised three children. He was gone a lot on business, and that, among other things, eventually took it's toll. At age 54 he was a divorced man ready for a change. He bought a small trucking company based in Baton Rouge, and returned home to Louisiana. The trucking business, like most, is all about relationships. The Cowboy wasted no time getting to know the people. He started to expand the customer base beyond the Baton Rouge area. One of his first new customers was the feisty owner of a place called Mona's in Ferriday.

They met in Mona's former office. Ramos, as usual, had done his homework. He had been at Mona's over ten hours a day on average for almost three years. He knew the customers, he knew the employees, he knew the vendors and he knew the employees of the vendors. He had spent hours looking over the books and analyzing financial statements. He had no formal education in accounting, but he made up for it with his street smarts and willingness to ask questions and learn. He treated everyone with respect, and in turn he was respected.

Perhaps Ramos Mantilla's best trait, along with the self discipline, was his ability to understand people. He had very little ego himself, which seemed to allow him an almost unencumbered view into the contents of the soft tissue between the ears of others. The Cowboy was no slouch at this himself, plus, he had a lot more life experience and business experience than Ramos. His combination of smarts and people skills is what had allowed him to become The Cowboy in the first place. There was a difference though, and this difference is where Ramos found his edge. He was young and hungry. He poured himself into understanding the business of Mona's, and as part of that, he poured himself into understanding the business of the Cowboy. He wasn't interested in conquering any of the worlds outside of Mona's, he just wanted to be as good as he could be within his own world. He was prepared.

After the small talk, Ramos began. "I want to talk business with you. As you know, Mona has decided to retire and I am taking over the store. She's been very good to me. I have a lot of respect for her. I also have a lot of respect for you. Your business success is the result of your hard work and good decision making, and I admire that very much. My story is pretty simple really. I came here from Peru with not much education or the ability to speak English. Mona's is the only job I've had. It's been tough at times, but I've managed to do okay. My only goal is to help take care of my family and to help improve the lives of my friends from Peru who live in this area, if possible. I have no …". The Cowboy cut him off.

"I'm pretty sure I knew all that, Ramos. I appreciate the kind words, and I respect you also. Now, what do you want to talk about"?

Ramos immediately realized he had talked too much. He was so intent on letting The Cowboy know that he wasn't a threat that he had crossed the line into what the Americans would call Bullshit territory. No more Bullshit.

"We're not using your company any more. I plan to use my own people and my own trucks to supply our seafood and produce at Mona's. It's better for me that way. I will have more control over what we buy and how much we pay. I have friends in Morgan City that I'll buy seafood from directly. A lot of our produce will come from our own garden, the rest we will take care of. I mean no disrespect in any way to you or your people, I'm just doing what I think is best for my business".

He was not looking at the Cowboy, he was dead still, eyes fixed on nothing, speaking calmly and respectfully. The Cowboy had been looking at Ramos from the start. He said nothing for a minute, just staring at the side of Ramos' face, then he looked away, stood paused a moment with his back toward Ramos, then slowly turned back toward him. Ramos hadn't moved. The Cowboy began in a condescending tone and manner.

"Son, I admire your gumption, but I'm thinking maybe you don't know who you're dealing with. I've paid my dues. I have a lot of friends around here. It's pretty tough to make it in business without friends. It's about more than just delivering seafood and produce, I take care of people. We take care of each other. That's the way business is done. Now, you and I can go two ways with this. We can help each other, or you can..." This time it was Ramos who cut the Cowboy off in mid sentence. Sitting in the same spot, hadn't moved. Speaking in a normal voice.

"You're right, your drivers aren't just delivering seafood. This morning one of your guys dropped off some Red Snapper just up the road in Natchez. He climbed back into the truck with an envelope under his arm. He counted out hundred dollar bills, sitting in his truck, in broad daylight. Kinda careless. Another one is making a delivery right about now just outside Baton Rouge. He has no clue what he's delivering, but it's more than just seafood. He's supposed to be making child support payments in two states, neither of which is Louisiana. He gets paid cash. He keeps his mouth shut. There are two sheriff's deputies who caught some very impressive fish last summer in Costa Rica. They had a big weekend with some very pretty girls. Lots of expensive Champagne and Cuban cigars. They didn't pay a dime for the trip. They both have families and are barely making ends meet. One is past due this month, once again, on both truck payments". A pause. Ramos turned his head, not fast, not slow and looked the Cowboy dead in the eye. Totally without expression. His own eyes void of anything except a cold, unflinching stare.

"I'm thinking maybe it's you who doesn't know".

The Cowboy quietly conceded the Mona's account to the new owner. Ramos didn't make a big deal of it, and he never mentioned the episode to anyone. Over time, the Cowboy came to be an admirer of the young Peruvian, and on more than a few occasions helped out when Mona's needed something on short notice. It seemed to be that way with everyone. Ramos was unyielding when he had to be, but never took advantage of anyone and was generous to a fault. He inspired the Peruvians. Gave them confidence. He was their unquestioned leader. Because of his reputation and generous nature, people sought him out. Not just Peruvians, but anyone who needed help or advice, or anyone who needed an advocate, especially poor people and those who for whatever reason had nowhere else to turn. His role became not unlike that of a local Mafia Don, minus the bad part. He didn't squeeze anybody. Just the opposite really, he never accepted any form of payment from someone who was sincere and needed help. It was just how he rolled. Funny thing. Nobody among his friends and customers had ever seen Ramos Mantilla lose his temper, act violently or even raise his voice in anger. Maybe they had heard stories, or maybe it was something else, the reason doesn't matter, he was the man. Although his bad side had not been seen, it was understood that it wasn't where a person wanted to be. Just the way it was.

PART 4

Nikki, Rafa and The Guv

CHAPTER 14

As murders go, this one was pretty clean. One shot to the chest. No sign of struggle, Not a big mess, just some blood and stuff to clean up. The chair would have to go. The blood stains on the floor were not that big a deal, they could be removed or the boards could be replaced. The apartment could be rented to someone new in a matter of days. But that wasn't going to happen. This was a murder scene. Just down the street from Oaklawn Park. The dead guy was at the track almost every day. Not just during the live meet, but almost every day, period, rain or shine. He was a horseplayer. It was his passion. He was good at it. Some guys live their whole lives without passion, or maybe just without finding their passion, maybe not caring to try to find it, maybe being scared of it, whatever, there are endless possible explanations, none matter, it's just not there. Ernest Hemingway Cole wasn't that way. He had a passion. It was Horse Racing.

The gun was a 22 caliber, no more than a peashooter according to some, but pretty effective when the bullet pierces the left ventricle. There was no gun found. No sign of forced entry. Forensics experts spent days going over every inch of the apartment. They found very little of significance. Ernie Cole died with over $1,400 in his front left pocket untouched.

There was a half full cocktail glass on the table beside the chair, and a newspaper in his lap. A copy of the Daily Racing Form was on the floor. It was as if he just died suddenly while sitting in his favorite chair, having a drink, catching up on the news and getting ready for another day of racing at Oaklawn. Just like any other day. The problem was that his heart didn't just stop beating of it's own accord, it was forced to stop beating because of a 40 grain piece of lead that came in unannounced and shut down the party, then and there.

Speculation was that the Police were not telling the whole story, that Ernie Cole was a spy, that Ernie Cole had ties to the deepest darkest corners of the criminal underworld and that when it all came out he would make the venerable Al Capone look like a choir boy. He was killed Sunday night, which was pretty good timing as murders go. Oaklawn Park didn't have live racing Monday and Tuesday. Ernie had a lot of friends at the track. It gave them a couple of days to get over the initial shock and try to get ready for the Wednesday race card. That Wednesday, the flags flew at half staff. There was already talk that Ernie deserved to be remembered in some special way, maybe even name a race in his honor. The shock was felt especially hard on the backside of the track, where the horses live and where the dedicated people who love the horses live and work with them. The ones that get a very small paycheck and no recognition. The ones that start their day, every day, before sunrise. They do the jobs that others don't want to do. They clean out the stalls. They feed and water the horses, groom them, exercise them, look after them 24/7, 365. They take care of the horses, and they take care of each other.

Ernie's best friend at the track was one of those people. Ernie called him The Governor. Nobody knew why, including Ernie. The South Americans who worked on the backside found it funny, and they started calling him Governor also. Being from New York, Ernie didn't have a trace of a Southern drawl, but that didn't stop him from doing his best impersonation of a born and raised Southern aristocrat when he pronounced The Governor's name. He emphasized the first syllable, held it a little longer than necessary, skipped the second syllable altogether, then totally ignored the O and the R and replaced them with A and H, so the end result was Guvnah. When the Spanish speakers started impersonating Ernie impersonating a Southerner, it got crazy. They eventually all just called him The Guv.

Ernie had lived in the apartment for almost five years. Before that, it was seven years in a condo that he bought when he moved to Hot Springs. He lived modestly, but was generous. He was a big tipper and had been known to buy more than one round of drinks after a winning day at the track. He was unassuming and had an easygoing manner. It was hard to imagine anyone that would want him dead. On most days he walked to Oaklawn from his apartment five blocks away. A lot of days he would be there for early morning workouts, have breakfast with the Guv in the track kitchen, walk back home and then return for first post in the afternoon. He would take his usual spot among the regulars on the track level, in close proximity to the paddock, the track apron outside and most important, the large bank of television screens that showed the simulcast signals from thoroughbred tracks all over the world. He was a horseplayer. He was not a degenerate gambler. There's a difference. More to the point, he was not just a horseplayer, he was a professional horseplayer. He made a living betting on horses. The true professional horseplayer is a rare breed, there are a lot of pretenders. Ernie was no pretender. He made his money the old fashioned way, he worked for it. Not in the conventional sense, nothing conventional about it, but it was work just the same. It required discipline and patience, traits that are in short supply among degenerate gamblers, but are part of the price of admission into the rare air of the winning horseplayer.

Ernie had a back story, but he shared it with very few of his cronies at the track. One of the few was The Guv, who had a past of his own. Ernie and the Guv were tight. Soul brothas. They trusted each other. That was big. A man needs somebody he can trust. Another unspoken rule among gamblers is that you don't talk about your problems, we all have them, nobody wants to hear about yours. The racetrack regulars are no different in that respect than those of other gambling venues, large or small. The racetrack and the poker table are different places, but when the horses are about to hit the stretch, or the cards are about to hit the felt, they are one and the same. Time and place are irrelevant. Nobody gives a flying fuck where you went to school or how many charities you gave to last year or how far along your sister's cancer is. In that moment, you get a respite from those things. Just the way it is.

The Hot Springs police wasted no time interviewing the first, most obvious person who might have some insight into the life of Ernie Cole, The Guv.

"Let's start with what we know, which is not much. Ernie Cole was murdered. You were his best friend. Do you have any idea who did it or what might have happened"?

The Guv had done his best to prepare himself for the interview. It was not, technically, an interrogation. They had told him he was not a suspect, but he knew that meant nothing, and could change in an instant for whatever reason they might choose. He had spent time himself in the pokie when he was just a kid. He was wary. But he also wanted to help.

"No, I wish I did, he was the best friend a guy could have. He had no enemies that I know of. I still can't believe he's gone. It will never be the same".

"For the record, we have to ask you some things. We have no reason to think you had anything to do with it, we're just doing what we have to do". The Guv just nodded, slowly. "When did you last see Ernie Cole alive"?

"Sunday afternoon, about 3:00, we had a horse running in the 7th race, we watched the race together, then I left the track for the day".

"Did you talk to him at all at any time after you left the track"?

"No".

"Where were you from the time you left the track until 10:00 the next morning"?

The Guv looked at the police detective. He didn't like the question, but he understood it had to be asked. "I was at home. I cooked dinner and watched a movie. Went to bed around 10:00. Got up at 5, was at the track before 6. Mondays are light days for us, there's no racing. I was at the barn until about 11, I called Ernie about playing golf and didn't get an answer. Had lunch in the track kitchen. Got the call about Ernie around 11:45".

"Did you talk to anybody at all Sunday night"?

"My brother called, we talked about twenty minutes, probably around 7 That's it".

"What movie did you watch"?

"Hangover II, not as good as the first one".

There was a pause. The detective was trying to decide how to proceed. The Guv spoke.

"I didn't kill Ernie. I loved the guy. You're wasting your time on me".

The detective knew he was telling the truth about not being the murderer, he just did. He was not at all convinced, however, that he was wasting his time talking to the Guv. Somebody killed the man. There had to be a reason.

"Who were his closest friends other than you"?

"The man had a lot of friends, everybody on the backside loved him. He was like one of us. We were his family, really. He was pretty tight with a few of the horseplayers. We had a poker game, every Thursday night. Ernie loved poker, he was good too, except when he had too many Budweisers, then he was pretty much like the rest of us, win some, lose some".

"What about his past,. did he ever talk about his ex wife, his son or his career on Wall Street"?

"Not a lot, but we were tight, we talked about everything. He was a fun guy with a great attitude. He didn't waste much time talking about the past. He was all about living his life to the fullest every day. It wasn't often that we talked about those things, but when we did he was honest and candid, as always with Ernie".

"So is there anything that you know of in his past that would possibly cause someone to want him dead"?

"No".

The detective looked at the Guv, paused for a long time, then turned away as he exhaled a deep sigh that showed his frustration with the lack of any clue about the direction the investigation might take. He turned back.

"He was your best friend. We could use your help".

The Guv nodded. Said nothing. Something about the situation made him pause. It was a feeling. He had felt it before, many years before. In a small room, talking to a man. He had learned a few things since then. This wasn't the same man, but it was the same feeling. He would help, but he was going to be very careful.

CHAPTER 15

Nikki's phone buzzed during her real estate law class mid morning Tuesday. She glanced and saw that it was Gabriela. She returned the call on the way back to her apartment.

"Hey girl, saw you called, was totally engrossed in an explanation of one of the nuances of some arcane law that originated as a result of a dispute between two well heeled landowners over mineral rights to the sediment and shit in the creek that separates their properties".

"I say we split the creek down the middle, you own the stuff on your side and I own the stuff on my side".

"Not so fast senorita, there's a whole gravel bar on your side covered with rocks that include a bunch of crystals and stuff, maybe even diamonds. They obviously came from a large rock formation on my side, upstream from the gravel bar".

"I don't give a rat's ass where they came from, they're on my property now, so they're mine".

Now Nikki was tired of the legal talk, she just spent a whole class listening to it.

"Whatever, I got plenty of diamonds anyway".

They both laughed. Then Gabriela switched gears.

"Hey, I read something this morning in the news that I thought might interest you. I don't want to bring up an unpleasant topic, and maybe you saw it yourself, but if not I think you should at least take a look at it".

"At what"?

Gabriela experienced a moment of apprehension, then continued. "There was a murder Sunday night in Hot Springs Arkansas. The guy was involved in horse racing and was a big gambler apparently". She paused again.

"What about it Gabby"?

"He was a well liked, older, divorced white man who used to work on Wall Street".

Nikki said nothing for several seconds. "What else do you know"?

"Nothing really, it was a brief story. I'm sorry to bring it up, but I thought I should mention it".

"It's okay, I understand...I'll check it out".

Nikki headed straight home and jumped on the internet. Two years ago, she had spent many hours searching for information, any information, that might help her find out what happened to her father. *It was frustrating. It was heartbreaking. She got nowhere. She didn't want to revisit those days. She had no desire at all to read about someone else being murdered. Someone who quite possibly had children close to her age. She didn't want to go there. But she had to* go there. *The time she spent with Anna was fresh on her mind. It was heaven sent, she was heaven sent. Nikki thought after Anna's visit that she might have closure, yet here she was, wondering if there could possibly be a connection between the murder of her father and this man in Hot Springs Arkansas.*

She spent the next half hour reading the online reports of the murder. Nothing she read made her think there was any connection to Gib. There were certainly similarities, primarily the combination of Wall Street and Horse Racing, but there were many more differences. The obvious one was that in Hot Springs there was a body, and a bullet hole. Ernie was dead, no doubt about it. That was a much different starting place than a totally unexplained disappearance. Ernie was a horseplayer, a professional gambler, who left Wall Street fifteen years ago. He was born into a privileged life in New York City. Gib was an unassuming Southern boy who made his way in the investment business by working up through the ranks. He had never even been to Wall Street until a month before he disappeared. Still, they were both dead, and there were a lot more questions than answers.

Decision time. To delve further into circumstances around the unfortunate and quite sudden demise of Mr. Cole, Nikki would have to risk scraping the scab off a wound that she had only very recently allowed herself to think might be healing. Such is the stuff required of persons of character, to make the hard choice. In spite of the similarities, should she dare peek into the abyss, to willingly enter a place that would undoubtedly be inhabited by those prone to malevolence? To what end? Redemption? There was none to be had. A lessening of the pain of another? Maybe. Solace for having tried? No, not really. What then? Nikki made the decision. She said a silent prayer for Ernie Cole and those who loved him. She would not get involved. That was that.

It was five dollar pitcher night at the Taj, albeit Dixie. She was ready for a cold one, but she would have to wait until five o'clock. Predictably, her afternoon class was a drag. The guy was brilliant, but dull as a dime store butter knife, and he insisted on taking roll every class. To top it off, he wore a bow tie and seemed to purposely buy pants an inch and a half too short. How could she possibly be expected to learn anything in such an environment?

The first plastic cup of cold Dixie lasted about as long as a fourth quarter lead of the Saints in the eighties. Reggie and Gabby took notice. Nikki poured another and dispatched of it in the same manner. Reggie was having happy visions of crazy drunk sex later. Gabby's thoughts were more grounded. She knew Nikki well, when the girl started pounding beers like this, there was something going on. They had not yet had the chance to discuss the murder in Hot Springs, not that they should, but she had just told Nikki about it that morning, Nikki had spent many days and weeks in agonizing desperation, trying to figure out what really happened to her father. She had guzzled Dixie then. She was guzzling Dixie now.

The Wednesday race card at Oaklawn was a pretty typical mid week affair, lower and mid level claimers with a couple of nice allowance races late in the card. Ernie's murder was the topic of conversation among almost every segment of the race crowd. There was wild speculation, as well as the garden variety gossip, but there was no logical explanation. Ernie Cole was murdered. How in hell could that happen? It just didn't make sense. The obituary in the paper was brief, but well done. The funeral was announced for Friday morning, with visitation Thursday evening at a local funeral home, a half mile from Oaklawn. The body would be cremated. That decision was made by Hayden, as were all the others, since he was the only family member. Hayden had important stuff to do in Boston. His flight back would leave Little Rock a couple of hours after the funeral, which was going to be a short and sweet graveside service for family and close friends. True to form, Ernie's will was a simple, hand written list of his wishes, signed by him and witnessed by a couple of his buddies at the track. It was in his safe deposit box. There was not a lot of discussion about what might be in the will. It baffled, and disgusted, Hayden, but from all indications, pickings were going to be slim for the heirs.

The visitation was well attended. The Mayor, several city council members, business leaders, even a Congressman. They all looked solemn and pained to see Ernie go. Not a single one even knew him. Only two had ever met him, neither remembered it. It didn't seem right to have only one person in the receiving line, so it was suggested by the funeral home that one of Ernie's close friends join Hayden. Of course that was The Guv. They made quite a pair, Hayden and the Guv, a fair haired New Yorker who not so discreetly was repeatedly sneaking a look at his smartphone, and a swarthy Peruvian who not so discreetly was repeatedly checking out the Congressman's young trophy wife. The New Yorker wore a frown of which he was unaware. The Peruvian wore a woody, of which he was not only aware, but quite proud. He knew Ernie would approve.

The graveside service the next morning was indeed short and sweet. The Chaplain at Oaklawn, who was not an ordained minister, or affiliated with a church, delivered the eulogy, and did quite well. His name was Martin Carrington. He was early fifties, and retired from the family insurance business which his father started. He announced at age 41 that he felt called to devote his full time and energy to motivational speaking, as well as sales and leadership training. He was endorsed by the Fellowship of Christian Athletes, and frequently incorporated scripture and biblical principles into his talks. He was a smart dresser and a card carrying

Republican, who never passed on the opportunity to rail against the moral decline of American culture, and enthusiastically support any and all of the true American Patriots.

It was a cold morning, the gathering was small, gone were the Congressman, the Mayor and the other luminaries. Everyone at the graveside had a personal connection to the deceased. Except one. A very pretty dark haired young lady who respectfully listened to the eulogy, and even appeared to have a tear rolling down her cheek as she turned to leave. She spoke to no one. She had every intention of leaving Hot Springs and returning to New Orleans without delay. It wasn't to be. As she started her car and turned her attention to cranking up the heat, she was startled by a woman in a pant suit and overcoat standing just outside her driver side window, trying to get her attention without scaring her in the process. After her initial surprise, she decided the woman was almost certainly no threat, and lowered her window just enough to talk to her. As she did, she saw the badge on her belt.

"Sorry to startle you mam, I'm Detective Kay Delacio with the Hot Springs police department. Would you mind if I asked you a few questions"?

Nikki didn't think, she just responded. "Of course, I mean, of course not, what's it about"?

"Can I inconvenience you to ask that we go inside to talk"?

"I guess so, where would that be"?

"Here, there's a room in the office we can use. Don't worry, we don't think you've done anything wrong, we just want to talk".

"Okay, should I follow you there"?

"Yes, thank you".

Five minutes later they were in the small meeting room. The detective began. "Again, I'm sorry for the intrusion. Let me tell you why we're here. Ernie Cole was murdered, I assume you know that".

"Yes".

"What's your name, and what connection do you have to Mr. Cole"?

Nikki sighed. She was okay with the question, but she knew there was some explaining to do, and who knows where it would lead or how long it would take. "My name is Nikki Carter, I didn't have any connection to Mr. Cole".

"Okay, so why were you at the graveside"?

Nikki took a deep breath and exhaled slowly. "My father disappeared over two years ago. His name was Gib Carter. I have it on good authority that he was murdered, but I can't prove it. He was in the investment business, like Mr. Cole, his murder involved a connection to horse racing, like Mr. Cole".

Nikki started slowly shaking her head, trying to keep her composure. The emotion was real. The detective knew it, but she had a job to do. She needed answers. "Can I get you some water or coffee or something"?

"No, I'm okay".

"Where do you live"?

"New Orleans, I'm in law school".

"So you drove from New Orleans to Hot Springs for the graveside service"?

Nikki nodded, "yes".

"Did you know Mr. Cole at all, had you ever met him or talked to him"?

"No".

Detective Delacio was an experienced police officer, intuition told her that Nikki Carter was telling the truth, and that she would probably not be any help at all in the investigation, but she was not quite to the point that she was going to mark her name off the list. It would help if she would just talk, and maybe she could be on her way back to New Orleans. She was on the verge of tears, and she felt sure there had been many tears before. She didn't want to push her over the edge. Just before she opened her mouth to ask another question, she got her wish, Nikki talked.

"I've never heard the name Ernie Cole, and I had no connection with him whatsoever. I read about his murder online. A close friend of mine in New Orleans saw the story and told me about it. There's really no reason to think there's a connection, but I couldn't get it out of my mind, so I got up early this morning and drove up here. I figured that if I didn't I might always wonder about it. At the graveside I realized there was no need to stay, and I'm hoping that I won't always feel the need to turn over every leaf looking for answers, it's too stressful and painful, I just want to let it go".

"Let what go"?

Nikki turned her head, looking into the thin air with faraway eyes. "Not knowing why my father had to die".

"You said he was murdered. Was there an arrest made"?

"No. Officially he's still just disappeared, but he was murdered".

Kay Delacio was quiet a moment. Something was obviously wrong here. Maybe this young lady had convinced herself that she knew what happened because she couldn't bear to think that her father had just walked away. It wouldn't be the first time. Then again, maybe she really did know. She certainly seemed confident of it. Either way, there was unfinished business. However, that unfinished business was not her, Kay Delacio's, responsibility. The business of investigating the murder of Ernie Cole was. Still, no way she was just going to dismiss this young lady's comments about her father.

"How do you know"?

Nikki looked away. "I just do. I know they killed him. I just don't understand why. I mean, I sorta do know why, but I don't understand it, and I guess I never will".

"Have you told the police what you know"?

Nikki sighed. "I shouldn't have brought it up. It doesn't matter now. It has nothing to do with Ernie Cole".

The detective thought for a minute. "Nikki, it's none of my business, but who have you talked to about this? If you don't want to answer it's okay, but this is pretty heavy stuff to keep bottled up inside".

"I know, I know, it's complicated".

"Nobody needs to carry an unnecessary burden. Life is too tough as it is. Promise me you'll talk to somebody about it".

"I've talked to somebody…". She seemed to want to say more, but stopped short.

"I'll tell you what", said the detective, "let's put that aside for now, we can come back to it later if you want to. I have a couple of more questions. I'll make it quick".

"Okay".

"Have you ever heard of a guy from Peru they call The Governor"?

"No".

"Have you ever been to Oaklawn Park"?

"No".

"Okay, that's okay, you can go. Just don't leave town without telling us".

Nikki looked at her with eyes full of a combination of concern and incredulity, mostly the latter.

Detective Delacio quickly said "I'm kidding. I'm sorry. I shouldn't have said that. Just a little bit of police detective humor". She paused

"Really, I'm sorry, that wasn't very professional. Here's my card. If you want to talk for any reason, please call me".

"Okay".

"Nikki, I want to make sure you understand something".

Nikki just looked at Kay Delacio, not sure what to expect next from her. The detective continued.

"First, you're not a suspect, not even close. Second,

I'm serious about your needing to talk to someone you trust about your father. You don't know me, but I have a lot of experience in these matters. I'll be happy to listen. I mean it. Off the record and totally confidential, you just let me know. Any time, day or night".

"Thank you, I appreciate that very much".

They stood. Kay Delacio looked at Nikki, then gave her a quick hug. "Drive carefully".

"Okay, thanks".

Hayden was glad to be back in Boston. The only business left in Arkansas would be to settle the estate. That could take a while, so he busied himself with other things. Ernie had a safe deposit box at a downtown bank. The Guv told Hayden he thought the will was there, but he wasn't certain. As close as they were, Ernie and the Guv didn't talk much about money, except as it related to horse racing. It was just the way they rolled. Ernie always had a wad of bills in his pocket, and he paid cash for almost everything. A lot of gamblers are that way. An investment portfolio is great, a bank account is necessary, but cash is king.

Hayden wasn't a part of that world. His was more conventional, and respectable. He marched to the beat of the drummer who strikes the drum according to the rules, with precision and skill, the right way. The way that is tight, refined, impressive to those who know the difference between a rag tag street band and a group of trained adherents to a higher standard. He was living a life of purpose and meaning. He was doing important things, things that mattered. He wasn't sure how his father had gotten so far off course. He thought it was sad. Living in that apartment, hanging out at the racetrack every day with that bunch of ne'er do wells and misfits. He knew his father wasn't a bad person, a kind soul in fact. He figured there must be a reason for the decisions his father had made, however misguided they were. It reminded him that he must remain diligent, lest he himself should wander down the perilous path that veered so, so far away from where a man should go.

As far as could be determined, Ernie didn't owe anybody any money. His utility bills were paid. His rent was current. He had no debts. Hayden settled up with the funeral home, and asked The Guv if he would clean out the apartment and do what he wanted with the contents. He arranged for a local lawyer to handle the estate, such as it was. Tuesday morning The Guv met the lawyer at the bank to open the safe deposit box. It was a small box. Inside was a plain white envelope with Will written on the outside. There was a diamond ring, which the Guv figured was Ernie's mother's, a small silver box with initials inscribed on the top and an old sterling silver charm bracelet, loaded with charms of all descriptions. The lawyer removed the items and opened the envelope. Inside, as expected, was a simple hand written will.

To Hayden: I Love You, the things in this box are yours. They were given to me by my Mother. I wish you many years of peace and happiness.

Any and all decisions concerning any and all of my other possessions are to be made by The Guv. I Love You my brother, and I miss you already. Tell all the boys I'll see them at the winners' window.

It was vintage Ernie, pure and simple. The lawyer looked a little perplexed. The Guv had a grin on his face and tears in his eyes. When *the eyes filled all the way, a few of the tears trickled down the face of the swarthy Peruvian.* He was in no hurry to wipe them off. The Guv immediately had a brilliant idea. There was going to be a funeral parade.

Saturday morning, after the early workouts and the necessary work was done, the group started to come together in the Oaklawn parking lot. Benny the Brickmason was on the snare drum, he got things started, Carl was next with his trumpet, which was surprisingly loud and clear, then everybody else pretty much just joined in. Carl had been practicing, but he only really knew two songs, When the Saints Come Marching In and Just a Closer Walk with Thee. They started on Central Avenue, right at the main entrance to the track, and headed toward town. It was a huge party. The Guv had no idea so many people would join in. They didn't have time to get an official parade permit, but the security guys at the track, many of whom were Hot Springs policemen, said it would be okay if they tried to stay mostly on the sidewalk. That was the plan, but it quickly turned into a full blown New Orleans style Funeral March, traffic in both directions came to a standstill. Some people even got out of their cars and joined in. Young and old, black and white, rich and poor, all joined in. They were twirling umbrellas, throwing beads and dancing in the street. Big Tony was banging on a bass drum he borrowed from the high school, there was a tuba, several clarinets, saxophones, and a guy nobody seemed to know playing the trombone like it was going out of style. A tall blonde was dressed like Miss America. One guy was dressed up like the Pope. The procession turned around three blocks away and headed back toward the track. When they reached the main entrance, Preacherman was standing on the top step, waving his hands to get everyone's attention. He had a hand held microphone hooked to a portable amplifier. When the crowd was quiet, he began. There was some concern among security that the revelry had gone on long enough, and they didn't want to have to interrupt the Preacherman if he got going like he could. They had no need to worry. Preacherman was certain he had the early Daily Double picked cold, and he hadn't made his bet yet.

He raised his hand and bowed his head. "To our friend Ernie, Rest in Peace, and in your own words, See You at the Winner's Window". There was an eruption of yelling and shouting and clapping. Ernie Cole would not be forgotten.

CHAPTER 16

Horseplayers are an optimistic lot. Every day at the track begins with anticipation of something good happening, or at least the possibility of something good happening. Not a bad way to start the day. Not a bad way to live life. It's the life Ernie chose once he was quiet and listened to his inner voice. Of course, it could be argued by someone with a different view that Ernie bailed out. On his career. On his family. On himself. But it's what's on the inside that makes the man, and who on the outside can possibly know what's on the inside?

The wedding was only a few months away and Nikki was starting to feel the pressure. Luckily, Reggie's mother was a sweetheart and didn't mind picking up the slack. They spent most of the day Saturday together, going over all the things that needed to be done. Nikki and Reggie had dinner at La Crepe Nanou, one of their favorite Uptown spots. There are no reservations, so they waited outside with the other devotee's of the small French Bistro. By the time they were seated both

Nikki and Reggie had dutifully prepared their palates by making their way through a bottle and a half of Sancere. The meal was delicious. Nikki was glad to be back in New Orleans, and she didn't intend to stray too far away for a good while.

Donald "Dub" Starkey was a young associate at an old money law firm in Hot Springs. He wasn't an experienced estate lawyer. He wasn't an experienced lawyer, period. He was barely out of law school. When Hayden asked some of his lawyer friends if they knew anybody in Hot Springs, AR, a suitable old money firm got the call. They handed the file to Dub. Dub scheduled a phone conference with Hayden and got the basics. Ernie and Hayden's mother divorced when he was four years old, so he had no memory of living with his father. Ernie spent time with him on the weekends when he was young, but during his teenage years he didn't see him much. His mother remarried during those years, and Ernie was mostly out of the picture. Ernie had money, and when his parents died he had a lot of money. Hayden never had to worry about money. He had a substantial college fund, and when he finished school it became his portfolio. Ernie would invite Hayden to visit him in New York, and on occasion he did. Their relationship was civil, but had no real substance. Ernie had decided to keep his crazy ass mother's book store in business, and he often spent time there doing heaven knows what. Hayden's mother had always warned him that Ernie was eccentric, and it wouldn't help his career to be cast in the same light, so he mostly kept his distance from Ernie. As it turned out, in Hayden's view, it was good advice. Ernie's reputation on Wall Street began to suffer.

It was said that he drank too much and some days wouldn't even go to the office. Eventually he and the firm agreed to part ways. The firm announced that Ernie was retiring to pursue charitable work like his father. Hayden laughed out loud when he saw the announcement. Ernie sold the Upper East Side apartment and moved into a place down the street from the book store. He invited Hayden to join him on a trip to Europe. He declined, too much going on. Hayden's next ten years or so were spent building his own career in Boston. Unfortunately, that came at the expense of his own marriage. At least there had been no time for children, and his replacement girlfriend had her own career, so everything was good on the home front, such as it was.

Dub was getting the picture. Ernie Cole's estate, and legacy, were, according to Hayden, tainted. He had risen very high on the food chain. He was a player. Then he threw it all away. Just like that. Wife, child, career. Lost it all. Painful to watch. Kinda like when you're driving and come across a bad looking accident on the side of the road. Keep moving folks, nothing to see here. If that was how Hayden saw it, that was okay with Dub. He was glad not to have to do too much fancy lawyering anyway, being new and all. It would be good to just handle the file for the firm, make a few bucks, learn a few things, and move on.

He should have known it wouldn't be that simple. It started when the light blinked on his desk phone. "Dub, there's someone here to see you, Mr. Zamfir". Dub turned his head and looked down, the way he did when he needed to dial through the memory bank. He was pretty sure he had never heard the name.

"Did he say what it's about"?

"No, he was very polite, just said he would like to speak with you. He's sitting in the lobby. Interesting looking guy, pretty easy on the eyes".

"Alright, I'll come see what he wants. Give me just a minute".

"Okay, just take your time".

He could almost see the grin on her face. Dub Starkey didn't have many people walk in off the street and ask for him by name. In fact, it had never happened. His job was to help the partners work through their files. There wasn't the time or the need for him to try to develop his own clients just yet. He was pleasantly surprised that he had someone waiting for him, but also a bit apprehensive that he had no idea who the person was or why he was there. The young man rose to greet him.

"Hello, I'm Dub Starkey, how can I help you"?

"Mr. Starkey my name is Rafa Zamfir, sorry for the intrusion. Is there a place where we can talk? I'll only take a few minutes of your time".

"Of course, we'll use the conference room".

Dub led the way and waited for the man to be seated, then sat across from him. He was indeed strikingly handsome. Black curly hair, dark, deep set eyes. A simple silver loop earring in his left ear. He had smooth olive skin and a pleasant face, from the Mediterranean maybe.

"Okay, what can I do for you"?

"I understand that you're the attorney for the estate of Ernie Cole".

"Well, I'm working on it, the lead attorney is one of the senior attorneys here, I'm an associate working with him".

"I see. I saw your name and assumed you were the main guy, but that doesn't matter to me, I'm happy to talk to you".

The young man was indeed polite, but Dub wanted to get on with it. "What was your relationship to Mr. Cole"?

Rafa Zamfir paused. "He was my father".

Dub's initial reaction was not much of a reaction at all, he just looked at the young man sitting across from him. There was no reason to doubt him. It was a surprise, certainly, but there was no reason to think it mattered much. The estate didn't appear to be complicated. There wasn't much money, there weren't feuding family members, no problems. Still, he sensed that there was more to be said, and maybe discovered. True that.

"Okay, tell me more. Why didn't we know this"?

"I can't answer that. It's an unusual situation, but I certainly haven't tried to keep it a secret. I didn't find out who my father was until I was fourteen years old. I was born and raised just outside of Paris. I lived with my Grandmother. She's a wonderful lady. She's lived a very hard life, as a member of the Roma community in France. My mother wasn't around much, she had problems and was not very stable".

Dub held up a finger as if to say he wanted to pause the conversation for just a minute. "Let me make a suggestion. First, how long will you be in Hot Springs"?

"Not long, but I can stay a few days, if I need to. I'm not expecting you to just drop the other stuff you're doing for my benefit, I just want to make sure I take care of whatever I can before I leave town".

"Fair enough, give me a minute". Dub started to get up, then stopped. "How about having a beer after work today, that way you can give me the full story. We can meet in the lobby of the Arlington Hotel at five o'clock. Is that okay"?

"Sure, works for me".

The Arlington is quintessential Hot Springs. It sits at the end of historic Bath House Row, on Central Avenue, aristocratic and proud. It may not be in the league of the world's great luxury hotels, actually it's not even close, but it matters not, the old girl rules the roost in this town. It's like an old painting that, with it's crackled texture and deep subtle colors, has, over a long time, attained the patina and countenance of a masterpiece. It's history, like the town's, is colorful. Tales of gamblers and gangsters abound, woven into the fabric of the place, and into the memories and musings of those who have spent time there, or wish they had. For those who prefer worn marble stairs and old brass handrails over newer options, there is a lot to like, not the least of which is the huge, regal, wrap around porch that begs both guests and passers by to sit, sip a cool one, and participate in a moment of calm. The porch is not the kind you see on a graceful old white wooden house as you drive through the historic districts of quiet Southern towns. Those are wonderful, and evoke feelings of family, friends and summertime. The Arlington porch does that too, but on a grander scale, and in a more inclusive manner. It's not one family's home, it's home to every person who decides to have a seat and savor a respite from the worries of the day. It's big, expansive, made of stone and tile, with a high ceiling and wide open space between large, arched columns. It could be in Rome, Paris or Istanbul, but it's not. It wraps around the front of the Arlington Hotel in Hot Springs, Arkansas. Once through the door, the large porch gives way to the large lobby, friendly and welcoming. A bar lines the wall on the right, just the way it's supposed to in a place of lives lived well, and otherwise. On the far left is where the band plays, and has played, long into the night for many, many galas, graduations and occasions of conviviality for decades. The registration desk is at the rear of the grand space, along the back wall, as it should be in a civilized public house.

Rafa was perched on a bar stool, drink in hand, people watching, when Dub arrived. "Whatchya havin Mr. Zamfir"? was the barrister's greeting.

"You mean, what was I having", answered Rafa, after removing the empty Pilsner glass from his mouth.

"I stand corrected", conceded Dub. Then to the bartender, "two more of those please".

After the second beer, Dub changed to the subject at hand. "So Rafa, are you sure Ernie Cole was your father"?

"Positive".

"Pardon my bluntness, but why are you here? Are you hoping for an inheritance"?

Rafa paused as if to consider how to best answer. "I wouldn't turn it down".

"Why did you come to me first, instead of the police"?

"I read your name, so I looked you up, and I'm not that crazy about the police".

Dub leaned back and motioned to the bartender that it was already time for another cold draft. "Is there a particular reason why that's so"?

"I just don't totally trust them, that's all, no big deal".

Dub sat and looked at the young man, "You do realize there's a murder investigation here"?

"Yes".

"So how about this, why don't you tell me about yourself, and your father, and why it is that you're just now showing up, a week after his funeral, and we'll go from there".

"I just showed up because I just found out he was dead, but okay, I'll start from the beginning. Are you at all familiar with the Roma people"?

"Do you mean Gypsies"?

"Yes, although we don't call ourselves that, we prefer to be called Romas".

"Sorry, I meant no disrespect".

"No problem".

Dub was listening to Rafa more as a drinking buddy than a lawyer. The story was interesting, and it certainly might change the dynamics of Ernie's estate, but at the end of the day what would it matter? There was no estate, to speak of. There was, however, a murder investigation involving this young man's father, and that was reason enough to listen closely.

"I was born in a Roma community just outside of Paris and raised by my grandmother. It was not the best life, but it was all I knew, so I was good with it. My grandmother was a good woman, she wanted me to have a better life, she did her best to try to make that happen. I didn't see my mother much. I suppose she meant well, but she couldn't stay away from trouble. She made poor choices, especially in men. She was involved with drugs. You get the picture. She kept telling me that things were gonna change, and she meant it, but they never did".

Rafa needed a bathroom break, when he returned, Dub had relocated to a table in a more secluded part of the lobby, against the wall, a little better place to talk. "Keep going", said Dub, "I want to know how you got from there to here".

"Well, as I said, my grandmother was determined that I was going to have a better life than she and my mom had. She made me stay in school, insisted that I study and read a lot, and did her best to keep me out of trouble, which for the most part she did. I never knew anything about my father, but I wanted to. I started asking questions, and got few answers. I finally got out of my mother that his name was Ernie and that he was an American businessman".

"Hold on a second", said Dub, "are you telling me that your mother knew who your father was but didn't tell him he had a son"?

"Yes".

"Why? I mean, I'm not saying it's wrong, it just seems, I don't know, unusual".

Rafa looked at Dub for what seemed like a long time without saying anything. "I'm not sure I really know. Doesn't make much sense to me either. I suppose she had her reasons. Anyway, I was able to find out who he was".

Dub just listened.

"We were poor, my Grandmother and I. She worked hard and got paid very little. She made sure I had hot meals to eat and clean clothes to wear, and that took a lot. As I say, I hardly knew my mother. I was the youngest child, and I barely knew the names of my brothers and sisters, some I never laid eyes on. I'm not complaining, just telling you how it was. My grandmother was a very determined lady. She decided that I was going to be different than my older siblings. She sacrificed a lot, I owe everything to her. I'm not going to let her down".

"What do you mean by that"?

"I mean I owe it to her to finish my education and get a good job and make a life for myself that she will be proud of. More than that, I want to honor her hard work and sacrifice".

"Is she still living"?

"Yes, but barely. She's 81 years old and has severe dementia. She hardly knows anybody any more. It's sad, but she's had a long life and hasn't left anything on the table, and she's been loved. That's a pretty good life in my book, but it's been tough, really tough. That's why she was so determined that I would have it better, she knows how life can beat a person down, and keep him down. Her dream is my dream".

Dub was getting the feeling that somehow the story was going to end up having to do with money, it just felt that way.

However, he wanted to let Rafa get to the point, if there was one, on his own. "Tell me about you and your father, did you have a relationship with him"?

"Sort of, it depends on what you call a relationship".

"I'm listening".

"Well, as I said, I was fourteen when I found out who he was. I wrote him a letter and told him I wanted to meet him. It took him by surprise, of course, and he was skeptical. But he knew it was possible because he had had a short fling with a woman in Paris who could easily have been a Gypsy. I included my phone number in the letter, and he called me. It was weird, and awkward. He wasn't rude, but as I say, he was skeptical. After we talked for a while, he asked me to send a hair sample, so that he could test for a DNA match, so I did. It took a few weeks, but he called again and said the DNA was a match. I met him in New York a week later. I was surprised at the way he looked. He seemed too old to be my father. We had great meals, and he showed me around the city, or at least part of it. It was amazing, didn't seem real". Rafa paused and took a swallow of his beer.

"Did you ask him for money"? Dub said, matter of factly.

Rafa was taken aback for a moment. "No, but we got around to discussing it".

"Keep going".

"He talked a lot about the importance of getting a good education. He said that if I did well in high school he would pay for me to go to college. I told him all about living in the Roma community. Like most people, he had a preconceived idea about us that was not very flattering. I'm pretty used to that, but I was surprised that a man of his intellect would not be more insightful regarding the life and history of the Roma, especially considering his experience travelling in Europe. Anyway, he was reluctant to give me money, I suppose because he wasn't sure he could trust me or my motives. He did give me a thousand dollars cash. I didn't ask for it, he just gave it to me. He said to be sure to take care of my Grandmother, and that he would help her if she had health care issues. So, that's how we got started as father and son".

"How old are you now"?

"Twenty six".

"So that was twelve years ago, about the same time that he moved to Hot Springs. How often did you see him after that"?

"Not often, about five or six times. Every couple of years he would pay to fly me to New York. We kept in touch, mostly by email".

"Did you like him"?

"Good question. I respected him for helping me without my asking, and I think he really did want me to do well, but I never felt really close to him. He was a decent man, but it always bothered me that he might just be helping me out of a sense of obligation".

"Did you try to get close to him"?

Rafa shrugged. "I don't know. At first I did, but eventually I came to appreciate his financial help, and we both kind of understood that that was just how it was".

"Did he pay for college"?

"Yes, Paris-Sorbonne University, computer science degree, then I decided to go to graduate school at NYU. He paid for all of it. I'm through with my degrees, but I'm still at school writing a paper on Algorithmic Logic that I hope to present this fall".

"And he paid for everything, school, place to live, meals, everything"?

"Yes".

"That's a lot of dough".

"Yes".

"Do you have enough money to finish the paper"?

Pause. "Not exactly".

"Well, that's a problem isn't it"?

Pause. "Yes".

Dub ordered another round, and asked for a menu.

Rafa was quiet. After the beers arrived and the server left, he looked at Dub.

"It doesn't make sense".

"What doesn't make sense"?

"You're saying there's not much of an estate".

"That's right, as far as I can tell".

"Then, where did the money come from"?

"What money"?

"The money he was sending me, five grand a month, where did it come from"?

"He was sending you five grand a month? Damn. That's a lot of cash. His rent was probably five hundred a month and he was sending you five grand. That really makes no sense".

"Yeah, that's what I'm saying".

Dub looked at Rafa. There was something wrong. He didn't know what it was, but he trusted his instincts, and his instincts left no doubt. This young man appears out of nowhere, says Ernie Cole is his father, has been getting five thousand bucks a month from him, a man he hardly knows, a man, supposedly his father, who was murdered in cold blood and has been dead less than two weeks. He hasn't asked a single question or made a single comment about the murder. His only concern is the cash. Not good. Not right. He spoke.

"You need to talk to the police".

"Yeah, I figured I should do that".

"I mean now. Let me ask you something".

"Okay".

"What is going on with you"? The draft beer had loosened his lips, had widened the parameters within which he was discussing the late Ernie Cole. The jury was still out, hell, was barely in session, concerning this young man, Rafa Zamfir. He needed to know more, a lot more.

"What do you mean"?

"Your father was murdered. Doesn't that mean anything to you? Aren't you sad, or mad, or something? You're acting like he was just a paycheck to you, nothing else".

Rafa wasn't sure how to react. "Look, I just got through telling you that I tried to have more of a relationship with him. It was his choice to keep his distance. I wasn't happy about that, but I accepted it. What else was I supposed to do"?

"I'm not talking about that part. I'm talking about right here, right now. The man is dead, was murdered for God's sake, doesn't that matter to you"?

"Of course, calm down man".

"Calm down my ass, let me tell you something. A lot of guys get dealt a bad hand in life, maybe you're one of them, doesn't matter, you gotta play the cards. You've played your's pretty well so far, but not by yourself. You've had two people in your life who gave you the help you needed, one is dead, the other almost dead. You're up against it now Cuz, you're out of money and out of prospects, so you come sniffing around here to see what you can find. You didn't bother with the funeral and you haven't bothered with the police, you came straight to me, straight for the money. Well guess what, it ain't gonna be that easy. This party's over, I'm going home".

Dub pulled a couple of twenties from his pocket, tossed them on the table and headed for the door.

Hayden got the call from Dub the next day.

"Just got a minute Dub, you need me"?

"I'll make it quick. A guy showed up at my office yesterday claiming he's Ernie Cole's son. His name is Rafa Zamfir, grew up in Paris, says your dad was sending him money to go to school. I'm not sure what to make of it, I told him to talk to the police, after they check him out I'll get back with you. Just wanted to let you know".

Silence.

"You still there"?

"Yeah, just thinking. My father lived in Paris for a while after the divorce. How old is the guy"?

"Twenty six, about to finish graduate school".

Hayden silently shook his head. "Guess I should have figured there could be some crazy shit involved". There was more
than a hint of disgust in his voice."I'm sure the guy has a story.
We'll deal with it".

"I've heard part of it. It gets crazier…..He's a Gypsy".

CHAPTER 17

Nikki was sitting at a table with some of her Law School buddies. It was on the large front porch of a hotel on St Charles Avenue called, appropriately, The Columns. It was New Orleans all the way, cocktails in the afternoon, huge old live oak trees framing the view of the streetcars passing back and forth, in no particular hurry. Lots of Mardi Gras beads hanging from the live oak branches, each, no doubt, with a story. Languid, bluesy jazz playing somewhere in the background. Clinking glasses, laughter. People taking the time to be people, with all the burdens of the day still there, but set aside for a while.

She loved all of those things, but her mind wasn't fully engaged there. It wasn't even in New Orleans. It was in Hot Springs. She knew almost nothing about Ernie Cole, but he was dead, and there were questions. If he had children, they would be fighting the pain. Been there, done that. Maybe still there.

After several nights of fitful sleep, Nikki made the call. To Detective Kay Delacio, Hot Springs PD.

"Detective Delacio, this is Nikki Carter, do you remember who I am".

"Of course, good to hear from you, please call me Kay".

"Okay, thanks Kay, do you have a minute to talk"?

"Absolutely, just let me get to a little better location, hold on just a minute".

The detective walked outside and had a seat on a low retaining wall bordering one side of the patio behind the police station.

"What can I do for you"?

"If your offer is still good, I'd like to talk".

"It's still good. And it's still off the record".

"Any progress on the investigation"?

"No, I wish there was. Some folks around here are kind of edgy, and I guess I can't blame them".

Silence.

"Relax Nikki, talk to me, about anything……*I'll tell you what*, I'll do the talking, jump in when you're ready".

"Okay", replied Nikki, "I'm such a wimp".

"Wrong, I've interviewed a lot of wimps. You may be scared, or whatever, but you're not a wimp. Hundred percent sure about that".

Silence

"I'm going to tell you a story, just sit back and relax".

"Okay", said Nikki, followed by a short, nervous giggle that was important, because it told Kay Delacio that she was gonna be okay, and probably would open up given a little time.

"I had a teacher in the fifth grade that chewed tobacco".

Laughter from Nikki.

"She was a sweet lady, and I guess she thought we didn't know, but everybody in the school knew. It didn't matter to us, but it mattered to her. We respected her, so nobody said anything about it. She kept chewing, and we kept ignoring. She was a damn good teacher. I had a good year".

"Did she spit"?

"No, that would give her away. She made do with tissues. She used quite a few".

"That's disgusting".

"Naw, it was just how she rolled".

More laughter.

"So, Nikki, tell me what's on your mind".

"Well, I guess it's sorta two things".

"Alright, what are they"?

"I keep having this nagging feeling that I should talk to somebody about what I have learned about what happened to my father, in case it could possibly help with Mr. Cole. I don't have any reason to think it will, but I would hate to wonder later if I could have helped".

"That's understandable, what's the other thing"?

Pause.

"I'm guessing it also has to do with your father, but not Ernie Cole".

"Yep".

"Here's a suggestion. You tell me everything you want to about your father, in confidence. We'll leave Ernie Cole out of it for now. Don't worry about all the details the first time through, just tell the story, and I'll ask questions when I need to. There's no right or wrong here, I just want you to talk".

Pause.

"Okay".

"And Nikki, you don't have to start out telling me about what happened. Tell me about him, anything about him. I'm sure it will be worth listening to".

Nikki immediately felt better, more relaxed, and started to talk.

"It's okay. I want to tell you about it. One of the worst things about what happened is that it sounds so bad, disappearing after he wired ten million dollars to an offshore account. He made a big mistake, but he wasn't a crook. He was a man of character who made a huge mistake that cost him his life. It's hard to imagine how it could have happened, but it did".

"Do you know what happened? What really happened"?

"Yes".

"Do you want to tell me"?

"I think so, but not right now".

"That's fine Nikki, I can wait. But listen to me and please, please trust me on this". The detective had Nikki's full attention.

"You have to talk about it. What's done is done. You can't change it. A part of your father is alive and well in you. Talk Nikki, please".

Nikki's voice started to crack, and the tears started to roll.

"Can you come to New Orleans"?

"Done".

They met in City Park, a quiet place away from the hotels and the distractions of the city. They strolled for a while, chit chatting about stuff that didn't matter, then sat on an old stone bench.

"Good choice for an important meeting", said the detective, in a deadpan manner.

"Okay, I get it, I shoulda booked a meeting room in the Ritz Carlton, my bad".

Subtle chuckle from Detective Delacio. "I believe what you said about your father".

"What part"?

"That he was a man of character".

"Thank you".

"Look, I know it's not pleasant, but tell me what happened to him".

Nikki took a deep breath, let it out slowly, then began, and for almost an hour, with only an occasional pause, and only an occasional comment from the detective, told what she knew of the last few weeks of Gib Carter's life and about her meeting and talking with Anna. Told her everything, almost. Kay Delacio was impressed with Nikki's resolve, and confidence. She was beautiful, she was sincere.....She was not telling the whole story. Somehow she knew. She just listened, and waited.

Nikki was talking and thinking at the same time. Not really thinking, more like hearing/feeling the thing she was fighting. The name. Silas Greer.

"How bout a beer"?

"How about several beers"? replied Nikki.

They walked across the street and sat at an outside table facing the park. One thing about The Big Easy, it doesn't take long to find a watering hole. Beers were served. The mood lightened.

"Why did you call me"? The question came out of left field, as intended.

"What do you mean"?

"You're holding something back, what is it"?

Nikki had to decide, as we all do, part of being human, part of the deal, step up, deal with the hard stuff. Take the bat in your hand and step up to the damn plate. Kay Delacio's instincts were right. Nikki was holding back. Nikki stepped up.

"I know the name of the person who had him killed".

Now we're getting somewhere. Hot Springs Arkansas may be a small town, but Kay Delacio was no hick town detective. She, herself, was a person of character, like Gibson Carter. Her motive was pure. She felt Nikki's pain, her reluctance, her fear. She wanted to help. She wanted the truth. She got it.

"Nikki, your father, God rest his soul, is smiling right now, you can take that to the bank. Tell me what you know".

She did. The effect was immediate. Tears came in torrents.

The detective took her hand, held it through the tears.

Good for Nikki. Good for Detective Delacio. Probably not good for Silas Greer.

CHAPTER 18

Rafa was not happy. It never occurred to him that his father, Ernie Cole, was anything other than a wealthy guy who made a fortune on Wall Street, retired, and lived the way he wanted to live, playing the ponies and travelling when he felt like it. Now he's dead, and the lawyer says there's not much cash. How in the hell could that be? This trip to Hot Springs was supposed to be a formality. Show up, prove Ernie was his father, get the cash. He figured it would take some time, but there was nothing much he could do about that. It seemed reasonable to him that, since he had been getting five thousand a month, he would continue to get that amount every month until he was totally through with school. That was now far from certain. He only had a couple of hundred bucks to his name, and the rent would be due soon. Not good.

The conversation with the police only added to his frustration. It took almost all day. Back and forth, question after question. Rafa was uneasy. Not only were there questions about the money, but these guys were treating him like a suspect. The frustration was not his alone. The whole police department felt it too. It had been almost two weeks without an arrest, or even a serious suspect, the people of Hot Springs wanted the case solved, the sooner the better. The day ended about as bad as a day could end. He got a call from Paris. His grandmother had passed away. Rafa Zamfir buried his head in his hands and cried. Alone.

Kay Delacio returned to Hot Springs from New Orleans late in the day. She was tired. Went to bed early. Had to get some rest. The next day would probably be stressful. The Hot Springs Police Department seemed to be spinning it's wheels. The Ernie Cole case was getting tougher by the day. They were anxious for her to interview the victim's son. Maybe she could do a better job, after all, she was the lead detective on the case.

The last thing Rafa wanted to do the next morning was go to the police station and answer more questions about his relationship with Ernie Cole. He couldn't imagine what new stuff they wanted to talk about, it seemed that they had covered it all already. Detective Delacio sensed that may be the case. Not her first rodeo. True to form, she went to Plan B. When Rafa walked in, she took charge.

"How about some breakfast"?

They sat across from each other at the Waffle House nearest the track. Kind of a pedestrian breakfast, even for a Gypsy, but that didn't matter. He had two eggs over easy, bacon and dry wheat toast. He drew the line at grits, just couldn't go there. What are grits anyway? One of Rafa's issues, among many, with

Western Culture, especially American Culture, was the propensity for obesity, or more to the point, the lack of discipline regarding food and health. It wasn't so much that the Roma people were healthy eaters themselves, it was that they didn't have a choice, they ate what they could get, which sometimes was not very much. Americans eat what they want, and throw away what they don't want, simple as that.

The breakfast conversation was light. Next stop was Oaklawn Park. Barn 52, The Guv. The detective wanted Rafa to spend some time with his father's best friend. There was really no plan, other than to let them talk.

The first thing Rafa noticed about the Guv was that he was not an American, he was different. Dark, tanned skin, deep wrinkles in his face and around his eyes. Soft eyes. Smart, but not bookish. Self assured, but calm. Kind, but wary. Comfortable in his skin, but a man who, in the words of Clint Eastwood, knows his limitations. A man who deserved respect. A man who got respect.

The first thing the Guv noticed about Rafa was that he had confident eyes. The fact that he was a Gypsy didn't faze him, he knew that part already, but Ernie's boy had confident eyes. The Guv didn't show it, but he liked that. Reminded him of Ernie. Ernie didn't talk much about Rafa. He had told the Guv he had a son who was a Gypsy, but not much more. Part of his past. This wasn't the past. The young man was here, now.

"Sorry about your father, it's still hard to believe. You doing okay"?

"Yes, thank you".

In that moment, Rafa changed. It was subtle, and it wasn't so much that he changed, it was that his perspective changed. Ernie Cole was his father, the DNA said so, but about all that had meant was a monthly check. He didn't know if this man, The Guv, even knew about the monthly check, suspected he didn't, yet he was acknowledging Rafa's loss.... A man only has one father.

"You ever been around horses"?

"No".

"Come on. I'll show you around".

The Guv spoke English well, but with a definite Spanish accent. They walked inside the stable area, and Rafa came face to face with his first thoroughbred race horse. He was a six year old gelding who had run the day before in a mid level claiming race. Finished third. Hit the board, as horseplayers say. He was all silky, chestnut colored muscle. And big. A beautiful animal. Rafa was impressed.

"He ran yesterday", said The Guv. "we're just letting him walk a little in the shedrow".

"He's so big", said Rafa.

"Yeah, he can run too. I wish I had a bunch more just like him".

"How many horses do you have here"?

"Thirty one right now. It's always changing. We lose one or add one. That's the way it is in this business".

"Seems like a lot of work".

"Depends on what you consider work. It's our life. It's not for everybody, but we're horse people, it's what we do".

Rafa wasn't sure what to think about The Guv. This was a
man whose life was taking care of horses, that was pretty much
it, but he seemed to have no desire to do anything else.

"I guess if you're happy doing it, it doesn't matter what you
call it", said Rafa.

The detective was not a horse person, but she knew a few
things about people. She was almost certain that neither of
these two had anything to do with the murder. She still had a
lot of questions for them, but this wasn't the time.

"How about I just let you guys hang out for a while? I have
some stuff I need to do that will take me most of the day. I
would like to spend some time talking with both of you together. Can I come back and do that here at three o'clock this
afternoon? Is that okay"?

"Yes, that's okay", replied the Guv, without looking at
Rafa.. " We'll just meet right back here at three".

"Great, thank you. See you then".

The Guv looked at Rafa and nodded toward toward the
track. "Let's go watch some workouts".

They walked to the rail and stood silently watching the
horses for a couple of minutes. Rafa broke the silence.

"Was he good at picking the horses"?

The Guv nodded. "The best".

Silence.

"You see that filly by the rail, across from the seven eighths
pole, the one with the reddish streak in her mane"?

"Yeah".

"She's one of our's. A nice three year old making her first start this weekend. Her name is Miss Betty Jo".

"She's beautiful, they all are. I've never seen thoroughbred horses up close".

"They're easy to get attached to. They have personalities".

"What's Miss Betty Jo's personality"?

The Guv smiled. A happy, knowing smile, with something behind it. "Pure sweetness".

Rafa looked out at the track, the horses, the exercise riders, the rich brown sandy dirt, the green grass, the blue sky. For the first time he saw something there. Something that might bring a man back, day after day.

"Who did it Guv? And why? Doesn't make sense to me".

"Me either. I don't know who or why just yet, but somebody did it, and there's a reason".

Rafa asked the Guv the question he had asked himself many times. "Where was the money coming from"?

"What do you mean"?

"He had money, right"?

The Guv slowly turned and looked away. When his gaze returned to Rafa, it was cold and hard. "What are you after"?

Rafa looked at him, uneasy, but said nothing.

"Ernie Cole was a man of integrity".

"I'm not…".

"Hold on. I'm not through. We need to get straight on a few things".

Silence.

"You're father was a damn good man, as good as I've ever been around. He had his ways, like all of us, but he had the strongest sense of right and wrong of any man I've ever met. And he was tough. Nobody fucked with Ernie Cole. He had a heart as big as the sky, but he would tell a man the way it was, whether the man liked it or not. He was different, but that's who he was. Some guys don't have the courage to be who they really are, so they compromise. Not Ernie. He was the real deal. Not all good, but a lot more good than bad. And all real".

Silence.

"You missed the funeral. No fucking card, no flowers, nothing. Then you show up and start asking about money. Nobody around here even knew you existed. I knew because Ernie told me, but nobody else did that I know of. Even his other son, Hayden, didn't know. That's okay, not your fault, but if you want to be treated with respect, you gotta give us a reason to think you gave a shit about Ernie, and son, you haven't gotten off to a very good start in that regard. Now, here's what we're gonna do, we're going to talk, me and you. When the detective comes back around, we're gonna talk to her. You may or may not ever get another fucking dime, right now I couldn't give a shit, but you're going to talk to me, and I hope you have the gonads to do so without an attitude".

Rafa stood looking at the Guv. He didn't think, he just reacted. He spoke in a low, even tone, as if his words were bubbling up from a hot cauldron, and the cauldron was deep..

"He didn't care about me. He didn't care about my mother. He didn't care about my people. I was on the payroll, simple as that. And only because he didn't have a choice. He grew up rich. In New York. In America. He made big money on Wall Street. I know who he was, I did my homework. He came to Paris, threw money around and had a big time with an exotic looking Gypsy woman. My mother. I wasn't born rich, I was born in a Roma community outside of Paris, to a mother who would entertain rich American men just to get a few bucks so she could buy something to allow her to escape, even for a few hours, the hell she was living. I would probably be the same way if it weren't for my Grandmother. She wouldn't let that happen. She had nothing. Nothing. Because she gave it all to me. Just to give me a fighting chance".

Rafa's voice became forceful, his whole person indignant.

"Don't tell me about the character of Ernie Fucking Cole. He led a charmed life compared to my people, my Grandmother, God rest her soul. Ernie Cole was my father, but he wasn't one of my people. Like I said, I was on the payroll, simple as that. He didn't want more than that, so why the fuck should I act like he was more than that to me? I'll help you, because I want the money. Just the way it is".

It was the Guv's turn to react. "Well you ungrateful little son of a bitch. You think you're the only one who's ever been dealt a bad hand. I grew up in Peru. In a shack. Hot meals were hard to come by. I did what I had to do. Got busted and sent to prison when I was fifteen years old. Spent five years there. Got the shit beat out of me so many times I lost count because I wouldn't bend over and just take it up the ass. Never got even a letter in prison. I got out and made it into America. No family, no nothing. I started shovelling horse shit at the racetrack, and was glad to do it. My wife took my three kids and left twenty years ago. I'm lucky if I get to see them once a year. I'm not complaining. Just the way it is.........Everybody's got a fucking story".

There was a long, long pause. The words, like raindrops on the ground, had to settle where they would.

Rafa spoke softly.

"My Grandmother died last week. I'll never see her again. When I go back, I want to make sure she has a headstone on her grave. And fresh flowers". Tears rolled down Rafa's face.

The Guv reached over, put his hand behind Rafa's neck, and gently pulled him close. He leaned into him until the top of his forehead rested against the side of Rafa's head.

"She's gonna like that".

They stayed that way until Rafa's tears stopped, and he was calm. The Guv spoke.

"Let's go have a beer".

"What about the detective"?

"She can wait".

Twenty minutes later they were bellied up to the bar in the Longshot Saloon. The Guv held his mug of draft beer up, indicating a toast. Rafa complied. Their mugs touched.

"To your Grandmother. May her love for you forever be a part of who you are".

"Let's make a deal", said the Guv, "Whatever we talk about is between me and you, period. You know computers, you understand technology. I need your help. I will share things with you, but only if I have your word that you won't share any of the information with anybody, including the police. Especially the police. Are we good so far? Can you do that"?

'Yes".

"A hundred percent"?

"A hundred percent".

"I think I know who killed your father".

Rafa had no reaction at first. It had been a helluva day already, now this. He spoke. "Why haven't you told anybody"?

The Guv looked him straight in the eyes. "They won't like it. They won't believe it. I don't trust them".

"Who is them"?

"The police, the Mayor, the people with money, pretty much everybody".

Chapter 19

Nikki's phone buzzed just as she was sitting down for dinner with Gabriela's family. Chicken Marbella, one of her favorites. It was the Detective. She let it go to voicemail. After dinner she found a quiet spot and returned the call.

"Nikki, can you talk for a few minutes"?

"Yes, of course".

"I think you should make a trip to Hot Springs. The FBI wants to talk to you. I haven't told them anything. They know I interviewed you the day of the funeral. They asked me about it. I told them you were not a suspect and had no connection at all to Ernie Cole. Everybody is uptight about this case. They are working every possible angle, and regardless of my conversation with you, they want to talk to you themselves.

Also, as I told you, I have never heard of Silas Greer and have no idea who he is. However, I did some checking. He's a very dangerous man. I don't know too many details, but what I do know is that he lives somewhere in the Caribbean and is involved with a lot of unsavory people. He could be a Mafia Kingpin or just a businessman, I'm not sure, but whatever he is, he's right at the top and controls a lot of illegal activity. He owns a few casinos, including Burnham Glen. He could be into drugs, I don't know. A hell of a lot of cash flows through his organization, wherever it comes from. We can talk more about that later in person, I'd rather not discuss it any more than that on the phone. Are you okay with coming to Hot Springs in the next couple of days"?

"I guess so, if that's what you think".

"I think you should come meet with them. If you don't, they will wonder why, and there's no need to give them any reason to do that. Ernie's son Hayden is going to be here at about the same time. If you want to talk to him I'll try to arrange it. I'm sorry to make you drive to Hot Springs, but I think it's what you should do".

"Okay".

The drive was no big deal. Although it was eight hours, it was just driving. The thinking about things was a big deal. She wished that could be an eight hour inconvenience. No such luck. It was there, for as long as it took, period. Thinking about Gib. Thinking about Silas Greer. Enough time had passed that she could get on with her life, she knew that, and that was no small thing, but she couldn't shake the thought of her father's last moments on this earth. What were they like? Was it pure terror? How long from the instant he knew it was over, until it was over? Was there any time at all? Sweet Mother of All Gods, she hoped not.

No person is without fault, or without fear. Courage is not courage without the fear. Without the fault, there would be no need for religion. We all struggle. Just the way it is.

They met in a crummy room in a crummy building somewhere in Hot Springs, Arkansas. The two FBI guys were there to talk with Nikki Carter, something they both viewed as a waste of time. The local police detective, Detective Delacio, told them as much. But there was pressure from all sides to solve the murder of Ernie Cole, so there they were. The questions were routine. The answers were the same ones she had already given. Not a lot of progress was being made. Then the tone changed. They asked a question about Gib Carter. Not directly, but it might as well have been. They started poking around and talking about similarities between Ernie and Gib. It was as if someone had flipped a switch and the dull, tedious business of the murder of a two bit horseplayer in Hot Springs had changed into the investigation of the still unsolved case of the disappearance of Gib Carter and his ten million dollar stash. The agents were now focused, but Nikki wasn't about to be a pawn in their game.

Maybe it's the Ying and the Yang, who knows, but the increased interest of the interviewers pretty much perfectly coincided with the decreased interest of the interviewee. These guys were talkin, but they weren't sayin nuthin. They probably weren't bad guys. Probably had families and maybe even went to church, but there were things going on inside the head of this pretty woman that they would never know. There was plenty she didn't know also, but there were a couple of things she did. These guys were clueless, and a waste of her time.

"How'd it go"? Detective Delacio was on the phone, anxious to get Nikki's take on the meeting with the FBI agents.

"Frustrating. Accomplished nothing as far as I could tell. They seemed to be going through the motions. I hope I'm through with them".

"Did they seem satisfied that you had no connection to Ernie Cole"?

"I guess. They were a lot more interested in my father than Mr. Cole. That would have been fine with me, but they had no idea what questions to ask. Seems like they would have done their homework a little better, but I'm thinking they didn't do any homework. It was just another day on the job for them. At least it's over with".

"Well, I wish it had gone better, but you did accomplish something, even though it doesn't seem like it. The Hot Springs police department will probably mark you off their list for good, and the FBI isn't likely to come back around after this Hot Springs case is done".

"Okay, well, at least that's something".

"Relax, have a cocktail, Hayden and I will meet you in the lobby at six thirty".

"Alright, thanks".

She did have a cocktail. It was good. She had two more. Talking with the FBI makes a girl thirsty. Her dinner companions were right on time, just as Nikki was being served number four. Hayden Cole's visit to Hot Springs was supposed to be short and sweet. Meet with the lawyer, make sure the Gypsy wasn't a problem, handle anything else that needed his attention and get the hell out of town. The short part was no problem, his flight left from Little Rock early the next morning. The sweet part was another matter. The day had been anything but. It was hard to believe Rafa Zamfir was his half brother. The guy didn't even own a car. His clothes looked like they came from the discount rack at the thrift store, which they had. He had an earring and long hair. He wore prayer beads. Worst of all, he didn't know his place. The guy had been getting five grand a month, for God's sake, and he had done nothing to deserve it. Unless, of course, you count his being born into the Lucky Sperm Club. He was living in America, going to school in America and he had no respect for America. What the fuck is wrong with this picture?

They found Nikki sitting at the end of the bar. Hayden was immediately impressed. The detective made the introductions.

"Hayden Cole, Nikki Carter".

"Good to meet you Nikki".

"Good to meet you too. thanks for letting me join you".

Hayden maintained a calm, professional demeanor, but inside his head there was an excited little voice. "Whoa dawg! What have we here? Bingo Baby". Lights and bells and buzzers were going off in his head as if he had hit the jackpot on a progressive slot machine. Men are such primitive beings when it comes to the opposite sex. He had just met this woman and in his mind he already had her naked and begging him to stick it in deeper and do it harder and please, oh God never stop.

Nikki was duly impressed herself. Hayden Cole was a handsome man. Well dressed, self assured, probably wealthy. She would let him have his little fantasy, but that would be it. There was no chance he would see the naked Nikki, this day or any day. Kay Delacio, no wallflower herself, wasn't sure whether she found Hayden's abrupt change amusing or disgusting, but this wasn't her first rodeo, and she knew what multiple cocktails could do to a girl's judgement. The first thing she did, after ordering a drink of her own, was order a platter of appetizers for the table.

Nikki looked at Hayden. "So what do you do in Boston"?

"I'm a partner in a Real Estate Investment Trust. We primarily own medical buildings and doctors' offices in the Boston area. We also own the management company that manages them. We are a private company, but are in discussions now to do an IPO. It keeps me on my toes, but I enjoy it".

An hour, and two more cocktails later, the appetizer plate was bare, with Nikki having done most of the damage. The conversation, such as it was, centered on Hayden, his business and Boston. It was all about Hayden. Ernie's name never came up, not once. Nikki was fading, her eyes heavy. Kay knew more conversation was pointless, so she suggested to Nikki that she call it a night. Nikki, without hesitation, rose, shook hands with Hayden, thanked Kay and headed upstairs to her room.

Hayden, smooth as an old Sauterne, merely shifted his gaze from the lovely young New Orleanian, to the newly appreciated, sophisticated and beguiling Hot Springs police detective. She was concealing an amused smile behind her passive eyes.

He was transparent, but he had a cute dimple, and the night was young.

The first order of business for Nikki the next morning was breakfast, and she knew just the place. The Pancake Shop is on Central Avenue, across the street from The Arlington. To say it's been around a while would qualify as an understatement. The day it opened FDR was in the White House, and the menu has hardly changed since. The orange juice is fresh squeezed, the pancakes are made from scratch and served with butter and warm maple syrup. The ham and sausage are the kind Grandma served. Don't bother trying to make a dinner reservation, they don't do that. This is a breakfast joint.

As Nikki lingered a bit with coffee and the Sentinel Record, she overheard the news. There was an arrest in the Ernie Cole murder case. She paid the check and hurried across the street. She turned on the television in her room and switched to the local channel.

The Hot Springs police chief was answering questions from the local media. He had already made his official statement. Nikki grabbed her laptop and did a quick internet search to get the story. The arrest was made that morning. A thirty three year old local man who had been in trouble before, but nothing even close to this. He had a history with drugs, and had been in and out of rehab three times. He hung out at the racetrack, and knew almost all of the regulars. He was well liked by most of the guys, and was friends with Ernie. There were occasions when he would get drunk and a little loud and rowdy, but he was never violent, quite the opposite really, he was a funny drunk. Nikki had read enough. She packed her bags and headed to The Big Easy. Didn't even stop at the front desk, the FBI could take care of the bill.

The eight hour drive back to New Orleans gave her time to work some things out. Some of those things she had pretty much worked out already. She had done what she knew she had to do. She had gone back to Hot Springs and talked to the FBI, and she had at least tried to talk to the son of Ernie Cole. What a joke that was. His father was murdered. In cold blood. Why and by whom were mysteries, and this shithead was having dinner and drinks and doing his best to weasel his way into the pants of one or both of his dinner companions. He gave no indication at all that he was the least bit concerned about what happened to his father. What a prick. What a fucking prick.

She kept driving. And thinking. About Gib, about her father. How sad she would be, how utterly devastated and sad she would be if she thought Gib was disappointed in her because she wasn't doing anything to solve the mystery of his death. That thought was something she couldn't handle. It was the one, irrational or not, that would keep her up at night.

Nikki had never known trouble, or hard times. There was almost no conflict in her house growing up, other than the occasional family squabble, which never amounted to much. There were differences of opinion, of course, as is always the case when learned people discuss things, but underneath it all was the bedrock of love and commitment, each unconditional and unquestioned. Her mother and father were both gone, but the bedrock was still there. It made no sense to her that Ernie

Cole's son appeared to be unfazed by the sudden death of his father, especially given the tragic manner in which it happened. She prayed for strength, and peace of mind, the former being more attainable than the latter.

CHAPTER 20

Lonnie "Spud" Harrison was having a bad day. He had a little bit of a hangover, but no big deal there, he was used to it. The bad part was that he had been arrested for murder. It all went down so fast he hardly had time to think. They showed up at his apartment at the ungodly hour of eight o'clock in the morning. Had a search warrant. Searched his car. Found a gun under the seat. Twenty two caliber, a popgun. He had never seen it before, but they said it was his and that he had used it to murder Ernie Cole. Before he knew it he was in cuffs, headed downtown. He had time to think now, plenty of time, he was in the pokie. He had been there before, in the pokie, but only for a short stay, for getting drunk and acting a fool, smoking weed, that sort of thing. This was his first murder. Actually, it wasn't his first murder, because he didn't do it. All he could do for now was talk to himself. "I ain't never come close to killing nobody, never even been in a half decent fight. But that don't matter. They got their man. All the rich folks are happy as hell. The streets are safe again. Sombitch, this ain't good".

Word travelled fast, just as Spud knew it would. By that afternoon it was all but a done deal, the trial, if there was one, would be just a formality. It was indeed surprising that Spud was the guy, he and Ernie were friends. But as they say with murder, it's almost always somebody the victim knew well. The arrest was all the talk among the guys at the track, but horse-players being what they are, as soon as the horses left the gate in the first race, it was pretty much business as usual. Run you sombitch run.

Around Hot Springs there was almost a palpable sense of re-lief that an arrest had been made. Around Barn 52, the mood was less than celebratory, and the sense of relief was missing. In it's place was something quite different, the sense of urgency. Inside that barn, far away from the steps of the police department, the official statement and the media coverage, was a man who knew the killer of Ernie Cole. The killer wasn't Spud Harrelson, it was Martin Carrington. All he had to do was prove it.

Rafa and the Guv had worked out a deal. Each had some-thing the other needed. The Guv needed Rafa's brain, more specifically, he needed Rafa's knowledge of the world of Cyberspace. The Guv had thought almost incessantly about how it all went down, not just pulling the trigger, but all the stuff that had to happen before the trigger was pulled. He was a wise man, but his education came from the life he had lived, from the streets of Peru to the stable area of Oaklawn

Park, and many, many places and people in between. He knew people. He didn't know computers. Rafa knew computers. Rafa was flat broke. (There's broke, as in, "I can't go on the golf trip this time guys, I'm fuckin broke", and then there's the broke that's not mentioned because no good can come of it because it's so not where a person wants to be and it's just better left alone, it's unsavory nature fully understood but mercifully unrecognized. Not just broke, flat broke). If he was going to stay in Hot Springs any longer, he needed a job and a place to stay. The Guv knew where Rafa could get those things. At Barn 52. The Guv arranged for Rafa to have a place to stay on the backside, among the horse people. He could eat meals in the track kitchen. He had to pull his weight around the barn and help with whatever job was needed, which he gladly did without complaint, but his main job was to use his brain and his knowledge of computers to help The Guv figure out what led to his best friend being found tits up on the floor of his apartment, with no pulse.

Late that afternoon there was a meeting in Barn 52, a closed door meeting. Not just closed, closed and locked, Presiding over the affair was The Guv. In attendance were a small group of men and women, five in all, who were the members of El Consejo, "The Council". The full name was El Consejo de Ancianos, "The Council of Elders". They were the ruling body of the Backside, period. They didn't wield much, if any, power outside of their domain, but inside, they ruled.

They shared a level of commitment to each other that was nothing short of remarkable. These were people who helped each other, probably because not doing so was not an option. They were pretty close to the bottom of the food chain. All were Hispanic. They cared nothing for the trappings of American society. It wasn't that they didn't like Americans, it was that they couldn't relate to them. These people were the working class, pure and simple. They weren't just poor, they were poor and they were outsiders. They had come for the chance to earn money, and that's what had kept them here. They were tough, resilient, proud. The Guv didn't mince words.

"What is said here today stays with us. Period. Does everyone understand that"?

All heads nodded yes.

"As you all know, there has been an arrest in Ernie's murder case. The police have Spud Harrelson in jail. Everybody seems to think there's no doubt that he's the guy. I'm pretty sure he's not. Problem is, all I really have to go on is my instincts and some things that I've observed. I'm going to share with you today what I think and what I plan to do about it. My loyalty is to the people in this room, and all of those whom you represent. Without you and your's I have nothing, and no chance. With you and your's, we, together, I believe, can make things right. For Ernie. You're not going to like most of what I have to say. I only ask that you listen and give your consideration to the plan".

No response, nothing to say yet for the El Consejo. The Guv continued.

"This is the part you're not gonna like, might as well put it on the table right now. I think Martin Carrington killed Ernie".

El Consejo, indeed, was not receptive to the theory, as predicted.

The Guv knew that he needed to be calm and confident, and present his case in a logical manner, so that the others might respond to his reasoning, and not be too influenced by his obvious emotional connection to Ernie Cole.

"First, I think he did it for money. As you all know, Martin Carrington is the Oaklawn Chaplain. The chaplain has, because of the nature of the position, a certain amount of built in credibility. Most people assume that a chaplain is either a member of the clergy, or at least in some way associated with a church. Not the case with Martin. He's not an ordained minister, has never been to seminary and is not associated with a church, other than as a member. He retired several years ago from his family's insurance business, after his father passed away and the business was sold to outside investors. I am told by several different people that know him well, that Martin didn't want to leave the insurance business, but the new owners didn't give him a choice. They didn't want him. So, he officially retired, and started spending his time promoting his sales training and motivational speaking business. The assumption is that he was a successful insurance executive, and now he's teaching others how to succeed also. Now, I'm not suggesting that Martin Carrington didn't have a successful career in the insurance business, he did. What I am questioning is how he did it. His father started the business and built it into a large agency. Martin joined him at age thirty, after spending six years in college and another six years trying to make it as a professional tennis player, which didn't work out. He began calling on his father's clients and selling them life insurance. Then he started combining life insurance and mutual funds, and then he started doing seminars in churches, supposedly offering financial advice based on Biblical Principals. He was slick. Talked well. Dressed well. Said all of the right things. Lived in the right neighborhood. Associated with the right people. You get the picture. When his father's agency was sold, and the new owners didn't offer him a position, he decided to concentrate on his speaking and coaching sales people. He eventually landed a job with the Fellowship of Christian Athletes, primarily as a spokesperson and fund raiser. That's how he became associated with Oaklawn Park, and the jockeys group".

At that point The Guv paused and looked at the others. "I think Martin Carrington had money problems. He was on easy street when he had his father's business to feed off of, but that went away. He spent a lot of money maintaining his lifestyle and maintaining his fucking image".

He paused again, and reminded himself that he needed to keep the personal feelings out of it. But it was hard. He continued.

"As you know, Oaklawn has a fund that was set up years ago to give financial assistance to the backside workers and their families. I don't have to tell you that it's a big deal, to all of us, to have that extra money. The money in that fund comes from three places. The city contributes, a portion comes out of the betting handle and the rest comes from local churches. Horse racing is a big deal in Hot Springs, as we all know. It's in everybody's best interest to keep it going strong. That money comes directly from the payroll department of Oaklawn. In addition, there is another charitable fund that is sponsored by the Fellowship of Christian Athletes, and the distribution of that money is overseen by the Oaklawn Chaplain, Martin Carrington. It's not clear exactly where that money comes from, and it's not a set amount, as you know. All we are told is that it comes from anonymous donors who want to help. Of course, nobody is too concerned with where the money comes from, we're just grateful to have it".

The Guv paused once again. He had their full attention.

"I believe somehow, Ernie was involved with Martin Carrington and the FCA, maybe as one of the anonymous donors, I'm not sure, but they were connected in some way, and it cost Ernie his life. Maybe it sounds crazy, but I don't trust Martin Carrington. He had money problems, he had access to money and he knew Ernie. Ernie ends up dead, for no reason anybody can imagine. I don't know what happened, but I think Martin Carrington is responsible". Pause

"Which brings us to the reason I asked you to join me here today. I'm trying to figure out what happened to Ernie. I am not talking to the police about Martin Carrington. They don't want to hear it. They have their man. I don't trust them anyway. You all have met Ernie's son Rafa. As you know, he's living on the backside and helping us in Barn 52. Rafa is a very smart young man, and he knows more about computers and cyberspace than anybody else I know. He and I are working together trying to trace the FCA money trail. Where it comes from, and of course, who it comes from. It is already proving to be very difficult, which only adds to my suspicions about Martin Carrington. The source of the money that comes from Oaklawn is right there to see, totally transparent. The source of the money that comes to us from the FCA, is just the opposite, anonymous, and so far, untraceable. They are not required to tell us the source of the money, supposedly to honor the wish of their donors to remain anonymous. We haven't said a word about this to the FCA or Martin Carrington, or the police, for obvious reasons. We don't want anybody to have any idea what we're thinking and doing. It's just between us. I'm here today to ask you to please give me your blessing to find out the truth about the FCA money, and about Martin Carrington. If we, Rafa and I, are unsuccessful, or if we find out we are wrong, that will be the end of it. I give you my word on that. If we find out we are right, and can prove it, we intend to see to it that Martin Carrington is made to answer for what happened to Ernie. The risk for you, and us, is that if we are wrong, and the FCA finds out what we're doing, we probably would lose the FCA money for good, and I know you don't want that. So that's it, and now I ask you, do we have your blessing"?

CHAPTER 21

Nikki got the call mid afternoon on a Tuesday. It was a number she didn't recognize, and she was in the library, so she didn't answer. They didn't leave a message. A few hours later there was a call from the same number. Again she didn't answer, but this time there was a voice mail message. He said his name was Rafa and he was calling to ask a favor, and to please call back. She erased the message. Next there was a text message. Rafa again. The message was polite. He said Ernie Cole was his father and he just wanted to talk to her for a minute, if possible. Nikki wavered, but after a while she called the number. Rafa thanked her for returning his call. He had a kind voice. She relaxed a little. She remembered Hayden's condescending comments about the half brother he never knew he had. A Gypsy.

"How can I help you"?

"I'm hoping that you might be able to help me with some information. I know this sounds crazy, but I want to come to New Orleans and talk with you. I'll meet you somewhere. You can pick the place. I would tell you more now but I'd rather not do that on the phone. I'm sorry to call out of the blue with such a request, but there's a good reason for my doing so. If, after you hear what I have to say, you'd rather not talk further, that's the way it will be. I promise you that. If you feel more comfortable bringing someone with you, someone we both can trust, that's okay, but I would rather it be just us. I'd like to come as soon as possible, tomorrow would be great, but I understand that's asking a lot of you. Now, I don't want to pressure you into anything, so I suggest this, think about it, and if you're okay with having a meeting, text me back at this number with a time and place. As I said, I know it sounds crazy, but it's important to me".

Rafa, finally, was quiet for a moment. He had been so anxious about making the call that he realized now that he had just blurted out the words without even giving her a chance to say anything.

"I thought they arrested somebody", said Nikki.

"Yes, they have", he replied. Pause

Nikki sighed. "Okay, I'll think about it and let you know".

"Nikki", said Rafa, then paused. "Thank you".

They met on the riverfront, ironically not very far from where Gib had spent time two years earlier pondering the pros and cons of betting a large sum of money on a horse race. Crazy, this thing we call life. He sat on a bench and watched a tugboat pushing barges around in the Mississippi River. She said his name as she approached, cautiously. He immediately rose to greet her and instinctively held out his hand. She took it and they shook hands briefly, informally. Her face was pure, classic, relaxed, straight walnut brown hair. Full lips, high cheekbones and an easy confident smile. But it was the eyes that got him. Blue/Gray. Absolutely, stop the presses, oh my god, Gorgeous.

His return smile was muted out of deference and respect, but was there just the same. His manner was similarly understated. Respectful. Appreciative that she would take the time to meet with him on such short notice. She noticed these things. His look was close to what she had expected, dark curly hair, olive skin, but it was the eyes that got her attention. Dark, deep. Very dark. Very deep. Rafa motioned slightly to the right with his thumb.

"That's a damn big river".

Nikki laughed. "That's why they have these damn big levees".

They both laughed. Easily.

"Thank you for coming".

"You're welcome".

Pause

"Do you have any idea why I'm here"?

"Not really. Not really sure why I'm here".

"Can we walk"?

"Sure".

They started strolling along the riverfront.

"I'm trying to find out what happened to my father. They made an arrest, but I think they have the wrong guy".

Nikki was quiet, then she realized Rafa might be waiting for a reaction. "Why is that"?

Pause

Rafa stopped walking. "Can we find a place to sit, in the shade"?

"What about just grabbing a table somewhere"?

"Okay, whatever you prefer".

A few minutes later they were sitting in a hole in the wall bar on Decatur Street. The place was less than half full. Pretty quiet, but there was some lively chatter across the room. They ordered at the bar, two draft beers, Stella Artois. They touched glasses.

"Welcome to New Orleans", said Nikki. "Whatever you want to tell me or talk about is okay. It's safe with me. I don't know how much help I'll be, but I'll listen".

"Okay, thanks".

Pause

"You were about to tell me why you think they arrested the wrong guy".

Rafa smiled and made a little bit of an almost chuckle sound. Just enough to say, alright, hold your horses girl, I'm getting to it. "Actually, it's more like we think they have the wrong guy. And really, it's more like he thinks they have the wrong guy. But I agree with him, and that's why I'm here".

It was Nikki's turn to offer a muted laugh and feign exasperation. "Well, I'm glad we got that straight. Now maybe you can tell me the story. Look, I could care less about all the bullshit formalities and correctness. I'm pretty sure I'm on your side, so just tell it like it is. I'm listening".

He looked at her. This chick was unbelievable. Not just pretty. She was smart and confident as hell. Man oh man. I gotta concentrate. More serious now.

"The other person is a guy they called The Guv, short for governor".

"Hold on a second. I think I've heard that name before".

Nikki thought back. It was when she was being questioned the first time, at the cemetery, by Detective Delacio.

"Do you know Detective Kay Delacio"?

"Yes, I've talked to her".

"I went to your father's funeral. She saw me there and questioned me afterwards about my reason for being there and about any relationship I had with your father. After I told her I didn't know your father she asked me if I had ever heard of The Governor. I told her no. Who is he"?

"He was my father's best friend. He's from Peru. He works at Oaklawn Park as the manager of a stable of thoroughbred race horses". Pause. "Why were you at the funeral"?

Nikki took a deep breath and exhaled slowly, looking at Rafa. "I don't know".

"What do you mean, you don't know? It's an eight hour drive. There had to be some reason to drive that far to a funeral".

"It's not any kind of big deal. Does it really matter"?

"Yes. It matters. If it's no big deal, then just tell me".

"Okay. I read about what happened to your father and I couldn't get it out of my mind. I kept thinking I should do something. I couldn't help wondering whether there could possibly be a connection between what happened to your father and what happened to mine. They were both in the investment business and both had a connection to horse racing. I drove to Hot Springs the morning of the funeral. There weren't a lot of people there. I didn't know anybody. The weather was bad. I decided there was no reason to stay, so right after the funeral I got in my car to go home. As I did, Detective Delacio approached me and said she'd like to talk to me. She asked some questions about why I was there. I didn't have a reason other than what I told you. I felt kind of stupid, honestly, but she was very nice and we ended up talking a while about my father".

"Pretty ironic. You went to the funeral for no real reason. I had a real reason and didn't go".

"Yeah, ironic. Keep going. Why do you and the Governor think they have the wrong guy"?

"Because, it doesn't make sense. First, let me give you some background. I was fourteen years old when I met my father for the first time. It was a surprise to him that I even existed, my mother didn't tell him she was pregnant. Crazy, I know, but that's another story. I found out who he was and got in touch with him. I eventually went to New York and met with him. He was nice enough, but didn't really want to develop a close relationship. That was hard for me to accept, and I had some pretty strong feelings about it. Bad feelings. It seemed to me that he was a rich American guy who found out about a child he didn't know he had, a child that resulted from a weekend of debauchery with a Gypsy woman in Paris, and the only way he knew to deal with it was to offer the kid, me, some money and hope he went away, which I basically did. He gave me five thousand dollars a month to pay for my education and living expenses. That was pretty generous, I know, but I needed it to pay my way at a top tier American University, and it was always a struggle to make it work. We didn't talk much. I didn't want to. As far as I was concerned, he was a paycheck, nothing more. I had mixed feelings. I grew up in a Roma community, not much more than a camp. My Grandmother raised me. It was a very big deal to her that I got a good education. She wanted me to have a better life than what she had. Ernie was my meal ticket, as you say in America, and for that I was grateful. But, I felt like he considered me a lower class person. Not American, no pedigree, not one of his kind. A Gypsy. He would help, out of a sense of obligation, but that was it. He didn't want me to be a part of his life. I wasn't good enough. That's how I felt. I used it as motivation. I wanted to show him that I deserved better. That I was more than good enough, and smart enough. The pedigree I couldn't do anything about".

"And you graduated from college"?

"Yes, from Sobourne, a University in Paris". Pause. "With honors". Pause. "I'm not bragging. It's part of the story".

Nikki couldn't help but smile. "I understand. Don't worry about that".

"Okay. Well, I'm getting to the point".

"Look, just tell me what doesn't make sense. I might not understand yet, without all the details and background, but that's okay. I want to know. I'm with you on this so far, and

I want to know the whole story, but just tell me what doesn't make sense".

"He was giving me five grand a month, every month, like clockwork. Now he's dead, and there is no money. Where did the five grand a month come from"?

"Okay, look, I understand that part, but I'm still trying to understand why you think they have the wrong guy".

"The guy they arrested is a local thirty three year old man. Single. Lives in an apartment at his Mother's house. He's had problems with booze and drugs. Can't hold a job. You get the picture, not exactly a pillar of the community. But everybody likes the guy, and he's never been in any serious trouble. Got busted for marijuana about ten years ago, that's it. Never been to prison, no DUI's, nothing".

"The news reports say they found the gun in his car. How does he explain that"?

"He swears it's not his, never seen it, doesn't own a gun. They say it's stolen, no serial number".

"Okay, I think I follow that, but I'm wondering what it is that you think I can do to help you. I don't know any of those people, I didn't know Ernie and I met you an hour ago".

"Sorry, I was just trying to explain, and I guess I'm not doing a very good job. Here's the deal. This is why I'm here. The Guv thinks Martin Carrington killed Ernie".

Nikki started shaking her head slowly. An eye roll would have also been appropriate, but she spared him that. She says in a series of slow, descending, staccato-like syllables, running low on patience, "who is Martin Carrington"?

Pause

"I'll tell you that in a minute. I'm here because I need help understanding the financial and legal worlds that I think my father was involved in, especially offshore investment accounts. I want to know how they work, how they're created and how to find out who's behind them. Maybe I should have just told you that on the phone, but I was afraid you might not want to talk about it, and I figured if we talked in person it might help my chances of getting your help".

"What makes you think I can help with that"?

"I heard that you had been in Hot Springs. I remember when your father disappeared. It was a pretty big story. I did some reading about it".

Rafa stopped for a moment, looked away, then back at Nikki.

"I know you probably don't want to talk about this. I guess that's why I've been beating around the bush. I don't know anything about your father other than what was reported in the news, and I'm sure a lot of that could be inaccurate. I read that there was a secret offshore account involved, and they suspect it had to do with gambling. I'm wondering if my father was involved in something similar. There's no evidence of it that I know of, but it seems to me there has to be some money somewhere that nobody knows about". Pause. "Look Nikki, maybe I made a mistake by calling you. If so, I'm sorry. I can't blame you if you're not happy about it. I'm frustrated. It seems the more I learn about offshore accounts, bogus corporate accounts, private investments, secret accounts, numbered accounts, the more confused I get. I thought you may be able to relate. Maybe I should have minded my own business".

Nikki sat still, faraway eyes, expressionless, hearing what Rafa was saying, but only in the strictest sense. Technically, she heard the words, entering her ears and causing her eardrums to do whatever it is they do to notify her brain that words have arrived, but hearing and listening are not the same thing, the former requiring no intent. She heard the words, at least her brain heard the words, but they had to take a seat and wait in the part of the brain that is accommodating in that way. They were on hold. The part of the brain required to listen was busy. The boss was on the phone. The heart, the soul, the spirit, the core, call it what you will, the boss, was talking. When the boss talks, you must listen, just the way it is.

Chapter 22

After what seemed liked ten minutes, but was actually about thirty seconds, Rafa stood. "I'm going to get us another beer".

The bar was about half full now, starting to get the vibe of a French Quarter watering hole warming to the end of the work day. After a couple of steps toward the bar, Nikki spoke.

"Get us a shot too".

It was more of a command than a request. Rafa wasn't sure what to think, but he got the feeling that new ground had been broken, or was about to be. Nikki took a tug on her beer, swallowed, put it down. She reached for the Tequila, knocked it back without hesitation. Returned the shot glass to the table top, took a breath. She spoke deliberately, eyes fixed on the table top.

"I'm not ready to tell you everything about my father, I may never be, but there are a few things we need to get straight". Pause. "He was a damn good man. He made a big mistake, a huge mistake, and it cost him his life. He did something bad, but he was not a bad man. The offshore account he sent money to was just a number to him, nothing more. It was an account set up by evil people to support their evil ways. He didn't know that, at least not at first. When he found out, it was too late, the money was gone. When he tried to do something about it", she paused, not moving a muscle, transfixed, alone in her world, "they killed him", pause, "just like that".

Rafa didn't say a word, he just sat, looking at Nikki, who still had not moved a muscle, looking down, staring, unblinking. After a moment, he spoke softly. "I'm sorry".

After a few more moments, he could see Nikki breathing a little harder, the muscles around her mouth tensing slightly, followed by a teardrop tumbling from her cheek. Her head bobbed, she leaned forward, resting her face on her hands on the table, and cried.

Chapter 23

When Rafa opened his eyes the next morning, it took a few seconds to figure out where he was. He recognized nothing. Then he got it. He had slept on the sofa in Nikki's apartment. The details of the afternoon and night before were fuzzy, at best, but he remembered Nikki insisting that they do another shot or two, then taking him to some place in the French Quarter. He couldn't remember the name of the place and had no clue exactly where it was, but he did remember singing and dancing were involved, and of course more drinking. They eventually walked to a hamburger joint and got a sack full of burgers and fries, then rode the streetcar back to her place. He vaguely remembered sitting on her porch and talking, but that was it. He awoke on the sofa, fully clothed, with an aching head. The apartment was quiet, with no indication that Nikki was awake yet. He walked out onto the porch and looked around. The magnificent Live Oak trees beckoned, so he took a stroll down the sidewalk toward St Charles Avenue.

Along the way he stopped for coffee and sipped it as he me-andered along. He loved New Orleans. He felt more at home there than any other place he had been in America, not even close. When he returned to the apartment, Nikki was stand-ing in the kitchen, making coffee. Her hair was a mess. Her eyes were a little puffy, and appeared to be not totally focused. Her face was flush from sleep. No makeup. Wearing shorts and a tee shirt. Her legs were perfect. Her breasts, although on the small side, were enough to notice, especially the way they pressed against the tee shirt just enough to make it clear that she hadn't bothered with a bra. She had told him during the course of conversation the day before that she was engaged, but his bulging manliness had no recollection of such a thing.

She spoke. "I think I owe you an apology".

"For what"?

"Everything from about early afternoon yesterday until about now".

Rafa laughed. "Apology accepted. It was really a drag hang-ing out with you and partying in the French Quarter".

"Well, I guess if you had fun it wasn't all bad".

"I had fun". There was a slightly awkward moment of si-lence. Rafa could tell she wasn't sure what to say next, so he bailed her out. "I'm going back to Hot Springs. If you want to talk more, we can do it on the phone. I hope you will, but I un-derstand if you don't". He paused. "Just so you know, I admire you for saying those things about your father".

She looked at him. Earnestly. "Thank you".

"I better get going, thanks for letting me stay here".

"You're welcome".

He smiled at her, then turned to leave, walking toward the door.

"Rafa".

He turned back toward her. She walked to him, standing hesitantly, then reached to hug him. He wrapped his arms around her and pulled her close. She nuzzled against him. He felt her closeness, her breasts firm against his chest. They stayed that way a few moments, then released, not lingering or making eye contact. Then he looked at her again with a devilish smile.

"I always knew I would like New Orleans".

She smiled back. "I'm glad you do".

As he opened the door, she spoke again. "Rafa".

He turned.

"Be careful. Be very careful".

The ride back to Hot Springs was uneventful, which is expected when you go Greyhound and leave the driving to them. Rafa had things to ponder, no doubt, but he was having some difficulty focusing on anything other than Nikki Carter. When she said goodbye and hugged him, did she really press herself, firm nipples and all, against him? Or was he imagining that? Her eyes and skin and hair were the best of the best. Her smile was magnetic, unforced. And she was smart as hell, maybe smarter than he was. But, oh yeah, she's engaged. Damn. She's so fine.

Nikki had her own thinking to do. Part of it involving Rafa. He was different than what she had expected. He was so smart.

She never thought of Gypsies being smart. His skin and hair and eyes were perfect. It felt good to hug him goodbye. Did he hold her a little tighter and longer than necessary, or was she imagining that? He's a Gypsy, not a U.S. citizen. And anyway, I'm engaged.

Chapter 24

The live race meet at Oaklawn Park begins in January and ends in mid April. Winters in Hot Springs, although mostly pleasant, can be cold at times, with overnight temperatures below freezing. Multiple days below freezing can cause the ground to become frozen and hard. Not good for race horses. As a result, the January/February schedule at Oaklawn is at the mercy of the weather, and there are days when the track is closed. So, not surprisingly, the mood at the track brightens when the calendar turns from February to March, and to the beginning of Spring.

The Guv was looking forward to the races on the first Saturday in March. The barn had a promising three year old that had been a bit of a late bloomer, running once as a two year old, beaten twenty lengths after a bad start, and missing the board in his first start of his three year old year, a Maiden Special Weight at Fairgrounds. They dropped him into a Maiden Claimer the second day of the Oaklawn meet. He won easily. He came back barely two weeks later and won an allowance race by five lengths. Next he got to the wire first in another, tougher allowance race. Three for three at Oaklawn. He was training great during morning workouts, so they decided to enter him in the Rebel Stakes, a traditional Oaklawn stakes race for three year olds that is the last important prep race for horses hoping to run in the Arkansas Derby a month later. A win in the Arkansas Derby would then be followed by a spot in the starting gate at Churchill Downs the first Saturday in May, in the Kentucky Derby. Lofty goals, for sure, for any horse, but especially for one who had yet to run in his first stakes race.

The Rebel was the ninth race on a ten race Saturday card. The feature race is almost always the next to last race of the day, any day, at any thoroughbred track, anywhere. Just the way it is. Attendance was about 22,000 on a beautiful early Spring day. Horse racing in general may be in decline, but not in Hot Springs, Arkansas. The Guv, always cool, never rattled, was nervous as hell, pacing back and forth like a father outside the delivery room. Finally it was time, and they led their horse, Demopolis, over to the paddock to be saddled for the Rebel Stakes. The Guv had on a suit, a borrowed suit, that almost fit. The young jockey couldn't help but grin when he walked out of the jockey's room and saw the Guv standing in the paddock dressed like a preacher on Easter Sunday. The horse was thirty five to one on the tote board as the bugler called them to the post and they started the post parade. The Guv liked to gamble, like most horse people, but he didn't have Ernie's passion for handicapping or his knowledge of betting strategy, so he had simply walked to the window and put fifty bucks "across the board" on his horse. He could almost hear Ernie scolding him for making such a pedestrian bet and not at least trying to make a little money on the race by playing some exotics. The whole idea of Ernie not being there still didn't seem real, and it pained The Guv to think about the fact that that was never going to change. Demopolis broke well but got shuffled back to sixth entering the first turn. The jockey, a young Peruvian who had ridden Demopolis in his last three wins, guided him to the rail on the turn to save ground. Along the backstretch he felt the horse relax and establish his rhythm, which was important if he were to have a chance against these stakes horses. At the quarter pole, he asked Demopolis to pick up the pace, which he did. At the top of the stretch he was fifth, but gaining ground. In mid stretch the young jockey found himself boxed in on the rail, without running room. He angled Demopolis to the outside and asked him for his final kick to the wire. The horse responded, and surged past the fourth place horse. He was gaining on the leaders, but ran out of room. He crossed the wire in third, beaten two and a half lengths. He didn't win the race, but it was a strong effort against the best three year olds on the grounds. The guys from Barn 52 were disappointed not to win, but happy, very happy, with the way Demopolis ran. There were smiles all around. The Guv's show ticket paid him $285, he sure wished Ernie was there to see it.

Rafa didn't have a mutuel ticket on Demopolis. He had never bet on a horse race in his life. He had always held his father's penchant for betting on horses against him. He judged it to be a frivolous pursuit, without merit, unsavory. It had never occurred to him that handicapping and betting on horse races could be anything other than a bad habit. Now that he had spent time around horse people though, he was starting to see it in a different light.

Thoroughbred handicapping is tough, and most would say that is an understatement. As hard as it is to handicap a horse race, handicapping alone doesn't get the money. It's also necessary to know how to bet. That part of the equation takes place at the intersection of the enigmatic worlds of odds and probabilities. The horseplayer who understands these concepts and uses them to bet is still not guaranteed a profit, but at least he stands a chance. All others can only hope for a timely visit from Lady Luck. Ernie Cole was one of the rarities, a winning horseplayer. Rafa had been of the opinion that all horseplayers, almost by definition, were losers, not just losing bettors, but losers, in the broad sense. It takes a pretty solid person to admit he was wrong about something, with no caveats. Rafa was beginning to realize, and admit to himself, that he might have been wrong about horseplayers in general, and one in particular. He found himself wanting to know more, about the world of thoroughbred racing, and about that person, his father, who was the exception to the rule.

Ernest Hemingway Cole was not a likely candidate to become a professional horseplayer. He was born into privi*lege, and grew up that way, in New York City.* Working on Wall Street wasn't a dream for Ernie, it was the normal course of things. He had never even been to a thoroughbred track before his visit to Oaklawn Park with Lobo and his cronies. Many years after that experience, he still remembered the fun he had that day. And not just the fun, he remembered the vibe. The vibe was good. When he returned to the place more than thirty years later, the vibe was still there, and it was still good. At first he just hung out and watched the races, betting when he felt like it, with no particular strategy and no particular plan to develop a strategy. That changed. He was losing, and that wasn't okay. He began to study the Daily Racing Form and reading about thorough-bred handicapping. He met some of the regulars at the track, and listened to them talk. He read books and went to seminars. He was hooked. He was well suited for the life of a horseplayer. Very smart, strong willed and savvy, yet disciplined. He was good with numbers, and his years on Wall Street had taught him a lot about how to determine fair value and the nuances in-volved in evaluating the all important risk versus reward prop-osition that is the cornerstone of both places, Wall Street and the Race Track. Above all, though, it just felt right. When he was at the track, he felt good. When he was at Oaklawn Park, with all the characters and all the sights, sounds and smells that went along with being there, he was where he wanted to be, and in no time, when he was there, he was home.

Nikki was tired. She and Gabby had played two sets of ten-nis against a Tulane basketball player and his girlfriend. The girl-friend was a marginal tennis player, at best, but her boyfriend was six feet seven and loved to come to the net and force you to get a shot by him. It seemed at times as if his wing span covered the entire court. Nikki and Gabby held their own against the big guy, but he eventually wore them down with his endless attacks at the net, and they decided two sets was enough. They sat and drank much needed water. As they cooled down, Nikki checked her phone. She had a missed call that made her pulse quicken. She had been wondering if he would call. She told herself that if he did, she would try to help him if she could, but it would only be because she should, not because she wanted to talk to him again. She was willing to help, she wanted to help, but no way she was going to get personally involved with Rafa. That's what she told herself.

She waited until she got home to return the call.

He wasted no time answering. As he said hello, he was wearing a Gypsy grin.

"Hello Rafa, it's Nikki, I saw that I missed a call from you".

"Yes, I couldn't stand it, I had to hear your voice".

Nikki laughed. "I believe you like the Southern girls, Rafa".

"OMG yes", he replied, mockingly. "Especially the ones with tattoos".

Nikki laughed harder. She had a small Fleur de Lis tattooed low on the back of her neck. A group of her classmates at Tulane had decided, after several pitchers of Dixie on tap at the Taj, that they needed to get tattoos to show their unwavering support of the New Orleans Saints during their run to the Super Bowl in 2010. It was no more than an inch and a half from top to bottom, but it was there, and Rafa had noticed.

"They won the Super Bowl, it was worth it. Besides, everybody says it's cute".

"No argument here".

"What have you been up to? Do you have news to tell me"?

"Not really. As I said before, this offshore account stuff is confusing as hell and I was hoping you wouldn't mind if I talk to you about it and get your opinion on a few things".

"I'll help if I can, but as I also said before, it's not easy getting the information you need. Why don't you just tell me where you are with it and we'll go from there".

"Okay, my father, Ernie, I'm just going to call him Ernie, okay"?

"Of course okay, you don't have to explain".

"Ernie was giving me five thousand dollars a month to live here and go to school. I told you that, right"?

"Yes, you told me that".

"Alright, five grand a month may not be big money, but it's not chump change either".

"Agreed".

"Now, setting aside the five grand a month for a moment, Ernie was also a very successful money manager on Wall Street for almost thirty years. He made a lot of money. In addition to that, he was the only child of a very wealthy New York City family, his father having made his own fortune on Wall Street".

"Okay".

"I have met with the attorney handling the estate, the Guv is the executor. As far as anybody knows, Ernie had very little money. His bills were paid, his rent was current and he had a few thousand dollars in the bank. That's it. He wasn't getting a Social Security check, no retirement check from Wall Street, nothing. How can that be"?

"Strange. So you think there was some sort of offshore account involved"?

"I don't know, but there has to be something. The five grand didn't appear out of thin air each month".

Nikki thought for a moment. "Rafa, exactly how did you get the five thousand a month? Was it a direct deposit into your account? Was it the same day of the month every month"?

"The money didn't come directly to me. He arranged it with the school that he would put $5,000 a month there. They took the tuition, room and board and all that out each month and I got the rest, usually about a thousand a month, it wasn't exactly the same every month because of fees and stuff that were deducted some months".

"How did you actually get your part of the money each month? Did it come to your bank account automatically"?

"I don't have a bank account. I have a prepaid debit card. Each month, after the school is paid, my portion of the five thousand goes into my account at the school, then I transfer it to my prepaid card and that's where I got my spending money".

"When did the last payment hit the account".

"The first of February".

"Are you sure"?

"Well, yes, it was paid as usual and I put my part on the card".

"What about March"?

Rafa's brow furrowed. "He wasn't alive in March".

"Have you looked at it in March"?

"No, but hold on a minute and I will".

He grabbed his laptop and pulled up the account. Nikki waited, then heard Rafa say to himself, "Holy Shit", then return his attention to the phone. "There's nine hundred sixty one dollars in my account, how can that be"?

"Is that about how much it usually is"?

"Yes, but how did it get there"?

"Can you tell at all where the money comes from? Is there some sort of entry that shows the source of the money"?

"There's a reference number, that's it".

"Is it five thousand, exactly, every month"?

"Yes".

"And it's the same day every month"?

"Yes, the first day of the month, unless it's a weekend or holiday, then it's the next business day".

There was a long pause.

"Did he ever say anything to you about how long the payments would last?, like, until you graduate or until you get your Masters Degree"?

"No, we didn't talk about it, I always just figured it would be as long as I'm in school, or maybe until I get a job. As I said before, we didn't talk much. I didn't appreciate the way he treated me. It was as if I was an inconvenience to him. But I was glad to have the money, so I didn't make a big deal of it. I figured two could play that game, so I more or less quit thinking of him as my father and just considered him a source of money. I wish he would have talked to me more, but he didn't. He just didn't seem to be interested".

"Or maybe vice versa from his point of view".

"What do you mean"?

"Well, from what I know and what you've said, you may have had more of a chip on your shoulder than you realize. Could be that he was at least a little wary of your motives, understandably, and felt your animosity. Maybe he decided to just be your benefactor and leave it at that because he could tell you resented him and he didn't want to deal with your attitude".

Rafa's skin bristled, but he could see her point. He didn't know how to respond right away. Nikki continued. "Look, I barely know you, but it doesn't always take a long time to get the essence of a person. I'm pretty sure you have strong character, but that's only because you allowed me to see the real you, whether you intended to or not. Maybe that didn't happen with your father. It's not hard to imagine that it wasn't easy to be relaxed and open with him when you met him for the first time. He probably felt the same way. All he knew about you was what you allowed him to know, which I'm quite sure wasn't much. When I met you in New Orleans, you were sweet and kind. You treated me with respect. You were relaxed and smiled easily. One of the things I like most about you is that you don't try to be anything other than yourself".

Nikki stopped. She realized she was preaching to Rafa, and that it probably sounded like she was blaming him for the way Ernie was toward him. She paused, then continued, in a much softer voice. "I sound like your mother, scolding you for something that happened in the past. I'm sorry. I wish I had met your father, but more than that I wish that he could have known you better, ...the real you".

Rafa was quiet.

"Rafa"?

The silence on the other end of the phone made Nikki wish she had just kept her mouth shut. It all happened so fast, they were talking about the money and all of a sudden she starts throwing her two cents in and acting like she knows some shit about the relationship between two people she barely knew, one she never even met. As if she were the fuckin wise wizard woman. She wanted to just push the rewind button and return to the point right before she said everything she just said. She wanted a redo. Funny thing about words, though, you can't take them back. They are what they are, good or bad. Just the way it is.

"Rafa"? Nothing. "Rafa talk to me please". Nothing. There was a sigh of exasperation from Nikki. It was plenty loud to hear, and certainly would have been heard, if there had been anybody to hear it, which there wasn't. Rafa was gone.

CHAPTER 25

The Guv had a lot on his mind. There were only a few weeks left at The Oaklawn meet, then the stable would be moving to Kentucky for the Churchill Downs summer meet. He always had a touch of melancholy when it was nearing the time to leave Oaklawn, it was his favorite track, and Hot Springs was as close to a home as he had, but this time it was more than just sentiment that gave him pause, he had unfinished business in Hot Springs, important unfinished business. The rapscallion, no, that descriptor wasn't strong enough, the detestable Martin Carrington had murdered his best friend and gotten away with it, so far. The Guv had to bring the truth to light. The backside workers, including the Guv, needed no convincing. Carrington, the track chaplain, the Christian leader, the benevolent one, had a way about him, intended to nurture affinity among the believers, that bred dislike and distrust among those who saw through such feckless pretense. Still, that sentiment doesn't go far by itself in a court of law, nor the court of public opinion.

There needed to be more, something concrete. The Guv needed proof. His sense of urgency was compounded, and the task
at hand was made immensely tougher, when he awoke on a
Thursday morning to the news that Lonnie Harrison had confessed to the murder of Ernie Cole.

Martin Carrington got the news Thursday morning, like
everybody else. He was less surprised than most, and more
pleased than all. He reminded himself to keep his serious face,
and to avoid the topic of Ernie's murder, just as he had done
every day since it happened. He had almost convinced himself,
through his twisted sense of self importance, that he had simply done what was necessary, and in the end everybody would
be better off because of it. Ernie Cole, likable as he was, was
nothing more than a two bit gambler who had lost his way.
Likewise Lonnie Harrison, a ne'er do well who had squandered
every opportunity to be something more than a sluggish weed
head. He, Martin Carrington, wasn't happy about the misfor-
tune that came the way of Ernie and Lonnie, but life's not fair,
and he didn't make the rules. He promised himself that he
would never forget the sacrifice those guys had to make so that
he could keep to his task of making the world a better place. A
noble man.

What a bunch of bullshit. What he should have been thinking about was the fukkin Guv. The Guv was a man, a real man,
not because he was some kind of badass, but because he had
the ability to just be who he was, and to allow others to do
the same. Not just a real man, a real person, able to love, able
to laugh and care, and get pissed off and show it, and get up

every morning and get on with it, living life, giving an honest effort every day and not complaining about it, although at times he had every reason to. Able to have a best friend, a real best friend who he loved to the core and the best friend knew it, and loved him back the same way. They don't give that away at the county fair for putting a quarter on a color. It's real, and beautiful and rare, and better than a million zillion dollars and a whole shit load of gold and precious jewels. That's what the Guv had, and the bogus mofo Martin Carrington should have been worried, very worried, but of course he wasn't because his head was so full of himself that he couldn't see what he should have seen. He killed the Guv's best friend. His ass was grass.

Lonnie's confession was the news of the day. Almost everyone was relieved that there wouldn't be a trial, especially the Oaklawn management and the city leaders. The less publicity about the incident the better. The race meet had been very good, as always, great racing and big crowds. Excitement was building toward the last week of the meet, called The Racing Festival of the South, when Oaklawn closes out it's live race season with a series of big races, ending with the Arkansas Derby on the last day. The confession would allow the murder of Ernie Cole to gradually be relegated to the back pages of the newspaper, and eventually become just another part of race track lore.

The streetcar meandered along St Charles Avenue, rocking from side to side and making the familiar clicking noise as the driver started and stopped to allow passengers to get on and off. New Orleans was coming alive with Spring. Azaleas were in bloom. Majestic live oaks took on a fresh green glow. The garden district, just down St Charles Avenue from Nikki's apartment, was vibrant with color, the green grass glistening. Nikki loved New Orleans in the Spring, but this morning she hardly noticed her favorite change of season. Her attention was elsewhere, or nowhere at all. The stuff in her head didn't require any effort, it was there whether she wanted it to be or not. She had a debate going on there. Should she be mad at Rafa, or should he be mad at her? Then there was the other thing. The thing that was lingering. The thing she knew would never go away. Silas Greer.

Nikki, by nature, was kind, like Gib. But whereas he at times was too nice for his own good, she had a healthy dose of guile, and had no trouble showing it when necessary. She was glad she had the bastard, Silas Greer's, name, but when Anna gave it to her, she, Anna, made it very clear that she did so reluctantly, because no good could come from trying to exact revenge from the man. Nikki understood that. It really didn't require much convincing when you threw in the fact that because of Silas Greer, and whoever or whatever he controlled, her father's bones were lying on the floor of the Atlantic fukking Ocean. Still, it wasn't okay to just let it go. It would never be okay to just let it go. Letting it go was not an option, because even if she wanted it to just go away, it wouldn't. It never, ever would. Which brought her back to Rafa. He was from a different world, a different culture. Hard to imagine growing up as he did, being raised in a Gypsy community and never even knowing his father. He, Rafa, had his own issues, but he was brilliantly smart, and for whatever reason, money or something else, and she was deciding that it may indeed be something else, although at first it was the money, or a combination of the two, who knows, whatever the case, he was determined to force his father's killer to face the music, to answer for what he did, whatever that meant, and whatever it took. She, Nikki, on the other hand, had the name of her father's killer. Maybe not the person who did the deed, but the person who controlled the person who did the deed. The guy that gave the order, the big man, the boss. She had his name in her hip pocket, and she wasn't doing a damn thing about it. That, by God, was about to change.

Nikki's phone buzzed, bringing her out of her thinking place and back to the present. It was Rafa, right on cue.

"Well, you are indeed still alive and kicking. I thought maybe someone kidnapped you or something".

"Okay, maybe I deserve that, but you were pretty hard on me, as I recall". Pause. "How are you" ?

"Great. Just riding the streetcar and thinking about which five star restaurant to choose this evening. I think I might go with Commander's Palace. It's been a while and the garden district is so nice right now".

"Damn, do you need a date?, I can be there in about eight hours".

Nikki laughed. It felt good to do that. "They don't serve hamburgers you know".

"No prob, I was thinking along the lines of turtle soup and a plate of oysters. Maybe a bottle of something from the Loire Valley, that should work fine. Look, can you talk a minute"?

"Yes, but I really am on the streetcar, so it may take me a minute to get situated".

Nikki walked to the rear of the car, and at the next stop stepped off, onto St Charles Avenue. She walked across the street and sat on the steps of an old stone building with a plaque that said it housed the headquarters of some multi-cultural alliance nobody has ever heard of but has a damn nice building in which to do it's thing.

"Sorry about that, now I'm good".

"What are you doing on the streetcar in the morning? are you playing tourist"?

"Not exactly, I met my study group for breakfast and now I'm headed back to Tulane University, the mother ship".

"Okay schoolgirl, I have another favor to ask, and you may not want to hear it, but let me explain for a minute, okay"?

"This sounds familiar, and why do I think there might be a not so relaxing trip to Hot Springs Arkansas involved"?

"Just keep an open mind please, I'm serious about this".

"My mind is open, let's hear it".

There was a moment of silence as now Rafa recognized a familiar tone, and decided in that split second to get to the point first, then explain, unlike before.

"I do indeed want you to come to Hot Springs".

Nikki sort of laughed, but it was a muffled type, not the spontaneous ha ha ha. That's the good kind, the kind that tickles the soul and lightens this thing we call life, and nourishes the good karma. You can't laugh and frown at the same time, can't be done. That's a beautiful thing. People pay other people to make them laugh that way. Crazy, but good crazy. Nikki's laugh wasn't that kind, it was the manufactured smart ass sarcastic kind, which is also kinda cool, if done correctly.

"Is this a joke?, I seem to be laughing".

"I thought you might appreciate my getting to the point for a change".

"Excuse me, but I believe I was the one who was a step ahead of you. I told you what you were going to say before you said it, Gypsy Boy".

Nikki immediately wished she could take that back, once again. But of course, once again, she couldn't. There was a very tenuous, but short, pause.

"Are you through with all that bullshit? Can I state my business"?

Long pause.

"I'm sorry I called you Gypsy Boy", pause, "I'm serious".

"No prob, I'll probably call you worse than that at some point, maybe pretty fucking soon at this rate".

Nikki laughed, the real thing.

"State your business Mr. Zamfir".

"We need help Nikki".

"Who is we"?

"The Guv and I".

"Okay, keep going, lay it out there".

"The Guv is driving himself crazy (probably a pretty short drive, Nikki thought, but didn't say it) trying to figure out how Martin Carrington killed Ernie. That's bad enough, but now, maybe you haven't heard, that Lonnie dude confessed to the murder, so as far as the legal system is concerned, and just about everybody else for that matter, the case is closed".

This was news to Nikki, and now she was fully engaged in the conversation.

"If he confessed, does the Guv think he's not telling the truth? why would he do that"?

"I don't know, I don't know what to think, but what I do know is that there's no doubt in the Guv's mind that Carrington's the guy, and he's not going to give up until he proves it".

"What do you think I can do to help?, we've kind of already been through this".

"We've kind of been through it, but it's time to get down to business. The Guv is executor of the estate, but he has no clue exactly what that means or what that allows him to do, and he won't admit it, but I think he's intimidated by it all and embarrassed to ask for help. He's a wise man, but he's not very educated. He's lived almost his entire adult life in America, but he's never really assimilated into the culture. He's an American citizen, and proud of it, but he lives and works with a bunch of Hispanics, mostly Peruvians. Anyway, you get the picture. I'm trying to help, but it seems I'm more frustrated and confused now than when I first got involved with all of this. You're smart, you know how the legal system works, you're an American, you are well spoken and confident, you're very pretty and you have that Southern charm thing, you know what I mean, should I continue"?

"Please do, but first repeat that last part, I like the way it sounded".

Ignoring her smart ass reply, he continued. "So will you help us"?

Nikki exhaled loudly, signalling the angst that she was feeling.

"If I say no, are you going to take all that stuff back"?

"No, can't take back the truth".

"I'll come to Hot Springs Rafa, but just because I do, don't think the answers are going to be easy to find. It's probably going to continue to be frustrating, and it's possible that you'll never get to the truth, but I'll help, and if we both give it our best shot, maybe we can get it done, I hope so".

"Man, you don't know how happy I am with that. Thank you Nikki. Thank you very much".

"You're welcome. I guess I better go get packed, I'm headed to Hot Springs. Do they still sell those corned beef sandwiches? I hear they're pretty good".

"Damn right they do, they'll be on me".

"I'll have to take care of a couple of things before I leave, but if I can leave at a decent hour tomorrow, I will".

"Be careful driving. Let me know when you hit the road. I really do appreciate it Nikki. The Guv is going to love you".

"I'm sure the feeling will be mutual. I'll talk to you tomorrow".

Chapter 26

The Guv was indeed impressed. He knew from Rafa's description of her that Nikki would be attractive, but he also knew the fickle nature of what a man likes about a woman, and vice versa. He needn't have been concerned about that, she was a keeper. Oh hell yes she was.

Rafa made the introduction. "Guv, this is Nikki Carter. Nikki, this is the Guv".

"Very nice to meet you Nikki, I've heard a lot about you".

Rafa immediately wished the Guv would just be his boot wearing, rough edge self and not try to act as if he were the fucking ambassador to the backside.

"Thank you, I've heard about you too".

As she said that, Nikki glanced at Rafa with a hint of a smile. It was nothing more than a genuine response to a warm greeting from the Guv, but to Rafa, there was no doubt she was letting him know that now she knew he had talked incessantly about her since their last meeting and that he was totally smitten and couldn't stand the thought of living his life without her. These silly little things we do, we humans, especially when it involves tiptoeing around and looking and listening and trying to decide how close we should get to the thing that attracts us and scares us at the same time. Wanting to have some confirmation that what we think is there is really there, and not just a sliver of fool's gold.

The Guv, the chivalrous one, wasted no time seeing to it that Nikki was set up comfortably in her luxury suite on the backside. It had been his suggestion that they offer her a free place to stay for a day or two, or more, however long didn't matter, at the track. It wasn't exactly the Ritz Carlton, but the women saw to it that there was a nice clean room for her when she arrived. Nikki was more than impressed by the hospitality she was shown. She didn't yet totally understand the dynamics of the racetrack community, and never would, but she would come to understand a few things. Number one, these were hard working people with a tough life. They were real. There was something to them. Number two, they were one big family, mess with one, mess with all, which lead to number three, the most important of all, as it pertained to her and the reason she was there. Ernie Cole had been considered family. What these people lacked in money and status, they more than made up for with passion and tenacity. Getting to the truth about Ernie was big, very big.

Mornings start early on the backside. A damn rooster would need an alarm clock. Not exactly what Nikki was used to, but she didn't complain. By the time she had finished her coffee and a few bites of breakfast in the track kitchen, in which she was treated as if she were a member of the royal family, she was joined by Rafa and the Guv.

"Let's get this girl some riding gear and see how she does on the back of a thoroughbred", said The Guv, looking at Rafa, then to Nikki.

"Good idea", replied Rafa.

"Don't think so, boys, I'm a city girl. I do kinda like those boots though", Nikki said, eyeing The Guv's well worn cowboy boots. "Can I get some with spurs"?

"Absolutely", replied The Guv, with a chuckle.

The Guv and Rafa wasted no time finishing breakfast, after which they walked with Nikki out to the track and watched a few horses going through their morning workouts.

"They're beautiful", said Nikki.

"Yes they are", replied The Guv.

Rafa broke the mood. "Alright folks, we have work to do, let's get to it".

There was a small meeting room near the track kitchen. The Guv didn't want to draw attention to what they might be doing, but there didn't seem to be any way to avoid it, so they just went in and closed the door.

The mood was more serious, with a little tension in the air. Nikki sensed that the two men needed some direction, so she spoke first, which suited them both just fine.

"Let's start out by making sure we are all on the same page and agree on what we're trying to do. I'll give you my take on things, and ya'll can correct me if I'm wrong or you disagree or whatever. Is that okay"?

Heads nodded. It was.

She looked at The Guv. "You think this man, Martin Carrington killed Ernie".

Pause, The Guv answered. "Yes".

"Tell me, in your own words, why you think so. Don't worry about trying to convince me, I'm on your side, just talk".

Rafa had a feeling, a good feeling, that now, right now, they were taking the first few steps toward something that was a big deal. Not just for himself and The Guv, but for Nikki, the backside family and anybody else that found themselves having to fight for the truth. The Guv took a deep breath and exhaled slowly.

"Martin Carrington is a sorry sack of shit, he's smarmy".

He paused and looked at Nikki, then Rafa, as if he were waiting for a reaction of some sort. Rafa's mouth started twisting. He turned his head as if he were trying to shake it off, which he was, but it wasn't to be, he couldn't stop it. He burst into a fit of laughter that made his gut heave and it took a good thirty seconds for him to catch his breath, at which point it started all over again, which of course led Nikki to laugh, and finally The Guv joined in. Laughter is indeed contagious. Rafa finally composed himself enough to speak.

"He said he was smarmy, fuckin smarmy, where'd you get that Guv?, you must have been waiting all weekend to lay that on us. Did you look it up on Wikipedia or what? He said he was smarmy. Smaaarmyyy, oh shit, Ha Ha Ha Ha Ha".

"It ain't that damn funny", The Guv broke in, "don't matter where I got the word, that's what the sombitch is, smarmy. He's smarmy and he's a sack of dog shit and he needs to pay".

"Alright", said Nikki, "got it, keep going Guv".

The Guv exhaled again, seeming to have a hard time finding the words.

"Look", said Rafa, "how bout I tell you about that smarmy fucker and The Guv can break in whenever he wants, is that okay Guv"?

"Have at it".

"Okay, first, it doesn't make sense that Lonnie killed Ernie. They were friends. Ernie helped him out now and then, gave him odd jobs and such. Nobody that I've heard from has ever seen them have a cross word. For that matter, as far as I can tell, nobody has ever seen Lonnie have a cross word with anybody. There's no motive. I don't think he did it. Martin Carrington, on the other hand, by all accounts, was having trouble maintaining his lifestyle without the Insurance Agency paying his way. Ernie had money, at least I think so, and I've thought about it an awful lot. He led a simple life and kept a low profile in Hot Springs. That was his choice, the way he wanted it, but he made a lot of money on Wall Street. He was an only child and his father was filthy rich. They owned real estate in New York City alone worth many millions, plus a place in Italy and who knows where else".

"Wait a second", said The Guv, so they did.

"Here's how it is. Martin Carrington is a sorry piece of shit, period. He's a fucking fake. He comes around here passing out a few bucks and acting like he's a servant of the Lord. Gives advice to the little people. Talks with a voice that's all serious and shit, very sincere. Dresses like he just stepped out of a damn men's magazine, that prick. Of course, when Ernie was around he was different, because he wasn't the big dog then. He wouldn't dare show his true colors to Ernie, because Ernie was the money man, and he had to keep the money flowing, to buy those clothes and drive that car and wear those fucking cuff links, that prick".

"Okay Guv", interjected Nikki, trying to suppress a laugh. "We get the point, and we agree, although I've never met the man, I know the type. We need to focus, though, on whatever facts we have. I'm getting the impression that Martin Carrington is a pretty smooth operator, what..."

"Pretty smooth prick", said The Guv.

Now Rafa jumped in. "Guv, we're with you, hundred percent. He's a prick. That's a proven fact, he proves it himself every day, but being a prick is not against the law, we..."

"Must not be, else that sombitch would be serving a life sentence in San Fukkin Quentin". The Guv couldn't resist.

Rafa and Nikki looked at each other, then at The Guv.

"I know, said The Guv, I'll be quiet. Continue".

Rafa did. Looking at The Guv and speaking with a new sense of urgency. "Like Nikki said, we need facts Guv. We gotta focus on the facts. We haven't gotten very far, and Lonnie has cut a deal with the suits. Most people just want this whole thing to go away. We have work to do".

The Guv, now totally serious, looked to his right, toward the lovely femme fatale from New Orleans, "tell me what to do Nikki, I ain't quittin til I nail that bogus pile of donkey dung".

Nikki, as any newly minted lawyer would, produced a legal pad. "Let's get started, we're not leaving here without a plan".

CHAPTER 27

That evening, some of the guys who worked for The Guv fired up the grills and loaded them with burgers and smoked sausages, onions and peppers. There was potato salad that Nikki loved. It had fresh corn, hard boiled eggs, cilantro, cumin and and some sort of South American style Aioli that was spicy and delicious. There were several coolers of beer, and the Spanish music was kickin. Nikki was tired. The day had been long and stressful at times but they had made some progress. The biggest thing was that Detective Kay Delacio was now going to help them. Already she had talked to someone at NYU about Rafa's account, and they promised a reply within twenty four hours. Amazing the different reaction you get when you identify yourself as a police detective on official business. If they knew where Rafa's five thousand a month came from, that could lead to them to other assets. It was a start.

Dub, the newbie lawyer working on Ernie's estate, seemed to be in over his head, but he was basically working for Hayden anyway, so they didn't share anything with him, and would only call him when they didn't have a choice. They weren't necessarily concerned that Hayden was a problem, they were pretty sure, in fact, that he had no inclination to be further involved at all. Now that Lonnie had confessed, Hayden could all but forget about the hick town of Hot Springs, Arkansas. Dub could let him know when the estate was settled and that would be that. Still, best to keep a low profile, and only involve Dub and/or Hayden when they had to.

The financial office at NYU wasted no time honoring the request of the law woman. The Detective received the email late in the day, and just happened to see it when she checked her inbox the last time before leaving the office. It was brief: Detective Delacio, Mr Zamfir receives a direct deposit of $5,000 each month into his account at NYU. It comes directly from United Casualty Insurance Co, Des Moines, Iowa. There was a policy number referenced on the original paperwork, it is SL2333809. This is all of the information provided to us by Mr Zamfir and the insurance company. As we discussed earlier, NYU has a very strict policy regarding safeguarding the personal information of our students, especially financial information. We respectfully ask that you help us honor that commitment, as we know you will. We are pleased to comply with this request and hope you find the information helpful. Please let us know if you need any further assistance. Kindest Regards, Dr. Regina Kulotta, Student Finance Director, NYU.

A quick internet search produced the contact info for United Casualty Insurance, offices were closed for the day.

Nikki slept late the next morning, if you call 7:30AM late. Her first decision of the day was to take four Ibuprofen. Her head was a bit fuzzy after the impromptu party the night before. If there were any doubt whether the backside crowd knew how to have a good time, all doubt was gone. They did. It was fun, but Nikki awoke with a not so good feeling, along with the headache. This not so good feeling had nothing to do with overindulgence, nor with the murder case, certainly not with Rafa. The first part of the evening was nothing but fun, drinking beer with a shot or two of tequila in there somewhere, laughing and talking. The language barrier was a little bit of a problem for some of the backside crew that hadn't learned much English, but they made do. It was obvious that they loved Rafa. At one point, after the dancing started, he broke into some crazy looking thing that was supposed to be a Gypsy break dance, although she doubted what he was doing had ever been seen anywhere near any Roma community anywhere, then he shifted into his version of a more traditional Spanish Gypsy Flamenco, this time he was joined by a beautiful young lady who, Nikki suspected, was not a stranger to Rafa. The dance was lively and entertaining, if short on skilled Flamenco, and it served to heighten the festive mood among the group. Nikki herself eventually joined in, along with almost all the others, as the party intensified and the night wore on. The fact that Rafa was dancing with a beautiful girl, and obviously enjoying it, was not what troubled her. After all, it was a party, there was dancing. What did bother her was the feeling that maybe she was missing out on something. This was living. A little crude, maybe, but these people, this evening, were alive. With passion, for life, for each other, and their life together. What could be more precious than that? New Orleans had the same vibe, living life today, right here, right now. Nikki loved that about New Orleans. She loved that about these people. Then what was the problem? what was she missing out on? Certainly not Rafa.

United Casualty Insurance Company was not as forthcoming as the detective had hoped, at least not initially. The information was available, but of course there were documents that needed to be completed and properly notarized, to protect the client, etc. etc. The fact that she was a police detective investigating a murder didn't carry as much weight as she thought it would, so she went to Plan B and asked to speak to an officer of the company. After a series of short conversations with people who wanted no part of it, she finally got the head of the legal department on the phone, at which point she was tired of being tolerated and shuffled along like an annoying little brother at the school carnival. She was ready for somebody to talk straight with her.

"Detective Delacio, this is Rudd Lancaster, sorry for the delay, how can I help"?

"Rudd, are you a decision maker with the company"?

"Maybe, I'll help if I can".

"I'm trying to get information regarding a policy issued by your company".

"Yes, I know that much".

"Okay, I know you have rules to follow. I'm a police officer, I respect that. Can I talk to you for a minute off the record"?

"Yes, I'm not promising anything, but I'll listen".

"I'm investigating the murder of Ernie Cole. I assume you know who he is".

"Yes".

"Here's the deal Rudd, and this is confidential".

"You have my word".

"I have reason to believe that Ernie Cole was murdered by someone who managed a scheme to steal money from him and got caught. Someone he trusted. I have no reason to think that your company had anything to do with it, other than you're the company, or one of the companies, that this person used to do whatever he did. I need help, I need information. I'm going to get it. If I have to get a court order and/or a warrant, that's what I'll do, but that takes time, and it's a pain in the ass. If you help me, I'll make sure you and your company get credit for doing so. That's a promise".

"Tell me more, what information do you need"?

"Whatever you have that might help. I know that's vague, but I'm following leads, and I don't have anything other than this one policy number".

"How can I verify that you are who you say you are"?

The detective gave him her badge number, social and driver's license number.

"I'll call you back in an hour".

It took fifty five minutes. Rudd had been around. He knew a homicide detective would appreciate promptness. He got voice mail on the first try. He told the detective that an email was on the way, with attachments that showed a scanned copy of the original application paperwork. He suggested that the detective call him after she had looked at the application documents. He reminded her, respectfully, that he was stretching protocol by emailing the documents, and to please use discretion.

That was no problem. Detective Delacio was stretching protocol a bit herself, maybe more than a bit. The Ernie Cole murder investigation was over. They had their man. He confessed. Case closed. So why is she still digging around and asking questions about stuff related to Ernie Cole? That wouldn't be an easy question to answer, if it were asked.

The first attachment she opened was a copy of the cover page of an annuity contract issued to Rafa Zamfir by United Casualty Insurance Company. It stated that Rafa would receive five thousand dollars a month for the rest of his life. Not bad, thought the detective. Damn good news for Rafa. The second attachment was a copy of the original application. It meant little, if anything to the detective, but she figured it might mean something to someone who knew what he was looking at, so she called her insurance agent and asked him to take a look at it. She forwarded the email to the agent, and got a call ten minutes later.

"Nothing out of the ordinary that I can see", said the agent. "What are you looking for"?

"That's the problem, I'm not really sure, but one thing I'm curious about is where the money came from. Anything you can tell about that from looking at the documents"?

"What do you mean, what money"?

"The money used to set this thing up, it had to come from somewhere".

"Well, there's not a copy of a check, so I'm not sure about that. Maybe it just wasn't included in these documents for some reason, or it could have been an electronic transfer".

"How would I know if it were an electronic transfer"?

"You probably couldn't tell from this paperwork. Have you talked to the agent"?

The detective was silent. Of course, she should have thought of that. It was probably just too obvious, which is often the case in any investigation, you're looking so hard for something hard to find that you overlook something right in front of you.

"No, damn, I should have thought of that. Let me see where that goes. I may call you back".

"No problem, any time".

The agent listed on the contract was Odell Donaldson. His office address on the application was in Grayson's Bow, a small town just outside of Hot Springs. The detective started to call the number listed, then stopped, and instead called Rafa.

"I need your help".

"Okay, you got it", replied Rafa.

"I have a name and telephone number, do you have something to write with"?

"Just a second", then, "yes, go ahead".

"The name is Odell Donaldson, the number is 501.328.9944".

Rafa repeated both back.

"Correct", the detective continued, "he's the insurance agent listed on your annuity paperwork. I want you to call him and ask for an appointment. Tell him you want to meet him and review the annuity, so you'll know someone you can call if there's ever a problem, that sort of thing. Just be yourself and ask the questions you would normally ask. And then, casually, almost as an afterthought, you know how to do it, just be yourself, ask him where the money came from. Now, he might not be sure what you mean, so just tell him, again, in your own way, that you don't really understand annuities that well and you're wondering how it all works. Make it a point to say that five grand a month is a lot of money for you, and you're wondering exactly where it comes from. Did your father pay a lump sum to the insurance company to set it up? Is the monthly payment guaranteed never to run out, as long as you live? That sort of thing. Questions that you really do have, so you don't have to fake it. Then ask him if Ernie wrote a check, up front, to the insurance company, and how much the check was for. All of these are legitimate questions, so you don't need to expect him to think anything is out of the ordinary. If he says there is a check, ask for a copy. If, for any reason he's not sure about it, tell him it's important that you find out because you and your attorney are working on the estate and you need to tie up all of the loose ends, make sure you've accounted for all of the bank accounts and so forth. Above all, we need to find out where the money came from. You don't tell him that, of course, I'm just telling you that. How we get there is not really important, we just need the information. Remember, you have every reason to ask these questions. You're the customer, you're father just died and you're trying to figure out the finances. It's the truth, simple as that. Sorry to go on so long, but I want you to be prepared. Now, ask me whatever you want".

"I think I get what we're doing, but let me clarify a few things before I call the guy".

"Absolutely, take your time. Let's talk about it".

They spent the next half hour discussing the details of the plan. When they were through, Rafa was ready.

CHAPTER 28

Rafa made the call. As he did he ran his right hand over the prayer beads on his left wrist.

"Is this Odell Donaldson"?

"Yes it is. Who am I speaking with"?

"I'm Rafa Zamfir. I have an annuity contract with your company, and I believe you are my agent. Is that correct"?

There was a longer pause than Rafa expected. "I'm not sure, I might be. Do you have a policy number I can reference? I can pull it up and tell you for sure".

Rafa gave him the number, and waited patiently.

"Okay, got it. You do have an annuity policy with me. What can I help you with Mr. Zamfir"?

"I assume that my father, Ernie Cole, set this up for me with you. Is that right"?

Another pause that seemed a little long, as if he was unsure how to answer. Rafa could feel the uncertainty, and the tension. He decided, without really thinking, to try to help the conversation along. "Mr. Donaldson, let me tell you why I'm calling, maybe that will help".

"Okay".

"My father is deceased. He was murdered. You may have heard about it"

"Yes".

"My father and I were not close. He was paying my way through school, and I appreciated it, but we didn't talk about it. I didn't know about the annuity, and now that I do know I'm wondering what else I don't know. My father was a very generous man. I don't know how much it took to set up the annuity, but I know it had to be a good bit. I'm helping with his estate. We're having a hard time making an accurate list of his assets. What I'm wondering, and the reason I'm calling you, is where the money come from to buy the annuity. Can you help me with that"?

"I didn't know your father, and I really have no idea about his assets". There was another pause, just long enough to be uncomfortable. The next words from Odell Donaldson were a game changer. It was a simple question, that told Rafa he had just hit paydirt. "Do you know Martin Carrington"?

It all went down quickly after that. Rafa managed to arrange a meeting that afternoon with Odell. He took the detective with him. It was a little bit touch and go at first. Odell wasn't sure what to make of it all and was wary of talking with the detective, but after some time, he came around. It became obvious to the detective that this man, Odell Donaldson, was scared. He had allowed himself to be used by Martin

Carrington, and was afraid of the consequences. Of course, every man is responsible for his own decisions, including this one, so he indeed had some things to worry about. He had made some pretty decent commissions by going along with Martin Carrington. He knew what they were doing could be wrong, but the money was too tempting and he chose to turn a blind eye and go along. The detective convinced him that, if he cooperated and helped nail Martin Carrington, his own misdeeds would not be vigorously investigated, and would probably be overlooked altogether.

It was time to get serious. The detective got straight to the point.

"Tell us about Martin Carrington. Tell us everything".

Odell swallowed hard. "I was introduced to Martin by a mutual friend at church. He said Martin was a part of FCA, liked doing business with good Christians, and had a soft spot for insurance agents who were good people but were struggling to make it in the insurance business, which I definitely was, struggling that is. Martin said he was working with a wealthy client who wanted to use the FCA to do some charitable giving, and wanted to be discreet, didn't want his buddies and those around him to know about it. He asked if I was interested in setting up an annuity for the client. Of course I was. Martin went on to explain that he would do it himself, but he wasn't going to because of the possible appearance of a conflict of interest. He said that if I would be the agent on the annuity purchase, he would handle all of the paperwork, meet with the client, get it signed, everything. All I had to do was submit it as the agent. It seemed a little too good to be true, or a lot too good to be true, but then he told me that I would only get 20% of the commission. The rest would go to the FCA, and they could use it however they wanted. Then it made sense to me why he was asking me to do it. He could help a struggling agent, help the FCA and help the client by keeping it all confidential. He, Martin, wasn't getting paid anything, or at least that was the way I understood it, which seemed like a really stand up thing to do and made me feel good about the whole thing". The detective and Rafa were both listening intently, both amazed and excited about the information flowing from this man. Odell took a sip of bottled water and continued.

"Martin got all of the paperwork for the annuity prepared and signed by Mr. Cole. All I did was sign the paperwork as the agent. I never met the man, which didn't seem strange to me, if indeed he was a wealthy man who wanted to keep his financial life private. It did seem unusual to me that he would purchase an immediate annuity on such a young person, but rich people tend to do things differently, so again I didn't say anything, but I was kind of curious about that".

The detective spoke. "Did Mr. Cole write a check to pay for the annuity policy"?

"No, he sent a wire transfer directly to the insurance company, a little over one million four hundred thousand dollars".

The detective's eyebrows raised involuntarily. "Do you have a copy of the wire instructions that might show us where the money came from"?

"No, that was all handled by Martin. I wasn't involved in that part of it. As I say, all I did was sign the paperwork as the agent".

"Is there a way that you can access that information now, as the agent"?

Odell looked at the detective, obviously feeling stressed and wishing the whole thing could just go away. "I don't know".

The detective was quiet. Thinking. It might not be such a good idea if Odell tried to get the wiring information anyway. It could raise a red flag that would alert Martin to the fact that there was some sniffing around going on. "Okay, let's forget about that for now". Then, out of the blue once again, Odell asked a question that caused the detective and Rafa both to snap to attention as if Sergeant Vince Carter himself had barked it out at the top of his lungs.

"Have you looked at the other account to see if you can get it from there"?

Pause.

"What other account"?

"The Bradenton account".

"Not sure about that one. Tell us about it".

"I just figured if you knew about the annuity you would know about the other account".

"We probably should, but we don't. Please tell us about it".

Odell relaxed a little, glad that the detective said please.

"It's the one we set up after the annuity. Martin uses it to give money to the workers at the racetrack. I don't totally understand how it works, I just do what he tells me to do".

The air in the room suddenly got thicker. Pulses accelerated. "So, it's not an annuity"?

"No, it's some kind of trust account that invests in mutual funds. It's for clients who want to make charitable contributions. It's tied in with the FCA somehow. Bradenton manages the money and sends the checks to the charity and all that stuff. Martin says it's better than a lot of trust accounts because Bradenton does everything and it costs less than setting up a trust at a bank".

The detective and Rafa were both quickly getting confused.

"Let's back up a minute", said the detective. "Let me see if I understand what you're saying, correct me if I'm wrong on something".

"Okay".

"You set up two accounts for Ernie Cole, at the request of Martin Carrington".

"Yes".

"Is it only two, or are there more accounts we don't know about yet"?

"Only two".

The detective paused, thinking through it and beginning to wish she knew more about the subject. "Do you have an account statement from the Bradenton account"?

"I can pull one up on the computer and print a copy if that will help".

"Absolutely, please do".

Odell logged into the Bradenton Investments website, printed the most recent account statement and handed it to the detective. It had the Bradenton Investments name and logo at the top. The account owner was listed as Ernie Cole Charitable Gift Trust. The account value was over twenty two million dollars.

The detective looked at Odell and shook her head slightly, while thinking. Rafa could see and feel the frustration, the detective's body saying what her voice wasn't.

Rafa was good at reading people. He was a Gypsy. He could do that. He could read the detective's palm too, but that would have been showing off, and it probably wasn't the right time for it. What he did do was speak up.

"Detective Delacio, excuse me for interrupting, may I have a word with you, in private"?

"Of course". She looked at Odell. "Let's take a ten minute break".

When it was just the two of them, Rafa spoke to the detective in a low voice. "I think we should talk about this before you ask him more questions. We need to find out as much as we can about this new account, then ask him what else we want to know. He's nervous, and I think he's pretty clueless about the whole thing anyway. He would probably appreciate having some time to calm down and regroup. We can start again tomorrow morning. What do you think"?

"I think that's a good idea. Let's do it".

A few minutes later the three of them were back together. The detective wasted no time. "We're going to stop here and call it a day. We'll reconvene here again tomorrow morning at eight thirty. Does that work for you"?

"Yes, that's fine".

"Good. Now Odell, please listen to me. Do not tell anyone you talked to us today, not even your wife, and especially not Martin Carrington. Are we clear on that"?

"Yes".

"One hundred percent clear"?

"Yes".

"This is very serious stuff. I'm not sure where this will end up, but we're going to get all the facts and see where they lead us.

Any questions"?

"No. I'm going to help you any way I can. I never was totally comfortable with Martin. I wish I hadn't gotten mixed up with him".

"Get some rest, we'll see you in the morning"

Bradenton Investments was a major player in the mutual fund industry worldwide. It was a privately held firm who hired only the best and brightest, many of whom never left. After several phone calls, the detective was able to get the help she needed. No mention was made of Ernie Cole or Odell Donaldson, just a request for product information. The young lady on the line was an inside sales support person who was a product specialist. She knew her stuff. The detective made it clear she wanted to know about one product, the Charitable Gift Trust. She and Rafa had spent time on the Bradenton website, and had a basic understanding of the product, but they were in over their heads when it came to the details of how it worked and how it was used. The young lady's explanation was confident and professional.

The Charitable Gift Trust was a donor advised gift fund, set up as a turnkey solution for those clients who wanted to set up a trust account for charitable giving, but wanted something simple and cost effective. She described a typical situation in which it might be used, but only after making it clear, with lawyer like precision, that she was not giving specific tax advice, only a generic explanation of the product. She paused and asked the detective if she understood that. She said she did. To Rafa, it was another example of how Americans go to great lengths, spending time and money, to protect themselves from getting sued, and then invariably when the shit hits the fan, they turn around and sue each other anyway.

The bottom line to the explanation was that Ernie gave away a huge chunk of money, but kept the right to decide later what charity or charities get a piece of the cash. Bradenton was managing the money and distributing a piece of it whenever instructed by Ernie to do so. Once the account was set up, gift recommendations could be made online. So, whenever he felt like it, for any reason, Ernie could go online and instruct Bradenton to make a donation to anybody he chose, as long as it was an IRS approved charity. It was all quite confusing to Rafa and the detective, but they continued to ask questions until they were satisfied that at least they understood the basics. What they didn't understand was how Martin Carrington fit into the equation.

They took a break for a bite to eat, then went back to work. Joining them were Nikki and the Guv. Nikki took the account statement and looked at the transaction history. Then she took a poster board and made a timeline of charitable gifts made from the account. A pattern quickly emerged. The main recipient of the money, almost the only recipient, was the local chapter of the FCA. Nothing wrong about that, the FCA was an IRS approved charity. Also nothing wrong with the fact that the local FCA chapter had a person with ties to the community on the payroll as a fund raiser. Nothing wrong with the fact that the fundraiser was also the official chaplain at Oaklawn Park. That person was Martin Carrington. Nothing wrong with it, but certainly curious considering the circumstances.

The Guv spoke up. "When the prick comes around like fucking Santa Claus, handing out the cash, is that where it comes from"?

Nikki, grinning, responded. "Good question Guv. Let's back up a bit and see if we can get closer to the answer. Exactly how did it work with Martin when he gave money to the people on the back side? Did he actually hand out cash? Was there any paperwork, some kind of receipt, anything? Just tell us as best you can how it works".

"I avoided the slime ball, but I got regular payments from the FCA on my card. I never got any cash".

"What card are you talking about"?

"When that ass licker came around the first time a few years ago, we had a meeting and he explained to everybody that the FCA was going to be helping the backside workers pay bills and stuff. He didn't say how much we would get, but we didn't complain, it was free money. He passed around a list that had everybody's name on it. He told us to find our name on the list, check the spelling and the family information to make sure it was accurate. He left the list and we all made sure our names were on it, then gave it back to him. A week or so later, we each got a prepaid cash card with our name on it. Then, the first day of every month, we got cash put on the card by the FCA. We were all pretty happy about it".

"Was it the same amount every month"?

"Yes, except not everybody got the same amount. It depended on the size of your family. And then sometimes there would be an extra payment that just showed up on the card. The way dickwad explained it to me was that every now and then somebody makes an unexpected contribution to the back side fund and they just passed it along to us. It always seemed a little too secretive to me, but as I said, nobody complained about the cash".

They all looked at each other. They were onto something, but so far it was too confusing to understand exactly what. Nikki spoke. "Okay, let's try to connect the dots and see how far we get. Ernie set up a charitable trust. The trust made regular payments to the FCA. The FCA made regular payments to the backside families. Looks to me like the payments to the backside families were coming from Ernie's trust". She looked at the others. Heads nodded.

"Yep", said the Guv.

Nikki continued. "Let's assume that the reason it worked that way was because Ernie wanted to help out the back side people, his people, but he didn't want them to know the money was coming from him. Martin is the logical person to be the go between. Ernie arranges with Martin to give money to the FCA, with the understanding that it would then be given to the backside families. Martin, of course, would honor Ernie's wish to remain anonymous, so he didn't tell anybody about the arrangement. That all makes sense to me, but it does nothing to explain Ernie's murder". She turned to the detective. "What are we missing"?

The detective responded, and her calm, professional demeanor lowered the anxiety factor a notch. "I think you're getting there. The money trail is not always easy to follow. Almost never is, really. But it's almost always a good idea to stay on it to see where it leads. There's still a lot we don't know about the money. We're pretty sure some money came from Ernie and ended up on the back side. It's the part in the middle that bothers me. We know how much money left Ernie's account and went to the FCA. We have the account history that shows that. We know some money left the FCA and went to the back side, but we don't know exactly how much. That part of the trail is fuzzy. We need to clear it up".

Chapter 29

Nikki spoke. "If the FCA is an IRS approved charity, aren't the financial records open to the public? Maybe we just need to request them".

A hint of a smile appeared on the detective's face, then was gone. She liked what she heard, but she was thinking several steps ahead, and she knew the danger there. "Contacting the FCA directly is a dicey proposition. It would throw up a big red flag for all to see, especially our friend Martin Carrington". She threw a glance at the Guv, expecting another wisecrack, but none came. "It's best if we can access the information without them knowing". Rafa started to speak, but the detective held up a finger, asking Rafa to wait one minute, then she paused and continued. "What I should say is that it's best if "you" can access the information without the FCA knowing. I'm in deep enough already, sorry, but I don't need to be part of that".

There was an uneasiness in the air, then Rafa spoke.

"Maybe I can help out there". He gave a sheepish glance at the others. Nikki was enamored by it, but didn't show it. "I have a couple of buddies that are pretty good at that kind of stuff. I could give them a call".

Silence, then the Guv broke in with his typical roguish aplomb. "You got friends that are fucking hackers"?

"I don't know that I would call them hackers", replied Rafa, "they aren't crooks, but they are hackers in the sense that they are pretty good at getting past firewalls and such, it's a challenge to them".

"Sounds like a bunch of fucking hackers to me", said the Guv, "just what we need".

Rafa looked at the detective, as if seeking approval, "should I ask them to help"?

Nikki spoke up. "Absolutely you should. Go for it. We gotta nail that bastard Martin Carrington. Don't tell your friends why you want to know, just tell them you need the detailed history of grants or payments or whatever you call them, to the Oaklawn backside, or better yet, get the entire list of payments, regardless of where they go, that way we'll make sure we don't miss anything".

The detective gave a slight nod. Approval given. Barely more than twenty four hours later, Rafa held in his hand a printout of the entire financial transaction history of the Hot Springs FCA, for the past three years. Four hours later they were still at it, and it felt like they had made very little progress. The money coming into the FCA from Ernie's charitable trust was easy to see. The money going from the FCA to the backside was another story.

Each individual recipient had his or her own ID number, without names, and each payment to each ID number was listed as a separate transaction. So, for every payment to the FCA from Ernie, there were over a hundred payments from the FCA to the backside. Nikki couldn't help but wonder if it was that way on purpose, so that it would be hard to figure out for anybody who came snooping around, but she tried to suppress that thought and just focus in on the money trail as it was. It was getting late, they were hungry and tired, so they stopped for the night and agreed to start again the next morning. The Guv and the detective both headed home. Rafa and Nikki headed to the Longshot Saloon.

Among the other perks of taking up residence on the backside at Oaklawn Park, is the ease with which you can slip across the street to the watering hole and not have to worry about driving home. Of course, for some, that proximity of pleasure is enabling, and as she crossed Central Avenue, it occurred to Nikki that, to a neutral observer, she might be considered one of those, in light of the fact that she had been at Oaklawn five days, and this was her fifth visit to the saloon. But she wasn't one to concern herself with such things, so she didn't dwell on the thought. In fact, it amused her, especially given the propensity for the moral majority to so willingly put New Orleanians on the wrong side of the ledger, so that upon examination at the pearly gates, they can be separated and banished to the gurgling lava pit that is the consequence of excessive merrymaking. It was late, and they planned to get an early start the next morning, so Nikki and Rafa showed restraint, ordering only one pitcher of cold draft, along with a platter of fried bar food to curb the appetite.

Rafa looked at Nikki. Her profile was regal. Chin, nose, lips and forehead in perfect proportion. Flawless skin. Her thick dark hair was pulled back in a ponytail, with a few strands of fine, wispy hair dangling sensually against the back of her neck. She felt his gaze, turned toward him, and instead of looking away, he smiled. He wasn't sure, but he thought she blushed slightly, making her even more irresistible, if that were possible.

Conversation came easily, as usual. Plenty of playful banter, along with reasoned debate about this and that, but not a word about the murder case. Rafa at one point took Nikki's hand, turned it so that it was palm up and, while staring intently, lightly traced the lines of her palm with his fingers. It felt good, very good, to both of them. It was nearing midnight, and the morning would come too soon, so they left the saloon and walked back to their home away from home on the backside. They came to Rafa's building first. He didn't stop, and kept walking with Nikki to her building. She wondered whether that fact was chivalry or lustful longing, and which she wanted it to be. As they reached the entrance to her building, they stopped. No words. After a long pause, he said softly, "you're beautiful". He reached, pulled her close and kissed her. His heart fluttered, in perfect rhythm with hers. For that moment, the world quit turning. Since approximately one hour after she first met him on the riverfront in New Orleans, Nikki had been both dreading and longing for this moment. In a perfect world, she would have already decided how to handle it. The world is far from perfect, and Nikki wasn't quite ready to deal with her feelings for the Gypsy, Rafa Zamfir. The kiss was as good as it gets. Nikki was practically melting. Their breathing was deep. Rafa pulled her closer. He began kissing along her cheek and neck. The passion was strong and getting stronger. He ran his hands along her back and to her sides, then he moved his hands up and gently cupped her breasts. Nikki felt a rush of desire that was almost unstoppable. But stop it she did. She put her hands around his wrists.

"I can't Rafa. I just". Pause. A loud sigh. "I can't". The world again stood still, this time for the wrong reason. Since approximately ten seconds after he met her on the riverfront in New Orleans, Rafa had longed for this moment, when he would hold Nikki, nibble on her ear, and shower her with kisses. There was never a second of dread. "Rafa", long pause, "I'm engaged", another long pause, the angst palpable, "I could never"....she grimaced.

Rafa looked at her, silently, then spoke softly, as if he were reminiscing about something many years past. "I've spent so much time thinking about you, every day since we met, every hour really". He closed his eyes, exhaled, and turned away.

She spoke, voice unsteady, "it wasn't wasted time".

He looked back at her. Incredulous. "How can you say that"?

"Rafa, please understand".

He stared at her with blank, sad eyes, "I understand".

He turned, steadied himself, and walked away.

She said his name. He turned his head slightly toward her as he kept walking. He couldn't see her face in the darkness, couldn't hear the trickle of the tears.

CHAPTER 30

The morning did indeed come early, but Rafa welcomed it after a fitful night of little sleep. He grabbed coffee in the track kitchen. The detective was waiting when he got to the meeting room, followed in minutes by the Guv. Nikki was absent. "Anybody heard from our girl"? The Guv asked.

The Detective said "No".

Rafa gave a seemingly disinterested shake of the head. Said nothing. The Guv was puzzled. He punched in her number on his phone. No luck. He headed for the door. Her car was not in the usual spot. The Guv had a moment of near panic, then he saw that it was parked just outside the door to her apartment. The apartment door was open, and as he approached, Nikki walked out, carrying a box. Not good. The Guv, never one to overreact, stayed true to form.

"Good morning".

"Good morning", Nikki replied. She continued to the car, set the box on the ground, and opened the car door.

"Can I help you"?

"I just have a few things, but thank you".

"Where you headed"?

"I'm going home Guv. I was going to come see you first. I guess you beat me to it".

"I wish you wouldn't, but I'm sure you have your reasons".

She looked at him, with no immediate response. He spoke again.

"I want you to do me a favor before you go".

Nikki loved the Guv, but more than that, she respected and trusted the Guv, and she knew the feeling was mutual. No way she would deny a favor to the Guv, regardless of what it was, within reason.

"Okay". Somewhat tentative.

"Can I buy you a cup of coffee"?

Nikki smiled. "Must be some favor".

What the Guv lacked in formal education, he more than made up for with people skills. He knew there was something wrong, and he was pretty sure it involved Rafa. It didn't take Sherlock Holmes to notice the chemistry between the two. He had stayed out of the way of it, but he was paying attention. He made the decision, which would prove correct, to not address the subject of Rafa directly. His instincts told him there was something else going on with Nikki, in addition to Rafa, and again his instincts were on target. The Guv had been thinking. Nikki had no connection to Ernie Cole, Oaklawn Park or anything or anybody in Hot Springs, Arkansas. She came to Ernie's funeral on the outside chance, a possibility, however remote, that there could be a connection between the murder of Ernie Cole and the disappearance of her father. There obviously wasn't, but that didn't stop her from hoping that there could be something she was missing. Her presence at the funeral drew the attention of the investigators, so, unwittingly or not, she became involved. The thing that was bugging the Guv was that the thing that caused her to drive eight hours to Hot Springs the first time, the mystery of her father's disappearance, seemed to have vanished into thin air. No mention of it. Didn't make sense. Nikki Carter's father was still missing, and yet, here she was in Hot Springs, Arkansas, racking her brain to figure out what exactly what happened that resulted in the murder of Ernie Cole, a perfect stranger until a few weeks ago. Whatever made her come to Hot Springs hadn't gone away. It was there. It was lurking. Had to be.

"Let's hop in my truck. I know a good coffee drinking place".

They headed down Central Avenue, toward downtown Hot Springs. He parked on the street in front of Bathhouse Row, an impressive group of old, ornate buildings that once housed the thermal baths that Hot Springs was noted for. Their grandeur was still intact, though only one was still a bath house. They stopped for takeout coffee, then walked past the bathhouses, up a wide brick stairway onto the aptly named Promenade, a brick and stone walkway which is set along the lower portion of Hot Springs Mountain, parallel to Central Avenue. They walked for a few minutes, then found a place to sit. The grass was beginning to turn green and the birds were chirping, pleasant reminders of Spring.

"They say a lot of famous people came to Hot Springs back in the day to take the baths. Maybe a few of them came for the night life. They say it was quite a place at one time".

"That's what I hear". Silence, except for the birds. "So, what's the favor Guv? You're acting kinda strange".

The Guv gave Nikki a wry smile. "I guess I'm not that good at this kind of stuff".

"What kind of stuff? What are you talking about"?

"First of all, I want you to know something. I admire you very much. You're beautiful, you're smart, but what I admire the most is your heart".

"I admire you too Guv, very much".

The Guv chuckled softly to himself, aware that he was acting like a school boy beating around the bush. It was time to get on with it.

"I want to talk about your father".

Nikki looked at him. Surprised. "Why are you making such a big deal about it"?

The Guv looked her square in the eyes. "Because it is a big deal".

Nikki suddenly wasn't too comfortable. No way she could know it, of course, but she was about to have a conversation that would change the rest of her life. She realized this was a different Guv she was talking to. He had been nervous about broaching the topic. That should have told her something. She was going to have to let him in. There is rarely, if ever, actually there is never, in the view of the one doing the letting in, a right time. Just the way it is.

Nikki, of course, stepped up to the plate. Eyes locked on his. "I guess you want the whole story".

He had a look she had never seen from him, something like very serious reverence. "Yes".

She started. It wasn't difficult. Maybe it was her trust in the Guv, or maybe it was simply the release of stuff that needed to be said. Whatever the reason, the words flowed. A lot of them. Until the hard part. The part that ripped her heart. At that point she started to struggle. The Guv struggled with her. They went down that path together, toward the thing that needed the light of day. The thing that couldn't be just buried and forgotten. It brought her to Hot Springs, and until it was dealt with, would never go away. By this time they were sitting close together. Her hand inside his. It was almost lunch time. Except for a coffee refill and bathroom break, they hadn't moved.

"I didn't know your father's disappearance had anything to do with horse racing. I can see why you wanted to know more about Ernie's story".

"Guv".

"Yes".

"You want to know what's bugging me"?

This is the point at which, normally, the Guv would unload buckets of sarcasm, but this was far from normal, and sarcasm had no place. "Yes".

"I've been spending all this time trying to help find Ernie's killer, and no time trying to find my father's, and I know who both of them are".

Nikki, amazingly, was not crying. Her words were profound, and the Guv let them settle, knowing their weight. After a minute, he held her hand in both of his, raised it to the side of his face, and gently squeezed. "That's a helluva burden to carry".

Nikki sat still, calm, looking away. The Guv let go of her hand, stood, then kneeled in front of her, put his hands on her knees, and looked up at that beautiful face. At first she didn't move, but then she slowly turned toward him. His mouth spread into a grin, then, as if he were poked with a cattle prod, he jumped to his feet, thrust his arms into the air and let out a yell like fourteen little kids getting what they wanted for Christmas. He jumped around, danced a jig and pretty much acted like a fool. Nikki looked around to see who might be witnessing this spectacle, because otherwise it would never in hell be believed. There were a few people within hearing and seeing distance, but nobody close by and nobody who was actually willing to watch. She scrunched up her face with mock incredulity, then lowered her head as if not wanting to look, then her shoulders started heaving, and she erupted in uncontrollable laughter, insisting that he stop embarrassing himself and her, while at the same time smiling and laughing. Kinda like when a little kid starts acting in a manner that is inappropriate, but funny, and his Mom tells him to stop, but you know she thinks it's cute, and he knows it too, so he just pours it on, causing her to then have to actually get control of him because it's gone too far, and the kid ends up pissed off because it's not fair, and he may be right.

The Guv grabbed Nikki by the hand. "Come on, let's get a bite". They walked across the street to a small deli with a few tables outside. They had sandwiches. The Guv insisted on sharing a slice of caramel pie, so they did that too. Then, as if the break in the action never happened, he got back to the conversation.

"Why are you just now telling me this"?

Nikki looked at him. Having to reset her frame of mind to serious mode. Before she could answer, he negated the need.

"Forget that, doesn't matter". Pause. "I want you to tell me the rest. Now".

"I'm not sure what the rest is, Guv. That's what I've been struggling with. What to do".

"Okay, let's back up a second. Let me see if I understand where you are. You're saying your father didn't just disappear, he was murdered".

Pause. "Yes".

"And you know who did it"?

"More like who had it done, but yes".

Pause. "Damn". Long pause. He looked at Nikki, who was looking away. "Tell me about it. Explain how that is, and why you're keeping it to yourself".

Nikki took a deep breath. "He got involved with some bad people, really bad people. They're involved with the Russian Mafia. He didn't know that. He made a bad decision. He lost ten million dollars on a horse race. Crazy, I know, but it happened. It's complicated, but the end result was that they killed him and made it look like he stole the ten million and disappeared.

Somebody who was part of it told me what happened. That person gave me the name of the man who is responsible for having him killed, and warned me that no good would come from trying to do something about it. That's where I am. I have the name, but I don't know what to do with it. I'm scared to do anything, and I'm terrified of just doing nothing".

Crazy indeed. The Guv studied her. "I'm going to make a phone call. Stay right here, I'll be back in ten minutes".

Nikki nodded. "Okay".

The Guv returned, sat, and looked at Nikki. "I want you to go somewhere with me".

"Okay, where"?

"Ferriday, Louisiana".

Nikki looked at him. "Are you kidding? Why"?

"I want you to meet somebody. An old friend. Someone who may be able to help".

Chapter 31

An hour later they were on their way. Nikki driving, the Guv riding shotgun. Nikki had protested the trip a bit, once she thought about it, but she relented without too much of a fuss when it became obvious there would be no denying the Guv. He insisted that his friend, a trusted fellow Peruvian of some apparent import, could be a great help, after hearing her story, if he were so inclined. An onlooker would have thought it quite remarkable that Nikki would so readily agree to embark on a trip with a man old enough to be her grandfather, and who looked every bit a grizzled horseman, with his ruddy complexion, deep lined face and well worn boots. And she with the look of a Countess on casual day. But she had promised, and although she knew this wasn't the original favor, she was good with it. A road trip with the Guv.

On the road, they talked about everything except Gib Carter. Nikki played the Guv some of her music, and sang along on some. He didn't have his music, so he just sang a few songs. In Spanish. His voice was strong and he seemed to hit every note. The more he sang, the more animated he became. Nikki laughed and smiled for many miles. She had never been around the Guv away from the track. It was an experience she would treasure for years to come.

They rolled into Ferriday just before cocktail hour. The mood changed a bit. It was still good, but they were there for a reason, and there was a layer of apprehension in the air. The Guv directed Nikki through the small town, to the Southern edge, and down a series of roads that led to an old plantation home, surrounded by the remains of an old plantation. The driveway was fine crushed stone, as was the walkway leading to the front door. The house itself wasn't an expansive landmark, like the ones visited by tourists in Natchez. It was modest in comparison, but to Nikki it had all of the look and feel of an old Southern Treasure, with the weathered patina that can only be found in a place like this, lived in and loved by families who didn't need anybody to explain to them the joys of accordion music and sucking the heads of crawfish. It was two stories, all wood except for the old brick foundation and the four chimneys. It was white, and had been painted more than a few times with varying degrees of attention to detail. The result was a rich ivory color that bore the evidence of summer and winter, but not neglect. There was no huge wrap-around porch or multiple balconies, none needed. The front porch was of the utilitarian type, large enough to accommodate family and a few friends. The front steps leading up to the porch were just wide enough for the old gossips to come and go without breaking formation. Majestic live oaks flanked both sides, and back, and front, as well as the long straight walkway that lead to the front steps. All in all, a masterpiece.

As Nikki and the Guv stepped out of the car and turned toward the house, an older black lady appeared on the porch, waving enthusiastically.

"I'll be damned", said the Guv, "that's Luevada, still kick-in". He quickened his pace and greeted her with a huge smile, followed by a huge hug. "Luevada this is Nikki Carter, Nikki, this is the one and only Luevada. All I gotta say is don't piss her off".

"Don't you listen to him Nikki, he's just being crazy. Pleasure to meet you. My, you are a pretty girl. Ya'll come on in. I'll tell Mr. Ray you're here. Nikki, the powder room is the first door to the right of the stairs".

"Thank you Luevada". She looked at the Guv. "I LOVE this place".

He chuckled, "good, so do I".

Luevada reappeared, "he's sitting out back. Can I fix ya'll a drink"?

"Damn right you can. What would you like Nikki"?

She hesitated a second. "I'll take a beer if you have one, thank you".

The Guv glanced at Nikki, shook his head, then looked at Luevada. "She drives all this way, to the damn Plantation, and orders a beer".

"And she's gonna get a damn beer too. You can fix your own. ... Rude".

Drinks in hand, they stepped out back. Once again Nikki was mesmerized by the simple warmth and beauty of the place. The back porch was bigger than the front, and screened in. Three steps led down to a patio area that was designed for comfort and obviously well used. Large river rocks formed the patio itself, blending into a large area of packed, crushed stone underneath a canopy of live oaks. There was an old brick grill, and adjoining it on one side was a stone and brick pizza oven with a stone chimney accented with old Peruvian glazed tiles. There was a group of mismatched chairs near a fire pit. Underneath the trees was a large stone table, with chairs all around. Sitting in a comfortable looking chair was a thin, weathered looking old man with thinning hair and a pleasant face. He had a ruddy complexion similar to The Guv, and confident eyes, although one eye drooped noticeably. As they approached, he stood and embraced the Guv in a manner that made Nikki realize just how close these two men were. The Guv, his arm still draped over the shoulder of his friend, made the introduction. Nikki Carter, Ramos Mantilla.

Ramos took a step toward Nikki, and offered his hand. She took it, then he brought his other hand up and held her hand gently in both of his. His smile and sincere eyes made her relax. He liked her immediately. They sat and talked. When it was time for another drink the Guv stood. "I'm making this girl a drink, the hell with the beer".

"Don't forget your old pal here", said Ramos, "the usual".

"No, not the usual, we're sharing a drink, the three of us, and I'm making it".

Ramos half rolled, half closed his eyes in mock disgust. "Oh shit".

Nikki giggled.

Ramos looked at Nikki. "I know Hector brought you here to talk about your father. We'll do that tomorrow. Okay"?

Nikki smiled. "Okay". Pause. "You called him Hector, is that his real name? I've never heard it".

"Yes, around here he's Hector". This time Ramos smiled. A proud, satisfied smile.

The Guv reappeared with the drinks, on a tray. Three glasses of Champagne, and three shots of Tequila. Nikki looked at him. She spoke as a nose in the air aristocrat, with an exaggerated Southern drawl. "Why, Hector, those aperitifs do look delightful, you shouldn't have gone to the trouble of preparing such a classic combination".

The Guv was taken aback slightly, but recovered in fine style, as always. He grinned and nodded slightly, "Hector at your service, my lady".

All three touched the tequila shot glasses and knocked them back. The boys looked at Nikki. They both said, almost in unison, "Damn".

Ramos was radiant with pleasure. Not just because he was enamored with Nikki, but also because he enjoyed seeing Hector having fun.

They finished off the Champagne, and Nikki said, "I'm switching back to beer, I can't keep up with you boys".

The back door of the house opened and out walked four men carrying cardboard boxes of food from the kitchen at

Mona's. Each one greeted The Guv with a full hug, pats on the back, handshakes, the whole nine yards. Nikki thought it was kind of a cross between a greeting between close friends and a show of respect for a visiting dignitary. They started putting the food out on the concrete table, only to be stopped by Luevada, who walked out with a tablecloth.

"You damn rednecks have a lady in the house, get that stuff off the table and let's do this right". A few minutes later the tablecloth was on the table and it was covered with plates, silverware and all sorts of delicious looking food. To top it off, Luevada put a flower vase in the middle with fresh flowers. "I picked those myself", she said to Nikki.

"I love them, thank you", Nikki replied.

Luevada turned to leave, "I'm out of here, ya'll a bunch a drunks".

Somewhere along the way the music started, upbeat Latino style, of course. The four Peruvians each grabbed a beer and joined in the party. Nikki was thoroughly entertained by the animated conversation among the guys. At first, to accommodate her, they spoke English, but that didn't last long, and soon the Spanish was flying. She was so used to the Guv speaking English that is seemed strange to hear him carry on with his buds in rapid fire Spanish, but she thoroughly enjoyed watching it. At one point Ramos actually jumped up and started dancing a jig. Nikki immediately joined him. The others clapped and whooped it up, Peruvian style. The Guv and his buddies knocked back another shot. Ramos took a seat, rested a while, then stood and sauntered off to bed, sleep would come easily this night. The food was untouched, and there was no indication the boys would be interested any time soon, so Nikki just fixed herself a plate and enjoyed a moment of calm. Then, following Ramos' lead, she left the party and went inside to the guest room and a much deserved rest.

Nikki slept well. When she awoke she had one of those moments, when you first open your eyes in the morning and you're in a strange place, that caused her to glance around the room and wonder, for a split second, where the hell she was. Then she relaxed and took it all in. She walked over to the window, pulled the curtain back and looked out. It was barely daylight, but she had a good view of party central, the back yard. She smiled. As she walked into the kitchen, she was greeted by The Guv and one of the guys from the previous evening. They were about to leave for Hot Springs.

"Good morning princess".

"Good morning. How are you boys feeling this morning"?

"Like a million bucks", the Guv replied. "Would you like coffee"?

"Yes, thank you. I can get it". She poured herself a cup and joined them at the kitchen table.

The Guv looked at Nikki and nodded toward his companion. "Gabo is taking me back to Hot Springs. He looks for any excuse to go to the track. I told him we have a good filly running today in the fifth race. He's already counting the cash".

"You're leaving now"?

"In a few minutes, yes".

Nikki gave the Guv a sad look. Said nothing at first. Not sure what to say. The previous twenty four hours had been so much fun, she hadn't prepared herself for this moment. It was hard to think that she wouldn't be seeing him any more. "When will I see you again"?

"I don't know, but there will be more opportunities. I can't go too long without seeing your smiling face".

Pause.

The Guv's friend, Gabo, judged it to be a good time to check that the car was ready to roll, and he left the room.

Nikki walked over to the Guv, he stood, and without a word she hugged him tightly, not letting go. "I'm going to miss you Guv".

"Me too sweetie. Be careful driving to New Orleans".

"I will. Let me hear from you Guv".

"You will, and that goes both ways".

As she pulled away, she looked him in the eyes. "Thank you".

He hugged her one last time. Said nothing. Turned away while he could so that she wouldn't see the tear on his cheek.

Rafa was struggling. He kept looking at the numbers on his spreadsheet and they all kept working out. He had accounted for all of the money going to the FCA from Ernie's Charitable Trust, and all of the money going from the FCA to the Oaklawn Park backside, and there was no indication that anything was wrong. No money was missing, nobody was complaining, nothing. He kept rolling it around in his head, and it kept coming up the same way. He discussed it with the detective. She was just as perplexed as Rafa, plus, she was working on other cases, so she wasn't able to do much other than offer encouragement. Then there was the Nikki thing. The heavenly kisses he shared with her were the real deal, no doubt about it. You can't fake that stuff. She was engaged, he got that. She didn't want to be unfaithful to the guy, he got that too, and admired her for it, but there are some things you just can't deny. Their mutual attraction was one of those things, and she was denying it. It wasn't as if he was convinced without proof. The way she kissed him that night was proof enough. Just was. Just the way it is. So how could she possibly decide to just let that go? No way she could. But she did. Gotta deal with it.

The human brain is pretty amazing. It can do a hell of a lot on it's own, when left alone to do it. But many times the rest of the body just can't seem to get out the way. We throw up all sorts of obstacles. Stress, anxiety, call it what you will, it gets in the way. The harder we try, the tougher it is. Sometimes we just need to back off, give it a rest and let the brain do it's thing. That's where a good night's sleep can come to the rescue, sometimes. That night must have been one of those times for Rafa Zamfir. When he awoke, one of his first thoughts put him on the trail that would ultimately lead him and the Guv to paydirt. The thought was simple. The names. What if some of the names were bogus? Rafa called the Guv. He didn't worry about the time. He knew there was approximately zero chance the Guv was still sleeping. Of course he was correct. The Guv answered at four forty six in the morning, a little concerned that there must be something wrong if the kid was up at that hour.

"Everything alright"?

"Damn Guv, can you at least say hello, or would that be too civilized for you"?

"Hello, fuckwad, everything alright"?

Laughter on Rafa's end. "Yeah. I want you to do something. Do you have a computer handy"?

"I am a fucking computer".

"Well, okay then. We're in business. I'm going to email you the list of names associated with Barn 52 that the FCA's records show have gotten payments from Ernie's trust. If there is also a printer handy, maybe you can stick your dick in it and print the names. I want you to verify that the names are actual people who work for you, or have worked for you. I'm wondering if maybe some of the names are bogus, if not on the Barn 52 list, then maybe one of the others".

The Guv thought for a minute. "That's pretty smart for a damn Gypsy. Send it on over, I'll check it out and call you back".

Fives minutes later the Guv held the list in his hands. He quickly scanned the names. Nothing unusual. He went back over them, slowly. All were legitimate. He called Rafa. "These names check out, all of them". Pause. "Do you have the same thing for all of the barns"?

"Yes, I think so".

"Send Barn 38. I'll call you back".

Most of the names on the Barn 38 list were familiar. A lot of them were Peruvians who were good friends with the Barn 52 guys. There were some names that the Guv didn't recognize, but that was to be expected, there are always new faces around the barns. He thought for a second, then called Francisco Perez, the Barn 38 manager.

"Frankie, this is the Guv, you got a second"?

"Sure, brother, what's going on"?

"I'm trying to make sense of some stuff I've been working on. It involves the Martin Carrington situation. I know you probably don't want to be involved with it, and that's fine with me, I just want some information, off the record".

Francisco didn't say much, he was wary, just like everybody else. He didn't give a rat's ass about Martin Carrington, he thought the guy was way too arrogant for his own good, but there were a lot of people on the backside who wanted to leave well enough alone. The Guv spoke again before his friend had a chance to get cold feet.

"All I want to do is read you a few names and get you to tell me if they work for you or not. That's it. It won't go further than me".

"Totally off the record, right"?

"That's right. This conversation never took place".

"Okay".

There were nine names the Guv didn't recognize. He named the first six. All were employees of Barn 32. The seventh name was one Francisco didn't know, was not associated with Barn 38, but was on the list of people who got paid through the FCA. The last two names were legitimate, like the first six. The Guv double checked the name in question, just to make sure. There was no question about it. Fransisco didn't know who he was.

The Guv called Rafa back. "Are you by yourself"?

"Yes, why"?

"We have to be very careful with this. Don't let anybody have any idea what we're thinking, not even the detective. In fact, especially the detective".

"Okay, no problem, what did you find out"?

"There's one name on the list of people from Barn 38 that appears to be bogus. I'm not sure yet, but I'm thinking we may be onto something".

The Guv gave Rafa the name. "See if you can get your hacker buddies to check this guy out. We don't need to be jumping to any conclusions, and Rafa, listen to me. Absolutely one hundred percent this is just between me and you. Understand"?

"Yes, one hundred percent".

Pause.

"Rafa".

"Yes".

"Damn good job. Ernie's gone. Martin Carrington is going to have to answer to us".

Chapter 32

Nikki and Ramos started their conversation with small talk, but it wasn't the usual small talk, the kind that doesn't mean anything, it was much more than that, because both were curious about the other, and knew there would be more to this relationship than just making a new friend.

"I love this place", said Nikki.

"Thank you, it has a little history behind it. Back in the day, when cotton was king, a Louisiana man had a pretty good size operation here. This was his house. Having one of the big plantation homes didn't mean much to him I guess, he was just a farmer with a lot of land. Almost all of the land was eventually sold off, all except for the house and a few acres around it. I moved into the house because it was close to the store and nobody lived here. Then a lady that worked for me, who had four children, needed more room, so I offered to let them live here. It worked out well for all of us. The kids were good ones, for the most part. Their mother kept them in line and made them help around the house. I ended up being almost like a father to them. Three of them went to college, the other one is in the military. Their mother died a few years ago. They come back to see me a couple of times a year. I miss them, but I'm glad to see them doing well. Luevada comes for a few hours every day during the week. She pretty much rules the roost around here, which is fine with me. The crowd at Mona's knows they're always welcome here, as long as they act right, and Luevada sees to that. It's like one big, extended family. I like it that way. Now, it's your turn to talk. Tell me about yourself".

Nikki looked at Ramos, not really knowing where to start and feeling a little inadequate compared to him.

"Hector tells me you're in law school", he said, helping her along.

"Yes, at Tulane. Almost finished, thank goodness".

Nikki was silent for a moment. Ramos patiently gave her time to gather her thoughts.

"Can I tell you something"?, she asked.

"Of course, whatever you want".v

"I'm not totally sure why I'm here. The Guv, or Hector.."

Ramos broke in. "Call him the Guv, no problem".

"The Guv said he wanted me to talk to you. I guess about my father, but I'm not exactly sure why, and, I'm not sure what to tell you".

She was struggling a bit, and Ramos didn't want that. He was pretty sure she would relax and talk from the heart, in time, and he didn't want to make her any more uncomfortable than she already was, but he also knew that the sooner they broke the ice, the sooner they could have a real conversation about her father.

"Let's back up a minute. Hector and I go way back. He probably didn't tell you this, but we were in prison together in Peru. We were young men once, believe it or not".

Ramos saw a flicker of a smile.

"We came to Louisiana together. He's like a brother to me. Hector is a good man, better than I am. I think the thing I like best about him is that he doesn't judge other people, period. At the same time, he doesn't worry about others judging him, period. He tells it like it is. It's not always the easiest or best way, but it's his way. I respect him for that".

Ramos was silent for a moment, stared straight ahead. "I went to prison for killing a man. I was sixteen years old. He abused my mother. Beat her up one too many times. I killed him. He deserved it. I don't regret it, but I'm not proud of it either. It was something I had to do, and I did it. He was a powerful man in Peru, and some of his powerful friends wanted revenge. They tried to have me killed, and almost did, but I survived. I learned the hard way that there are bad people in the world. I don't know why that is. I trust a few of my closest friends, like Hector, but nobody else. Every person I meet, I respect, but view as a possible threat until I know for certain otherwise. It's not a good way to live, but whether it's the life I chose, or the life that chose me, it is what it is. It's my life. One good thing, I suppose, is that now I don't fear any man, and people around here know that. The reason that's good is because it gives them confidence. They know there's somebody that will take up for them. Americans that were born here take a lot of stuff for granted. I'm not complaining, I'm just telling you how it is. I understand it. My people, the Peruvians, and their extended families, they don't ask for much, they just want a fair chance to make a life for themselves. They come to me when they have a problem or need help, and I try to help them. That's the way it's been for a long time now. That's why Hector brought you here. It's the first time that's ever happened. Means a lot to him, so it means a lot to me".

There was a long pause. Then Ramos slowly turned toward her, and said in a soft, low voice, "tell me about your father Nikki".

The mood had totally changed. Ramos had done a masterful job of getting to the heart of the matter at hand, without making Nikki do it herself. There was no need to beat around the bush.

"Do you know anything about the story of what happened to him? It was all over the news, so I figure maybe you know a little bit about it, like pretty much everybody else does".

"I know a little, and I did some reading about him after I knew you were coming, but that doesn't matter to me, just start wherever you want to, I'll ask questions I'm quite sure".

"Okay". Deep breath. "He was a wonderful father, and a wonderful person. My mother died about five years ago of breast cancer. She was wonderful too. It was pretty hard on him, but he got through it. I'm an only child, so we spent a lot of time together, before and after she died, but after she died we were closer than ever. I adored him in every way. He took a new job and moved to New Orleans a few years ago. An old friend of his is President of an investment firm there, and he offered my father a job as the chief investment officer, which was a pretty big deal. He took the job and moved from Mobile to New Orleans. I was already at Tulane, so of course I loved it. We spent time together going to restaurants and stuff. Anyway, the new job involved more travelling than he was used to, and he loved it. One of his first big trips was to New York, representing the firm at a conference that included a lot of the big players in international finance. He stayed at the Waldorf Astoria and had a busy weekend that included meeting a young lady from Russia named Natalya. She worked with a Russian Bank called Stezlaus Bank. She was gorgeous, and fun, and my father was totally smitten with her. They basically spent the weekend together. She was divorced, with no children, so it wasn't scandalous or anything like that. Through her he met the movers and shakers at Stezlaus Bank, and that's more or less when the trouble started".

Nikki paused. Ramos got her a glass water to sip on. "Take your time Nikki, you're doing great. Don't worry about all the details, we can go back and fill in if necessary".

"Okay, thanks. Anyway, these guys liked my father, and by the end of the weekend they had become friends. When he left New York to return to New Orleans, he figured he might never see any of them again. He wasn't thrilled with that because he really liked Natalya, and she liked him, but it was just kind of the way it was going to be. A month or so after he got back to New Orleans, he got a call out of the blue from Natalya. She

invited him to a long weekend at some fancy resort in Greece
I've never heard of. Some rich guy got engaged and the Stezlaus
Bank was throwing him a big party. Well, he went, and by the
end of the weekend two things had happened. He officially fell
head over heels in love with Natalya, and the Stezlaus Bank
retained the New Orleans firm as one of it's money managers.
The result of that was that they wired the firm two hundred
million dollars to invest, with the understanding that my father was going to do the investing. What he didn't know, but
she did, was that Stezlaus Bank was connected to the Russian
Mafia".

Nikki paused, and as if on cue, Ramos asked his first
question.

"What do you mean, connected to the Russian Mafia? in
what way"?

"The bank is owned by the Russian Government, and is
split into two parts. The part my father and his firm were doing business with is legitimate. They basically manage the government's money, and they hire people like my father to help
them invest it. The other part is the mafia part, and I don't
know much about it, but they're involved in all kinds of stuff,
including offshore gambling and money laundering, which is
the other part that my father got involved with".

Nikki was pained to say the words. Her father, Gib Carter,
was involved with offshore gambling and money laundering.
Sounds so bad. Is so bad. It had been almost three years, but
hearing herself say the words made it seem like yesterday.

Ramos noticed. He always noticed.

"How is it that you know all of this Nikki"?

"Natalya told me, except her name is not really Natalya, it's Anna. She travelled from Russia to New Orleans to tell me about it. It's all still hard for me to believe".

"I understand. It's quite a story. I know it's not pleasant for you to talk about it, but I think it's good that you are, and I appreciate very much the fact that I'm the one you're sharing it with. Hector told me you're special. You are. I would have known that without his telling me. Take your time and tell me what you know Nikki".

Nikki spoke with more resolve than before. "It's important that you understand something". Pause. "He loved Anna, and she loved him. Crazy, I know, they had spent a total of five or six days together. But sometimes it happens that way. I'm sure about it because she told me, and she didn't just tell me, she showed me. She travelled from Russia to New Orleans to make sure I understood the truth. She didn't do that for herself, she didn't do it for him". Pause. "She did it for me". The first tear, a drop of pure crystal love, dropped from her cheek. "The ten million dollar part is confusing to me. I sort of understand, but not really. I'll do my best to explain that part".

"Okay. Just tell me in your own words. It doesn't have to be perfect, I just want the story".

"There is a guy they call Shanghai who is an expert horse race handicapper. He's affiliated with Burnham Glen Casino near Boston. Stezlaus Bank owns Burnham Glen, not officially, of course, some non descript legal entity owns it, for the record, but Stezlaus Bank owns the legal entity, and so they own Burnham Glen. It takes a lot of digging to figure that out, but I know, because I did the digging. On the way back from Greece, on the private jet, owned by Stezlaus of course, one of the Stezlaus boys told my father about this guy Shanghai. He also told him, bragging I guess, about the huge horse race bets they made with some super exclusive offshore gambling house, also, as it turns out, owned by Stezlaus, using Shanghai's picks". She stopped for a moment to make sure Ramos was following the story. He was.

"The next part is the crazy part, the part that doesn't make sense. A group of the Stezlaus guys have a Tuscan Villa that they own equal shares in. They hang out there, entertain I guess, whatever you do when you own your own Tuscan Villa. One of the guys wanted out, and they offered his ownership share to my father. Only problem was, he didn't have the money. He made a good living, better than most, but these guys had serious cash, and he wasn't in their league. But, he wanted a share of the villa so that he could spend time there with Anna". Nikki took a deep breath and let it out slowly, not enjoying the retelling of the story.

"So, he bet ten million dollars on a damn horse race, using the Stezlaus Bank's money to do it. He was going to use the winnings to buy the share in the Tuscan Villa". She frowned and shook her head, then continued. "He wired the ten million to an offshore account. His horse lost the race. Ten million dollars disappeared into thin air, just like that. Of course he was practically out of his mind trying to decide what to do about it. Everywhere he turned he hit a brick wall. His friend that told him about Burnham Glen and Shanghai said there was nothing he could do about it, as if he had lost ten dollars, not ten million. He did the only thing I guess he figured he could do. He went to Burnham Glen to look for answers. He booked a room, but he never made it there. They were one step ahead of him. I suppose they could tell he wasn't going to be denied an explanation, and they figured they had to keep him quiet, so they took care of him. He was last seen at the airport in Boston. Hasn't been seen or heard from since. They killed him Ramos, in cold fucking blood". Nikki wasn't crying now, she was tired of crying. She wanted somebody to pay, and for the first time, she didn't feel the least bit bad about admitting it.

Ramos showed no sign of emotion. He had quietly listened, now he spoke calmly, with no wasted words. "Hector told me you know the name of the person who you think is responsible".

At first she didn't respond, then she said matter of factly, "Silas Greer".

Chapter 33

The Guv rolled in just after lunch. Rafa was at the barn waiting for him. He was holding papers in his hand. The Guv motioned him into the barn office, and closed the door.

"You look like you have something to show me".

"Yep, like you said Guv, I think we're onto something".

"Tell me about it".

Rafa held up the papers. "This is a list of all of the people from Barns 41, 42 and 43 who have gotten at least one FCA payment in the last two years. There are over a hundred and forty. As you know, those three barns are part of one of the largest racing stables in the U.S. I got my boys to see if they could secretly access the stable's payroll records, then I compared the lists. Out of one hundred forty four names that received cash from Ernie's trust, only one hundred thirty one were on the stable's payroll at any time during the last two years. That's thirteen names that apparently got cash that weren't supposed to. Thirteen fucking names Guv. Maybe there's an explanation, but it looks pretty bogus to me".

The Guv looked at Rafa, the wheels in his head turning. "That piece of shit had a gravy train straight from Ernie's trust to his back pocket. Do you have the amounts of money that those people got"?

"Yes, but I have to go back through the transactions and match the names to the totals. It gets a little confusing because of all the numbers, but it's all there, and I'm working on it".

"Okay, Rafa, I know you're tired of me saying it, but please make absolutely sure nobody else knows about this. There's no telling what that pencil dick is capable of, he's pretty damn slick. And, there will be a hell of a lot more people that want to believe him than want to believe us".

Ramos and Nikki strolled into Mona's as if they owned the joint, which they did, or at least he did. Ramos couldn't suppress a smile as he escorted Nikki to a table for lunch. The employees and regulars who were there were very much impressed, and most were smiling at the sight. It was kind of like your grandfather having a date with a cheerleader, except not weird like that would be. They knew who Nikki was, and knew he wasn't trying to fool anybody into thinking he had suddenly ventured into Hugh Hefner territory. She was enjoying the attention and thought it was sweet that everybody was smiling at Ramos sporting a young hottie into Mona's. Ramos made introductions as the others randomly came by the table. He was obviously the patriarch of the place and was held in high regard by every person there. Nikki thought to herself how very cool it was just to observe the man and his environment. Ramos, as usual, was not just spending idle time enjoying lunch, he was also thinking, and had been all morning. He was going to do something to help Nikki, that was a given. The question was, what would that be?

Ramos Mantilla knew the pain of losing a father. He knew pain from a lot of stuff, but that was his life. This was Nikki's life. He wanted to help, but he also wanted to make sure that anything he did now wouldn't cause problems for her later. She was young. Her future was bright. After she gave him the name Silas Greer, he spent some time on the internet seeing what he could learn about the man. There wasn't a whole lot there, but the more he learned about Stezlaus Bank and Burnham Glen Casino, the more certain he became that the waters Mr. Greer was accustomed to swimming in were deep, dark, and most of all, dangerous. Ramos was seventy eight years old. He had made it a point his whole life to take care of himself, and his health was good. He still exercised, but his troubles in prison had left their mark. He had chronic back problems, and he walked with a noticeable limp, the result of being stabbed numerous times in the lower back and left leg many years ago. He weighed one hundred fifty two pounds, and his calm demeanor was anything but intimidating. Those who knew him, or knew of him, knew those things were deceiving, and that being his enemy was a losing proposition, but Silas Greer wasn't among that group.

Ramos never planned to be a powerful man, it just worked out that way. When he took over Mona's, he was just trying to make a go of it. He worked as hard as any man, but he wasn't ambitious, he just didn't know any other way, and he didn't want to fail. He started his seafood business because he wanted to have the best seafood possible at Mona's. It ended up being one of the largest seafood distributors in Louisiana. He sold it to a group of guys that worked for him. He made money on the sale, but could have made much more. He wanted to help them, so he did. Now they take care of him. Mona's gets the best seafood available, period. He was a quiet man most of the time. In a discussion about anything serious, he would allow others to speak first, measuring them and their words. When he did speak, his calm and confident manner only served to enhance his reputation as someone who commanded respect by just being himself, and as someone who feared no man. In the early days at Mona's, he took care of both his customers and his employees. Of course, in turn, they were loyal to him and to Mona's. People would seek his advice on all sorts of stuff, and in time he became the one they would turn to in times of trouble. One example was a situation that developed with a local group of Peruvian women who worked as house-keepers at a nice hotel in Natchez. They were hard workers, but most were undocumented, so they were always scared of be-ing found out and being punished or even deported. The hotel took advantage of this and gave the Peruvian women the least desirable jobs and work schedules, and no vacation. For a long time they didn't complain, but eventually a few of them got up the courage to talk to Ramos about it. He scheduled a meet-ing with the owner of the hotel, bypassing the hotel manager altogether. After the meeting, the women all got a raise and the work schedule was changed so they each had every other week-end off to spend with their families. The women, and their families, were of course extremely grateful to Ramos for help-ing them. He expected nothing in return, it simply made him smile to see them happy. That's the man he was.

In time, it became common knowledge that any Peruvian that needed an advocate for any legitimate reason, need only to call on Ramos Mantilla. He was like a mafia boss, but with several differences. He wasn't involved in any illegal activity, nobody paid him anything for protection and he didn't get in-volved in politics. He was a proud Peruvian, pure and simple. You mess with his people, you mess with him.

The situation with Nikki was different. She wasn't Peruvian, or even South American, and what happened to her father was totally outside his domain. The most important dif-ference, though, was that this was a friend of Hector's. Hector had never asked him for a favor. He wasn't asking now, not directly, but he wanted to help Nikki, so he came to Ramos.

When they returned to the house Ramos took his usual after lunch nap. Nikki sat outside and read a book, soaking in the mild Louisiana Spring day. She wasn't sure what the result of meeting this man would be, but she was very sure that being with him was time well spent. When he awoke from his siesta, he joined her in the back yard. Within a few minutes Luevada walked out of the house.

"Ya'll shook things up at Mona's, I've already heard all about it. Mr. Ray and his new young girlfriend". She laughed. "News travels fast around here Nikki".

"I see that. Maybe I should have held his hand or something to make it seem more real".

Now the three of them were laughing. Ramos chimed in. "Nobody in that place thinks I'm Nikki's boyfriend, I promise you that. They just want something to gossip about".

"Well you damn sure gave them what they wanted then", replied Luevada. Still laughing. "Ya'll okay? Can I get you anything? You want coffee Mr. Ray"?

"I guess so. Nikki, would you like coffee or something else to drink"?

"Do you have hot tea"?

"Sure, as long as you like Earl Gray", answered Luevada.

"Sounds great".

Luevada delivered the beverages, then turned to go back inside. "Let me know if you need anything else". She paused for a moment, then started walking, "lovebirds". She let out a laugh that was louder than before. Ramos just shook his head and chuckled.

Ramos spoke, and as soon as he did, his tone and facial expression told Nikki that the serious discussion had resumed.

"Nikki, I want to ask you some questions. I'm not sure where this is going, but I want to have as much information about Silas Greer and what happened to your father as possible".

"Okay".

"You said he wired ten million dollars to an offshore account".

"Yes".

"Explain to me how that money could just disappear. Was it some kind of secret, numbered account or something? It seems to me in a serious criminal investigation somebody would have to explain where the money went".

"I know". Pause. "Believe me, I know. The FBI spent months trying to find the money. I spent months trying to find the money. The account was bogus. The offshore sportsbook was bogus. Stezlaus Bank has a network of numbered offshore accounts that they use for money laundering purposes. When you trace the money trail to one of these accounts, you find that it's owned by some generic sounding holding company that nobody seems to know anything about". Pause. "My father, in the normal course of things, would never consider wiring money, any amount of money, to an offshore address he knew nothing about, no way. But the circumstances behind that wire transfer were much different than the normal course of things. He was in a different place, emotionally. He was blinded by love". She was trying to hold back tears.

Ramos spoke. "Life would be easier if we all did what we should do all the time, but it wouldn't be much of a life. I have no doubt your father was a good man. I'm sure of it". Pause. "Even good men screw things up sometimes. He wasn't the first and won't be the last. Just the way it is".

"Most of them don't lose their life because of it", said Nikki, with a sharp tone, no emotion.

Ramos wasn't expecting that kind of response. He looked at Nikki for several seconds. "No, they don't".

The Oaklawn Park meet was winding down, only two more weeks, plus The Racing Festival of The South. After that, the barns empty out, the crowds go home, and everybody waits until the following January to do it all again. The backside crew moves on also, sort of like a travelling show, to the next track on the circuit. Once again, a tough way to live, but they keep doing it, it's who they are, thoroughbred horse people.

The fact that the Oaklawn meet would end soon gave the Guv and Rafa a greater sense of urgency to expose Martin Carrington for who he really was, a murderer. Rafa had spent hours examining the FCA records, and cross checking the names of backside workers with the names on the FCA list. There were discrepancies, but the numbers worked out. Rafa was certain that Martin was skimming money from the trust, using the bogus names to do it, but he wasn't sure how. Then it hit him. Again, it was so simple and obvious. The money the FCA gave to the backside workers was deposited onto cash cards issued to each person. The names on the cards were irrelevant. The cards didn't even need names on them, but by putting the names on them, they were more personal, and theoretically, the cash on the card was the property of the person whose name was on the card. In reality, though, it was simply a cash card, which meant that Martin could use the bogus cards the same as if his name were on them. Simple as that. He gave the list of names to the FCA, they issued the cards and distributed the cash to the individual cards. The barns had no reason to question anything. All of the names on the list were getting their cash. Martin had in his possession somewhere in the neighborhood of twenty bogus cards, each one getting re-loaded every week with more cash.

Rafa was excited, and pissed off even more than ever. The Guv was right. That prick had a gravy train going directly from Ernie's trust into his back pocket. He wanted to talk to the Guv right away, but the Guv was busy in the paddock, putting the saddle on the promising young filly he had told his friend about. Rafa decided to do what any person with half a brain would do in that situation. He bought a beer and a corned beef, put a ten spot on the filly, and settled in to watch her run.

Ramos spoke, "Nikki, I want you to stay here one more night. You can leave in the morning. Between now and then I want you to tell me everything you know about Stezlaus Bank and Silas Greer, every little detail you remember. Then I want you to do the same with Anna and all the people at Burnham Glen. I'm not the best with computers, and I don't have a clue about secret offshore accounts, but I know a few things about people".

"Okay", long pause, "Ramos, I have to tell you something".
"Alright".

"I'm worried about causing trouble with these people. What's done is done. I know my father, and I can just picture him right now begging me to just let it go, because he's afraid of what might happen to me if I seek revenge or try to get some kind of justice. The whole thing has been one long nightmare, and I can't help feeling that if I stir things up, the nightmare will continue, and maybe get worse".

Ramos sighed heavily, stared straight ahead for a while.

"I don't have all the answers Nikki, not even close. For your sake I wish I did, but I don't. You have to decide what's best for yourself. Life is tough that way". Long pause. "If you ask me not to be involved, then that's the way it will be, and I will respect you for that, one hundred percent. But I know, and I think you know, it's not that simple. They killed your father, that will never change, no matter what anybody does. What I want", Pause. "for you, for him and for Hector, is to restore his good name. Not back to where it was. That's not possible. He was a flawed man, like all of us. That you have to live with. But as it stands now, he stole ten million dollars and disappeared into the night. That's not true. It's a lie, and I want to help you correct it. I don't know if I can, It's a scary proposition, for me as well as you. I can't sugarcoat it Nikki. It's a risk, but I believe it's a risk worth taking". Pause. Ramos shakes his head. "Life's not fair. I'll help if I can. It's your call".

Nikki's composure waivered, and she began, slowly at first, to sob. Then she gave in, and cried and cried and cried.

The filly ran second, beaten by a half length. Rafa looked at his mutuel ticket, then tossed it in the air and let it flutter to the ground. Part of the ritual at the track. Let those babies fly. Get those sombitches, those losing tickets, away from you immediately, and get on with the next race.

The Guv was duly impressed with Rafa's progress. They both knew, though, that there was still a lot of work to be done. They were close to having solid proof that Martin was stealing the money, but that was just part of the puzzle. The other part was going to be tougher, proving that Martin pulled the trigger.

It was after dinner. They were once again in the barn office, door closed. The Guv spoke. "I'm guessing somehow Ernie knew, or maybe suspected, that Martin was skimming money. He confronted Martin with it, and that prick was ready with the pea shooter, fucking coward".

"Makes sense to me, but how do we prove it"?

"I don't know, but one thing is certain. If we're right, Lonnie didn't do it. But Lonnie has confessed that he did do it. Something's gotta give".

"Do you think it's possible that for some reason Lonnie confessed to killing Ernie, but he really didn't?, why would he do that?, there's got to be more to it".

The Guv sat silently, thinking it through, elbows on desk, chin in hands. He stood, crossed his arms, looked down, mouth tight, then breathed out, relaxed his face and looked at Rafa. "Tomorrow I'm going to the jail to have a discussion with Lonnie. We'll see what he has to say".

CHAPTER 34

Nikki was counting the miles, wishing they would click off a little faster, or a lot faster. It was an easy drive, Ferriday to New Orleans, but today it didn't seem that way. She was exhausted. Mentally. Emotionally. She just wanted to relax and not think at all, about anything. Ha ha.

She had good reason to be mentally spent. Ramos asked question after question, even taking notes as he went. Most of it was no fun, some painful, reliving the visit to Burnham Glen, the conversations with Clarence and Shanghai and the rest. The human mind, and healthy human spirit, is pretty good at leaving the bad stuff behind, the details anyway, and those were exactly what Ramos wanted, details. Beneath it though, after the exhaustion has come and gone, is the therapeutic value of sharing the stuff, good and bad, that is there, and always will be, with someone who not only listens and cares, but who also has a fierce belief in the good, and the guts to do battle with the bad. The last hour of her drive home was not spent thinking about just her conversation with Ramos, though, she was also savoring a genuine New Orleans roast beef PoBoy, with debris, from her favorite hole in the wall joint just around the corner from her apartment. The corned beef at Oaklawn was excellent, but this was the mother's milk, just the way it is.

Lonnie wasn't used to having visitors. He had lots of friends, but they weren't real big on just dropping by the joint for a chat. Just as well, really, as far as he was concerned. It was just too awkward. He was thirty three, he would only be forty eight when he got out, possibly even forty three if he got paroled the first go around, plenty of time to start over.

One of those friends was the Guv, but he wasn't one of the few that might, occasionally, just show up. The Guv and Ernie were tight, really tight. Lonnie couldn't think of many, if any, good reasons why he would be here right now.

"Hey Lonnie".

"Hey Guv, what brings you to this fine establishment"?

The Guv, being the Guv, didn't even consider saying anything other than the straight up truth. "I don't think you killed Ernie".

Lonnie looked at the Guv as if he were waiting for more, but that was it. "Why do you say that"?

"Number one, I don't think you would and I just don't think you did, but the main reason is that I think Martin Carrington did it".

It was obvious that Lonnie was surprised at the statement. His mind immediately went to the possibility that he could actually be looking at a chance to get out. But he was not going to be jumping to any conclusions, he needed to figure out what was going on, so he played it cool. "I don't understand. I haven't heard you say that before. Why are you saying it now"?

"I'll tell you, but first I want you to tell me the truth. Did you kill Ernie"?

Lonnie didn't blink. "You could have told me you were coming Guv". The Guv said nothing, also didn't blink. Lonnie broke eye contact, looked to the side, then back. "What is this all about Guv? I cut a deal, here I am. Why are you acting this way"?

"Because you didn't kill him Lonnie, Martin did, and he needs to answer for it. I don't know why you decided to cut a deal, that's your business, but because you did that fucking scumbag gets off scot free. That's not right. I have my reasons for being upset about it. Ernie was my man, my best friend in the world. Martin Carrington killed him Lonnie. Are you just going to let him get away with it"?

"There's a lot you don't know Guv".

"No shit, Sherlock. What I do know is that you're going to tell me, right now, did you kill Ernie"?

Lonnie glanced around, wishing the Guv would just go away, but knowing that wasn't happening. Lonnie wasn't a bad seed, he was just someone who always seemed to find trouble. His role models weren't exactly Ozzie and Harriet. His father was long gone. He, his mother and cousin had a small time drug dealing operation, mostly weed, that had grown big enough to get the attention of the local police. The cops knew half the customers, and considered them pretty much harmless, so they looked the other way. Lonnie had been to rehab twice, but could never quite get over the hump. He had twenty five grand in credit card debt, no job and no prospects. He hung out at the track, and in spite of all his faults, was well liked by almost everybody. It came as a surprise when they found the gun in his car, but most people just figured it was another chapter in the crazy story that was his life. Lonnie proclaimed his innocence, but it didn't look good. He didn't have an alibi. He had, once again, been stoned, drunk and passed out at home the night of the murder, but nobody could vouch for that, and when the murder weapon turned up in his car, his world started closing in pretty quickly. One day, after they got absolutely nowhere trying to get a confession, the cops started playing hard ball. They started talking life in prison, maybe even death penalty, but the clincher was when they said his mother was next on their list if he didn't cooperate. There was pressure to solve the case, and he was their man. The District Attorney waltzed in and acted like Lonnie had just hit the fucking lottery. He was offering him a deal. Fifteen years, possible parole after ten. His mother and cousin would go on the do no disturb list. All of his debt would disappear. He even hinted that Lonnie might be sent to a low risk prison that had access to the Oaklawn Park television signal. Lonnie took the deal. The case was solved. Everybody relaxed. That is, almost everybody.

The Guv stared a hole through Lonnie, then his look changed to one that was less threatening. His eyes were pleading."Lonnie, please, please, I swear on a stack of bibles, I swear on Ernie's grave Lonnie, it will never go further than me. It's between you and me, on my honor Lonnie. Did you kill Ernie"?

The Guv was locked in to Lonnie's eyes. Lonnie looked like he was about to cry. His face twitched slightly. He bit his lip. Said nothing. Broke eye contact and tried to calm himself.

"Tell me Lonnie. Do it for Ernie. Lonnie, please, just tell me the truth". Pause. "Please". Long pause. The Guv closed his eyes.

Visitation was over. A guard came to take Lonnie away.

Lonnie glanced at the Guv. Saw him that way. Felt the pressure on his heart. On his soul.

"For God's sake Lonnie, for Ernie Lonnie, did you do it"?

Lonnie was walking away. Tormented. He stopped, turned back, looked at the Guv, and shook his head, no.

By the time Nikki unlocked her apartment door, Ramos was well on his way toward finishing the first draft of a plan. He had spent hours mulling over the possibilities, but he kept coming back to the simplest approach, just go see Silas Greer and ask for the money back. It also seemed like the craziest approach. Ten million was mucho dinero. No way he would just say "okay, here you go". So what then? What to do when he said no? That was not so simple.

Ramos, although his reputation was that of a powerful man, had not been in a position that required him to use that power in a long time. He didn't think of it as a bad thing, the fact that he lived his life now as a kindly gent, he liked it. He had never aspired to power and influence, it came to him because of circumstances and the way he handled them. Funny thing about power though, it has proven time and again that it can change a man. As Ramos did his homework on Silas Greer and Stezlaus Bank, he began to feel a twinge of something familiar, something on the most base level of a man. A slight little twinge of adrenaline, or something similar. It felt good, but it also worried him. Was he getting excited because he might have the opportunity to inflict pain, physical pain, as he had before, many years ago? Or, was he just getting excited about the prospect of helping Nikki? The thought of killing a man, or being killed, didn't scare him much. The thought of the possibility that he might want to kill again, that he was excited by it, was a totally different thing. It terrified him. And try as he might, it was not a thought that could be simply dismissed. It terrified him, but it didn't deter him. He had a job to do. Not literally, but that's the way he viewed it. His own demons were just another aspect of that job that had to be dealt with.

Another challenge for Ramos was the fact that, after prison, he had never had to deal with an adversary away from his home territory. Silas Greer lived and worked in The Cayman Islands, a well known tax haven and home to many financial entities of all types. Ramos thought he could deal with the Caymans. It wasn't home, but it was in the Caribbean, not half way across the globe, and they spoke English. There was nothing, on the surface, that connected Silas Greer to Stezlaus Bank. The company he controlled was called Transcon Holdings, pretty generic by almost any measure. Ramos knew he was way out of his league when it came to the subject of International Finance, so he made no attempt to understand it. Good call. The maze of money behind the facade of Transcon Holdings would be a challenge to even the brightest and the best who had spent their lives in such places. Money laundering was another matter, he understood that, at least the basic concept. Transcon Holdings was one big money laundering machine, and that's all he needed to know.

The offices of Transcon Holdings were on the eighth floor of a ritzy, yet understated building connected to a ritzy, understated hotel and resort complex in Georgetown, Grand Cayman. His was a life of privilege, but Mr. Greer valued his privacy.

Inside the complex, he had a luxury condo, a driver, and all the amenities he could possibly want at his beck and call. He could leave his office and walk to his condo without ever leaving the grounds, or without ever even stepping outside. His favorite amenity, so to speak, was a mid thirties vixen who lived, oh how convenient, in a luxury condo of her own in the same complex, owned, of course, by Transcon Holdings. Nice.

Nikki was busy trying to restore some order to her life. She was supposed to finish law school in less than two months. She met with her advisor, and they mutually agreed, with the school's blessing, that she would finish the following semester instead. They allowed the current semester to not count at all, and assured her that she was in good standing with the school. She was also supposed to be married soon, but that date had already been postponed, and no new date had been set. Her fiance, Reggie, was not happy with the situation. She understood. For about six months she had been, literally and figuratively, in another place, and it wasn't clear what the implications of that might be, to either of them, so things needed to settle out before new plans were made. Intertwined in there, somewhere, was the other thing she had to deal with, if she was honest with herself, before she could move on. Rafa.

Ramos, being slight in stature, had learned a long time ago to make up for it with superior knowledge, preparation and when necessary, cunning. He poured himself into learning all he could about Silas Greer and Stezlaus Bank. It wasn't easy. They were very private, and careful to protect themselves from any threat, from wherever it might come. He had some things in his favor. He was an old man, who appeared to be almost frail. His English was good, but there was no mistaking his hispanic roots. His dress and manner were not only non threatening, but humble. Perhaps his most disarming trait was his calm, almost meek demeanor. It was easy for him, because it was his natural way. He spent hours doing his due diligence. He wanted to know as much as possible about every aspect of Transcon Holdings, Burnham Glen Casino and Stezlaus Bank. Most of all, though, he wanted to know about Silas Greer, not just about the businessman Silas Greer, but about the man, his personality, his habits, and above all, his biggest weakness. He took a two day trip to Georgetown, Grand Cayman to scout it out, he dressed like an old hippie, complete with dreadlocks, and familiarized himself with the area, paying cash for a cheap room in a cheap hotel. The next day he was dressed in an Italian suit. He walked into the Transcon Holdings building as if he owned the joint, never made eye contact with anybody, checked it out to his satisfaction, then did the same at the adjoining resort hotel. He spent extra time at the airport and surrounding area. He wanted to leave as little as possible to chance. After returning home to Ferriday, he asked a young Peruvian computer expert, who had a dubious reputation as a hacker, to help him. He was amazed at the information the young man was able to provide him about Silas Greer and his world, more than he really needed, or wanted, to know. He was every bit as sinister as Ramos had figured, maybe more. Ramos knew men of that type often would, because of their outsized egos, lose touch with the mundane details of life that most people have to deal with. Therein Ramos found the weakness he was looking for, and as he explored it, another one emerged, also typical of the narcissistic, macho male. The irresistible allure of a beautiful woman. He was still a ways from being ready to have a conversation with the man, but he was getting there.

Rafa was frustrated. He had no doubt that Martin was skimming the cash, but he had no iron clad proof, and no proof at all that he was Ernie's killer. On top of that, the Guv was acting funny. He had been to see Lonnie, but he wasn't saying much about it. When Rafa asked questions about the meeting, he was evasive. Didn't make sense. After a time, the Guv finally told Rafa that he had promised Lonnie that he wouldn't share what they discussed with anybody, and that he intended to keep the promise. Admirable, except we're talking murder, not some family secret.

The deposits were made to the cash cards every Friday. There was a Mexican restaurant and grocery store within walking distance of the track. Most of the backside workers bought groceries there, or on occasion ate meals there. The owner of the place allowed the Oaklawn workers, with any purchase, to get as much cash back as they wanted without a fee, as long as the cash was on the card. Most of the workers would make a purchase there, and get cash back, almost every Friday. The people at the store got to know the names of a lot of the Oaklawn group. Rafa showed the owner and his employees a list of names he thought were bogus, and asked him if any of the names were familiar. None were. Then he had an idea. If Martin was skimming cash, he would want just that, cash. If he used the cards themselves to make purchases, there would be a paper trail, but if he got cash from an ATM and then made purchases, he was good to go, no paper trail.

Martin's office was in a nondescript building not too far from his home. Rafa didn't have a car, so he borrowed the Guv's truck. Friday morning he parked a safe distance away from Martin's home, and watched as he left the house and drove straight to the office. Mid morning he left the office, stopped by the post office, then drove to an upscale specialty grocery store and deli. He went in, and immediately went to the ATM machine at the front of the store. Rafa couldn't get close enough to see the card, but if the time it took Martin to retrieve his cash from the machine and count it was any indication, it was a large withdrawal, probably the maximum allowed at that machine. He did some shopping, buying just a few items, then left. His next stop was a large and busy gas station/truck stop. This time Rafa followed him in, staying just far enough away to not be noticed, but close enough to watch Martin, once again, head to the ATM machine and make what appeared to be a large cash withdrawal. He paid cash for gas, pumped it, and left. The third stop took the cake. Oaklawn Park. He strolled in, said hello to several people, stopped for a short chat with the comely young filly getting the gift shop ready to open, then, bingo, headed to the ATM for another cash withdrawal. He then headed to the track offices, presumably to do something important, but more likely to curry favor for his selfless devotion to the lost souls of Oaklawn Park. Rafa was no saint, wasn't even a Christian, but his heart was pure, and he admired people of integrity. He didn't admire Martin Carrington.

Chapter 35

"**Mr. Ray, you're** up to something. I don't know what it is, but it's something. If you need my help with anything, you know you can count on me".

"Thank you Luevada, it's nothing important enough to involve you. But I am planning a trip. I'll probably leave early next week. Not sure how long I'll be gone. I know I can count on you to look after things around here while I'm gone. That's pretty important to me".

"Where you going"?

"It's better if I don't tell you that. It's an important business trip. If anybody asks, you can just tell them that".

"I don't like the sound of it, but I'm sure it's important, as much time as you're spending getting ready. Just be safe, okay"?

"Okay, I will. You don't worry".

Ramos kept to the task. He studied Burnham Glen and Stezlaus Bank. Burnham Glen was easy, just a matter of putting in the time to learn what he needed to know. Stezlaus Bank was another story. There was a lot of stuff he just didn't understand. There were layers of security and seemingly endless subsidiary companies. If that weren't tough enough, the people involved were one big jumble of Russian names and job titles. He decided to simply avoid anything more than just a mention of Stezlaus. He had the names of a couple of people at the bank if he needed to mention them, but he hoped he wouldn't. His focus was going to be on the man, Silas Greer. He had plenty to be worried about. Silas Greer was big time. He had two bodyguards that stayed with him during the day, all day, every day he was at work, sometimes after hours if he wasn't inside his compound. Inside, the security system was virtually impenetrable, so he felt safe enough to move around on his own during his leisure time inside the perimeter of his compound, which included the office building and the luxury hotel. The rest of the resort was not as secure, but was still gated and monitored twenty four seven, three sixty five. He had a home in London, and his wife was there. He had a private jet that took him anywhere in the world at a moment's notice, but he didn't use it much. One of his bodyguards was a very menacing looking man. Large, huge muscles, thick neck, permanent scowl, intelligent eyes, just the kind of guy you would expect. The other was different. Younger, average size, good looking, cocky. He was his wife's nephew, so he was family, but not by blood. Silas didn't like him. Too sure of himself, with an attitude of invincibility, but he was loyal, so he stayed.

Ramos spent a lot of time on the phone and the computer, arranging his trip. He wanted to eliminate as many variables as possible, so he kept at it, hoping for the best, but preparing for the worst. He arranged to have some of his connections in Peru help him. He swore everybody to absolute secrecy. He racked his brain, over and over, trying to think of anything that could go wrong, and what he would do if it did. He booked multiple hotel rooms, flights, excursions, car rentals, limousines, dinner reservations. He bought at least two of every conceivable electronic gadget that he might need. He had his own story for why he was there, and two back ups. He prepared for rain, sun, wind, daylight, dark. His mind never quit preparing. Would have made a hell of a Boy Scout.

The day before he left he spent time at Mona's, having lunch and visiting. It made him feel good. He called the Guv.

"Hello my friend, how are the ponies doing today"?

"Good, I'm getting nervous, big week coming up, we're running four of them. They're ready, but I'm not sure if I am".

Laughter. "Relax Hector, they will do well, I'm sure of it. Put a few pesos on all four for me. I'll collect next time I see you".

"You got it".

"I called to tell you I'm going on a trip. I'm going to try to help Nikki. I don't want to tell you more than that, for your own protection, you know what I mean".

"Shit, I don't like the way that sounds. You don't owe me anything, you know that. I was hoping you might be able to help her, but I don't want you to put yourself in danger, and neither does she, I promise you that. Are you sure about this"?

"Yes, totally".

"Have you told her"?

"No. I want you to do that".

"Son of a fuckin bitch. She's going to be scared to death for you. Damn, damn, damn, why did I get you involved? What the hell am I supposed to tell her"?

"Calm down, you'll figure it out. Just be truthful".

"How can I be truthful when I don't know where you're going and what you're going to be doing? The truth is, I wish you would seriously reconsider. I can't stand the thought of something bad happening to you Ramos. Son of a fucking bitch. Why did I call you? Can't you send somebody else to do the dangerous stuff?, or just forget that altogether and try to work something out behind the scenes". Deep sigh. "Man, oh man".

Pause.

"I'm going because I want to go Hector. That's the truth. I appreciate your concern, and I love you for it, but this is my decision. It's a blessing to meet Nikki. Period. I've thought this through, over and over. I'm prepared. Trust me on that. I love you my brother, and I'll see you soon".

Long Pause.

"Ramos". The Guv was foundering, wanting to say something, but not finding the words. His voice was beginning to crack. "Be careful".

"I will, don't you worry".

Rafa was so disgusted with Martin Carrington that it was all he could do to stay out of the way. He wanted to confront the man, right then, right there. He really, really wanted to kick his ass, beat his ass to a pulp, right then, right there. He didn't. He left the front side of the track, headed to the backside, and made a beeline to Barn 52. The Guv was nowhere to be seen. He asked around and was told that the Guv had taken the afternoon off to take care of some business in downtown Hot Springs. Strange. Not like the Guv to take a whole afternoon off. He started to call him, then changed his mind. Let the man do what he needed to do, they would talk later. It was lunch time, but he wasn't hungry, so he did the logical thing, walked across Central Avenue to the Longshot Saloon, and bellied up to the bar.

After two beers, he started to relax, after three, he found his groove. The bartender knew Rafa wasn't driving, so the fourth was on the house. He was chatting with the bartender, watching the crowd, and as he started on number five, out of nowhere, he thought of Nikki. He was crazy about her. He couldn't help it. And he had been sure she felt the same way, but here he was, on a bar stool in Hot Springs, and she was in New Orleans, with no plans to return to Arkansas. He was still having a hard time understanding that. He tried thinking of other things. No luck, he had Nikki on his mind. Nikki. She was so damn fine. When he kissed her his heart skipped a beat. And she kissed him back, really kissed him back. And she held him, and he held her, close. And she was so damn soft and warm. And he could hear her breathe, and he could feel her breathe. Damn. Nikki. Damn. After the fifth beer the bartender brought out a plate of fried mushrooms and put them in front of Rafa. It took him seven minutes to eat all of them.

He paid his tab and walked back across the street. Post time for the fifth race was fifteen minutes away. If he were his father, if he were Ernie, he would head to the betting windows. But he wasn't, and he didn't. He didn't watch the race at all. Just didn't feel like it. Nikki. Damn.

The Guv was dreading the call, but once Nikki was on the line, he relaxed. "Hey Nikki, this is your old friend, Guv".

"Guv, I miss you terribly, please tell me you're coming to New Orleans for a visit".

A happy chuckle. "No, but I like the way you think. I need to work on that".

"Yes you do. I'm not kidding. Promise me you will Guv".

Nikki could practically see the smile on the Guv's face.

"Okay, I promise".

"Woo hoo, party time. Make room for the Guv".

Laughing. "You're sweet, girl".

"So, what's up Guv"?

Pause. "I just want to let you know that Ramos is arranging a meeting with Silas Greer". The Guv, astutely, didn't pause for a reaction, but kept going in a conversational tone. "It probably will happen next week. He asked me to tell you, because he was afraid you might think he's doing it because you expect him to. That's not the case. He likes you a lot Nikki, and he wants to help. He does stuff all the time to help people. It's who he is. I told him you would be concerned for his safety. He knows that. That's the other reason I'm calling instead of him. You need to trust me on this Nikki, he's going regardless of all that, he wants to, and that's the way it is". Silence, broken by the Guv. "You okay?, talk to me".

"I don't know what to say Guv. I'm really, really afraid of what might happen". Pause, sigh. "It terrifies me. He hardly knows me. Those people are bad Guv".

"I know that. He knows that. I had the same reaction. It terrifies me too. But Nikki, listen to me. Win lose or draw, this is the way it has to be, and whatever happens, never doubt that". Pause. "And, Nikki, however bad they are, they're not as bad as he is. I'm not kidding".

Nikki was crying. Said nothing.

"You okay girl"?

Pause. "I guess so".

There were two weeks left in the Oaklawn meet. This one and the next, the Racing Festival of the South. Rafa was getting anxious. He hadn't really given much thought to what would happen at the end of the race meet, but now it was a very big deal. After the Oaklawn meet, the Guv would be gone to Kentucky. Almost the whole backside would be gone, to Kentucky and elsewhere. Following the ponies.

There was absolutely no doubt in Rafa's mind that Martin was the guy. He knew the Guv was just as certain, but for some reason he seemed to be dragging his feet. He wouldn't talk about his meeting with Lonnie, and he seemed distracted, as if he had something on his mind. But what could possibly be more important to him than finding Ernie's killer? It was time to have a talk.

The Guv was at the barn, talking to one of his guys, when Rafa walked up. They both looked at him.

"Sorry to interrupt", said Rafa, then he looked at the Guv. "Can I talk to you for a minute after you're through"?

"Of course, I'll just be a minute".

One minute was more like five, not bad for the Guv. He joined Rafa on the rail watching the morning workouts. "How bout breakfast, on me"?

Rafa grinned at the Guv's magnanimous offer to spring for a four dollar breakfast at the track kitchen. "Sounds good, let's do it, maybe I'll get pancakes".

"No, don't think so, this ain't fucking Waffle House".

Rafa laughed. They sat near the rear of the dining area, away from those with a curious ear. "What's on your mind, young man"?

"Funny, I was going to ask you that. It seems to me you've been distracted Guv, which is none of my business really, except that I want to nail Martin Carrington, and it might be a lot harder to do after the live meet ends in a couple of weeks. Do you agree"?

"Yes. There are two reasons I've been distracted, one of which has to do with Martin. The first, which doesn't, is that I've been talking to Nikki about her father, and as a result I introduced her to a friend of mine you don't know, named Ramos Mantilla. Do you know the story of Nikki's father"?

"Yes".

"I didn't until last week. When she told me the story, I thought of Ramos, so I took her to see him. Sounds crazy, but I thought it was worth letting them talk. Now I'm sort of questioning that decision. Anyway, that's the first reason. The second, more relevant reason, is that I'm not sure what to do about Martin".

"What do you mean by that"?

"Well, you know how crazy this town is for horse rac-ing. Oaklawn is the crown jewel. Anything that's a threat to Oaklawn is a threat to half the people in Hot Springs, probably more. Martin doesn't work for Oaklawn, but he's the official track chaplain. You may think that's a crock of shit, and it is, but it means something to a lot of people".

"Wait". Rafa interrupted. "What are you talking about Guv? I never in a million years thought I would say this, but you sound like a damn politician. That scumbag put a bullet through Ernie's heart. Killed him in cold blood. And he's still strutting around in his ostrich skin fucking boots acting like nothing's wrong, like it's our damn good fortune to be some-where in his realm of influence. This piece of dog shit is going to answer for what he's done, and he's going to do it real damn soon. I love you Guv, and I admire you for helping Nikki, but she's not the only one who lost a father. If you're having second thoughts, that's fine, I'm sure you have your reasons, but I'm not, and I swear to God, I'm making Martin Carrington pay, with or without you".

The Guv put his head in his hands, looked down, eyes closed.

"If that sombitch is still strutting around a week from to-day, have at it. Conversation's over, get out of here".

Chapter 36

Ramos didn't like flying. He preferred to stay on the ground. He was okay with being on the water, but that didn't work for him this time, so he booked a flight to Georgetown, Grand Cayman. It was a lovely place, the weather almost perfect. Wouldn't be a bad place to hang out if he were so inclined. He wasn't. He had a job to do.

They all met at the Sand Dollar, a vintage seaside inn, according to the description on the internet. They could have just said it was a kinda cool, old cheap ass place to stay, reasonably clean and convenient to the honky tonks on the outskirts of town. They didn't say that, but they could have, would have been more accurate. It was just what Ramos wanted. An out of the way, low profile place to hang out for a couple of days and get ready. There were seven Peruvians in all, including Ramos, staying there, all under assumed names. All with full credentials if they were to need them. The third day, Ramos would move to a different location, a room reserved using his real name in one of the nicest hotels on the island. He was planning to never spend the night there, but he had a reservation, and would be registered there if anybody checked. The Peruvians were there to help Ramos with his plan. He only knew one of them, one of his cousins named Enrique. Enrique was very bright and totally trustworthy. Four of the others were a Peruvian family. Mom, dad and two children. That's what they were supposed to be anyway. In truth, they weren't that at all. They were Enrique's recruits. Their only job was to look and act like a family on vacation in Grand Cayman. The other was a con artist and thief, who was highly skilled at covert tactics, including gaining entrance to places thought to be too secure to do so. Ramos had hired him, at no small price, on the recommendation of several people who knew about such things. Enrique's job was to be ready, at a moment's notice, for any contingency, including one in which Ramos' plan fell apart and the other six would leave the island without him.

They had a cookout under the stars, just like they often did in Trujillo. There would be a growing tension among the group over the next two days, but for now the mood was relaxed. Ramos told them that they wouldn't discuss anything serious that evening, but would get down to business the next morning. That allowed them all to enjoy a pleasant evening, which they did.

They met the next morning in Enrique's room at the Sand Dollar. Ramos did the talking. His self assured manner and calm demeanor gave the rest of them confidence. He went over every detail. It would have been tedious if it weren't for the way he engaged each one of them in the discussion. After a while the kids were allowed to leave the room and have some time to themselves. Ramos then matter of factly explained to the adults, in general terms, what the goal of all this planning was. As he put it, it was to restore the good name of Gib Carter, by getting the people he was meeting with to rectify a wrong that was done several years ago that resulted in the death of Mr. Carter. He never mentioned Silas Greer, Stezlaus Bank or Burnham Glen Casino. Everybody in the room understood that if he wanted them to know something, he would tell them, otherwise, they just needed to follow instructions. They were all glad they were on the same side as Ramos Mantilla.

CHAPTER 37

One thing about New Orleans, they know how to eat. More than that, they take the time to eat, and drink, and cook, and enjoy the company of others who also like those things. The Big Easy.

On St. Louis Street in the French Quarter is Johnny's Po Boys. It's been there since 1950. It's a damn good place to eat. The proprietors are third generation New Orleanians. Don't bother bringing your credit card, they won't take it. Cash only. There's no pretense here, just the real deal. Red beans and rice, po boys, gumbo. Order at the counter.

Nikki and Gib were regulars. Nikki took the streetcar, Gib walked from his office. They would meet at Johnny's. There was almost always a line, but that was okay, it was worth the wait, and it gave them more time to talk, and laugh. Gib was funny, a little goofy maybe, but in a good way. He made Nikki smile. She missed him terribly. Always would.

Nikki was nervous about Ramos going to see Silas Greer. She couldn't bear to think about the possibility that it wouldn't end well. She barely knew the man, Ramos Mantilla. She tried to put it out of her mind. She needed a respite. She hopped on the streetcar and headed to Johnny's. Ordered a fried shrimp poboy, walked to Jackson Square, and had lunch. The day was sunny and mild. The Big Easy vibe was alive and well. There was a lady near her with a table set up for tarot card reading. She certainly dressed the part. Long hair adorned with ribbon and falling over her shoulders. Loose gold and red dress. Necklaces, bracelets, rings. Weathered face and deep, dark eyes. It occurred to Nikki that she looked like a Gypsy, which of course made her think of Rafa, her Gypsy boy. When she thought of Rafa she didn't just think something, she felt something. She kept telling herself that it would go away, that feeling, but so far it hadn't. She had sort of made a deal with herself, she would have fond memories of Rafa, the way he lived life, laughed. He was so damn smart, how was that possible having grown up in a commune? Probably not fair, calling it a commune, he called it a Roma community. She was still engaged, and was going to get married, she was sure of it. That's what she told herself. The wedding hadn't been cancelled, just postponed. Reggie, her fiance, was a great guy. They would have a great life together, she was certain of it. The lovemaking with Reggie was pretty good, and probably more civilized than making love to Rafa would be, that's for sure. Crazy ass Gypsy.

The Gypsy was doing some reflecting of his own. It was frustrating, doing all that work, having all the proof they needed to at least get Martin in big trouble for stealing money from Ernie's charitable trust, and just sitting on it. He hadn't spoken to the Guv in two days, which had never happened before. He was thinking he might as well pack his bags and get out of town, like Nikki did. Nikki, damn Nikki. Maybe he had misread her, maybe she was just like a lot of the other American girls he had met, nice to look at, fun to engage in a bit of repartee with, but not too interested in dating a Gypsy. It didn't really matter, he was focused on the one thing that did matter, redemption, for Ernie, for his father. Nikki was old news. Good riddance. Damn Nikki. He was better off without her, of that he was certain.

CHAPTER 38

The relaxed mood at the Sand Dollar was gone, replaced by butterflies in the gut of the crew, like athletes get before the big game. Only this wasn't a game. This was for keeps. Ramos had butterflies too. The difference was, he liked having butterflies. Kept him focused on the task at hand.

A few miles offshore was a boat, a nice charter boat, ready for action. On board were three Peruvians. The boat was outfitted for upscale clients to do first class fishing. The name, "Salty Girl", was painted in bright blue across the transom, at least it looked that way. Actually, "Salty Girl" was painted on a high tech sheet of white plastic material that was expertly applied to the boat, over the other name, the real name, "Trujillo Mamasita". The men on board didn't know Ramos Mantilla, but they knew plenty about the man. They were being paid well to make sure there were no problems. It was all business. They took no chances.

Enrique and his crew had an easy job, just be in the right place at the right time, and look and act like tourists.

But Enrique knew, like Ramos, that just because a job seems easy doesn't mean you don't have to be prepared. They had rehearsed the plan, they had rehearsed the contingency plan, then they had done it all again, over and over, just to be sure.

Ramos wasn't acting like himself. He was having a hard time escaping the feeling that he might be making a mistake. He turned to his trusted friend. He called Hector. "You got a minute to talk"?

"Of course, how are you"?

"Good, I guess. Seems like everything is going about as well as I could expect, but I have this nagging feeling that maybe I shouldn't be here at all, that I might be making things worse for Nikki. And, maybe I shouldn't be putting these other people, the ones from Peru, at risk".

"Have you said anything like that to them"?

"No. It's been all business".

"Good. I think it's best for you to figure this out yourself. If you need to cancel the whole deal, no problem, but they don't need to be in on it".

"I agree with that".

"One thing I learned from you a long time ago, is that you have to trust yourself. When you told me you were going to see this man, Silas Greer, you were very decisive about it. You had the confidence and determination that I've seen in you many times. I have total confidence in you, but it doesn't matter what I think, it matters what you think. Something else you told me, many years ago. Every man has fear, but not every man has courage".

Ramos laughed, which the Guv was glad to hear. "Sounds like something I would say".

"Look, quit overthinking it. Sleep on it. Trust yourself. You'll do the right thing, whatever it is".

He took the advice. Tried to sleep on it, but sleep didn't come right away. What did come was a memory of earlier days in Ferriday, when he first took over Mona's. All the Peruvians were proud of him. Proud that Mona's was owned by a guy from Peru. The locals admired him. He was fair in all of his dealings, just as fair as a man can get. But he didn't put up with any bullshit, and everybody knew it. The crew at Mona's was one big family, with locals and Peruvians treated the same. These thoughts brought a calm to Ramos, and made him smile to himself. Nikki wasn't a Peruvian, but it didn't matter. As far as he was concerned, she was part of the family. It also made him smile when he thought of Hector, the Guv. Some guys live their entire lives without having a friend like him. Then he let his mind drift, and soon fell into a baby's slumber.

The next morning they assembled for breakfast, and Ramos was his usual, calm self. The chatter was lively, none of it having anything to do with the reason for them being there. The hay was in the barn, as they say, and they were ready.

"Salty Girl", was on a slow cruise toward the main marina in Georgetown, Grand Cayman. They were picking up a family of seven, including Grandpa, and taking them on a first class fishing excursion. Like all fishermen, their hopes were high for a successful trip.

Chapter 39

Nikki had never been known as a party girl. She loved a good party, it just didn't define who she was. She was funny and engaging, but those traits were never forced or used as part of an agenda. She was Nikki. Not a sorority girl, though she had friends who were. Not a social climber, not because she decided not to be, she just wasn't wired that way. She was Nikki. There was a part of her that some considered antisocial, and maybe to some degree it was so, she loved to read and spend time by herself, and she was fiercely independent. She had the self confidence to be who she was, not really rebellious, but not afraid to buck the system on occasion. Her best friend was from Honduras, and two of her roommates as an undergraduate were black. They loved her, and she loved them back. She was a liberal, in most every way. Initially she decided on law school so she could fight for those less fortunate, and without a voice. Like many before her, that idealism had been tempered by the harsh reality of the system. It disgusted her to see how the charitable giving and not for profit sectors of the business and legal worlds were just as ruthless as the profit seeking money grubbers who bore the brunt of social denigration for acting the same way, but without the buffer of pretense. Her most serious relationship, before Reggie, had been with an associate professor at Tulane. He was thirty four, and married. She was twenty. She seduced him. He couldn't resist. She was careless and selfish. Got pregnant. Had an abortion that Gib never knew about. The professor was divorced soon after the affair ended. Nikki got an A in the class. Not her finest moment. It weighed on her. We're all flawed. All have baggage. Just the way it is

Nikki wondered what heaven is like. She believed there was a heaven, and that's where Gib and her mother were. She grew up Methodist, member of the church and all that, but it really wasn't her thing. To her way of thinking, it made no sense at all that each religion had it's own little book of rules, it's own version of the truth, it's own version of what happens when you die. How could they all be right? How could all but one be wrong, and the right one was the Methodists? Don't think so. The only thing that made sense to her, not just book sense, as they say in the South, or common sense, the thing that Samuel Clemens lamented the lack of, but the sense that has no origin other than the soul, the gut, gut sense, was that all of the big, grand religions, the mom and pop religions, the Vatican and the mud hut, were the same, all of us seeking something that doesn't exist, except in the heart and soul of a woman, or man. Call it faith, call it love, truth. Call it what you will, it's there, and nowhere else. Just the way it is.

She had read a story once that stayed with her. She saved it, and had reread it many times. On occasion she would share it with a friend. It did a better job than she seemed to be able to do of stating her way of looking at the world. She called it the Mexican Fisherman Story.

The American investment banker was at the pier of a small coastal Mexican village, when a small boat with just one fisherman docked. Inside the small boat were several large yellowfin tuna. The American complimented the Mexican on the quality of his fish, and asked how long it took to catch them. The Mexican replied, "only a little while". The American then asked why he didn't stay out longer and catch more fish. The Mexican said he had enough to support his family's immediate needs. The American then asked, "But what do you do with the rest of your time"? The Mexican said, "I sleep late, fish a little, play with my children, take siesta with my wife, Maria, and stroll into the village where I sip wine and play guitar with my amigos, I have a full and busy life".

The American scoffed, "I am a Harvard MBA and could help you. You should spend more time fishing, and with the proceeds buy a bigger boat. With the proceeds from the bigger boat you could buy several boats. Eventually, you would have a fleet of fishing boats.

Instead of selling your catch to a middleman, you would sell directly to the processor, eventually opening your own cannery. You would control the product, processing and distribution. You would need to leave this small, coastal fishing village and move to Mexico City, then LA, and eventually New York City, where you will run your expanding enterprise". The Mexican fisherman asked, "But how long will this take"? The American replied, "Fifteen to twenty years". "But what then"? The American laughed, "That's the best part. When the time is right, you announce an IPO and sell your company stock to the public. You would make millions. You would be rich". "Really? millions?, then what"?

"Then you could retire and move to a small coastal fishing village. You could sleep late, fish a little, play with your kids and take a siesta with your wife Maria. In the evening you could stroll to the village, sip wine and play your guitar with your amigos".

She loved to travel. Loved learning new things, seeing new things, meeting new people. Between her freshman and sophomore year at Tulane, she went to Europe with two other girls. They started in London and ended in Madrid. They spent a lot of time in Paris and Rome, especially Paris. Nikki loved Paris. Everybody loves Paris, but Nikki REALLY loved it. She appreciated New Orleans even more after that trip. It was the most like Europe of any place she had been in the U.S. Whatever her future path would be, she promised herself that it would include time spent in Europe, especially Paris. Yes it would. Hell yes it would. Life is short. You gotta stop and smell the roses.

Rafa would miss Oaklawn Park, and Hot Springs, but he was ready to move on. He was frustrated with the Guv. Didn't get it, why he wasn't doing more to nail Martin's ass. And all while Martin is still sucking cash. Spending it on fancy boots and fucking cuff links. Fellowship of Christian Athletes my ass. It was the Martin Carrington show. No fellowship to it, and worse, a slap in the face of all good, solid Christians who actually do give much more than they take.

He thought of New Orleans. He would like to go back there. If he stayed in America, that might be the place, either there or New York. Made him think of Nikki again. Shit, shit, shit.

CHAPTER 40

The preparation was done. It was almost show time.

Ramos was alone. Walking on the beach. Funny thing about the beach. Those that grow up near it, like he did, don't spend much time there. Those that grew up and live inland, away from the big water, spend big bucks year after year coming to it, to hang out by it. As a little boy he did spend time with his buddies, fishing, shrimping and crabbing, but that came to a halt when he went to prison. In fact, he hadn't held a fishing rod since then. He thought to himself that if all went well later that day, and he found himself aboard the Trujillo Mamasita, he might just wet a hook.

The Guv was in a closed door meeting inside the administrative offices at Oaklawn Park. He was asking for a favor, which was a rarity for the Guv. He was talking with Katarina, the voluptuous young vixen who served as the host of the Oaklawn replay show. He leveled with her, straight off the bat.

"This is absolutely just between us girls, okay"?

She looked at the Guz quizzically. "Okay Guv, of course".

"I need help with something, and I think you're the best person for the job. I'm going to tell you about it. After I do, if you don't want to be involved, just tell me and that will be the end of it. Okay"?

"Okay".

"I want you to make a phone call to Martin Carrington. Tell him we, Barn 52, are selling forty percent of a promising two year old colt. He will probably have his first start late this summer, maybe Saratoga. We're selling ten percent shares. Two are committed. We have two left. We're offering him one of those shares".

"That's it"?

"There's a little more to it, setting a time for him to come to the barn to look at the colt, but that's it".

"Why do you want me to do it"?

"I'd rather not get into it any more than that. Just one phone call. It's important. You can say no. I won't hold it against you".

"I'll do it Guv, for you"

Chapter 41

Ramos entered the lobby of the building as if he were just another guy with business to tend to, which he was. He calmly approached the the security desk, which ran almost the entire length of the back wall. It had an entrance on each side which led to a bank of elevators. Every person that entered or left had to wave an ID card in front of a scanner. There was a small sign that read, Visitors Please Register Here. He was politely greeted by an attractive young female receptionist. "Good morning, how may I help you"?

Ramos smiled slightly and nodded. "Good morning, I would like to see Mr. Silas Greer. I don't have an appointment, and he's not expecting me. I was hoping he might be willing to give me just a few minutes of his time. I'm a retired restaurant owner from the U.S. and I have a small favor to ask".

Every word was rehearsed. Ramos knew there was no way he would walk in and be escorted to the office of Silas Greer. The only chance he had was to appear totally harmless and unaware of who Silas Greer actually was. He knew the more information he gave them the better. He spoke softly, and did a good job of appearing to be a little old man who knew he was out of his element and probably had to work up the courage just to enter the building. He literally held his hat in his hands, and stooped just slightly to appear as docile and clueless as possible, without overdoing it.

"What is your name sir"? This was good. A name would make it a little harder for her to just send him away.

"Ramos Mantilla". He took a half step back, nodded again very slightly and gave her a hint of a sheepish smile. He didn't know it, but the young lady had a grandfather who she adored that lost his fight with cancer just a few months earlier. It never hurts to catch a break.

"Let me see what I can do Mr. Mantilla. Why don't you have a seat", glancing in the direction of a small cluster of chairs in the corner of the lobby.

"Thank you".

He sat facing the receptionist and waited. There was a Wall Street Journal on the table next to him. He picked it up and positioned it so that he could keep an eye on things, while appearing to read the paper. After a few minutes, the young lady walked over to him.

"Mr. Mantilla, Mr. Greer is on a conference call for the next thirty minutes to an hour. Is there something that one of his assistants can help you with"?

This is where Ramos shined, and where his preparation once again made a difference. He gave no indication at all that he was anything other than a kindly gent. Maybe a little different, but absolutely no threat.

"I'm okay young lady. I may take a stroll for half an hour and return. Is that okay? I would like to have a short chat with Mr. Greer. I won't take more than ten minutes of his time".

"Well, okay. I think that's fine. I'll see if I can get you in to see him, but I'm just the receptionist, so I can't promise".

He stood and placed the Wall Street Journal neatly back on the table. "Of course. You're sweet. I appreciate it".

He took a step toward the door, then stopped and turned toward her before she walked away.

"Are you by chance familiar with the book Silent Dream, by Nicholas Trafford"? He smiled. She smiled. Funny how that works.

"I don't think so. Should I be"?

"No, not really, you're kind of young for that one. I just remembered that Trafford spent a lot of time in Georgetown. I always figured it was the Washington DC Georgetown. It just occurred to me that it actually might be this place. Anyway, just a thought".

Silas Greer was an educated man. A voracious reader, he studied literature in college and had a rather short list of favorite authors. Nicholas Trafford was on it. Probably wouldn't matter at all, but if the young lady mentioned Ramos' comment to Silas Greer, it could make a difference. Worth a shot.

Ramos stayed gone for almost an hour. Sitting just far enough away from the building to not be noticed, he kept an eye on those who came and went. When he reentered the building, he simply went over and had a seat just as before. A patient man.

The receptionist had kept an eye out for him. The old man was sweet, but clueless. She didn't know what went on behind the closed door of the offices of Transcon Holdings. She was okay with that. She was paid well to not know.

"Mr. Mantilla, he knows you're here. Is there something I can get you while you wait. Coffee? Water"?

"Thanks, but no. I'm okay".

Ramos didn't appear to be paying attention to anything other than his immediate surroundings, which, of course, wasn't the case at all. There was security everywhere in the building's lobby, some obvious, some not. He knew because he made it his business to know. They were watching. He never looked directly at them. He read the Wall Street Journal, and waited. Eventually he looked up to see a large, very imposing looking man walking toward him. The man was polite, but didn't smile. He was the professional body guard for Silas Greer. He didn't bother to introduce himself.

"Mr. Mantilla, Mr. Greer sends his regrets for not being able to meet with you today. Perhaps you can call the office tomorrow and arrange a time to come back. He welcomes the chance to meet new people, and looks forward to meeting with you, but it's just not possible today". Total, fucking, bullshit.

Ramos, of course, was ready with a reply. "I see. Unfortunately, I have a flight that leaves in a couple of hours, so maybe we can try another time. If you could, though, maybe you can give him a message for me".

"Certainly, I'll be glad to".

"I have a dear friend who told me a story. I'm sure it's not true, but he insists it is. He's a gambler and a horseplayer. He says there is a guy at Burnham Glen Casino named Shanghai who is the best handicapper on the planet". Before Ramos got the next word out, the big man spoke.

"Wait a second. You're losing me. Do you have a message for Mr. Greer"?

Ramos looked at the man. Time to fish or cut bait. "Yes. I want to talk about Gib Carter".

Silence. "Okay, I'll pass that along". The bodyguard turned to walk away, without another word.

"And Pietro Ferretti".

He stopped. Bingo. He walked back toward Ramos, glanced around to see who might be listening, then said in a low voice. "Who the fuck are you"?

"A friend of Gib Carter".

The man said nothing. Ramos added. "I just want ten minutes. I'll settle for five".

"You'll settle for whatever we give you, if anything. Wait here".

It didn't take long. The receptionist walked over to him.

"Mr. Mantilla, Mr. Greer suggested that you wait in one of the small conference rooms. If you'll follow me, I'll take you there. First we need to register you as a guest".

Ramos signed the guest register, showed his driver's license, which she quickly scanned, and was given a guest badge to wear while in the building. She pressed her security card to the reader. The door opened. Ramos was in. Again she offered something to drink. Again he declined. She smiled at Ramos, closed the door and left. The room was indeed small, but comfortable and first class in every way. Within minutes the door opened. The big man was back.

"He wants to see you. I hope you know what you're doing. Empty your pockets on the table". The big guy frisked Ramos, just like in the movies. "Follow me".

The last week of the Oaklawn race meet was underway. The Guv had plenty to occupy his mind. The first of Barn 52's four horses was running in the Bayakoa Stakes, a sprint race for fillies and mares. She had been training well, and they had high expectations for a good showing. She broke out of the gate well, and after a quarter mile was in third, five lengths behind the leader, who appeared to be setting a suicidal pace, but less than a length behind the second place filly, and just to her outside, what horseplayers often refer to as the garden spot. At the quarter pole the leader began to back up, as expected, and the pace quickened. At the top of the stretch, the Barn 52 filly put a head in front, then half a length. She appeared to be putting the other filly away, but at the sixteenth pole they were back to almost dead even. They sprinted to the wire. Too close to call. Photo finish.

Photo finishes are hell on a horseplayer. More often than not, when two horses are battling, one will start to pull away in the stretch, and when that happens, almost always that horse wins. One of the traits of a truly great racehorse is the ability to battle, lose the lead, and get it back before the wire. That doesn't happen often. Most of the time the horse who gets overtaken is done. Even more unusual is the occasion when two horses engage in a head to head battle that lasts half the race or more, and stay that way to the wire. Probably the most notable example of this is the duel between Affirmed and Alydar during the Triple Crown races of 1978. Affirmed won all three races, and the Triple Crown. Alydar was second in all three, battling every inch of the way. Both are considered among the all time greats. Both gave it absolutely all they had to give. You can't ask for more than that. But sometimes they battle and you just can't tell who won. So you have to wait for the finish line photo. Losing is no fun, every horseplayer knows the feeling. Part of the deal. But losing a photo is like losing and getting punched in the gut at the same time, ask anybody.

The tote board flashed the result. Second place for the Barn 52 filly. Damn, damn, damn. What a bunch of shit. Screw horse racing.…..Who do you like in the fifth?

The Guv was disappointed. More for the fillie than himself. Crazy, but you work around horses all the time and you get that way. Besides, they had won their share of photos. Tomorrow was another day.

Indeed it was. The next day Barn 52 had a six year old warrior in an optional claimer, for a claiming price of seventy five grand. He had fourteen career wins in forty five starts, one of which was an ungraded stakes at Lone Star Park in Texas. This was another sprint. He was ahead by a length at the quarter pole and never looked back. Win number fifteen. Thank ya. Thank ya very much.

It was a relief for the Guv to get the win. He was smiling on the way to the winner's circle, he smiled for the picture, and he was smiling as he lead the winner back to the barn. It felt good to smile. Damn sure did. You have to enjoy the wins, smell the roses, taste the champagne when you can. Soon enough, it's back to the grind.

The day ended on another high note for the Guv, when he got a call from Katarina, the Vixen. Martin Carrington sounded excited about the possibility of investing in his first race horse, and he would be at Barn 52 the following Thursday afternoon to take a look at the promising two year old colt.

Ramos entered Silas Greer's office in the same manner he had entered the building two hours earlier, with a humble, unassuming manner. Both bodyguards, the big ass enforcer guy and the cocky pretty boy, were there, and apparently planned to stay in the room. Silas Greer was sitting at his desk, and didn't bother to stand or offer a handshake. "Have a seat Mr. Mantilla. You are quite persistent. What can I do for you"?

"I want to talk to you about Gib Carter. I assume you know who he was".

"I know who Mr. Carter is".

"He was a good man, admired by everyone who knew him. He made a poor decision, a terrible decision. What he did was wrong, and inexcusable, but he didn't deserve to die for it".

Ramos paused, looking straight into the eyes of the man, Silas Greer. He was calm. Didn't waiver. Took his time. "I'm an old man. I come to you..."

"Mr. Mantilla". The young cocky fellow interrupted Ramos in mid sentence. "You said you wanted to ask a favor. You're running out of time. You should probably get to it".

This was a moment Ramos would never forget. The moment of truth. He had travelled a long way to face this man. Ramos' eyes never left Silas Greer. He totally ignored the young punk, and he took his time.

"I come to you, with all due respect, to ask you to help me restore Gib Carter's good name. You can do that by returning the ten million dollars to Boardman and Company, where it belongs, and by issuing a statement making it clear that Gib Carter didn't steal the money".

The young guy actually laughed out loud, the big guy snickered. Silas Greer showed no reaction, but he broke eye contact with Ramos and looked over icily at the young bodyguard, said nothing, looked back. He spoke. "Mr. Mantilla, according to reports, Mr. Carter wired ten million dollars of his firm's money to some sort of secret offshore account. Neither he or the money have been heard from since. Hard to figure, but that sort of stuff happens all the time. If you think for some reason I'm responsible, you're wrong. Surely you didn't think you were going to walk in here and leave with a check for ten million dollars. Now why don't you tell me who you are and why you're here".

"I am who I say I am, and I believe you are indeed responsible. There's a lot I don't know, but there are a few things I do. Gib Carter made friends with some people associated with Stezlaus Bank. They retained him and his firm, Boardman and

Company, to invest two hundred million dollars of the bank's money. Gib bet ten million of that on a horse race. Stupid. Totally wrong, but he did it. He lost the bet, and the cash was gone. That part is not your fault, it was his. But then, when he, Gib, started questioning things, he hit a stone wall. He went to Burnham Glen Casino to try to get some answers, probably starting with this guy, Shanghai. He disappeared somewhere between the airport and the casino, and hasn't been seen or heard from since". Ramos paused for a breath. "Mr. Greer, it's not my intent to do anything other than get the ten million back and set the record straight on Gib Carter. Other than that, your business is your business, and as far as I'm concerned it will stay that way. I ask you now, please, do the right thing. Will you do what I ask"?

Silas Greer was a very savvy business man. He knew he had a problem, but he was not sure yet how big of one. He sat thinking, for what seemed like a long time. The ten minutes were up. That was irrelevant now. "Why did you mention the name of Pietro Ferretti"?

Bingo. At least now Ramos knew he had something to work with, and could possibly get the job done as easily as just sitting here and talking with the man, Silas Greer. Not likely, but at least possible. Ramos measured his words, still speaking in the same manner, with respect and humility. The body-guards were now as quiet as church mice. Ramos took a deep breath. "Well, as I said, I'm only here on behalf of Gib Carter. I'm not certain about the role of Pietro Ferretti. It's not my business, but I'll tell you what I think if you would like me to".

"I understand, and I would like you to".

"Pietro Ferretti was careless. Had problems, drinking, maybe drugs, gambling, the usual stuff. He came from big money, really big. Family money. The family ran into some serious problems. The money was still big, but not as big. He wasn't smart enough, or disciplined enough, to see that it might not last, probably because he never had to work for it. Sure enough, the gravy train dried up. Not completely, there was still plenty left for the average international playboy, but he had more expensive tastes than most. He told Gib about Shanghai, maybe on purpose, maybe not, doesn't matter. Gib has the brilliant idea of making a quick five hundred grand, betting on a horse race with somebody else's money. Personally, I think, as they say in America, he was letting his little head do the thinking. Doesn't matter, he did it. Pietro was his one and only connection to the offshore gambling shop, which was probably not a gambling shop at all, but part of a myriad of money laundering vehicles for Stezlaus Bank, and, of course, Transcon Holdings".

Ramos paused. The two goons were staring at Ramos, slack jawed, listening. Silas Greer sat quietly, listening. Ramos kept going.

"Pietro got drunk and told Gib things he shouldn't have, about Shanghai and big horse racing bets. Also told him about a Villa in Tuscany. Gib says he wants to bet ten million on a "sure thing" horse race, one of Shanghai's picks. Pietro knows he screwed up by telling Gib too much, and he doesn't want the Stezlaus boys to know, so he used his own bogus offshore account, gave the wiring instructions to Gib, and waited. He didn't have to wait long. Gib wired the money. The people at Gib's firm didn't question it. He had two hundred million of new money to invest, so they expected him to be putting it to work. As soon as the money hit the account, Pietro moved it to another secret offshore account that he controlled. After Gib lost the bet, Pietro saw an opportunity to make a quick ten mil. Nobody knew about Gib's bet but him, so he just pocketed the cash. Pretty slick, except Pietro hadn't really thought it all the way through. He was probably also letting his little head do the thinking. He assumed that Gib was a jet setter just like he was, and like it or not, he would just have to absorb the ten million dollar loss. His assumption was wrong. Gib was actually just a good ole working boy from Alabama, who happened to have a job investing money for rich people. He lost the bet on the "sure thing". Then, as they say in the South, he went ape shit. He got no answers from Pietro, so he did the only thing that made sense to him, he went to get some answers. He went to Burnham Glen, only he never made it. I'm not sure how he did it, but Pietro managed to get Gib on a plane headed to Russia. The plane landed in Russia, but Gib wasn't on it. He was taking a nap on the floor of the Atlantic fucking ocean. Now, I'm quite sure I have some of the details wrong, but I don't think I'm too far off the mark. The point is, Gib Carter was murdered and Boardman and Company is out ten million bucks. As I said, Gib was wrong, and stupid. He deserved to pay a hell of a big price for it, but he didn't deserve to die. And he wouldn't have, if not for Pietro Ferretti and Stezlaus Bank".

Pause. "And you". Pause. "I can't bring Gib back, but I can get the ten million back, and that's why I'm here".

Silas Greer was himself a cool customer. He had been in plenty of tight spots. He didn't flinch. His mind was working as fast as it could, trying to decide how to handle this particular tight spot, but on the outside he appeared unfazed by the story. He even managed a short chuckle. "Well, Mr. Mantilla, that's some story. I am impressed. Unfortunately, you're asking me to do something that's not possible, even if I thought the story might be true. You have misjudged me and Transcon Holdings. We do have a relationship with Stezlaus Bank, a very good relationship. If you do a little digging, you'll find that they are one of the largest, most respected banks in the world. Their reputation is beyond reproach, as is ours. My sympathy is with the family of Gib Carter, it must be very painful to not know where he is, dead or alive. I'm sorry, but I cannot grant your request. As I said, surely you didn't think you would walk in here, tell your story, and I would stroke you a check for ten million bucks".

"Of course not, I was pretty sure you would want to wire the money. Here are the wiring instructions". Ramos slid a piece of paper with the instructions across the desk. Silas Greer ignored it.

"Get the fuck out of here".

"I figured you would need some time to think about it, so I'll give you forty eight hours to give me a final answer. I think that's reasonable".

"You have your final answer. It's no. Get the fuck out".

"Very well". Pause. "Just so we're clear, if you were to change your mind and wire the money, that would be the end of it, as far as I'm concerned. As I said earlier, your business is no concern of mine, I'm just trying to do what I can to restore the good name of Gib Carter".

Chapter 42

During his prison stay, Ramos learned some things. One was how to breathe. He learned that staying relaxed in tense situations was a big advantage. He exercised his mind and body, meditated, practiced breathing. He found that by being well conditioned, and breathing properly, he could keep his pulse rate low and relax his whole body. He practiced. He learned. He became quite good at it, breathing. It served him well.

Ramos stood, calmly, and walked toward the door. The big man was standing there, holding the door open and glaring at him. Ramos never even glanced his way. He walked through the door, through the receptionist area, into and out of the elevator, signed out with the receptionist in the main lobby, and exited the building. His demeanor was the same as it had been since he first set foot in the building, perfectly calm and at ease.

He walked out of the building, went to the taxi stand and requested a taxi to the airport. He was glad there wasn't a taxi immediately available. A short wait would give the man time to think.

The ride to the airport was a quick one. He didn't see anybody following them, but then again, he was very careful not to appear to be watching, so it was possible he just couldn't see them without looking around. He arrived at the airport, paid the fare and stood outside the small terminal. He was looking at his phone, but he was also scanning the area as best he could. He was beginning to think he would need to go to plan B, when he saw the car pull just barely into view and stop. Two people inside. Not what he figured, that both of them would come, but also not a big problem. He walked inside the terminal and immediately turned left. About twenty five feet to the left were steps that led to the main level. The building was curved, just enough that at the top of the steps it was possible to look through the window and see along the outside wall to the entrance to the short term parking area. He quickly walked up the steps, turned and looked. The car was turning into the short term lot. He changed course and walked through the door that led to the parking area. Nearby was an area designated for bikes and mopeds, which were popular on the island. He went to a metallic blue colored moped, opened the top of the carrier on the back, and removed a bag that looked like a small overnight bag. He nonchalantly removed several items from the bag. He removed a large, tropical looking shirt and quickly put it on over the shirt he was wearing. Then he put on a floppy old man's hat, replaced the bag, and casually walked toward short term parking. The items from the bag were in his pockets, a very sharp knife, a small, folding hatchet and a package of syringes, along with three vials of solution. He was concerned about the timing, but he didn't need to be. The boys were not in a hurry.

After Ramos left the office, Silas Greer had immediately told the young bodyguard to follow Ramos and make sure he got on the plane, then he told both of them to go, just to make sure. They thought it was a waste of time, but they went. As they were leaving, Silas Greer gave them an ominous warning. "Be careful. That little old man could be a problem. Don't leave until you see him get on the plane and the plane leaves the ground. He has way more information than he should have. That bothers me".

The boys were hanging back a little. They weren't happy about being there at all, and figured if they had to wait until the plane left, they might as well have a few cocktails at the bar while doing so. They figured they would wait until Ramos had gone through security, and was at his gate, then they could relax at the bar until his plane started boarding, make sure he was on it, then leave. No problem.

Ramos leisurely walked across the short term parking area toward where the car was parked. Another man, probably on business and in a hurry, walked past him, got in his car, and left the lot. Once he was several parking spaces away from the car, Ramos ducked down and carefully made his way closer, being very careful to not be seen or heard. The boys were sitting, chit chatting. Ramos worried that something might be wrong. He was surprised that they were just sitting there. He waited, and hoped that he hadn't made a mistake by thinking this part of the plan would work. He pulled out a syringe and filled it with solution. For better or worse, it was showtime. After what seemed like five minutes, but was only about two, the young one turned off the car and started to get out. Ramos was there, waiting. At the same time the driver's door started to open, he covered the last few feet. As the young bodyguard stepped out of the car, Ramos buried the syringe in the back of his leg. The young punk yelled, grabbed the back of his leg, and went down. The big man reacted by cussing and calling his name, with no answer. He looked around anxiously, suddenly aware of danger. He grabbed his gun, stopped, and called the name of the young guy again, with no response. He looked around, saw nothing. He opened the car door, paused, then stepped out, gun in hand. Ramos had quietly moved around the back of the car and was waiting next to the passenger door. As the big man stepped out of the car and started to stand, Ramos made his move. With all of the force he could muster, he swung the hatchet and buried the leading edge into the shin of the right leg of the big man. The pain was so excruciating, and the damage so severe that the big guy never stood a chance. He hit the pavement hard. As he did, before he took another breath or had another thought, Ramos pulled his head back and with calm precision, slit his neck, the razor sharp blade of the knife easily slicing through skin, blood vessels, larynx, trachea and esophagus. Warm blood flowed. Dust to dust.

He then returned to the young one, cocky no more, grabbed his hair, pulled his head back, and slit his throat. Game over.

Ramos then quickly, but calmly, removed both diamond stud earrings that the young one wore, and slid them in his pocket. This was the riskiest part of the plan. If someone had pulled into the lot, or walked out of the terminal into the lot at the wrong time, he would have had to go not only to plan B, but maybe C or D or further down the alphabet. But the odds, not by accident, were in his favor, and ninety seconds after it started, the deed was done, and Ramos Mantilla was strolling through the parking lot. A cute little old man in a garish shirt and floppy hat. He walked to the moped, climbed on, and puttered away.

Silas Greer told his secretary and the rest of the staff they could go home early. He wanted some time to himself. He started by doing an internet search of the name, Ramos Mantilla. At first he saw nothing that raised a red flag. His story about being a restaurant owner held up. He was from Peru. No surprise there. It wasn't until he saw something about Ramos spending time in prison in Peru as a young man that he began to be concerned. He read more. When he saw a newspaper story from many years before about the murder of a suspected mafia boss in Trujillo, Peru, he got a really bad feeling in the pit of his stomach. He called his guys at the airport. No answer. He tried again. He texted them. Nothing. Not good. He called a friend at the Georgetown police department and asked him to go to the airport and check on things. About twenty minutes later he would get the bad news, the horribly bad news.

About halfway between the airport and the marina, Ramos passed the policeman, heading the other way, to the airport. He would not be happy when he got there.

Ramos pulled into the marina, parked the moped along-side several others, removed his gear from the carrier, and walked toward the water. He was met by his companions from Peru. To an observer they were a lovely family of four, and two other friends. They all embraced. The kids obviously happy that Grandpa was going fishing with them. The blood on his hands and pants leg were hardly noticed. As he greeted one of the men, he pressed two diamond stud earrings into the palm of his hand. They chatted for a minute, then that man left. The others strolled down the dock, and climbed on board The Salty Girl.

The rest of the day was a blur for Silas Greer. He had to answer questions about what could possibly have happened at the airport. There were no shots fired, no sign of much of a struggle, just two lifeless bodies and a lot of blood. No indication of who was responsible, according to the officer. Silas Greer didn't need any help figuring out who was responsible. None at all.

Tourism and banking are both big on Grand Cayman. Two dead bodies lying on the ground, throats slit, may not be that great for business. Short term parking at the airport was quiet most of the time, but got busy just before flight arrival times. The officer didn't wait to decide what to do. Silas Greer had been good to him, very good. As quickly as he could, forensic evidence be damned, he drug both bodies as far out of sight as possible. It wasn't easy, especially the big dude. A truck entered the lot, the officer approached the driver, hoping to divert him away from the immediate area, but there was no need.

"Officer we're here to help. Mr. Greer sent us".

He hesitated a moment. The driver of the truck spoke again. "We take care of the Transcon Holdings aircraft. He called and said you could probably use some help".

The officer didn't like it, but he damn sure needed help. There was the driver and another man in the truck. Involving people he didn't know in something like this was not good, but the alternative at this point was probably worse. Probably way worse.

"Okay, get out of the truck and do what I say". Pause. "This is some bad shit, but if he sent you then we're going to do it. Understand"?

Both men said yes without hesitating. He led them to the scene.

"Help me put these bodies in this car".

They did the big man first. It wasn't easy. It was very messy. They closed the trunk. Put the little guy in the back seat. The officer looked at the driver.

"Pull the car out just far enough to get it out of the way. Then park your truck so that this space is blocked. Take the car to your hangar and park it where it won't be seen. Come back as quickly as you can, bring whatever you can to help us clean this mess up". He nodded to the other man. "Let's get to work. Follow me".

They went to the back of the police car. The officer opened the trunk and removed several orange cones. They placed them so that no cars could get close. Within an hour, the bloodbath no longer looked that way, just some sort of oil spill or something that needed to be cleaned up. No big deal. Within twenty four hours, the parking space and area around it would be pressure washed and back in service. Business as usual. Within another twenty four hours the car and contents would cease to exist, except as teeny tiny pieces, returned to mother earth.

Silas Greer, heartless as he seemed, had a soft spot. He treated his wife and children well, but they were in London. He had free reign in Grand Cayman. He needed a pretty girl to scratch his itch. She lived in a luxury condo in the same building as his. Convenient. He insisted she keep a very low profile, and she did. To his knowledge, only his closest confidants knew she even existed. She lived her life. He lived his. She made sure to keep him happy when he visited. Tonight he needed her. No problem. "Relax and have another drink. I'll take a quick bath and put on something nice. Just for you".

She was gorgeous, of course. No piercings, tattoos. Very little make up. Pure and natural. Breasts that hung down just enough when she was pleasing him, but otherwise full and firm. She bent over to kiss him, breasts beckoning, only partially concealed by expensive silk. He parted the silk, and buried his head in her loveliness. The powerful man, powerless to resist the world's greatest treasure.

After the opening act, she led him by the hand to her bed. She let the silk robe slip to the floor. His manliness was, as they say, so hard a cat couldn't scratch it. It was all for naught. He threw back the cover, and there, on his pillow, on his side of the bed, in his most private sanctum, were two bloody diamond stud earrings.

Chapter 43

The next morning, one of Silas Greer's people called the airport and inquired if a Mr. Ramos Mantilla was on a departing flight the previous day. The answer wasn't the one hoped for. Ramos Mantilla's flight left on time yesterday, but he wasn't on it.

Nikki thought she heard her phone buzz, but she was in no mood to answer. She was trying to sleep. With the break in her law school regimen, she had been keeping much later hours than normal. The previous evening she had dinner at Gabby's house. They had a few glasses of wine. It was late when she got home, but she wasn't very sleepy, so she watched a movie. Now the world was awake and she just wanted to sleep. The phone buzzed again. Again she ignored it. The third time she reached for the phone. All three calls from a local number she didn't recognize. Then she got a text. It said, "Nikki please call me, it's important. Roger Boardman".

She immediately thought of Ramos, and was alarmed. Her pulse rate quickened. She called the number. "Roger, this is Nikki, is everything okay"?

"Yes. Can you talk for a minute"?

"Of course, what's wrong"?

"Nothing's wrong Nikki. Hold one second. Let me get to my office". He practically ran to his office and closed the door. "Nikki, you're not going to believe this. A wire came into the bank early this morning from Stezlaus Bank, for eleven million dollars. A note was with it, I'll read it to you".

Mr. Boardman,

It is with sincere apologies that we send this letter along with a wire transfer of eleven million dollars to your firm, Boardman and Company. As a result of an internal audit, we discovered a very serious breach of bank protocol, which led us to the discovery of a fraudulent transaction involving your firm. A trusted member of our banking family, we regret to say, masterminded a scheme to divert ten million dollars away from your firm, and into his own offshore account. As part of the scheme, this person managed to make it appear that the perpetrator of the fraud was your associate, Gibson Carter. There is a lot we still don't know, but we do know that ten million dollars was stolen from your firm, and Gib Carter is not responsible.

Unfortunately, and it saddens us to say, we know no more than you concerning the whereabouts of Mr. Carter. We have asked law enforcement to investigate. They are concerned for the welfare of Mr. Carter, and suspect that he may have been the victim of foul play. The wire transfer is the return of the ten million, plus one million in interest that would have been earned if the the money had been parked in a money market fund.

We sincerely regret the damage that has been done, and promise to do whatever else is necessary to help restore the good names of Gibson Carter and Boardman & Company.

Sincerely,

Yuri Constanislav

Chairman, Stezlaus Bank

Somewhere in the world, some time very soon, Pietro Ferretti was going to have a very bad day.

Nikki was quiet, sitting on the edge of her bed in nothing less than stunned silence. She didn't know how to react. It didn't seem real. She was worried how it came to be. She was worried for Ramos. "Is it real Roger? Is the money really there"?

"It's real Nikki. We've moved the money to a separate account. It's all there. It's safe. I have acknowledged receipt of the wire and the note with Stezlaus Bank. I have had no discussion with them at all. I will call them, but not before I've thought through what to say. We need to issue some sort of press release here in New Orleans. I look forward to that Nikki, but it too can wait until we're ready".

Nikki said nothing.

"You okay Nikki"? You still there"?

"Yes. I don't know what to say. It's unbelievable. It's wonderful. I hope I'm not dreaming".

"You're not dreaming Nikki. Why don't you take a little time and when you feel like talking more, call me back. If you can make time to do it, I'd like for you to come to the bank. I want to make sure the press release meets with your approval before we go with it. I would like to do that before the end of the day today. Can you do that"?

"Yes, absolutely. Hell yes I can. Why don't we just set a time, I can be ready in an hour or so".

Good. Why don't you come at ten thirty"?

"I'll be there".

The Salty Girl made it's way seaward. All on board were in good spirits, happy to be headed home, to Peru. When the captain of the vessel said it was time, his mates removed the high tech piece of material from the back of the boat. The Salty Girl, just like that, returned to it's true self, Trujillo Mamasita. The Salty Girl sign was rolled up, placed in a heavy gage steel wire cylinder and tossed overboard. Smooth seas ahead.

CHAPTER 44

The story was on the front page of the Times Picayune the next morning. The headline said it well. "Sad but sweet redemption". The article recounted the story of Gib disappearing with the cash and the subsequent speculation about how he did it and where he might be. It also acknowledged that absolutely no person who knew the man could believe that he did such a thing, and that there had to be an explanation. But there never was, the case got cold, and most of the inevitable whispers were not kind to the legacy of the man. Then the article gave the good news. The money was indeed stolen, but not by Gib Carter. The money had been recovered, all of it. Gib Carter had been falsely accused, and his good name was now restored. That was the sweet part, the redemption. The sad part followed. Gib Carter is still missing, and was very likely the victim of foul play.

Nikki already knew the bad part, so it wasn't any more sad now than it had been. The rest of the news was indeed sweet.

Sweet redemption for her father. The picture looked bleak for a long time, but, sometimes... there's more to the picture than meets the eye. Hey hey, my my.

CHAPTER 45

Nikki's phone was working overtime. Calls, texts and emails were coming in from everywhere. She did phone interviews with two local news shows. It was all a bit overwhelming, and she really had not gotten used to the idea that the nightmare, at least most of it, was over. The more she talked about it and heard others talk about it, the better she felt. People really did love her father, and were genuinely happy to hear that good news had come Nikki's way.

There was more. Roger Boardman called her late in the day. Boardman and Company was announcing the creation of the Gibson Carter Scholarship. It was a memorial to Gib and his devotion to learning. The scholarship would be awarded each year to a student or students from the State of Louisiana who demonstrate high character and a desire to learn. It was being fully endowed with a two million dollar contribution. One million from Boardman and Company, and one million from Stezlaus Bank in Moscow.

"The official announcement will be made tomorrow. I wanted you to hear it from me first. We're using the extra million that Stezlaus Bank wired us, and we're kicking in another million. The firm's advisory committee met today. It was approved. It was unanimous. I'm happy for you Nikki".

Nikki was barely able to reply, her voice cracking.

"Thank you Roger".

She had held it together, emotionally, but no more. She cried. Beautiful, plump tears of joy.

And there was more. Crying. Good crying. The Guv called. He had a message from Ramos. He was in Peru. All was well. He planned to stay a while for a visit and would return to Louisiana soon. Sweet, sweet mother of all things holy. It may have been the best news of all.

Silas Greer read the news in the Times Picayune online. He wasn't happy. He wasn't sad. Just the cost of doing business. He was a little nervous though. He didn't care for another meeting with Ramos Mantilla. He was hoping, just like some other men of his ilk, many years ago, in Peru, that this was the end of it.

Martin Carrington was a beacon of virtue. Trust me, I'm a Christian, just like you. I work in the nonprofit world. We're not in it for the money, oh hell no. Just look at this photograph. Me and this famous athlete. People love me. I'm sportin some expensive clothes and car and shit, but the bible says that's cool. I'm helping a hell of a lot of people. Beautiful. Bottom line, I'm a player. Oh hell yes I am. Pass the peas.

Americans can't relate to Gypsies. That's probably not fair. Some can. Some of those that were at Woodstock can, maybe.

They looked like they could then, not sure about now. Maybe not. Probably not, but maybe. Some probably still do.

There is an old adage. "Under promise, over deliver". Similar is when a person says that another person "exceeds expectations". The Roma people shouldn't have much problem with the latter, because expectations are so low. Rafa Zamfir, a Roma, a proud Roma, promised nothing. There were really no expectations, either, except from himself. He had come to Hot Springs Arkansas to lay claim to his share of the estate of his father. He didn't mourn the death of his father. There was no grieving, except for that caused by the realization that the money wheel might have ground to a halt. When he closed his eyes, he thought of his grandmother, his saint, and knew that there was a reason to hope, and study and work and believe in all that could be, and by God, all that would be. He had no malice in his heart toward these Westerners who lived in big houses and went to work every day trying like hell to get the coin to buy an even bigger house. If that's their way, so be it, but it wasn't his way. His father, Ernie Cole had been one of those, he thought. All Rafa wanted was his rightful portion.

Funny thing though, it wasn't quite that simple. Imagine that.

It started with the Guv. Rafa's narrow view of his father didn't square with what he was hearing from the Peruvian gentleman. In fact, the Guv, who turned out to be his father's best friend, and didn't even have a high school education, mainly because he was in prison during the time that would have been his senior year, and was nothing more than a swarthy shit kicking hayseed who spent all day in the company of horses, absolutely loved the man, Ernie Cole. He even turned hostile when Rafa first met him and didn't show the proper respect for his late father. The kind of man Rafa thought his father was, maybe more accurately, assumed his father was, couldn't possibly merit the kind of love and admiration this caballero gave him.

It took some time, but Rafa widened his view, opened his eyes a bit, and began to see a different picture, a different Ernie. Once that happened, everything changed, and the Gypsy boy who had come to town with a chip on his shoulder, not only began to see his father in a different light, he also saw the Guv for what he was, a man of substance, of character, a man who had what they don't teach in school, what they can't teach in school, because it can't be learned, it has to be built, one tough day at a time. That man practically worshipped his father, so what must that say about his father, Ernie Cole?

The Guv was acting weird. The Barn 52 family, close as it was, could tell there was something up. They knew he was a little uptight about the horses they had running in a couple of the big races during the last week of the Oaklawn meet. But that wasn't all of it. They all were a little anxious about the upcoming races, part of the deal, but this was different. The Guv was more nervous than the rest, and that never happened.

He had been thinking about what he was going to do. Over and over. The Guv was a no nonsense guy when it came to business. Everybody knew it. He had a lot of street cred for the way he handled people. He was respected. He was loved. He was probably the most well liked guy on the back side. He was cool, the Guv.

He was all that, but now, he had to step out. Had to step out of that comfort zone that was so familiar. He liked who he was, loved who he was, but now, that wasn't enough. He had to do what he had to do, and there was no way around it. When he was in prison, when he met Ramos, he learned some things. He learned what courage was. He always told himself that he could and would take care of business, whatever that meant, when the time came. That timed loomed close.

He made the call to Nikki first.

"Hey beautiful".

"Guv, how are you"?

"Good. Trying to get these last two nags ready to run before we leave town. It's a never ending job. But hey, that's why I make the big bucks".

Nikki giggled. "I miss you Guv".

"Same here. You've been kind of busy haven't you? I heard about the scholarship. That's absolutely fantastic Nikki. You deserve it".

"No, he deserves it. None the less, it is special, very special. I can't thank you enough Guv".

"No need to thank me, but I appreciate it. I'm happy for you girl". Pause. "Now, I have something to ask you, and you have to say yes".

Nikki giggled again. The Guv continued.

"I want you to come to Hot Springs next Thursday. Our best horse is running in the Count Fleet Handicap. I want you here. Win or lose, we've got stuff to celebrate".

Nikki was silent a moment. She had been so busy and her mind had been so occupied, she had no clue if she had something she was obligated to do that day. It didn't matter. She was going to Hot Springs to see the Guv.

"I'd love to Guv, I wouldn't miss it".

They worked out the details. He told Nikki to meet him in the paddock before the race. Nikki wasn't sure why she was meeting him in the paddock, right before the race, but she was good with it. She couldn't wait to see the Guv.

The next call, the one to Rafa, was harder. He wished he didn't have to make it, and that Rafa would just show up and everything would be good. Ha Ha. No way. He had just told Rafa, a couple of days ago, in so many words, to shut the fuck up and let him take care of business his way. So that's the way it was going to be, which meant for him, the Guv, it was time to put up or shut up. He made the call. It turned out to be much easier than he expected. Rafa would be at Barn 52 Thursday afternoon.

Mothers say to daughters, when the young ladies are going through relationship issues, and some guy is acting weird and she thinks she's in love with him and the earth will stop turning if he doesn't fully return her profession of undying love and affection, and he's cool with the affection part, but they aren't in the same place on the love and devotion part, and the mother can see that, and she knows there is sadness ahead for her sweet girl, but the young one is new at the game, and blind to the pitfalls, and that her darling girl has to learn the tough lessons of love on her own, and there's really nothing she can do to help her through it, except to be there, which is big, really big, but seemingly, to the daughter, not near enough to assuage her aching heart and restore her faith in this love thing. And then, after a time, order begins to be restored. The daughter sees the wretch for what he is, and can't believe he had her hoodwinked so. That is the time when the mother tells her daughter the thing that would have fallen on deaf ears in the midst of the turmoil, but is now able to be recognized as sage advice from the bosom of the one who nursed her to life and offers the truest, purest love in the known universe. "Don't worry my dear, there are plenty of fish in the sea, and when the right one comes along, you'll know it".

Nikki's mother told her that. Now, here she was. Her mother was gone, and the deep pool in which lovers swim seemed murkier than ever. She was engaged, or maybe semi engaged, if that's possible. Her man, Reggie, was not happy with her entanglement in the stuff going on in Hot Springs, and she knew those feelings were justified, which brought her to the remembrance of another old Southern saying: Mama said there'd be days like this. There'd be days like this my Mama said. Mama said. Mama said.

Oaklawn Park, Hot Springs Arkansas, was alive. Winter had given way to Spring. The horses seemed to know that this week was special, The Racing Festival of the South. The big races, and the money and prestige attached to them, attracted new stables, and their best horses, to Oaklawn. Many would only be there a few days, just long enough to get acclimated to the track, run in a big race and head back to their permanent home, often as far away as California or New York.

Barn 52 was in transition, like most all stables at the end of a race meet. They were moving to Churchill Downs, and would be there until the end of June. Then it was on to another track. The life of thoroughbred horse people. The guys who worked with the Guv were a tight group, and they managed to find out that Martin Carrington was going to be at Barn 52 Thursday. They talked among themselves, and decided on a plan, just in case things went down the way they thought they might. Nobody said a word to the Guv about it.

Rafa's grandmother never had the talk with him. Never really had a reason to. He had his share of boyhood crushes on girls, and a couple of girlfriends along the way, but never anything that caused his heart any damage. When he came to New York to go to college, truth be known, he was intimidated by all of the smart, good looking American women. He got plenty of attention from them, hard not to with his own good looks and confident manner, but he mostly kept to himself, and when he did socialize with women, it was with the non Americans he had met on campus. He had a small group of friends. They were close and hung out together a lot. He wasn't totally anti American, but he was wary of them. He had always thought he would return to Paris after school, it seemed the natural thing to do. It was home.

He was beginning to rethink that. He had a class with an American girl from North Carolina. They studied together a few times. She was funny and smart. They started dating. He met her friends. They accepted him without reservation. She met his friends. They loved her. They were together as a couple for six months. She graduated and moved on. They promised to stay in touch, but after a while that fizzled out, as it usually does. There were no hard feelings.

His wariness was practically gone. He enjoyed getting to know Americans, and realized that he had a lot more in common with most of them than he had thought. Then came Nikki.

It was one thing to get to know an American woman in a familiar environment, at school, in New York. It was another thing altogether to meet her on her home turf, in the American South. The first time he saw her, on the riverfront in New Orleans, he was smitten. Funny though, it didn't cross his mind for a good while that there was a chance they would ever be more than friends. It just didn't. She was beautiful, likable, smart, funny. All the things any man would like, and there was something about her eyes that made him wish that somehow they would get shipwrecked on an island and it was just the two of them and they had to build a little hut and search for food and fight off the native people and in the mornings in the hut they would wake up and make passionate love for about an hour and a half, every single day. He pictured that, but that's all it was, a fantasy. The reality was different. They had something in common, murdered fathers, but that was about it. Not exactly the place you would chose to start any sort of serious relationship. But they weren't trying to do that, that never works anyway. They were trying to help each other get through stuff, and that's a healthy place to start.

His logical self said: Sure, she's hot, and she makes you laugh, but hello, she lives in a different world than you, and when all of this bullshit is settled she has a life waiting for her, a fiance for God's sake, and a career. What the fuck do you have to offer her? A devilish Gypsy smile and a future full of endless possibilities? Right. Get a grip. You've already made your move. She rejected it, sort of. Just finish up your business and get out of town. End of story.

His other self said: All that doesn't mean a thing. The pain of rejection has never been, and never will be, as bad as the pain of regret. Rejection is temporary, regret has a way of hanging around, always looking back. Listen to your heart. Trust your heart. Follow your heart. Go for it. Go for Nikki, and let the chips fall where they may.

The world is full of irony. One example was that in the Wednesday edition of The Hot Springs Sentinel Record, Martin Carrington was featured in a part of the paper that every couple of weeks spotlighted a local person and his or her wardrobe. Martin's picture was front and center, with his choice of clothes for the day, right down to his favorite ostrich skin cowboy boots. Lucchese Full Quill Ostrich Boots, with "Grosseto" Stitch Design. Just your everyday $549 shit kickers. The article quoted Martin talking about how he liked to dress well and how important it was to project a professional, successful image. He even went on to say that he used to sometimes accompany some of his salespeople to a nice men's store and help them with creating the right look.

One of the jockeys showed the article to the Guv, and looked for a reaction. The Guv scanned the article, then looked at the jockey, a slow grin moving across his face. The jockey started laughing. The Guv started laughing. The Guv put the article on the bulletin board for all to see, and gave the jockey a thumbs up. Not a word was spoken.

CHAPTER 46

Anna's new life, in her home town, living with her father, was working out well, better than she expected. She had good friends. And family. Her sister and brother in law were close by if she or her father needed help. She had a boyfriend. No surprise there, she pretty much had her pick. She didn't miss the bank, and the life that went with it. Not at all. She did, of course, miss having Gib in her life. It had all happened so fast, her time with Gib, and didn't last near long enough. It was almost as if the memory of their time together wasn't a memory, but a wonderful dream which filled her heart, then went away.

Anna had a spirit about her, one of the things that attracted Gib to her in the first place. During the short time that they had together, Gib nurtured that spirit. Gib was gone, but the spirit was still there. Yes it was.

Her trip to see Nikki had allowed her to quit blaming herself, or at least less than before. She thought of Nikki quite often. She had made the decision after visiting New Orleans that it was too much of a risk to try to maintain contact with Nikki. The mere thought of Nikki having to be concerned for her safety terrified her. It wasn't worth it. Couldn't take that chance. Non negotiable.

Anna, like most, kept up with the news by going online and checking out what was happening in the world. Every week or so she would check the homepage of The Times Picayune, in New Orleans, just to see if anything caught her eye. Suddenly, one day, it did. The most prominent front page story jumped off the screen as if it were a lightening bolt out of a blue sky. It was discovered that the guy who disappeared with ten million bucks, Gib Carter, was not the perpetrator of the crime, but the victim of the crime. This news was acknowledged by the Stezlaus Bank, in Russia, who took responsibility, and returned the ten million dollars, plus one million dollars interest, to it's rightful owner, Boardman and Company, in New Orleans. The report went on to say that Gib Carter was still missing, and authorities feared the worst.

During the following days and weeks there were many other articles detailing, as much as possible, the whole affair. Of course, the details were lacking, and always would be, Anna was sure of that. She couldn't imagine what possibly could have brought about the admission of involvement by Stezlaus Bank, and she was very surprised that the finger of blame was being pointed squarely at a member of the bank's trusted inner circle, Pietro Ferretti, from Sardinia, whose whereabouts were also reported as unknown.

Anna was thrilled for Gib. Thrilled for Nikki. But along with the satisfaction of knowing there was redemption for Gib, came the realization that she wouldn't share in it. Not in the way that Nikki would. She, Anna, would have the satisfaction of knowing that Gib, her Gib, now and always, would live in hearts and minds and historical accounts, not as a mysterious fraud, but as a good man who became entangled in the twisted web of fate. She took solace in that, but she also figured, in the part of herself that allowed her to do so, that without her having taken the risk of going to New Orleans, to tell Nikki the truth, it almost certainly wouldn't have turned out that way. She wasn't sure of that, of course, no way to be without knowing more, and she was not going to know more, probably ever. That was hard to take.

Recognition is something we all want, admitted or not, just the way it is. But what is it?, recognition, other than knowing that others know, and not just that they know, but that they acknowledge that they know. Anna did what she had to do. She was loyal and steadfast and brave, but without recognition. The only person who could give it, recognition, because she was the only person who knew, was Nikki. But even though Anna knew that Nikki knew, Nikki couldn't acknowledge that she knew, to others, so there was no recognition for Anna. Happiness and elation for Nikki. Nothing for Anna. It takes a person of character to deal with that.

It wouldn't take much. Something, anything, that would acknowledge Anna's part in gaining redemption for Gib. She couldn't blame Nikki for not trying to contact her. She had made it clear to Nikki the danger in doing so. It was her, Anna's, decision to not give Nikki her phone number or address or any contact information. She had even worried at times that it had been a mistake to mention her last name, although she doubted that Nikki remembered it. Her life in Russia was good. Nikki, she hoped, was safe. Gib's good name had been restored. There was a lot to be happy about, and grateful for. Anna had a checkered past, to say the least, and very few positive role models during her formative years. When she met Gib, she saw something she had rarely if ever been exposed to, the goodness of a person. She had no doubt she would meet Gib again, on the other side. That was something she believed and clung to, along with her unshakable belief in the good karma, that quiet river of goodness that flows in the world, and that flowed in Gib, and that maybe, hopefully, flowed in her.

Chapter 47

The Count Fleet Stakes is a six furlong sprint race for horses four years old and older. It's a graded stakes race, meaning it has the added distinction of being near the top tier of stakes races run in America. The purse is $300,000. It's not the biggest stakes race at Oaklawn, but it's one of them. Barn 52 had a four year old sprinter named Carnelian who was running in the Count Fleet. He was by Thunder Gulch, the 1995 Kentucky Derby Winner, and out of a mare who had limited success on the track, but was the dam of multiple stakes winners. Carnelian was Ernie's favorite from the start, and he didn't disappoint. He raced once as a two year old, finishing fourth. Then he broke his maiden in his first start as a three year old at Oaklawn in January. He quickly won two allowance races, both sprints, which prompted the barn to enter him in the Southwest Stakes, an Arkansas Derby prep race. The distance of the Southwest is 1 and 1/16 miles, 2 ½ furlongs further than the 6 furlong sprints in which he had been running. He led the Southwest at the quarter pole, but tired in the stretch to finish a well beaten sixth. They decided to give him a rest and shoot for the biggest sprint race for 3 years olds at Oaklawn, The Bachelor Stakes. He won the Bachelor by six lengths, and hopes were high for Carnelian being a major player among the best three year old sprinters in America. He had mixed results the rest of the year, his biggest win being his first graded stakes. It was at Saratoga in August. He won at fifteen to one, and did it impressively. For the year he had seven wins in fifteen starts, very good, but not as good as Barn 52 had hoped earlier in the year. His four year old season started out well, with an allowance win and a second place finish in an early stakes race at Oaklawn. Then he won a good stakes race for four years old, never trailing and pulling away in the stretch to win by three easy lengths. They gave him a short rest, then entered him in the Count Fleet Stakes.

Nikki's phone buzzed. She had gotten so many calls and texts and emails, she almost ignored it altogether, but the number looked familiar. "Hello".

"Nikki"?

"Yes".

"This is Ramos".

Nikki was shocked and thrilled at the same time to hear his voice. "Where are you"?

As soon as she asked the question, she wished she hadn't. It didn't matter anyway, she was just glad to hear his voice.

"I'm on vacation. I can't talk long, I just wanted to let you know I'm doing fine, and give you a message." Nikki paused, immediately concerned about what that might mean. Ramos seemed to sense her apprehension. "Don't worry Nikki. Nothing is wrong. I sent you a letter. You don't have to do anything other than read it. It's something I thought you might like to have".

"Okay. When can I see you"?

"Not sure, but I'll let you know. Don't worry about me, I mean that. Everything is good".

"I hope so. Please be careful. I can never thank you enough".

"You deserve it Nikki. I have to go. I'll see you soon".

Two days later a letter arrived. No return address. No post mark. No postage.

Nikki,
This is for you. Do with it what you want, or nothing at all, it's just something I want you to have.
Anna Lishin
Voskhod Ulitsa 121
Groznyv, Russia   488935

She lives with her father and works at a local elementary school.

That was it. Apparently delivered by someone other than the postman. Nikki folded the sheet of paper and held it in her hand. She would do something with it, but she wasn't sure exactly what, or when. Anna had warned her of the danger they both faced. Contacting her now was not an option, maybe later.

She felt sure Anna would get the news, and she hoped and prayed that it would comfort her, she deserved that.

The Guv was quiet. Not unusual, he wasn't one to chit chat about nothing, but this day he had been in his own world, thinking. It was Wednesday evening. The next day it would be time.

Funny how life is. You wonder sometimes, if circumstances had been different, would things turn out the same way? Or you hear someone say that if different decisions had been made, a different outcome would have resulted. Really? So you know for certain that if you change one thing, if you could go back and change one little thing in the sequence of events that have already unfolded, everything that happened after that one little change would have happened exactly the same as they did, even though something that came before had changed? Kinda like when a poker player throws away his starting hand and then, after all the cards hit the board, he acts like he's unlucky because he would have made a full house if he hadn't folded. Really? Okay, whatever you say. Fact is, you folded. Ante up.

The Guv was in a kind of self reflective frame of mind, and that was rare. One of the things he had loved about Ernie was the way he never lost his temper, never got flustered, never felt the need to beat his chest and act like a badass and let everybody know that it probably wasn't a good idea to mess with Ernie Cole. He didn't do that. He laughed. He listened to your bad beat stories. He took the time to talk and laugh with everybody, the big guy, the little guy and everybody in between. One of the guys would nail an exacta for fifty bucks and be beside

himself with happiness, slapping palms and hootin and hol-
lerin, and Ernie would be happy for the guy, not acting happy,
happy, and show it, all the time having his own winning mutuel
ticket in the same race in his pocket, worth a lot more than
fifty bucks, and never saying a word about it. That was him.
That was Ernie. A man you never saw act like a badass, but you
knew, you just knew, a man that it probably wouldn't be a good
idea to fuck with.

The Guv was the same way. Not exactly, that's not possible,
but close none the less. But as clearly as he could see that about
Ernie, he was blind to that trait in himself. Sometimes, when
a man has something to prove to himself, it matters not what
others think. They may not need proof of the thing the man
questions, but he does. He sees in himself a shortcoming, a
weakness. True or not, it is if he thinks it is, so he must do what
he must do. Just the way it is.

The Guv had two soul brothers, Ramos and Ernie. One
remained. The other was taken. The taker had to pay.

Thursday morning brought sunshine to Hot Springs. The
combination of Spring fever and racing fever brought thousands to the track. Oaklawn management opened the infield,
and it quickly filled with families and all sorts of race fans who
wanted to enjoy the races and a lovely picnic on the green grass
of the infield at the same time. The mood was festive. The
hardcores went about their business, glued to the simulcast
screens or the racing form, talking to each other about the action, ignoring the huge influx of casual racegoers and acting at
times as if they were inconvenienced terribly by the amateurs

and wannabes who crowded around the paddock and windows and betting terminals and beer stands and corned beef counters, and were totally clueless. All in all, as always, it was a marvelous day to be at the track.

Heading North from New Orleans, a sedan with just under two hundred thousand miles on the odometer was making steady progress toward Hot Springs, the driver was grooving to the sounds of Sir Walter Constantine and the Crescent City Playboys. Lawrence Welk they ain't. She was happy, and it felt damn good to be happy. She was also a little nervous, but it was a good nervous. In a few hours she would be with the Guv. That wasn't the nervous part. The nervous part was the possibility, she hoped a good possibility, that she would have another chance to spend a bit of time with the one she kept thinking about. The Gypsy. She hadn't been trying to think about him, just the opposite really, she had been trying to reassure herself that the path she had chosen, the one that didn't include him, was the right one, and part of that was not thinking about him. Now here she was, cruising, chillin, groovin. Thinking. And we danced all night to a soul fairy band....

Rafa had become, maybe not an expert handicapper, definitely not an expert handicapper, but a decent handicapper, considering it had been less than three months since he had watched his first horse race. More important, he had a pretty solid understanding of how to bet. He had heard the Guv say numerous times that Ernie wasn't the best handicapper he knew, but he was the best bettor that he had ever seen. When Rafa asked him to elaborate, the Guv simply said that Ernie wasn't afraid to pull the trigger when it was time, but the biggest thing was that he had the discipline to not bet at all if he didn't think he had an edge. Like most truisms, simple, but monumentally difficult for all but a few. Another thing the Guv said that stuck with Rafa, was that most of the time Ernie avoided betting the favorite. The second race Thursday was a Maiden Special Weight for three year old colts. The even money favorite was a first time starter with a fancy pedigree, from a high profile barn and a big name trainer. Just what the doctor ordered, an overbet favorite. Rafa used the the next three choices in an exacta box. The favorite loomed on the outside turning for home, but flattened out in the stretch and missed the board altogether. The third choice got up at the wire, with the fourth second. It paid a juicy ninety seven dollars for a two dollar ticket. Beautiful.

Rafa grabbed a corned beef, he was growing quite fond of them, and found a seat outside on the concrete steps facing the track. The next race was a route, which meant the starting gate was placed right in front of the grandstand. He loved to see the horses roaring out of the gate. He even enjoyed the traditional pre race routine, saddling in the paddock, the call to post by the bugler, the post parade, warm up jog and finally, in the gate and ready to run. As he watched the race unfold, he imagined what it must be like to ride such an incredible animal as a thoroughbred race horse, and what courage it took to do so.

Standing in front of him and to his left, not far from the rail, was a lovely young lady, mid twenties, dark hair, beautiful figure made even more so by the sundress she had chosen to wear to the track that day. Rafa couldn't see her eyes, but he had no doubt they were show stoppers. He thought of Nikki, and the best eyes ever, and hoped, in the name of all things wonderful and magic, that he hadn't seen them for the last time.

As the seventh race neared, Rafa was anxious. He wanted to head over to Barn 52 and hang out before the race, but the Guv had told him to be there right before the race, for what reason he didn't know, but he would do as requested.

The Guv had decided. It would be just he and Martin, man to man, hombre a hombre. No gun, no knife, no nothing, just man to man, solo hombre a hombre. It's not the way Ramos would do it. If it were Ramos, it would have already been done. If it were most men, it wouldn't have gotten this far, they would have let the cops handle it. But this wasn't any of them. This was the Guv.

When the Guv first met Ernie, he liked him, he got good vibes, but it wasn't anything more than that. It wasn't until he was around him a while that he saw all of the little things that made the man he was. Looking people in the eye when he talked to them, smiling and being pleasant to strangers, sauntering about, no hurry, calm, confident, not talking all the time, willing to just go along, willing to not just go along, unafraid, generous, soft spot for the less fortunate, for children.

The Guv would never admit it, but he knew it just the same, that Ernie, if he were still around, would describe his buddy, the Guv, very much the same way.

All that being said, the thing the Guv missed most about Ernie was not all that. It was the laughter. It was, above all, the damn pure joy of laughing. At anything. Being alive in the moment and laughing. He missed that. Laughing with Ernie.

Martin Carrington, esteemed Track Chaplin, was entertaining a few friends in a private box at Oaklawn. Not his private box, of course, the private box of a staunch supporter of the Fellowship of Christian Athletes, and all of the fine work that they do. The friends were not personal friends, they were friends of the FCA, and just happened to be among it's largest local donors. Martin told them that he was going to have to leave them for an hour or so before the seventh race. He explained that one of the stables, Barn 52, had asked him to come by before the race. He didn't say why. They really didn't care why. They were just glad he was going to be gone for a while so they could grab a few beers and make a few bets, like normal people.

Among Ernie's quirky ways, one of the most notable was his choice of headwear. When he first took up residence at Oaklawn as a confirmed horseplayer, he wore a visor. Then he would switch back and forth between a visor and cap. One day he showed up in a plantation style, wide brim straw hat. It was a little big, so he went to a smaller version, and that became more or less his trademark headgear. They didn't sell them in the Oaklawn gift shop, so he just cut out the Oaklawn logo from one of his older caps and superglued it to the front of his straw hat, on top of the generic looking band that was already on there. Invariably, a couple of people a day would comment on the hat, and eventually the gift shop wised up and ordered some in a similar style, with the Oaklawn logo on them. They sold out in a few days, and immediately became a regular item for sale in the gift shop. The locals called it the "Ernie". Ernie loved them, of course, but Ernie being Ernie, he couldn't just go with the off the shelf version, so he kept to the original look. He would buy an "Ernie" from the gift shop, then cut and glue an Oaklawn logo onto it. Nobody understood why, not even Ernie, but it worked for him, and he kept doing it.

Nikki hit the outskirts of Hot Springs with time to spare. As she cruised down Central Avenue and neared the track, she couldn't believe the number of cars she saw. They were everywhere. The parking lots were full. The side streets were lined with cars. People that lived nearby let racegoers park in their yards for ten bucks a pop. She found a spot on the street a full eight blocks away, and parked for free. The walk was no big deal to her, she enjoyed it. Once inside Oaklawn Park, she was amazed how different it seemed. The infield was full of people, the grandstands were full of people and the outdoor, trackside area was full of people. She felt like a beer, so she hit the nearest concession stand and then walked outside. The sixth race was twenty minutes to post. The Guv had told her he would meet her in the paddock before the seventh race, so she had time to relax and take it all in, and that she did. She thought about how unlikely it was a few months ago that she would be here, now, hanging out at a racetrack, and loving it. And not just loving it, but being a part of it. She felt good. She was nervous, but she felt good.

Martin Carrington felt pretty good himself. He had visited the backside at Oaklawn many times, in his role as track chaplain, but today was different. He was going there, or rather, he was invited there, as a successful businessman, to take a look at a racehorse. As he walked through the crowd, at trackside, where the scrubs hang out, he was glad to be only passing through. Most of these people, these unfortunate souls, betting two bucks at a time and getting half drunk and actually thinking they might walk away at the end of the day with a pocket full of cash, all the while knowing the water bill was due a week ago and the car's on empty and is past due for an oil change, and the rent will be due before the next paycheck. These people, who dress any old way and some probably got a tattoo while in the Navy. And one thing's for damn sure, above all else, there will be something on the grill tonight and the beer won't run out. And somebody's wife, or husband, will end up pissed off about somebody dancing with somebody or some crazy shit like that. And to top it all off, there's a decent chance a few of them aren't even in this country legally anyway. There's just no cure for stupid. No excuse for being a lowlife.

He thought about how glad he was to be above all that. He took a glance down at his boots. Nice. He thought about how cool it would be to go to the paddock before a race and stand next to the trainer and say a few things and the pedestrian sort of folks watching would wonder what he was talking to the trainer about, maybe giving him some instructions. After all, it was his horse. He thought about that. He didn't think about Ernie Cole. He had not one single thought of Ernie Cole.

That would change.

CHAPTER 48

I t was early afternoon, barely past the lunch hour at El Coche Comedor, Trujillo, Peru. Ramos sat at an outside table, in the shade, with a soft breeze. It felt good. He wore plain linen pants and a lightweight collared shirt. The shirt was loose and long sleeved, with the sleeves rolled up, and the top two buttons undone. Room for airflow. He was reading the newspaper, and beside him on the table was a novel he had started a couple of days earlier. Reading had become one of his favorite past times. He especially loved stories that were set in parts of the world where he had never been. He loved to picture in his mind the faraway places he read about, and appreciated the skill of a writer who could describe a place and make it real, as if the reader were there, and part of the story.

He was trying to sort it out, his feelings. His trip to Grand Cayman was fresh in his mind. It was a success, and that made him happy. Happy for Nikki and Hector. It felt good to do something that meant something. There was no good reason to ponder anything. He had a good life. Retired, plenty of money, lots of friends. He hadn't been looking for excitement when Hector called him about Nikki. The whole experience, from the planning to the doing, had just sort of happened, and only because it was Hector who called. Anybody else would have been turned away, no doubt about it. But he did it. Because it was Hector.

And maybe another reason. Maybe. That's what he was trying to figure out. He was uneasy. He worried that there was another reason. For wanting to do it again. To think, to develop a plan and execute the plan, to feel the excitement, to face the danger, and if necessary, to kill.

He had never killed a man who didn't deserve it. Did that matter? Did it make it okay? Maybe. Maybe not. He could think through it and decide, but whatever decision resulted from the thinking wouldn't matter, because it wasn't the thinking part that was the problem. It was the other part, and no manner of logic or self discipline could change the other part. It could be controlled, harnessed, kept in check, maybe. But it couldn't be eliminated. That was the scary part, it was there, and it wasn't going away. Maybe he didn't just kill people. Maybe he enjoyed it.

His thoughts were interrupted by a man who approached the table. "Senor Mantilla, I'm Carlos, good to see you, It's been a long time".

The man was Carlos Dominguez. He had no official status. Was not a business owner, elected official or any other important person. He was, however, the son of one of the most powerful men in Peru, Ramone Dominguez, the Ministro de Comercio, the minister of trade, for all of Peru. Ramos had not sought the attention of Ramone Dominguez. Had never met the man and had no intention to do so. They came to him. Word on the street was that Ramos Mantilla was visiting in Trujillo. That didn't happen often, and Ramone Dominguez didn't want to waste the opportunity it presented. After all the things he had heard about the man, the thing that mattered most now was that he, Ramone Dominguez, with all of his power and influence, was on the good side of the man, Ramos Mantilla. He sent his son to meet Ramos as a goodwill gesture. That's what they said. Possibly not the best idea, if he had done his homework. Ramos was not interested in being schmoozed. In fact, he was about as unschmoozable as a man could be. He needed nothing and wanted nothing. He wasn't opposed to meeting new people, making new friends, he enjoyed talking to people. But if there was the least bit of an agenda behind the new person, nothing good could possibly come of it. And there was close to zero chance that someone with a hidden agenda would be able to talk to Ramos for more than five minutes without being exposed. Never the less, here was Carlos Dominguez, son of Ramone Dominguez, about to have a seat at the table with Ramos Mantilla, and give it a shot.

Unlike them, Ramos had invested some time learning a thing or two about Senor Dominguez in advance of his meeting with Carlos. He would give the young man a chance to say whatever it was that he wanted to say, but he was pretty sure it was going to be a short conversation.

"It has indeed. Please have a seat and we'll order you a drink".

"Thank you".

Ramos remained seated. They shook hands and Carlos sat across from him. He glanced at Ramos' glass tentatively, unsure if he was having a cocktail or something without alcohol, then he ordered a beer. Ramos was silent. Carlos spoke.

"I appreciate your agreeing to meet with me. My father and I both have a lot of respect for you".

"Thank you. I've never met you father, but he certainly has a fine reputation".

Once again, Ramos was silent. Just sitting and looking at the young man. Carlos shifted in his seat, broke eye contact, wanting the silence to go away. Ramos obliged him.

"Is there something you want to talk about"?

It was a simple question, yet both men knew it was more than that. It was the point at which Ramos Mantilla took control. The point at which Carlos wondered why his father had sent him there and the point at which all bullshit stopped, and looked for a place to hide. The waiter returned with the beer. Carlos took a swig, set the beer on the table. Looked up, at Ramos.

"No". Pause. "My father just wants to be friends, and to let you know that he admires you and offers his assistance if ever needed".

"Okay. I appreciate that. You can never have too many friends. I'm only in Peru for a while. As you probably know, I live in the U.S. It's not likely that I would call on your father, but it's good to know I can if the need arises".

Surprisingly, Ramos raised his glass for a toast.

"To friends. To Peru".

Carlos touched the glass with his beer bottle. He was so relieved he was almost giddy inside. He nodded to Ramos and took a healthy gulp of beer.

Ramos changed gears. "Have another beer young man, and tell me what's been going on in Peru since I've been gone".

It was vintage Ramos. Going with the moment. Relaxed and in charge without acting like it. He had been drinking only water, but now he switched to beer also, and settled in for a chat.

Young Carlos, much relieved, spoke. "What's it like living in the U.S.? There seem to be a lot of people from Peru there now".

"There are indeed. It certainly makes it feel more like home. Although now, after all these years, it is home for me. I guess that's not totally accurate, no place will ever replace this one as my true home. Have you been to the U.S."?

"Yes, a couple of times. I like it very much, but I'm always glad to return here. The U.S. is such a big place, I can't imagine living there. I'm much more comfortable here, in Trujillo".

"I understand. I'm sure you have a good life here".

Carlos seemed almost embarrassed by the inference that he lived a life of privilege in Trujillo that almost certainly wouldn't exist elsewhere. He gave a slight shrug. "Yes, I suppose I do".

There was a short silence, then Ramos continued. "One thing I do miss about Peru is the mountains and hills. Louisiana is flat, which is okay, it's lush and green and there's plenty of water, but every now and then it would be nice to look up and see the mountains".

"Yeah, I didn't think about that, but I'm sure I would be the same way".

They continued, having a few beers and talking. When the conversation lulled. Carlos' demeanor turned more serious, as if he had something on his mind. Ramos, of course, knew that was almost certainly the case, and sat passively.

Carlos spoke. "I need to be honest with you. I do have something to talk about. I respect you and I appreciate your straightforward manner. I should be the same way with you, and I haven't been. My father didn't send me, but he knows I'm here. If it's okay with you, I would like to back up a bit. To the point at which you asked me if there was something I wanted to talk about".

Ramos looked at him with his usual relaxed face. "Continue".

Carlos licked his lips and took a breath. "I want to give you some background first".

Ramos showed empathy. "Just relax Carlos. I'm not going anywhere. Tell me what's on your mind".

"We're having problems with some people, especially one person. Our country is not a big player in the global economy, as you know, but that doesn't concern us, we're doing okay. What does concern us is our standing in the Latin American community. We are not respected as much as we should be by some of our Latin American neighbors. The person I mentioned is feared by almost everyone, in his country and ours. He makes people pay him for protection, but he offers no protection. He simply takes money from our people, and if they don't pay, he sends some of his men to do whatever they have to do to get the money. The police do nothing. They are also probably getting paid, and I'm quite sure are also scared".

"Okay, keep going".

"This is nothing new. It's been that way for a pretty long time. My father is a proud man, he loves his country and he wants the best for his fellow Peruvians, but he's old school, and he doesn't really know how to deal with these people. He knows that, but he won't ask for help. That's why I'm here. I might as well put it on the table. I want to know if you would consider helping us".

"Helping you do what"?

"Stand up to the bad guys".

Ramos looked at Carlos without expression. "What makes you think I can help you do that"?

"Because you've done it before".

"That was a long time ago. I'm an old man now".

Carlos started to say something, then stopped. Not sure what to say next. Took a deep breath.

Ramos said flatly, "Don't back down now. Say what you want to say".

Carlos gathered himself. "I know what happened in the Caymans".

Ramos showed no reaction. Didn't change expression. His mind was working. He had sworn them all to secrecy. Paid them well. He wondered who had told, but only for a moment, no matter now.

"You may know part of it, but there's a lot you don't know. I had a very important personal reason for visiting the Caymans".

Once again, Ramos had spoken evenly, unhurried.

Also once again, he had been brief and to the point, which gave Carlos little time to try to breath normally. When he did speak, it was with humility and recognition that the conversation had not gone as he had hoped.

"I guess we were hoping that you would judge our problem as worthy of your involvement also, as a Peruvian".

Again Ramos had no reaction. That is, no apparent reaction. There indeed was a reaction, just out of view of the young man sitting across from him. The young man, Carlos Dominguez, had no chance of seeing, or sensing, Ramos' reaction because he was too busy dealing with the turmoil inside his own head. The questions were coming at him, from somewhere inside, faster than he could respond. What the fuck am I doing, talking to this man? I've said too much, gone too far, acted like a clueless fuck. I am a clueless fuck. I wish I could just melt away, disappear into the safety of somewhere other than right here, right now. I should have known better. Maybe I should just get up and leave. No, not good. I have to apologize first. And what happens now if I've been disrespectful toward him and the apology would just be another stupid thing and end up being one more reason for this man to raise his little finger and smash me and my pitiful life into a million tiny particles of nothing? Oh shit, oh shit, oh holy fucking shit.

Ramos spoke. "Young man, Carlos, let us, you and me, talk about something. The situation you describe is, as you said, nothing new. Not in Peru, nor many other places in the world. Sad but true. It's not fair, but life is not fair. As a Peruvian, it hurts me as it does you. Most people are good, but some are bad, just the way it is. Fear is a powerful thing, and some people, like this man, use it to get what they want. But remember, fear favors no man. The bad guy knows fear too. We're all afraid of something.

Now, if I were to, as you say, stand up to this man, it may very well help, because he doesn't want trouble, he wants easy money. To him I would be trouble, and maybe he would fear me, maybe, and avoid me, but it wouldn't be the end of it, because soon enough I would be gone, and he would be back to his old ways, and you would still be afraid. I live in the U.S., in Louisiana. You and your father and your countrymen live here, in Peru. It is not for me to stand up to this man, it is for you".

Ramos had Carlos' full attention. To the young man it felt as if he had been walking a path that led to a place he had never been, a dangerous place to which he knew he had to go, and from which he knew he may never return. He said nothing. Ramos continued.

"You're the one who must decide. It takes courage. You have to let this man know that you are willing to risk it all. He has to pay. And he needs to know that if you fail, there is another man, the next man in line, who will do the same thing. And he will know that sooner or later, when his friends call him, there will be no answer".

Twenty minutes later, Ramos was again sitting at the table alone, reading. Carlos had thanked him, a bit awkwardly, and left. Ramos told him not to worry with the tab. He knew the Peruvian had not gotten what he came for, but he also believed that what he did get was something better, the cold hard truth. What he would do with it was up to him. Just the way it was.

The thoughts returned, the unease. He loved his life in Louisiana, his family in and around Mona's. It scared him to think of a life without that place and those people. But, but, always a but, there was that thing that he had to deal with, figure out, if he could. He had no children of his own. Not because he didn't want them, but because that option had been rendered null and void by the sharp edge of a length of hardened steel in a Peruvian prison, many years before. The surgeries in his back, lower abdomen and leg took their toll. The doctors told him at the time that he would eventually be able to father children, but it never worked out that way, and he had resigned himself to growing old alone. The actual being alone part didn't bother him. He enjoyed having time to himself, and he had plenty of company whenever he wanted it. What he didn't like was the thought that he would leave no legacy, and that there was nobody that really needed him, that depended on him. His life had been one challenge after another, always another hill to climb or battle to fight. When Hector called, something inside was awakened. From his first conversation with Nikki until the job was finished, he was a different person, a man on a mission. It was scary. It was dangerous. It made him feel alive. He had no desire to impose his will on someone just for the sake of doing it, none at all. But when there was an injustice that needed to be corrected, and it was his place to do the correcting, something boiled up inside and took him over. And gave no quarter.

CHAPTER 49

The first meal Ramos had after returning to Louisiana was red beans and rice with smoked sausage from Mona's. It soothed him. He had thought often about the Louisiana food he was missing while away. Shrimp, oysters and crayfish would almost always come to mind, but when he got back, it was red beans and rice he went to first.

Everyone was glad to see him, and he was equally glad to see them. After a long lunch he returned to the house, answered some emails he had neglected and caught up on the local news. Late in the day he settled into his favorite spot, behind the house in the shade of the oak trees, and sipped the first cocktail of the evening. The familiar surroundings relaxed him. The anxious thoughts and feelings of the previous days were mostly gone. Life was good, and he chided himself for having been so quick to worry unnecessarily. He thought of Nikki, and Hector, and the satisfaction of redemption. A contented smile crept across his face.

He thought about the tattoo. It was in the shape of a Samurai sword, only shorter and wider. The handle and hilt had decorative markings, and along the top edge of the blade was a simple border. He had gotten it a couple of weeks after he left prison, at a place in New Orleans. After the young tattoo artist had finished the sword, Ramos asked him to add two marks on the blade, near the hilt.

"What type of marks"? the young man had asked.

"Just marks, nothing fancy", replied Ramos.

The tattoo artist paused and thought a moment. "Like notches"?

"Yes", Ramos had replied, "like notches".

Before he left Trujillo this time, he visited another tattoo parlor, for the very small amount of new work that needed to be done. The tattoo was rarely seen by anyone except Ramos. He reached over with his right hand and pulled his left shirt sleeve up over his elbow. The Samurai sword was there, as before, only now with four notches.

He would rest, spend time with his buddies, enjoy life. He had been thinking about his conversation with the young man at El Coche Comedor. He would keep an eye on things in Peru, and the situation there that the young man described. It was his home country. After a time, If he thought he could make a difference, maybe he would lend a hand.

Chapter 50

The Guv really hadn't thought it through very well. After all the thinking and questioning and convincing himself of what needed to be done, he hadn't spent much time actually planning how to do it. It wasn't that he hadn't thought about it much, he thought about it all the time, but it wasn't logical thought, it was emotional thought. The guys understood that, and it concerned them, so they came up with a plan of their own. As always, they had his back.

The Guv was mad enough to kill Martin Carrington, and he knew the prick deserved it, and the guys knew the prick deserved it. Martin Carrington was a killer himself, and a thief, and a phony and a liar. But killing the man was not the way to go. Just wasn't. It would feel good in the moment, but it wouldn't be good after that, and the Guv knew it. He wanted the gutless prick to face the music, and pay the price, day after day, for many days to come. He knew Rafa was not happy with the way he had handled things lately, but the Guv had his reasons, and he knew things

Rafa didn't know, couldn't know, because he was young and didn't have the experience required. The Guv had experience, in America and in Peru. He had seen too many times that justice wasn't blind. It should be, it was supposed to be, but it wasn't. Just the way it is. His biggest fear with the Martin Carrington situation, if he relied on the judicial system to do what it's supposed to do, was that nothing significant would ever come of it. The lawyers would argue back and forth, and the ones working for the home team, in this case Martin Carrington/the FCA/the Republican movers and shakers club, and all those like minded folk who collectively form the bedrock of the Moral Majority, would see to it that the prosecutorial zeal of the government lawyers would not be allowed to sully the reputation of a fine Christian man like Martin Carrington, who has done more for the health and welfare of the low paid workers at Oaklawn Park than anybody else ever has, and on top of that serves as the Track Chaplin, without any compensation, for God's sake.

Because of that, he, Hector, aka the Guv, would take care of business his way, and eliminate any chance of the spineless prick Marten Carrington walking away without at least a smudge or two of blood on his pristine veneer, and a thorn or two in his bogus buttocks.

After the results of the fifth race were posted, Marten excused himself and started making his way toward Barn 52, making sure to catch the eye of and say hello to numerous deep pockets along the way.

At the barn, it appeared to be business as usual. It wasn't. Ironically enough, now it was the Guv who was relaxed, and the other guys who were all up tight. The trainer wasn't happy about the tension in the air, so he led Carnelian out of his stall and let him hang out further down the shedrow until it was time to lead him over to the paddock for the Count Fleet Stakes. The Barn 52 guys, plus a large contingent of their fellow backside workers, male and female, were going about their normal race day routines, but they all knew that soon, there would be nothing at all routine about what was going down inside Barn 52. They were worried about what could happen to the Guv, and although none would say it, they were wondering if he was ready. Not one among them had ever seen the Guv even so much as lift a finger in anger toward another man. It just wasn't him. True that, but when the quiet man, however rare and for whatever reason, unleashes what he's got, heaven help the other guy.

Marten approached Barn 52 in his usual, pretentious manner, making too much of an effort to be part of the backside family, while wearing ostrich skin boots. Don't think so dawg. Two of the more attractive Peruvian ladies, dressed smartly for the occasion, greeted him as he entered the barn area.

"Hello there Mr. Carrington. Glad you could make it by to see us. The Guv is inside, he said to show you in when you arrived".

"Thank you. You both look lovely today".

Marten followed them into Barn 52. The Guv was standing, looking at a sheet of paper he held in his hand. There was nobody else there, and no horses. The ladies left without another word, and as they did they closed the large barn doors behind them. Marten thought it seemed a little odd, for them to do that. The Guv looked up, toward Marten, with faraway eyes. Then he looked directly at him and then down at the sheet of paper.

"I've been looking over some stuff". Pause "Do you know a guy named Homero Perez"?

Marten immediately, involuntarily, only for a split second, showed panic. He recovered quickly, and managed to appear unfazed, but it was too late, his eyes had betrayed him. He squinted a little and made a face as if he was trying to recall the name, then shook his head. "Don't think so, but I'm not always that great with names. Why do you ask"?

The Guv didn't answer. "What about Enrique Castalano"?

This time Marten didn't flinch. "I don't know Guv, sounds a little familiar, but I can't say for sure. Am I supposed to know these people"?

The Guv looked Marten in the eyes, unhurried. "Yep".

"Is there something wrong Guv?, I thought I was here to look at your horse".

The Guv looked away for a moment. Took his time. Marten's pulse rate quickened. The Guv returned to Marten's eyes, locked in. "There is no horse Marten".

Marten's face tightened. He licked his lips, trying to stay calm and think at the same time. His brain was in overdrive, about to hit warp speed, and there was nothing he could do about it. The Guv just stood there looking at him, not moving a muscle, then he turned up the heat another notch, speaking in a flat tone, barely moving his lips.

"You gotta answer for Ernie".

Marten had no immediate reaction. Now he understood. No more posturing. The Guv wanted him to squirm. He didn't want to, but he did, his heart pounding. He couldn't take the silence. He spoke. "What are you talking about Guv"?

"You and your ostrich skin fucking boots, which, by the way, have horse shit on them, bought and paid for by Ernie". Pause. "That's what I'm talking about".

"Guv…".

"Shut the fuck up Marten". Pause. The Guv held up the sheet of paper. "You don't know those gentlemen I mentioned because they don't exist, at least not at Oaklawn Park". Pause. "That didn't stop them from getting paid though, did it"?

"I don't know what you're talking about Guv..".

The Guv cut him off, forcefully, "Marten!". Marten stopped talking and looked at the Guv. The silence was deafening, and there was nowhere to hide. The Guv stared at the Oaklawn Chaplin with penetrating eyes, and no fear.

"Do you want to die today? right here, right now"?

He bore into the soul of the pitiful man. The Guv was totally motionless. Breathing slowly, calmly, while Marten began pleading with his eyes, paralyzed with fear. Then he managed to respond feebly.

"No".

"Then admit to me right now that you killed Ernie".

Silence. The Guv starting to breath heavier. Running out of patience. Marten Carrington, now in full panic mode, unable to do anything but be his bogus self, tried to respond.

"You got it wrong Guv…".

The Guv had heard enough. He took a step toward Marten, adrenalin taking over, panther eyes, fist clenched.

Marten, out of options, quickly shoved his right hand into his front pocket. Just as quickly, he pulled his hand out, trying to grip the gun.

He never stood a chance. It happened fast. Real fast. Guv's boys took over. They were waiting, and watching. They had his back. They pounced. Marten got the gun out of his pocket, but that was it, he never came close to pulling the trigger. A professional jockey is a little quicker than an out of shape track chaplin. They hit his arm. The gun fell to the ground.

Marten, trying in vain to avoid the blow, instinctively moved his head back, away from the Guv. That, combined with the Guv's forward momentum and descending angle of attack, resulted in a fierce blow, flush against the left side of Marten's face. Ironically enough, the expensive designer glasses he was wearing, though responsible for multiple, deep lacerations, may have saved the sight in his left eye, and maybe his life. He was immediately knocked unconscious. His left eye socket and cheek bone were crushed. A rush of blood covered his face, and quickly formed a crimson pool on the barn floor. The Guv's forward momentum had caused him to lose his balance, and trip over Marten's limp body as it hit the deck. Barn 52 erupted in frantic activity. Jockeys, exercise riders, grooms, all rushed in. They grabbed the Guv and made sure he was through pummeling Marten. They needn't worry. It was over. The Guv lay face down, head on his arms, not moving, exhausted.

Two paramedics, having been asked by the boys to be ready, quickly entered Barn 52. They immediately tended to

Marten. It did not look good, but although blood was streaming from his nose and face, he would survive, physically.

The guys had helped the Guv to his feet and brought in a chair for him to sit in. He sat, staring blankly straight ahead. The Guv's main assistant, a strapping young man thirty years his junior, knelt in front of the Guv, then looked him in the eyes and clasped his hands. Then he reached down and placed his own hand in the pool of blood, feeling it in his palm and between his fingers. He gave the Guv a loving kiss on the shoulder, and turned to walk away. The backside guys then formed a line, single file, in front of the Guv. The first one in line knelt in front of the Guv, touched the blood, then hugged the Guv. It continued that way. Every one of them touched the blood and touched the Guv. It was a powerful display of respect, love and solidarity. They were all in this together, every man with blood on his hands.

As Rafa neared the barn, he noticed the main door was closed. He had never seen that. There was a paramedic's van parked outside. He hadn't seen that either. Inside, the paramedics had Marten, conscious but dazed, on a stretcher, an oxygen mask over his nose and mouth, and an IV in his arm. His ostrich skin boots splattered with his own blood.

Rafa walked into Barn 52, and froze. He looked at Marten, then looked at the Guv. The Guv had been sitting, motionless, unable or unwilling to say or do anything other than to just let it be. He looked at Rafa, and as Rafa walked slowly toward him, he stood. Both men's eyes overflowed with tears. Rafa made the first move. He opened his arms and wrapped them around the Guv. He laid his head on the Guv's shoulder. The Guv closed his eyes and held the boy tightly. He put his hand on the back of Rafa's head and pulled him closer. No words spoken. None needed.

When they ended the embrace, Rafa looked at the Guv. "I thought we had a horse race to watch".

The Guv threw his arm over Rafa's shoulder and they headed for the door. They walked out of Barn 52, arm in arm. The paramedic van, Marten Carrington inside, was gone. They headed toward the grandstand. At the end of the row on which Barn 52 was located, just before they turned left, two jockeys walked up. Each had a red streak on the side of his face, the blood of Marten Carrington. Each was wearing a goofy looking hat with an Oaklawn Park logo attached to the front, the trademark head wear of Ernest Hemingway Cole. They turned left. Lined up on each side of the shedrow was a long line of men, women and children, members of the backside family. They were all wearing an Ernie hat with an Oaklawn logo. Every single one.

It almost took Rafa's breath away. As Rafa and the Guv walked by, many of them, young and old, reached out and touched Rafa. It was simple. It was the most wonderful show of love and respect ever witnessed by anyone there. Rafa turned to the Guv. "In college, one of my roommate's father died of a heart attack, my roommate had a godfather, he was a man that loved him and had promised long before to always be there for him when needed". Pause. "Guv, will you be my godfather"?

The Guv stopped walking and looked Rafa in the eyes. "Yes. Yes I will". Rafa wrapped his arms around him and squeezed.

They walked toward the paddock. No longer arm in arm, they made their way through the crowd. The horses were walking onto the track for the seventh race post parade. Carnelian looked relaxed and ready. Rafa said. "It's too late to go the paddock, let's find a spot on the rail".

"I want to go to the paddock for a minute, then we'll come out here to watch the race". Rafa didn't argue. They entered the paddock area, which was almost empty, the horses and crowd having just left for the track.

Nikki was sitting on a bench against the wall, trying to convince herself that it was okay that the Guv was nowhere to be found. Something must have come up. She had been through so much. Maybe it was best this way. Rafa wasn't supposed to be there anyway, so no surprise not to see him either. She would head back to New Orleans, settle into her routine, and be glad for all the good things that had happened. She was almost ready to stand and walk away, when she looked up and saw them, the Guv and Rafa, walking toward her. Rafa couldn't believe his eyes. There she was. Smiling that smile. They had blood on their clothes, but right then it didn't matter. Nikki went to the Guv, hugged him and didn't let go. She looked at Rafa. He was smiling at her. "Hey", she said.

"Hey Nikki". He would have said more, but the words didn't come, and it didn't matter anyway.

"We gotta go outside", said the Guv, and he headed to the track. Nikki and Rafa followed. The horses had just left the gate when they found room to stand not too far from the rail. The Guv was glued to the action, to the number eight horse, his and Ernie's horse, Carnelian. He was running mid pack, fifth or sixth, down the backstretch. Nikki wanted to watch, but what she wanted more was for Rafa to look at her with those Gypsy eyes. She couldn't help herself. She turned from the horse race and looked at Rafa, at the side of Rafa's face, and just gave in to it, her yearning for another chance. He felt it. He was watching the race, but he felt it. His heart beat faster. Unable to do anything else, he turned toward her. The look in her eyes that moment was the greatest prize he could ever hope for, and one that would be a part of him for many, many years to come. He stepped toward her. The kiss they shared was pure bliss. Then another, and another.

Entering the stretch, Carnelian had four lengths to make up. He dug in. Driving. At the sixteenth pole, he was a length and a half behind. It was as close as he would get. He ran like a champion, but this day he wasn't the fastest. He hit the wire in third. The Guv couldn't believe it. He stood there, then lowered his chin to his chest, closed his eyes and frowned, feeling the pain of losing. He turned, reached in his pocket, pulled out his mutuel ticket and looked at it. Number eight to win. Damn. He looked up. Rafa and Nikki were together as one, looking exactly like what they were, two young people in love. A slow smile crept across his face. He glanced back at his mutuel ticket, then back at the lovebirds. His smile widened. He stood there for a moment, just looking at them. As he did he tossed the mutuel ticket in the air. It fluttered in the breeze, then gradually came to rest among many others, already there, on the ground, at Oaklawn Park.

Epilogue

It was a bright, sunny day in Groznyv, Russia. Anna sat on a stone bench, enjoying the sunshine while keeping an eye on the children, eleven of them, five and six year olds. Their boundless energy attested to the fact that they were happy to be outside, playing in the schoolyard, too young to be concerned about adult things. Several of them were sitting beside her or on another bench facing her, laughing and being silly, which made her smile. They loved Miss Anna, she was a fixture at the school, and had been for a long time.

A young lady who worked in the school office walked toward her, holding a package. "Miss Anna, this came in the mail for you, it was forwarded to the school from your old address".

Anna reached for the package. It was a large shipping envelope, the return address was New Orleans, LA, USA. Anna said nothing. Opened the envelope. Inside was a smaller envelope. Inside it was a note.

Anna,

I hope this makes it to you, and that you are well. Your trip to see me in New Orleans changed my life. You were a blessing to my father, and you are a blessing to me. I can never thank you enough. I have thought of you every day over these many years and have prayed for your happiness and well being. May God bless you with all of the love that you deserve.

Nikki

Anna's eyes filled with tears. Also in the large envelope, there was a stack of papers, copies of newspaper stories, pictures, announcements and such from the last twenty years. On top was a copy of the most recent article in the Times Picayune.

Boardman and Company, a local investment management firm, announced today with great pleasure, the twentieth annual recipients of the Gibson Carter Scholarship. They are twin sisters, Anna and Natalya Zamfir, of New Orleans. They are daughters of Rafa and Nikki Zamfir, and granddaughters of the scholarship's namesake, Gibson Carter. The firm endowed the scholarship twenty years ago to honor the legacy of Gibson Carter, a beloved fellow employee, father and friend. It is most appropriate that his own granddaughters now share in his legacy of love and learning.

Tears rolled down Anna's face as she was reading. The children, curious as always, were upset by the tears. A few began crying along with her, their beloved Miss Anna. When she realized they were upset, she turned to them, and through even more tears, smiled and let them know she was crying tears of joy. At first they didn't understand, but then they could see she was indeed happy with what she had read, so they were happy. She stood, raised her arms, and began to do a little happy dance, which made them do a happy dance, all over the place, with gleeful abandon.

Anna, filled with joy, watched the celebration. She reached into the pocket of her dress and brought her hands to her face, holding an old leather bookmark. Attached to it was a strand of ancient prayer beads. She kissed them and held them to her cheek. Then pressed them to her chest, to her heart, leaned her head back slightly and closed her eyes, still smiling. The beads were old and worn, each with a rich, ancient patina. One was an agate, a Solomon's Agate.

34436765R00305

Made in the USA
San Bernardino, CA
27 May 2016